CUPID CALLING

CUPID CALLING

VIANO ONIOMOH

CUPID CALLING
Copyright © 2022 Viano Oniomoh
All rights reserved.

Cover, Interior Design, and Illustrations by Viano Oniomoh
Designedbyvee.com

"Retweet" icon courtesy of Freepik.com

Without limiting the rights under copyright reserved above, no part of this publication may be reproduced, distributed, or transmitted in any form or by any means, including photocopying, recording, or other electronic or mechanical methods, without the prior written permission of the author of this book, except in the case of brief quotations embodied in book reviews and certain other non-commercial uses permitted by copyright law.

This is a work of fiction. All names, characters, places, brands, media, incidents, and events in this publication, other than those clearly in the public domain, are fictitious, and are the products of the author's imagination. Any resemblance to actual persons, living or dead, events, or locales, is entirely coincidental.

For more information, visit vianooniomoh.com

Published by Viano Oniomoh Adores.

Paperback ISBN: 9798353565338
Hardcover ISBN: 9798360174035

*Lovers of love and syrupy-sweet romance,
this one's for you.*

CONTENT NOTES

This book contains the following content that may be upsetting for some readers. For anyone who needs it, please scan the QR code below to take you to the page on my website where I list the content warnings.

Take care,
~Vee.

CONTENTS

ONE * 7
TWO * 15
THREE * 23
FOUR * 32
FIVE * 49
SIX * 59
SEVEN * 73
EIGHT * 81
NINE * 96
TEN * 106
ELEVEN * 115
TWELVE * 129
THIRTEEN * 140
FOURTEEN * 147
FIFTEEN * 158
SIXTEEN * 170
SEVENTEEN * 182
EIGHTEEN * 193
NINETEEN * 209
TWENTY * 225
TWENTY-ONE * 243
TWENTY-TWO * 259
TWENTY-THREE * 272
TWENTY-FOUR * 285
TWENTY-FIVE * 295
TWENTY-SIX * 306

TWENTY-SEVEN * 314
TWENTY-EIGHT * 328
TWENTY-NINE * 342
THIRTY * 364
EPILOGUE * 383

HOME | ARCHIVE | ABOUT US | CONTACT | SEARCH

"RIGHT IN TIME" DIRECTOR TO DIRECT NEW BACHELORETTE-ESQUE TV SERIES IN COLLABORATION WITH NETFLICKS

Director Ameri Shae just announced on twitter that she's teaming up with Netflicks to bring us a brand-new dating-themed TV series.

Written by Aisha Suleiman

[Photo of Ameri Shae provided by Ameri Shae.]

For those who don't know who <u>Ameri Shae</u> is (which, how the heck?) films like the box office show stopper *Right in Time* and the award-winning TV show <u>Salacious</u> should come to mind. As a brilliant up-and-coming queer, Black female artist and director, fans have been eagerly awaiting what next Shae has in store for the world.

Well, we're here to tell you that you need wait no longer! Shae has just announced via Twitter (see tweet below) that she will be collaborating with Netflicks once more to bring us *Cupid Calling*, a brand-new bachelorette-esque themed TV series in the style of a dating competition, where a group of bachelors will be competing for the heart of one bachelorette. The show, according to Shae, will hold "all the tropes we love (and those we love to hate)", while simultaneously feeling "fresh and new."

> **Ameri Shae** ✓ @AmeriMazing
> #CupidCallingisComing So excited to collaborate with Netflicks to bring this show to life! It's got all those tropes we love (and those we love to hate 😂), while still remaining fresh and new! I can't wait for y'all to see it!
>
> 💬 1.7k   🔁 8.5k   ♡ 17.9k

To absolutely no one's surprise, the second the news dropped, everyone on twitter subsequently began to freak out. The hashtag #CupidCallingisComing trended at number one on twitter for over six hours after the announcement.

Here are a few tweets that perfectly summarise our feelings:

> **Stream Dynamite by BTS** @cut13pat00t13
> A DATING THEMED TV SERIES DIRECTED BY AMERI SHAE IN COLLABORATION WITH NETFLICKS FINALLY SOME GOOD FUCKING FOOD #CupidCallingisComing
>
> 💬 55   🔁 543   ♡ 3.9k

> **jordin is broke af** @broklynites_
> nah y'all don't understand what this news has done for me like suddenly my skin is clear, my grades are up, my crops have been watered- #CupidCallingisComing
>
> 💬 101   🔁 2.3k   ♡ 5.7k

> **Mari Barry** 📌 ✅ **@diy_mariiii**
>
> 1) Bachelorette-esque TV show
> 2) Exclusive website where we can sign in and vote for our faves
> 3) Directed by Ameri Shae
>
> Need I say more? 😳 #CupidCallingisComing
>
> 💬 2.3k   🔁 10.8k   ♡ 22.7k

As popular youtuber Mari Barry stated in her tweet above, Shae and Netflicks plan to launch *Cupid Calling's* own official website, the countdown of which you can find here. On the website, fans and viewers will be invited to sign in and vote weekly for their favourite bachelors, which—you guessed it!—could affect the overall weekly eliminations! Subscribers will also be given exclusive access to episode highlights and summaries, extras and behind-the-scenes content, and much more.

Each contestant (of whom there will be 30, ranging between the ages of 25-35) will have an introductory video/highlight reel posted on the website; and to whet your taste buds, a brand-new bachelor will be revealed on the website every single day for thirty days after the website has launched; we can barely contain our excitement!

The Bachelorette herself, and the star of the show, will be the last to be revealed.

Don't forget to share your thoughts in the comments below! What are you looking forward to the most in this series?

17 COMMENTS **(CLICK TO SHOW)**

The official website for the CUPID CALLING series.

Cupid Calling

ABOUT | THE BACHELORETTE | THE BACHELORS | EPISODES | CONTACT | BECOME A CUPID

THE BACHELORS

COMING SOON

COMMENTS

 EGG
FIRST ONE HERE HA!

 238   15

 **SPANISH_PRINCE**
first bachelor reveal is next week I'm shaking

 101   8

 **JIMINLUVR**

AHHH I'M SO EXCITED I CAN'T WAIT

♥ 122   💬 12

[LOAD MORE COMMENTS ⌄]

ONE

"HI, MY NAME IS EJIRO Odavwaro—"

"Can you please try to sound more enthusiastic?" Ajiri interrupted, though she didn't lift her eyes from the camera's feedback screen. "And use your full name."

Ejiro wrinkled his nose. "Is that necessary?"

"Just do it, please." She gave him a brief glance and flashed an encouraging grin. "And smile small, abeg."

Ejiro sighed, then smiled brightly. "Hi! My name is Ejiro David Odavwaro—"

"The smile's too fake. Start again." That was Blessing, his twin's girlfriend. She was also staring into the camera's feedback screen, standing beside Ajiri instead of behind the lens, which was odd; this was Blessing's project, shouldn't she be the one filming? But what did he know?

"Starting over again in three, two—"

"Just *try* to act natural," Blessing said quickly.

"—one."

They were making him nervous with how seriously they were taking this. "Does it have to be perfect?"

Ajiri sighed at the interruption. Blessing's eyes snapped up to meet his, and she clutched dramatically at her chest, one of her hands holding a half-finished lime green smoothie in a tall *Adventure Time* plastic cup and straw, the other holding a piece of A4 paper with her project's questions printed onto it. Her lipstick was neon green today, making her warm brown skin pop.

"I can't believe you even have to ask that. Who do you think I am?"

Ejiro shook his head, but he was smiling, a little more genuinely this time. "Fine. Okay. Fine." He took a deep breath. Let it out slowly. It might be for a small class project, but that didn't mean it would automatically rid him of his self-consciousness. "I just don't know why *you* can't do it," he said to his twin, not for the first time.

Ajiri looked up at him, her expression soft. Unlike her girlfriend, she wore no makeup, her afro was buzzed short to her scalp instead of braided to her hips and dyed at the tips in a matching colour to her lipstick, and her skin was as cool and dark as her twin's. She flicked the button to switch off the camera and focused fully on him.

"Look, you just need to be yourself, okay? Don't be so nervous. And it can't be me because Blessing has used me as a subject far too many times now."

"Exactly. And it's not like it's going to go up on a billboard or something. It's just one assignment for one tiny class," Blessing added, before slurping really loudly on her straw.

Ajiri snorted. Blessing looked at her, then she snorted, too. Then they did that *thing*—the thing where they shared a look that meant they were having an entire conversation with their eyes alone—which made Ejiro feel like an interloper.

Ajiri raised her eyebrows. She was biting her lower lip and trying not to laugh.

Blessing looked guilty, though Ejiro couldn't discern why, her full lips also twitching. "What? It's for a *class project*." Something about those words felt fake, but Ejiro couldn't quite put his finger on what.

"Stop looking at me like that."

"*You* stop," Ajiri said. They both burst out laughing, leaving Ejiro wondering, as usual, what the joke was.

He tried to ignore that twisty thing inside his stomach, the thing he was pretty sure was an ugly mixture of envy and longing, but he wasn't sure he was successful.

"Ha, ha, okay, all right, let's get this over with, please and thanks."

The ladies stopped laughing. Ajiri cleared her throat.

"Look, think of it as an audition."

The women exchanged a quick glance he couldn't interpret.

"Yeah," Blessing said, a little slowly. "An audition for ... like, a dating show."

Ejiro raised both his eyebrows.

The two women were giving each other that amused look again, before Ajiri quickly looked away.

"An audition for a dating show," his twin repeated, radiating false calm and confidence. "Exactly."

Ejiro tried once more to read between the lines, but the women were suddenly stoic, watching him with unreadable expressions.

"Okay ... so, like, speed dating shows?" he asked tentatively.

"Exactly like speed dating shows." Ajiri was already switching the camera back on. "Imagine that this is a once in a lifetime opportunity for you to meet the love of your life; you have to give your audition tape your all."

The words made Ejiro flush, the colour thankfully hidden underneath his deep brown skin.

"Oh," he said. He cleared his throat.

A once in a lifetime chance to meet the love of my life, he thought with a madly racing heart, closing his eyes and pretending for a brief moment that the audition tape was real.

He opened his eyes and smiled softly at the camera. "Hi, my name is Ejiro David Odavwaro. I'm twenty-five years old, I live in Manchester, and I'm an assistant chef in *Ewoma's*, my uncle's restaurant."

The women glanced at each other with pleased and excited expressions. Ejiro's cheeks warmed further.

"Perfect," Ajiri whispered, her eyes bright.

He beamed. On the inside, the raw ache for an actual romantic and sexual relationship tried to claw its way out of his throat, but he swallowed it forcefully back down.

If only it could be this easy.

EJIRO HAD JUST FINISHED SETTING down the trays for table one and three when Damilola came into the kitchens, removing the top page from her handheld sticky notepad and pasting it onto the counter's surface.

"Two peppered gizzard starters, two plates of fried rice with plantain as main, and *one* chocolate cake with vanilla ice cream for dessert," she recited by rote before expertly taking both trays Ejiro had filled and heading back to the front of the restaurant.

Humming along to the radio, Ejiro took a second look at the sticky note before he began to prepare the meals.

"I will soon introduce those iPad menus," his uncle spoke from behind him, his Nigerian accent thick despite the many years he'd spent as a citizen in England. He was sitting on a small wooden stool, munching on packaged plantain chips. "What do you think, Eji-ji?"

The nickname, as usual, made Ejiro feel all warm and mushy inside. "I think it's a great idea."

"Abi? That way when people order, it will come straight to the kitchen, instead of having waitresses running up and down."

"Makes sense." Ejiro nodded.

They were silent for a few minutes, while the delicious smell of caramelised onions wafted into the air. He turned down the flame, then added the finely chopped hot peppers and tomatoes, standing well back from the pan as it sizzled when he gently stirred. When it was gently mixed and bubbling, he sprinkled in some spices: thyme, beef flavour cubes, salt, and a dash of mild curry, his secret ingredient.

The gizzard was already cooked and fried, so it just needed to be stirred in with the sauce and it would be done. While that was cooking, he started in on the vegetables for the fried rice.

"Your mother," Uncle Reuben said, making Ejiro's heart skip several beats. He hummed to show he was listening. "Has she called you recently?"

"No, she hasn't," he said, focusing extra hard on dicing the carrots.

His uncle's following silence felt heavy. Ejiro swallowed nervously. He nearly jumped out of his skin when his phone began to vibrate in his back pocket.

"Talk of the devil." Uncle Reuben laughed with delight.

Ejiro felt like he was drowning. Please God, not now; he wasn't *ready*—

Uncle Reuben stood, reaching for one of the aprons hanging on a peg by the back door. "You answer that, I'll finish up the order."

"But—"

"No buts. Go on."

Ejiro couldn't even take his sweet time walking outside because his uncle didn't take his eyes off him.

When he got to the tiny alleyway behind the restaurant, he began to pace, the vibration of his phone making his heart thump furiously underneath his ribcage. It was mid-April, but the cool air still had a lingering bite to it that Ejiro, as panicked as he was, currently didn't feel.

It's just until I get my citizenship, was what he'd told his mother. It'd been six months since his citizenship had been approved, and now she wouldn't stop calling, asking when he was coming home.

He didn't even know why he was panicking. He *wanted* to go home. Eventually. Right?

"I didn't send you to study abroad so you can just abandon your roots. Whether you like it or not, you are still a Nigerian, and you have duties to your country to uphold," was what she'd said when he'd first told her about his intentions to apply for citizenship. Somehow, even though Ajiri had told her the same thing, Ejiro was the one she'd had a problem with.

Then again, Ajiri did literally the *opposite* of anything their mother wanted; "became" a lesbian—even though it wasn't precisely a choice; got tattoos and a nose ring; decided to study Fashion Design for her Masters instead of something more science-y like Business Management, which she—and Ejiro, both at the request of their mother—had studied for her Bachelor's; got an internship with a fashion brand in the UK instead of going back home and "starting up her own local business"; and finally topping it all off by saying she wasn't ever going back to Nigeria, unless it was to visit. Their mother had obviously since given up on her.

Ejiro, on the other hand, just wanted to please her. Was that so wrong?

The phone had stopped ringing.

"Jesus Christ," he whispered, striving to think of an excuse for why he hadn't answered immediately.

He didn't know why the thought of going back home filled his throat with bile. His mother was all alone, she *needed* them. He couldn't just abandon her. Besides, it wasn't like he was doing anything worthwhile in the UK. Like his mother had said countless times before, the job with his uncle was just a courtesy because they were family; it wasn't a *real* job, and his work as a comic artist online—despite the steady income it brought—wasn't a *real* job either, merely a hobby.

The phone started ringing again.

"Jesus Christ," he repeated, with more feeling.

He ripped the device out of his pocket, closing his eyes as he answered.

"Hello?"

"Hi!" chirped a cheery, unfamiliar, decidedly English voice. "Am I speaking to Ejiro Odavwaro?"

She completely butchered the pronunciation of his name. He was too relieved at it not being his mother that he didn't bother to correct her.

"Yes, this is he." His accent subconsciously switched when he realised he may not be talking to another Nigerian.

"Hi, hi!" the woman repeated, her excitement doubling, if that were possible. "My name is Stacey Radcliff, and I'm a representative from *Cupid Calling*. I'm ringing you to say—I'm sure you can guess this already—that we absolutely *loved* your audition tape and we'd love it if you could come in for an official interview to discuss you becoming a part of the show!"

Ejiro's mind was completely blank. She was a who-what-now?

"I'm sorry, could you please repeat that?"

"Certainly." Stacey sounded amused. "I'm a representative for *Cupid Calling*. We loved your audition tape, Mr. Odaro, and we'd very much like to meet you in person to discuss you possibly becoming a part of the show."

Panic began to set in. He had absolutely no idea who on earth she was or what the heck she was talking about. Audition tape?

"Uh ... what show was that again?" *And it's Odavwaro.* They could pronounce Galifianakis and McConaughey but his four syllables were apparently a problem.

The woman still sounded patient as she repeated, "*Cupid Calling*, Mr. Odaro."

"Odavwaro."

"Oh, pardon me. Odavwaro," she echoed, managing to finally get it right. "Would you like me to call you at a later date? Though I do have to warn you, if you don't reply in the affirmative on your second call—or you miss it—we will be going with someone else for the show."

"I completely understand, thank you, I'm actually at work right now, so you understand—"

"Of course, Mr. Odavwaro. What would be a better time for you? We're free Monday through Thursday between the hours of eight in the morning till five in the evening."

"Oh, uh ..." He paused to think. Today was Tuesday. He had a day off tomorrow. "Tomorrow at noon sound okay?"

"That's perfect. I'll call you then. Congratulations once again."

The call ended.

What in fresh heck?

"Was that your mother?" Uncle Reuben glanced at him when he came back inside. He'd finished with the vegetables and had the rice already on fire. He was just dropping the plantains he'd diced into the fryer.

"Uh, no." Ejiro shook his head. "Just ... wrong number."

Uncle Reuben raised an eyebrow, but he didn't press for more.

It wasn't until it was closing time that it suddenly hit him.

That supposedly fake audition tape he'd recorded for Blessing's "school project" about a month ago hadn't been fake at all, had it?

His heartbeat skittered, then began to race.

Those lying, traitorous, *stinking*—

TWO

ASSHOLES. THE LOT OF THEM.

Eddy let out one of his loud obnoxious laughs, and Obiora felt the headache in his temples throb just a little bit harder. He stood off to the side of the small meeting room, making himself a cup of green tea since all coffee did was fuck with his digestive system. Which was incredibly saddening considering how much he loved the damn beans. But with how strung out he felt right now, he couldn't risk making even the smallest cup.

Mike said something, which made Eddy laugh again. Obiora pretended to be busy on his phone, but he was merely watching the time on the screen as his tea brewed. When he glanced up after a moment, unable to help it, his pulse jumped when he found Obioma, his immediate older brother, watching him with a concerned frown on his face.

Obiora tried to smile but ended up grimacing instead. He turned back to his phone before his brother could take it as an invitation to come over. The rest of them knew how he got around this time of the year, so they probably wouldn't even bother. But could he blame them, really?

Okay, so maybe his co-workers weren't exactly assholes. It was just, when his father called for meetings like these, they served to remind Obiora just how badly he didn't want to be here. And then the reminder was followed by an almost crushing guilt, which was then topped off with a choking amount of grief. And with the guys laughing and chatting and acting like absolutely nothing was wrong, it made Obiora want to punch a hole into the wall. Which, again, wasn't their fault.

Fuck. He adjusted the knot of his tie, his throat feeling tight.

He'd just squeezed out and dumped his tea bag when Osita Anozie came striding in. At sixty-two years old and looking forty, with a slightly balding afro he had shaved in a sharp crew cut, the imposing man stood at an unimpressive five foot five, with warm brown skin, a stocky build, and thick eyebrows in a perpetual frown. The sight of him made Obiora's shot nerves short-circuit themselves even more. The green tea suddenly smelled absolutely disgusting, his stomach heaving at the thought of consuming anything.

Emeka Ikem, his father's best friend and the executive partner for *Anozie & Ikem* followed behind, taller and darker-skinned than his father and no less imposing, with a close-cropped greying afro, and a completely full grey beard.

Obinna, his eldest brother, came after, pushing his glasses up his nose, his hands filled with papers and documents concerning the latest project he'd acquired.

The meeting didn't take very long, which wasn't surprising, but with how Obiora felt it might as well have taken ten years.

"This could be one of the largest projects we've taken on since Emeka and I opened this firm," his father finished. Emeka nodded in agreement, that perpetual smile on his face. "I want you all to do your absolute best. You have two weeks to send in your preliminary sketches. That's all. Obiora."

Obiora startled, his head shooting up. His stomach roiled painfully like he'd eaten something bad. "Yes, sir?"

"I need to see you in my office immediately."

He stood and left the room before Obiora could reply, Emeka and Obinna following behind. His eldest brother glanced back once, looking concerned, before he disappeared out of the meeting room.

Obiora could feel Obioma's eyes boring into the side of his head, but he refused to look in his other brother's direction, standing up and making his way to his father's private office.

He was breathing deeply and slowly, but it did absolutely fuck all to calm his racing heart. He didn't even bother trying to figure out why his father wanted to see him; it couldn't be about anything else, could it?

"Come in," Osita boomed when he knocked. "Please, take a seat."

Obiora obeyed, clasping his hands in his lap, looking down onto his father's polished mahogany desk.

"Obiora," he said, his Nigerian accent thickening as it did when he was emotional. Right now, he was radiating concern. "Talk to me."

Obiora swallowed. "Please daddy," he whispered, feeling like he was twenty-one and losing her all over again. He clenched his eyes shut. His left knee was bouncing almost without his control. "I don't want to talk about it."

His father sighed. "God really works in mysterious ways. This project landed at just the right time for you. You can really get into it, you know? Challenge yourself."

It took effort to keep his face from twisting into an uncomfortable grimace at the thought of coming up with plans and shit for this new building.

And then there was the guilt, rising and rising, threatening to cut off his breath.

"I know, daddy," he forced himself to say, knowing the gruffness in his voice would be attributed to his grief. "I'll do my best."

"If you need anything—absolutely anything—you know I'm here for you. As are your brothers."

Obiora finally looked up. His responding smile was small, but it was genuine.

"I know, daddy. Thank you."

Osita grunted, and that was the end of that.

Obiora left the office and walked straight to his cubicle, slipping in his earphones, one of the best methods to get the rest of his co-workers to leave him the fuck alone.

Time kept moving, yet it never got any easier.

ON MOST DAYS, OBIORA LOVED his mother's love and attention, but whenever the anniversary of Ada's death came around, her affection felt smothering in its intensity. Luckily for him, he had the best mother in the world, because she understood the moment he cut their visit short and said he was heading out.

"Hold on, let me pack some of the leftovers for you."

"Mummy, you don't need to—"

"You're talking to the air," she replied, already disappearing into the kitchen.

Obiora smiled fondly and shook his head. He followed after her, knowing if he decided to wait in the sitting room, she'd take her sweet time.

Ifeoma Anozie rolled the smooth balls of pounded yam into small, clear cellophane bags, then lovingly folded them tightly into a food warmer. She was generous with the meat as she scooped some Egusi soup from the pot—in fact, it seemed to be more meat than soup, from what he could see, which made him feel weirdly emotional, like he was going to cry. What was with African mums and thinking more meat would heal all wounds? Not that it didn't.

She followed him to the door.

"I will make pepper soup for you tomorrow. With goat meat. Would you like that, honey?"

He nodded, swallowing to rid the lump in his throat. "Thank you, mummy."

"We have lots of extra bedrooms, you hear? We're just thirty minutes away; make sure you come over if you're feeling somehow."

"I will."

"Good." She switched to Igbo, "I love you."

Fucking hell, he needed to get out of here. "Love you, too," he echoed, also in Igbo, then he was hightailing his way out of there.

ESTHER WAS LATE AGAIN. WHEN he got a confirmation text from her stating she wasn't going to be for another hour, he was filled with a mix of annoyance and gratitude.

I know what you're doing, he sent.

Whatever do you mean? She responded, ending the text with an emoji with a halo.

He'd half-expected her to use her wife or children as an excuse for her tardiness—it wouldn't be the first time—but it seemed today was one of those days she wasn't even trying to pretend. He replied with the poop emoji, then put his phone on silent, heading to the locker rooms to change and drop his things, his shoulders already feeling lighter.

When he came back into the main space, most of Esther's evening class were already there, waiting, some of them doing some mild stretches.

"All right, everyone, are we ready?" There were echoes of affirmatives around the room. Obiora clapped his hands. "Great. We'll do some basic cardio today. Remember to listen to your body, everyone. Understanding that you can't or might not be able to keep up with me is *not* a personal failure. Got it?"

"Got it," they echoed.

There were bright, eager and excited smiles all around, which filled Obiora with a sense of fulfilment no amount of projects from his father could ever hope to accomplish.

Obiora grinned at them, his grief, for the moment, forgotten.

"Cue the music."

"**YOU NEED A VACATION.**"

"**YEAH?** No shit."

Obiora took a gulp of water from his flask, then flexed his aching wrists and fingers, a sure sign he'd gone too hard on the punching bag. The gym had since emptied of Esther's class, only about three regulars left behind, all with headphones on and working on their personal routines.

"If you ask your dad, are you sure he won't let you off for a bit?" Esther prodded. She was on a mat beside him, doing her cool-down stretches. Her dark brown skin shone with sweat, and her maroon braids—pulled up into a tight bun—were beginning to come loose from her bright pink hair-tie.

"I don't want him to worry." He saw her roll her eyes in the reflection of the gym's floor-to-ceiling mirror and couldn't help but grin in response. "I'm serious. I ask for time off now and he'll think I'm dying."

Esther snorted, then laughed. "This isn't just about Ada."

His chest twisted painfully at the sound of her name spoken out loud, mixed with an insurmountable gratitude. Everyone else tiptoed around the subject, but even though it hurt, Obiora loved

Esther for never treating his girlfriend's death like it was a taboo.

"Oh yeah?"

Esther rolled her eyes again. "This is about you and how suffocated you feel at work."

Obiora stumbled on his way to the treadmill. "What? I'm not—what?"

"You work out when you're stressed." Esther finally stood, done with her stretching. "Over the past few—"

"I work out literally every day, Es."

"Don't interrupt. Over the past few weeks, don't think I haven't noticed you coming in here earlier and leaving later. Something's got you tense, and with the way you've been complaining lately about your projects and deadlines, I'm going to put all my money on it being your job."

Obiora swallowed, refusing to meet her eyes where she was staring him down through their reflections.

"You know I'm right," she said softly.

"Okay. Let's say you're right. What then?"

Esther crossed her arms. "Well ..."

Obiora fiddled with the settings on the treadmill until it was at a steady incline, and began to jog. "Well ...?" he echoed.

"I brought my camera," she blurted.

It took him a second to understand. "Oh God, Es, not this again."

"Come on! What could it hurt?" She started counting off on her fingers. "One, you'll get a vacation; two, you won't worry your family; three, you'll have an excuse to take some time off without feeling this completely misplaced sense of guilt every time you think about quitting"—Obiora's breath hitched—"and four, you just *might* fall in love."

He scoffed. "Not gonna happen. You know my heart belongs to one person and one person only." And that person was fucking dead.

Esther suddenly looked pissed. "I wish you wouldn't take that bastard's last words to heart. Nicholas was an *asshole,* Obi. He disrespected your boundaries and took advantage of you when you were—"

"Es." His voice was dark. "Drop it."

She took a deep breath, and let it out slowly. Then she smiled. "I've got my camera, and the questions downloaded on my phone. It won't hurt to at least send in your audition. What are the odds that they'd pick you, anyways?"

Obiora's eyes narrowed. Esther looked smug. She'd dangled it in front of him like a challenge, and fucking hell he couldn't resist a fucking challenge.

He switched off the treadmill. "Fine."

"*Yes.*" She pumped her fist.

He grabbed the towel she handed him to wipe the sweat from his face. "Are we doing this here? Now?"

"Why not? The gym *is* your natural habitat."

"Fuck off." He grinned.

She laughed. "No, but seriously. You're more comfortable here, so I thought, why not? We want this to be as authentic—as *you*—as possible."

He blushed, self-conscious. "Look, whatever, I'm only doing this to prove that I can, and that they *will* pick me."

"Sure thing, hot shot."

"I'm serious. We send in the audition tape, I get the call, and that's the end of that."

"Whatever you say, Obi."

Esther went to get her camera. Though he tried his best, Obiora couldn't pretend that the wild racing of his heart was solely as a result of the exercise he'd just completed.

Fuck.

THREE

EJIRO SAT IN ONE CORNER of the sitting room, holding a red party cup half-filled with plain Sprite, grimacing and bobbing his head awkwardly to the music. Ajiri was—of course—currently on top of the table in the middle of the room, winding her waist and soaking up the hoots and hollers from her girlfriend and the rest of their friends.

His contract forbade him from telling anyone about his involvement with *Cupid Calling* until after the show had finished airing—which, wasn't that a bit strict?—but of course Ajiri had managed to concoct some mildly believable reason to gather all their friends and throw him a going-away party. What had she said again? He was going on a romantic retreat? Top secret host and location, of course. It was close enough to the truth that he was sure when he eventually revealed it, it wouldn't feel like too much of a betrayal to the rest of their friends.

God, he hated parties. Even though it was just his, Ajiri's and Blessing's closest friends—there were about twenty people, at most—he just didn't know how to mingle in this kind of setting. But he knew Ajiri would be upset if he wasn't enjoying himself, so he stood and walked around from the sitting room to the kitchen, smiling and occasionally swaying to the music, and managed a quick chat with whoever was free. The best part of the night would come later, anyway, when the music and energy had died down and they started gossiping about nonsensical things or playing childish games like truth or dare until the sun rose, then after that they'd probably all go out to get some McDonalds. He loved *that* bit of house parties, which should say a lot about him.

When he was sure he had sufficiently socialised enough, he snuck off to his bedroom without anyone being the wiser, closing and locking the door behind him.

His lips twitched into a nervous smile and his heart began to race in the same vein when he switched on his laptop. He'd succeeded in uploading a new part for his comic earlier, both on Tapas and Patreon, and the best part of his day was coming back hours later to read the comments.

There were twenty-two comments on the latest update on Patreon; his patrons gushed about the update and wished him well on his "vacation", some even going so far as to tell him to "actually REST, Ejiro, and put the damn drawing utensils down". Grinning, his heart so freaking big, he read through and replied to them all, promising them that he would indeed take a break. He didn't think he was allowed any electronic devices during the filming anyway.

When he switched over to Tapas, he was met with the same level of excitement for the latest update, and more well wishes for his "vacation". There were about five hundred comments on the web comic site, but he took his time to read every single one, and replied to the ones he could. Some readers left more well wishes on his message board, and he took his time liking and replying to those as well.

When he was done, he felt a little raw. Every time he got sick or something else in his life happened that prevented him from updating, he'd always feel incredibly guilty, but his readers were always so, so understanding, which only made him want to work even harder so he deserved their trust and support.

He'd wanted to put his Patreon on hold—which would stop them from being charged monthly—for the duration of his filming with *Cupid Calling*—or for his "vacation", as he'd told them—but his patrons had adamantly refused. In the end, the general consensus was that they'd rather put their own patronage on pause if they couldn't afford it, and then continue their patronage when he returned. He didn't know what he'd done to deserve them.

The nerves Ejiro had been trying to put at bay rapidly returned. In about three days, he was leaving for Oxford to begin the filming for *Cupid Calling*. Even though he'd spent an entire day in the first week of June—approximately three weeks ago, now—doing a photoshoot, handing them his blood and urine samples to test for STDs, having yet another audition in front of like forty people—producers included—signing the confidentiality agreement, and then two weeks later getting a second call to confirm he'd been selected, it still didn't feel real.

He was going to be on an actual dating show established by the legendary Ameri Shae, director of almost all his favourite films and TV series. He kept refusing to think about it because the thought filled him with a strange, almost suffocating anxiety. He was an introvert, through and through; how could he have let Ajiri and Blessing talk him into this? It felt like he'd gone through the whole in-person interview in a mild state of dissociation.

Ejiro's phone began to ring.

Immediately, he knew who it was and his stomach sank. He had to take a deep calming breath before answering the phone.

"Hello? Mummy, mingwo."

"Ehen, vredo. Ejiro. How are you?"

"I'm fine, mummy," he said, forcing himself to smile so she'd hear it in his voice.

"That's good, that's good. How's everything? I just spoke with your Uncle Reuben so I know things at work are okay."

"Yes, they're fine, everything's fine."

"I'm just calling to talk about this your retreat. You said you are leaving in a few days, correct? Are you all packed?"

"Yes. And yes, I've packed." He hadn't, but he knew she'd nag if he said otherwise. His stomach filled with that weird sense of guilt and shame at lying to her, but Ajiri had been right—he couldn't tell her the truth. It was awful to admit it, but his mother couldn't keep a secret to save her life, especially when it came to her children's "accomplishments". So Ajiri had come up with a clever lie about it being a religious retreat, and how Ejiro was "straying from the light" and needed to be saved. His mother had prayed on the phone with him for an hour straight after he'd told her why he still couldn't come home.

"This is good," his mother was saying, back in the present. "I'm so happy that at least one of my children is still on the right path. Speaking of, how's your sister?"

"Still has a girlfriend," Ejiro said with a slight roll of his eyes, because that was probably what she was *really* asking. It'd been ages since she actually cared whether Ajiri was fine or not.

"I can't believe she's still insisting on this depravity." Ejiro's chest went tight and hot. "What does she want me to do? Does she want me to apologise or something? Why is she doing all these things just to hurt me?"

Ejiro wanted to say something, wanted to defend her, but as usual, when his mother went on a rant like this, he couldn't speak—he couldn't *breathe*. After Ajiri and Blessing had started dating, Ajiri had finally told their mother she was a lesbian. Their mother's response was to at first go on an angry bigoted rant, and when her anger hadn't gone through, she'd began to weep, hard and excessively, crying loudly about how Ajiri wanted to kill her before her time. Ejiro refused to imagine how she might've reacted if they'd told her Blessing was trans.

Ajiri had sat through her furious raving, silent and stone-faced, while Ejiro had cried throughout, so hard he'd ended up with a pounding headache afterward. He hadn't known why the rant had affected him so much; unlike Ajiri, he wasn't queer, but hearing those words lobbed at his only sibling and best friend had felt like having them lobbed at *him*.

"Anyway, let's not talk about her. How about you, Ejiro? Have you and eh—what's that her name?—Samantha ... have you and Samantha made up yet?"

The tight feeling in his chest was growing worse. "Mummy, it's been over two years since me and Sam broke up. We're not getting back together."

"But you were so perfect for each other," she said, mournfully, like he was purposefully breaking her heart.

I don't want to talk about this, he thought but couldn't make himself say.

"With the way things are going, am I ever going to have grandkids? Your sister is a lost cause. You're my only hope, Jiro."

That last part was said teasingly, so he dutifully forced a laugh.

"Have you booked your flight home? You said you'll come after the retreat, abi?"

"Yes. I told you, I don't know how long the retreat is going to take"—another lie Ajiri had helped him make up—"so I can't possibly buy any tickets. It'll cost too much to reschedule."

"All right, fine. It's getting late, so I'll say goodnight now. I'll call you tomorrow, yes?"

"Okay. Goodnight, mummy."

"Ehen. Goodnight."

She ended the call.

Ejiro dropped the device onto his bed. He pulled his knees to his chest, and just tried to breathe.

He didn't know how long he remained like that before a body thumping hard against his door jolted him out of it.

"Jesus," Ajiri muttered, sounding slightly drunk. "Ejiro? Are you in there? Why the fuck is your door locked?" He winced at the curse word. She did go a little potty mouthed after she'd been drinking. "What are you doing in there?" Her voice turned sly.

Ejiro quickly rushed to open it before she could say something embarrassing.

She swayed inside. He closed and locked the door behind her.

Ajiri tumbled onto his bed, shifting until she was resting against the headboard. "This isn't a good look, Ejiro. A whole party out there being thrown in your honour and you're here, sequestered in your bedroom. Haba." Unlike him, Ajiri had picked up the English accent fairly quickly, but when she drank, her Nigerian accent and mannerisms came out in full force.

She stared at him, and he blushed, shifting uncomfortably.

"What's wrong?" She frowned, squinting her eyes. "You've got that—that look on your face."

"What? What look? I'm fine."

Realisation dawned. "You spoke to mummy, didn't you." It wasn't really a question, so he didn't bother to answer. Ajiri kissed her teeth. "I'm so glad you're doing this *Cupid Calling* thing. You know, I was so afraid she was getting to you with her manipulation. Blessing and I were so sure that this was it—any moment now you'd actually pack your things and leave."

Ejiro bristled. "I have to go home."

"You *have* to or you *feel* like you have to?" Ajiri raised an eyebrow.

That strange mix of guilt and shame made his heart pound painfully.

Like she could read his mind, Ajiri snapped, "You don't owe her anything."

"I owe her everything," Ejiro argued. "She's done everything by herself—all her life."

When their father had died—they'd been too young to remember—she had refused to remarry, against the wishes of her family. Her own parents were dead, so her extended family—aunts and uncles—had taken it upon themselves to write her future.

They'd felt it was unseemly for a single woman to take care of two children alone—or, more likely, that a single woman *couldn't* and *shouldn't* take care of children alone—and had cut her off when she'd staunchly kept refusing their continuous offers of a groom. So she'd set out and proved them wrong, raising them both completely by herself. The only person who'd stayed by her side was her twin brother, their Uncle Reuben.

"She endured constant disrespect and abuse from judgemental Nigerian society, and worked endless tireless hours just to be able to send us to good schools abroad—"

"Which is her fucking *job*, Ejiro. In case you forgot."

"I—what? That's not ... how is that fair? How can you say that? Without her, you wouldn't even *be* here—"

"That's what parents are *supposed* to do," Ajiri said, getting up from his bed. Her nostrils were wide, fists clenched in her anger. "They're supposed to feed you, and clothe you, and do the best for you, because that is their job! They didn't bring you into this world just so you could repay them one day; that's not how unconditional love works."

"Well, fine," Ejiro snapped. "I'm still grateful to her, all right? I still appreciate everything she's done, and if going home is the one single thing she wants from me in return, then I'm going to give it to her. Can we—can we not, please? I don't want to argue."

Ajiri wiped the tears that had been forming in her eyes. Ejiro had to blink repeatedly to keep his own tears at bay. God, they were useless at arguing, or being angry in general. They almost always cried when they were this angry or upset.

His twin still didn't look satisfied with the outcome of their argument—they'd had it countless times before, and she was never satisfied—but as usual, she forced down her displeasure, inhaling deeply.

"Come on, then," she said, taking his hand. "We're all just about partied out, so we're starting a game."

"Oh? Game time already? That was fast."

"Shut up, Ejiro."

He laughed. Before they left the room, she stopped him, hugging him tightly, burying her face in his chest. They were about the same height—five foot eleven—so she had to stoop a little to achieve it.

"I love you, you know that right? I only say these things because I'm worried about you."

"I know," Ejiro said, his voice as thick as hers. "I know. I love you, too."

"Good. Now, back to the party! By this time in about two months, you'll hopefully be in love and engaged." She waggled her eyebrows at him.

Ejiro blushed. Despite his misgivings, he really *did* want to fall in love—desperately—TV show setting or no. He wanted what Ajiri and Blessing had; a connection so deep it was like they were sometimes extensions of each other. Something like the bond he himself shared with his twin, but held up with a different but equally profound kind of intimacy. Even the way they'd met sounded like something straight out of one of Ejiro's romantic comics.

They'd met two years ago, during Ajiri's final year studying for her Masters in Fashion Design, and Blessing's final year studying for her Bachelor's in Photography. They'd both had deadlines and had rushed to the MMU print shop to print out their portfolios at the same time. Ajiri said when their eyes had met that first time, she'd known.

As their works had printed, they'd kept glancing at each other and blushing, neither one brave enough to make the first move. They'd exited the shop at the same time, about to head in opposite directions when Ajiri had forced herself to stop and turn around, her lips parted to call out to Blessing, only to find that Blessing had stopped and turned, too, her mouth open to call out to her. They'd laughed, and the rest, as they say, was history.

Ejiro *wanted* that with a fierceness that was almost devastating. Once upon a time, after Ajiri had come out to him, and Blessing had mentioned being not just transgender but demisexual as well, Ejiro had wondered if he might be queer, too. But he'd written off his questioning as a longing to have something in common with his twin; he didn't think he'd ever been attracted to people other than women, and even though something about the way Blessing had described her demisexuality had felt—*right* to him, he'd dismissed it on the account of just how badly he wanted a deep sexual and romantic connection. Surely someone on the asexual spectrum wouldn't want such a bond as badly as he did?

He'd thought he'd had that bond with Sam, his first and only serious girlfriend, but that had ended in disaster.

He shook off his thoughts, returning himself to the present, to Ajiri, still in his arms.

"There are probably going to be a million other contestants, so, you know, no pressure."

"*Twenty-nine* contestants, not counting you." Ajiri winked at him. "That doesn't sound too bad. Trust me, Ejiro, once the bachelorette sees you? Once you see *each other*? That'll be it. As long as you're yourself, you'll have her swooning into your arms in no time."

FOUR

THERE WAS POSSIBLY NOTHING OBIORA hated more than lying to his family. It was a miracle he'd been able to secretly meet with his "handler" and the producers a few weeks ago for his in-person audition, and all the extras that came along with it. He'd gotten the confirmation call while he'd been on a lunch break at work and had managed to also keep that to himself until he could tell Esther, which, again, was a fucking miracle.

The guilt sat heavy in his stomach like a rock after his father mentioned—for what felt like the millionth time—how proud he was of Obiora for finally taking this step for his mental health.

"It's good," he repeated after they'd finished dinner. "I know a lot of people don't take this mental health thing seriously, especially Nigerians, but I don't want you to feel ashamed or uncomfortable, you hear? This is good."

"Thank you, daddy," Obiora said, ducking his head. The movement might have come across as bashful, but in reality, he was trying to hide his shame.

"Perhaps I can finally hope for some grandkids in your future, eh, obim?" his mother teased, standing up to begin clearing the table.

Obiora blushed, though his throat was thick with something bitter. He stood, as did his brothers, to help pack up the dishes and take them to the kitchen. "My future spouse could be a man, mummy."

"Ehen? Are you saying you won't adopt if that's the case?"

Obiora managed a small laugh. "Touché."

"So Nkem is not enough of a grandchild for you?" Obinna asked with a teasingly raised eyebrow.

"Don't go putting words in my mouth now."

They laughed.

"We should even be focusing on Obioma, sef," their dad added with a sparkle in his eye. "You and Anita have been married, what? Almost a year now? Should we be expecting any good news any time soon?"

"Daddy, please," Obioma said, but he was blushing.

They laughed again.

In the kitchen, they scraped off the bits of food still clinging to the dishes, then used paper towels to wipe their surfaces after. Even after telling their mother that it wasn't necessary to wipe the plates before putting them into the dishwasher, she was adamant the oils would somehow ruin the machine. It was tradition now to wipe their plates after eating.

"I'm going to head out," Obiora said when they were done, and the dishwasher was gently whirring.

"Really? So soon?" his father asked as Obiora walked into the sitting room, his mother and brothers following behind. Osita was already in his favourite chair in front of the TV, settled in for either the news, a sports channel, or a film; it all depended on his mood, and his wife's preference, of course.

"Yeah," Obiora answered, managing to sound perfectly sheepish, hands in his pockets. "I want to double check my stuff—make sure I have everything before I leave."

"Ah, ah, you're only checking your things now?" his father

scolded gently. "If you forget anything, you know you'll be on your own since you said they don't allow phones and such."

"I know, I know. I'll be thorough."

"What about you two?" Ifeoma asked, glancing at Obioma and Obinna in turn, her hands on her hips. "Will you be leaving early as well?"

His brothers glanced at each other, exchanging a look Obiora couldn't quite interpret, but made him feel strangely nervous.

"Yeah, we'll be heading out as well," Obioma finally said.

Obinna threw an arm over Obiora's shoulders, nearly making him stumble. The three of them were a perfect combination of their parents; tall, like their mother, and stocky and well-built, like their father, thanks to stable gym routines. They had their father's warm, brown skin, and their mother's loose, kinky curls.

"Yeah, we want to go drinking—spend some sibling time together before he leaves, yeah?" His eldest brother ruffled his hair playfully.

"Stop it," Obiora groaned, smacking his hand away half-heartedly.

"All right, then. Let me see you in the kitchen for a bit before you leave." His mother nodded at him.

The bitter taste in the back of his throat intensified. He left his father and brothers behind, following after her.

She turned to face him, a soft, concerned look on her face. "I hope we're not making you uncomfortable?" she said in Igbo, her voice pitched low. "You look worried."

Ah, shit. Curse his mother's uncanny ability to read him like an open book.

"I'm fine, mummy," he replied in English. "I'm just a little self-conscious about the whole thing, though not in a bad way." Fucking hell, the lies were going to make him physically sick—he could almost feel his stomach heaving.

"Mhm?" The sound was noncommittal. She placed both her hands on his shoulders, and stroked his arms gently. "The most important thing to us is your health. You know that, right? I mean, yes, we'd be ecstatic if you are able to find love again, but most of all, we just want you to *heal*—that's all. Don't feel pressured by my jokes about grandchildren, eh, obim?" *My heart.* She called all of them that, but it still managed to feel special every time she did, no matter who she was referring to.

Obiora smiled. He impulsively hugged her, silently apologising for lying.

He could feel her smile in her voice as she said in Igbo, "I love you."

"I love you, too, mummy."

"All right. I'll let you off now."

The brothers said their goodnights, and Obiora couldn't have left quickly enough.

When they were on the pavement, the three brothers stopped automatically, glancing at each other.

"*The Swan*?" Obinna said, his eyes dancing with mischief.

Obiora felt a faint sense of foreboding. He cleared his throat. "Uh, you know, you guys don't need to—I mean, shouldn't you be heading home—"

"*The Swan*," Obioma interrupted, looking just as devious.

"Fuck's sake," Obiora said.

"Language," Obinna scolded, without much heat.

Obiora had no choice but to nod in helpless agreement when his brothers looked at him expectantly. "*The Swan* it is."

The pub wasn't located too far off from their parents' abode, so they began to walk in its direction. Obioma and Obinna brought out their phones, presumably to text their wives about their whereabouts.

Obiora felt a slight pang, suddenly feeling, for the briefest moments, painfully alone. He shook it off.

The pub was busy when they arrived, though the crowd was still on the family-friendly side of it due to the early hour. The later it got, the more it'd be filled with university students looking to get drunk and have a great time, while the families dwindled down as they went off to bed to prepare for a new, tedious work day.

The music wasn't too loud, the sound of it almost overshadowed by the noise of the pub's patrons.

"I'll get the drinks," Obioma said, yelling slightly. "You get us a table. What'll you guys like?"

"Just a vodka and coke for me," Obiora said, not in the mood for anything fancy.

"Coke," Obinna said. After he'd gotten married, he used to only drink when they hung out during the weekends. Then after he'd had his daughter, he'd stopped drinking altogether.

Obioma nodded. "Back in a sec! Text me if you're gonna sit in someplace obscure."

Obiora nodded.

Obinna jerked his head in the direction of the pub's main room. "Up or down?"

Obiora looked around. "Up, I think."

They headed upstairs and found themselves a small table in the corner of the room. Obinna texted Obioma their positions as he'd requested.

"So. How's the little fireball?" Obiora asked, desperate to take control of the outing.

Obinna returned his phone to his pocket. When he looked up, there was an amused quirk to his mouth, like he knew exactly what Obiora was doing. "She's doing great. Same as she was the last time you saw her. Which was, what? Last week?"

"Yeah, yeah, I get it." Obiora slumped.

His oldest brother took off his glasses and held them up into the light, squinting at the lenses. Seemingly satisfied that they were clean enough, he replaced them on his nose. He met Obiora's eyes, and his expression turned serious.

Obiora swallowed.

"Let's wait for Obioma," he said, still watching him with that serious look.

Fuck me, Obiora thought, eloquently.

They didn't have to wait long.

"So," Obioma said the second he sat down, after passing them their drinks. "At first, Obinna and I thought maybe you'd come to us on your own, but since that's obviously not happening and you're leaving in two days …"

"Here we are," Obinna finished.

"Uh, what … what are you guys talking about?" He laughed awkwardly.

Wow. Smooth one, Obiora; they're definitely not suspicious now.

Obioma rolled his eyes, taking a sip from his drink—a vodka and lemonade on ice, with a wedge of lime on the edge. "Don't play coy. I mean, not that there's anything wrong with it, but do you really think Obinna and I believe you're going on some therapy retreat bullshit?"

"Language," Obinna said automatically.

They ignored him.

"Tell us what's really going on." Obiora opened his mouth. "The *truth*, Obiora." He shut it.

"Are you really going on a—what did you call it? A grief counselling retreat?" Obinna asked. He gave him the "concerned dad" look, the one that said no matter what Obiora said, he'd love and support him anyway.

Obiora's chest swelled with how much he loved them.

He took a large sip of his drink, grimacing a little. The ratio of coke to vodka was a little unbalanced; there was too much vodka.

"Fine, you want to know the truth?" His cheeks heated up, and his stomach roiled. "Don't make it a big deal, or whatever, I'm just— it wasn't even *my* idea—I'm only going along with it because I needed a break and I didn't want daddy to freak out—"

"Obiora." The dad voice again, except this time, it was in a tone that demanded answers.

"Fine," he repeated. His heart raced. "It's a dating show." He practically spat it out. Like ripping a Band-Aid.

There was a pause.

"It's a what now?"

Obiora could feel himself blushing harder. "You heard me. When Esther saw the casting call, she made me send in an audition, all right? And when I got the call back ... well. Here we are," he said sheepishly.

When he'd gotten the second call, he hadn't actually planned to go, not really. But then Esther had said, "You're right. It *is* a competition. If you went on without the intention to win, you probably wouldn't last a day." And Obiora had said "bet", ignoring the sparkle in her eyes that told him she'd said those words on purpose, because obviously the bigger issue here was the challenge underneath said words.

Plus, if he were really being honest here, he really did want a fucking break from his job.

No, not want. It was a *need*. He hadn't had a vacation in the past five years since he started working with his father, and by vacation, he meant a holiday by himself or with a lover, not one with his family, which they did at least once every year.

Esther was right. Working for his dad was becoming unbearable, even though acknowledging his stress only made him feel guilty. After Ada's accident, his dad had practically shoved the job in his face, and it had helped Obiora immensely in coping with his grief. He'd buried himself in the work, and it had felt like an escape—a much needed breath of fresh air.

How could he repay his father's kindness by up and quitting, just like that? And all because he wanted to become a fucking personal trainer? His old man wouldn't show it, but Obiora *knew* he would be disappointed. The man was already planning how his three sons would take over the firm the second he and Emeka retired, since his best friend didn't have any children of his own. The last thing Obiora wanted to do was break his heart.

"A dating show?" Obioma repeated. He looked like he was trying not to laugh. "Are you serious?"

"Stop mocking him," Obinna reprimanded. "What kind of dating show?" To anyone who didn't know him, he looked blank-faced, but Obiora knew his family like he knew the back of his palm. The bastard was also trying not to laugh.

"Go on. Laugh it out," he said with a tired sigh, groaning when Obioma did just that, startling the people sitting at the table over with how hard he chortled. "It's called *Cupid Calling*. It's new. The director is Ameri Shae."

Obioma abruptly stopped laughing. "Ameri Shae? *The* Ameri Shae?"

Obiora felt smug. "*The* Ameri Shae." He took a sip from his drink.

Obinna wrinkled his eyebrows. "Remind me what she directed again?"

Obioma looked appalled, like Obinna not immediately knowing who she was was the greatest crime known to man. "*Right in Time? Scandalous? Fly Off the Wall*? Any of those ringing a bell, old man? I know you don't watch a lot of TV, but *come* on."

"Yeah, yeah, okay," Obinna said, but he was grinning. It seemed to sink in, because his eyes grew wide. "Jesus."

"Exactly!" Obioma gasped, startling the table over with his loud voice, yet again.

"Lower your voice," Obiora hissed. "I'm on a contract; I'm technically not supposed to tell anyone."

"You devil." Obioma punched him playfully in the arm, but he dutifully lowered his voice. "Is that why you lied to us? Come on, brother, you know you can trust us with anything."

"I know, I know, and I'm sorry. I just didn't want it to be a big deal. And I didn't want mummy to think that doing this show means I'm back in the dating field." No matter how many times she told him she was only joking when she mentioned grandkids, Obiora knew, deep down, that when his mother said she wanted him to heal, her idea of that was probably him meeting and falling in love with someone new.

Yeah. Like fuck that was gonna happen. It didn't help that her older two sons were already happily settled.

Obioma looked confused. "I'm sorry, what? Then why the fuck are you doing it?"

"Language."

"I just need a break." Even admitting it filled his mouth with a sour tang. "I didn't want daddy to worry if I told him I want time off for no good reason."

"*Should* we be worried?" It was the concerned dad face again.

Obiora rolled his eyes. "No, you should not."

"Are you sure?" Obinna pressed. He had his arms crossed over his broad chest. "Why would you be wary of telling daddy you need a break?"

"Come on. *You* haven't taken a vacation from work since you started working, and you've been there *six* years longer than I have!"

Obinna's eyebrows furrowed. "That's not true. I've taken many vacations."

"Anything that has to do with your wife and daughter does not count."

Obinna flushed.

Obioma snorted.

"Don't you even start." Obiora zeroed in on him. Obioma gulped. "You're just as bad. The only time you took a vacation was when you broke your leg two years ago, and that's because daddy *forced* you to."

"Okay, so what?" Obinna said, scoffing. "Just because none of us have taken vacation time doesn't mean *you* can't."

Obiora mirrored his brother's pose, crossing his own arms. "You really think if I asked for vacation time, daddy would just be like, 'of course son, here you go', no questions asked?"

Obinna's chest puffed up defensively. "I mean, of course he'd have questions—"

"He'd freak out. Hell, *you're* freaking out, don't even pretend. You think something is seriously wrong, don't you?"

Obinna looked like he was fighting not to prove him right, but the ever-honest man couldn't help it, he blurted, "But why *do* you want to take a vacation?" and Obiora made a sound of triumph, while Obioma groaned in the background. Obinna ignored them. "Are you feeling overworked? *Is* there something wrong?"

"There we fucking go."

"Language."

Obiora sank into his chair. "I rest my case."

Obinna fiddled with a paper napkin, ripping it into tiny, neat squares. A bad habit he had when he was worried; he'd never really stopped since he was a kid. "So, you just want time off for ... for nothing? For time's off sake."

"Yes," Obiora lied. He forced himself to meet his brother's eyes, feeling sick as he did. Looking away would only have made Obinna refuse to let it go.

Obinna dutifully stared into his eyes for several moments, before giving a brief satisfied nod. "All right. Occasionally taking a break from work is a good thing. No matter the reason. If we count our spouses as reasons—which I am, don't interrupt—this means adding anniversaries, birthdays, and the lot—Obioma and I *have* had more vacations than you. It only makes sense that you should get time off, too."

"Great, good, fantastic. Are we done with the therapy session?" Obioma said with a roll of his eyes. "Can we please get back to Ameri *fucking* Shae?"

"Language."

Obiora grinned, shoving his discomfort to the side and grasping at the subject change like a drowning man grasping at straws. "I know, right?"

"Is it going to be like speed dating or?"

"Heard of *The Bachelorette*?"

"No way."

Obiora preened. Then again, Obioma was easily impressed, but he didn't let that stop him.

"Speaking of Ameri Shae, did you catch up on the last episode of *Scandalous*?"

They ended up chilling at the pub for another hour, before Obinna had to cut their outing short. Caroline, his wife, didn't like him coming home late. Anita, Obioma's wife, usually worked late hours—she was a nurse—so Obiora guessed she had a night shift.

They headed off the main road and back into the residential area toward their parents' house, since Obinna's car was parked there.

"Shall I drive you both to yours? I don't mind."

"Nah, I'll take a cab."

Obioma was on his phone. "I'm meeting Anita in town, so I'll take a cab as well."

"Right."

Obinna turned to look at him as they stopped by his car. "Even if you're doing this for the vacation time, maybe keep an open mind?" His eyes twinkled.

"Please stop." Obiora groaned.

Obioma looked up from his phone, a slow, playful grin spreading across his face. "Yeah," he drawled. "It didn't even hit me—this is going to be like *The Bachelorette*! You'll be competing for one gorgeous woman's heart—you should absolutely go for it!"

"Not going to happen. Goodnight." Obiora began to walk away.

"Aw, Obiora, come on!" Obioma called after him. "Think about it! Mummy and daddy would—"

"Obioma." Their eldest brother's voice was sharp. "Leave it."

Obioma sighed. "Fine, whatever. Just … Obiora?"

Despite himself, he stopped and looked back.

"Keep your heart open?"

Obiora made sure they saw him roll his eyes. "Goodnight."

"Goodnight," his brothers echoed, sounding amused.

As Obiora made his way to the main road, it was easy for him to ignore the rapid, almost excited pounding of his heart—an excitement of the possibility of falling in love with someone new—because it didn't mean shit. He'd tried to move on from Ada with Nicholas, and look how *that* had ended.

Nah, he was done denying his heart belonged to anyone but her.

And even if he *were* looking for love, the last place he'd look would be on a fucking reality dating show.

Ameri Shae ✓ @AmeriMazing

It's here! The moment you've all been waiting for. The first contestant for CUPID CALLING has finally been revealed! Check him out on the official website here: cupidcalling.com.

The next bachelor will be revealed same time tomorrow. 💘
#CupidCallingBachelorReveal

💬 2810   🔁 10.2k   ♡ 19.3k

The official website for the CUPID CALLING series.

Cupid Calling

ABOUT | THE BACHELORETTE | THE BACHELORS | EPISODES | CONTACT | BECOME A CUPID

HIGHLIGHT REELS

EJIRO ODAVWARO

Say hello to Ejiro David Odavwaro, AKA bachelor number one! Ejiro is twenty-five years old, works as an assistant chef at EWOMA'S, his uncle's restaurant in Manchester, and is an aspiring artist. During his spare time, he likes to draw comics and hang out with his twin sister and best friend, Ajiri, and her girlfriend, Blessing.

Ejiro, a painful romantic at heart, has always wanted to find love.

Let's hope he can do so with CUPID CALLING!

Click here to read the full transcript of Ejiro's Highlight Reel

COMMENTS

 **ANONCUPID_**

welp only one bachelor reveal and I've already got a fave lmfao

 2232   722

 **ABSTRACT_TIGER**

he's so shy and sweet I love him 🥺

 2089   512

 **BABYGIRL997**

He seems very honest. Very real and down to earth. Can't say much cause we need to see him in action, but based on this highlight reel alone, I hope he makes it far in the competition :)

 1937   380

 LOAD MORE COMMENTS

The official website for the CUPID CALLING series.

Cupid Calling

ABOUT | THE BACHELORETTE | THE BACHELORS | EPISODES | CONTACT | BECOME A CUPID

HIGHLIGHT REELS

OBIORA ANOZIE

Say hello to Obiora "Obi" James Anozie, AKA bachelor number seven! Obiora is twenty-six years old and works as a junior architect for ANOZIE & IKEM, his father's architectural firm in Sheffield. During his spare time, he likes to work out at the gym, and watch TV shows with his two older brothers, extended family, and closest friends.

Obiora has lost love, AND had his heart broken. He hopes to find something real with CUPID CALLING.

We wish him the absolute best!

Click here to read the full transcript of Obiora's Highlight Reel

COMMENTS

 FAKERAKE24

"I know what I'm here for. I know what I want. Everything else is just white noise." Jesus f*cking Christ I want to have his babies

 2877   806

 DELISHCUPCAKE

Ameri Shae is right we do love a resident bad boy with a broken heart haha I'll be rooting for him!!♥♥

 2323   771

 BANGTAN0613

He reminds me of my ex: handsome, sexy, confident, and cocky as hell. So, naturally, I hate him >:(

 2013   1090

LOAD MORE COMMENTS ⌄

FIVE

WELL, THAT HADN'T LASTED LONG. Ejiro's confidence, that is.

Be yourself. But try not to be too much of an introvert. Initiate conversations whenever you can. Ask questions; people love talking about themselves! And for God's sake, smile! You glower when you're nervous and it makes you look like a serial killer.

Ejiro inwardly shook his head, his lips quirked as he remembered Ajiri's words before he'd departed for the filming in Oxford, about a week ago. *Thanks a lot for the pep talk, Ajiri, but it's done f-all to help.*

He was pretty sure he'd looked like a cow when he'd filmed what Ameri had called his "highlight reel"; a Q&A style video he'd filmed with the director herself acting as his interviewer. It would act as an introductory video of him for the future fans, and would be released about a month before the show itself started airing, to give fans who to root for. After filming that, it had been a waiting game until today. The first official day of filming.

He'd been the very first bachelor to arrive; Ameri hadn't wanted the bachelors to meet until today, so their reactions to each other would be genuine. He'd counted his being the first as a good thing, because not only had he been able to make a hopefully good impression on the bachelorette, it had given him no choice but to greet the next bachelor to appear or risk coming off like an ill-mannered donkey.

And the bachelor after that, and the bachelor after that, and so on. But eventually, there'd been enough bachelors that they had begun to mingle with *each other*, and he'd sort of ... faded into the background.

The bachelors were loud and boisterous and knew how to control a conversation. Each time Ejiro tried to interject with something—tried to make his presence known—he was overshadowed by someone else. Eventually, he stopped trying, bobbing at the edges of conversations and grimacing awkwardly.

Now, he lingered by the long table holding the drinks and snacks, and couldn't, for the life of him, remember the names of any of the guys he'd greeted. He remembered the very first guy and that was only because his name was Adam—*like Adam and Eve*, Ejiro had told himself so he'd remember—and he had incredibly pale skin that clashed with his bright red hair and freckles.

The rest of them, though? Zip. A flush of shame and dejection warmed his cheeks. When he got as nervous as he was right now, he tended to operate on autopilot, so he wasn't entirely surprised that his brain was so busy trying to keep him from tripping all over his own feet that it hadn't retained a single lick of information from the entire past hour.

Had it even been an hour? It could've been ten minutes for all Ejiro knew, and his anxiety was what was making the seconds tick by slowly.

He had his first meeting with Sophia Bailey, the bachelorette, going for him—the way she'd looked at him from underneath her eyelashes when he'd first introduced himself, hugging her after her request, made his heart give a weird thump in remembrance. But it had been her awed and overjoyed reaction to the realistic painting he'd drawn of her that had sealed the deal. Ameri had shown him a surprise picture of her to end his highlight reel, wanting his unfiltered reaction for the clip. Sophia was so freaking gorgeous Ejiro hadn't resisted the urge to immediately put her likeness on paper.

But what if the other bachelors had done something equally or even more extravagant to capture her attention and he was forgotten?

She was here right now, making her way around one of the pools behind the house where the bachelors had congregated, cameras and lights following her as she talked to each bachelor one on one. Her pale blue dress glittered, complementing her full figure, and bringing out the rich plum shades underneath her dark brown skin. Her thick black hair fell in silky waves to her shoulders.

Ejiro felt like he was going to be sick. He'd slowly been gravitating *away* from her approach as all the endorphins from earlier fled from his system, leaving him feeling cold and exposed.

God, Ajiri would be so disappointed in him.

"You going to drink that?"

Ejiro startled, turning to look at who'd spoken. He felt his stomach sink—even further than it had already sunk every time a bachelor had walked through the back doors.

The stranger was ridiculously handsome, because of course he was. He was Black, with warm, dark brown skin and a riot of curls falling over his forehead, shaved close on the sides. Stubble artfully framed his square jaw—Ejiro didn't even know stubble could *look* artful—and when he smiled, a tiny dimple appeared on his right cheek.

Jesus Christ. If there was anything more attractive than two dimples, it was *one* single dimple. Ejiro felt the sudden urge to draw him, the fingers of his free hand twitching. He got the urge sometimes, when he met people whose features or mannerisms were so vibrant, he just *needed* to put them down on paper, to somehow immortalise their sheer vitality. The urge this time, however, made him feel slightly annoyed. He might as well eliminate himself right now.

A playful smirk curved the stranger's full lips—which didn't help at all with Ejiro's *I-need-to-draw-him-right-freaking-now* urge—and he nodded at the still full cocktail Ejiro had hovering in his right hand. "You've been holding that all night and haven't touched it. Unless I'm wrong and that is in fact *not* your first drink of the night. If so, please ignore me."

Ejiro smiled, a wobbly, self-conscious thing. "Ah. I don't actually drink ... I just—" *wanted to look like I was busy*, but that was kind of sad to admit, so he didn't say it out loud.

The man seemed to take pity on him, which made Ejiro feel pathetically grateful. "Not good with new people, huh?"

Ejiro laughed, though the sound was a tad self-deprecating. "That obvious?"

"The other guys have been talking."

Ejiro's eyes widened. "Oh dear God."

The man laughed, a full, hearty sound. "Don't look so worried. Some of the guys are trying to figure out who'll be going home tonight in the hopes that it won't be them. And since you've been trying to fade into the background—"

"Unsuccessfully, obviously," Ejiro interjected, "since you're here and everyone's talking about me."

He laughed again. "You've kind of been eliminated on the pure basis of your ... well."

"Boringness?" Ejiro guessed, cringing.

"Evasiveness," he corrected, looking amused, obviously only trying to be nice for his benefit.

Ejiro's stomach sank at the implication. Anxiety clawed up his throat like bile, and he tightened his grip around his glass to keep his hand from trembling.

If the other bachelors had already written him off as a lost cause, what were the odds that Sophia didn't feel the same?

His eyes darted in the bachelorette's direction. She was standing in front of the greenhouse—yes, there was a freaking *greenhouse* in the backyard of this mansion—her smile a little strained as one of the bachelors talked and gesticulated wildly at her. It was one of the blondes; there were about four of those, if he could remember correctly. He wondered if Sophia was uncomfortable because of the guy, or because of the cameras.

Probably the cameras. He looked away. Tried to take a sip of his drink and immediately grimaced and stopped in time when he remembered the alcohol.

He'd known it couldn't be this easy—why on earth had he let Ajiri talk him into this? At this point, he wanted this entire thing to be over and done with so he could go home.

"I assume you're only here to check out the competition, then?" Ejiro snarked in what was possibly a poor attempt to hide his dejection.

"Yup," the man admitted. Ejiro tried not to look too shocked at his honesty. His eyes twinkled as he added, "Or lack thereof."

"Ow."

The grin came back, dimple flashing. The man swirled his cocktail in its glass, the movement a little hypnotising. "I'm Obiora, by the way."

"Ejiro."

"Nigerian?" He looked excited.

"Born and raised." Ejiro couldn't help but smile back, his shoulders relaxing minutely. "I only got my citizenship about a year ago. What about you?"

"Second generation immigrant," Obiora replied, beaming. "My parents moved here in the late eighties with the dream of helping their families back home."

"Oh, big mood." Ejiro agreed, and Obiora laughed.

Then there was the sound of a huge splash, drawing their attention before Ejiro could add something witty, almost pathetically eager to continue the conversation in the hopes of making a new friend.

One of the bachelors had undressed and jumped into the pool in nothing but his underwear.

"Whoop!" he hollered, completely unashamed.

Ejiro grimaced.

"Not a good look." Obiora agreed.

"I said no."

That was Sophia, her voice firm. The backyard went completely silent.

The blonde she was talking to didn't seem to realise he was the focus of everyone's attention, his voice unbearably loud as he said, "Come on, don't be a wuss—"

He abruptly wrapped his arms around Sophia's waist, his grin wide and feral, his eyes dancing with mischief as he lifted her into the air.

Everyone seemed to know instinctively what he was about to do.

"Hey!" more than one bachelor, including Obiora, yelled, already making their way quickly across the backyard.

"Put me down," Sophia said, her voice cold. She'd gone dangerously still.

Ejiro hated confrontations. He felt sick, dizzy, but his feet took him in Sophia's direction as well, his worry for her overshadowing his fear.

"Come on—" the blonde was cajoling, turning in the direction of the pool, his arms tensing, getting ready to throw her in.

"Yo, did you not hear when she said to let her go?" Obiora growled, his voice dangerous.

"Maybe you should mind your business," the blonde taunted back, his grip on her tightening.

The tussle was quick. More than one person grabbed the blonde's arms, while others pulled Sophia out of his grasp and led her to safety.

"Jeez, I was only playing," the blonde said, but Ejiro could clearly see the discomfort in his eyes, the realisation that he'd gone too far.

The men sneered at him.

"Are you okay?"

"I'm fine, I'm fine."

There were too many people surrounding her.

"Can I have some space, please?"

The men immediately backed off. Sophia looked shaken. She turned and stalked back into the mansion. Some of the cameras, along with Ameri, quickly followed after her. The rest remained to film the aftermath.

Ignoring the cameras, the bachelors rounded in on the blonde.

"What the fuck is *wrong* with you?"

Ejiro took that as his cue to back off.

He glanced in the direction of the mansion, but knew Sophia needed her space, so he didn't approach it.

He was drawn to the greenhouse, leaving the bachelors arguing behind. Later on, when he'd do his commentary during the cutaway, Ameri would ask him why he hadn't said anything to Chad—of course the donkey's name was *Chad*—and Ejiro would admit he was awful at confrontations; besides, the other bachelors seemed to already have it covered.

The greenhouse was a thing of beauty, even from the outside. The doors were locked and it was dark, but Ejiro could faintly make out the colours of the variety of plants and flowers within. It would make a really romantic spot later on in the competition, which was probably one of the reasons Ameri must have chosen this mansion as the location.

His mind went to the comic he was writing on Patreon and Tapas. Things between his MC and love interest were building really slowly, but what if they had a moment in a greenhouse like this? Dubem worked in a flower shop, so it wouldn't be too farfetched. What if, when he finally asked Efe, his love interest, on a date, he took her to a greenhouse? And they had their first kiss?

Excitement made his blood race as the scenes bloomed in his imagination, bright and vivid—petals and greenery surrounding the couple in a tender embrace—and Ejiro's hands itched desperately for his drawing tablet.

"Pretty, isn't it?"

Ejiro jumped. Sophia laughed.

"Whoops, sorry," she said, still giggling. "Didn't mean to startle you."

"No, no, it's not your fault, I was lost in my own world," Ejiro said quickly, grinning, though her proximity made his heart pound for reasons other than her surprise appearance. Two cameramen hovered behind them, but he managed to ignore them.

She was here. She was talking to him. She'd ended her alone time and come straight to him, if the looks the other bachelors were giving him were anything to go by.

Please God—pardon my language—but let me not fuck *this up.*

"Are you okay?" he asked, frowning with concern. "What happened earlier was all kinds of messed up."

Her eyes darkened a little, but it thankfully wasn't aimed at him. "I'm okay. And you're right. That was fucking shitty. But at least we all have one less bachelor to worry about," she said with a conspiratory wink.

Ejiro blushed. He didn't think it was sportsmanlike to say anything bad about a competitor, even though it was a relief to hear.

"All this excitement has left me parched, though," Sophia said, one hand delicately touching the long arch of her throat.

God, she was gorgeous. He wanted to draw her again. She deserved to be a goddess in a fantasy comic. She shifted her weight from one foot to the other, and Ejiro winced, wondering if her feet hurt. She *had* been standing almost all night. He hoped the night would end soon, so she'd get some rest.

Then he registered her statement.

"Piña colada?"

"How did you know?" She looked surprised but extremely pleased.

Ejiro ducked his head. "Lucky guess." She might've been socialising with all the bachelors so far except him, but that didn't mean he hadn't been aware of her. "I'll, um, be right back."

"Thank you, Ejiro." Her eyes were dark, sultry.

Ejiro tried not to stumble, his stomach flip-flopping at the flirtation. "It's no problem at all."

He turned and headed quickly for the drinks table. He could see some of the staff running to and fro in the periphery, and discerned that they were probably going to place a fresh glass of the drink on the table before he arrived.

And he was right. A cue in the background told him to slow down. By the time he made it to the table, a camera following close behind him, a staff had edged the fresh drink onto the table, managing to smoothly avoid the focus of the cameras.

What did I tell you? Ejiro could hear Ajiri's smug voice in his head. *Just be yourself and everything will fall into place.*

He'd spoken to the bachelorette for the second time, and he hadn't messed up.

So maybe he wasn't as handsome as the other bachelors, and he wasn't as ... exuberant. Sophia still *liked* him. That was all that mattered.

He turned around, and felt the small smile on his lips freeze so quickly his face could have cracked with it.

He'd been expecting Sophia to be alone in front of the greenhouse where he'd left her—perhaps glancing in his direction, looking shy but expectant.

Instead, there was Obiora, down on one knee. The slit of her dress had been pushed aside to expose one of her long legs all the way up her thigh. Obiora was cupping her bare calf in one of his hands, the other gently, tenderly—*sensuously*—easing her shoe off her foot.

Her free hand held tightly onto his wide shoulder for balance. Throughout the entire feat, they didn't once look away from each other, the tension between them unmistakable.

Ejiro's vision went red, his grip tightening warningly around the glass he held.

Go to her, his mind screamed. *She asked you for a drink. Don't let him steal the spotlight!*

But Ejiro couldn't move.

He watched as Obiora took off the second shoe, saying something that made Sophia laugh shyly and duck her head.

When he stood, Obiora let his hand run up her leg and thigh in a movement that looked accidental, even distracted, but Ejiro *knew* it was intentional.

Sophia shivered visibly at the touch. Even a baby would have seen that it wasn't a shiver of revulsion.

Ejiro dropped the drink back onto the table with shaking hands, then he turned and walked straight into the mansion, leaving Sophia, the cameras, and the other bachelors behind.

SIX

"THANK YOU," SOPHIA SAID, HER eyes dark. "One more moment in these"—she gestured with a hand, holding up her honestly terrifying looking heels—"and I'd probably have committed murder."

Obiora laughed. "Well then. That means I've literally just saved someone's life. They're welcome." He winked.

She laughed so hard she began to snort. That he was the one who'd put that expression on her face filled him with a buzzing sense of pleasure and excitement.

He remembered how it had felt to hold her wide, curvy hips in his palms earlier, when they'd met at the top of the stairs leading into the mansion, and he hadn't resisted the urge to ask if he could spin her like a Princess. The feel of the warm, intimate press of her body against his afterward—the way she'd lingered, eyes sultry and dark with a mirroring desire.

Said eyes were just as dark right now. She was standing, hips cocked, back arched slightly, sensually pushing out her gorgeous tits.

Fucking hell.

Free vacation, Obiora reminded himself for the millionth time.

He couldn't let himself get side-tracked, no matter how sexy and lovely said side-attraction was.

Besides, this was how it always started. Distant compatibility led to mutual attraction led to long conversations, and then bam, he'd mention his dead girlfriend once—show that he still loved her, despite it having been five years since that fateful day—and that would be the end of that.

Obiora forced himself to look away, glancing around the backyard, and realised most of the bachelors were sneering and eyeing him frostily.

Oops. He winced. He hadn't quite meant to steal the spotlight like that, but he hadn't been able to continue pretending not to notice how uncomfortable Sophia had looked the longer the night had droned on and she'd been unable to get off her feet. She'd kept shifting her weight, grimacing when she thought no one was looking.

Well, *Obiora* had been looking. And if he'd used the opportunity to seal his spot in the competition, at least for the first episode, then so be it. From the looks on some of the other bachelor's faces, they did not approve of his methods. Ejiro was nowhere to be found.

Fuck.

He really *had* only meant to make Sophia more comfortable. Should he have waited until Sophia was done talking to Ejiro first? Yeah. Maybe. Most likely. Okay, yes.

But it was too late now. And honestly, it was a fucking *competition*; if Ejiro couldn't handle the heat, then it was good that he'd gotten himself the fuck out of the kitchen.

Sophia looked around, probably in search of the bachelor in question. The drink Ejiro had gone to get her remained untouched on the refreshments table.

"Did you by any chance see where Ejiro went?"

"Nope," Obiora answered honestly.

"Oh."

She looked disappointed, which made him feel a spark of jealousy, the competitive side of him rearing its usually ugly head.

"Want me to get you that drink?" he asked, desperate to get her attention back on him. "Maybe Ejiro needed a breather. I haven't spoken to him much, but from the brief conversation we *have* had, I can tell he's a little shy."

"He is, isn't he?" Sophia said, a little dreamily. Then she seemed to realise she'd said that out loud, and more importantly, *who* she'd said it to, and blushed, smiling brightly to cover it up. "Please. The drink, if you don't mind."

"Not at all."

Obiora made his way to the refreshment table, leaving his face deceptively blank, avoiding the glares of the more hostile bachelors. He grinned at the ones who winked or smirked at him, no doubt thinking the way he'd swooped in while Ejiro's back was turned was a brilliant move.

He felt another pang of guilt, which he aggressively shook off.

Keep your head in the fucking game, Obiora.

SIX BACHELORS WERE GOING HOME tonight, and Obiora was pretty sure he wouldn't be one of them. Pretty sure.

The thirty men stood in three neat rows in front of the mansion, each row lined sequentially from the bottom step to the third, so their faces would be clear for the cameras.

Sophia stood on the paved ground in front of them. By her side, away from the path of the stairs, was a long table holding a series of identical soft-pelt pink hearts the length and width of a palm, with golden arrows pierced through them. Before they'd lined up, the producers had given them magnets to keep within their breast pockets—they probably didn't want to risk using pins because it might take too long to pin, or worse, it could hurt someone.

Only twenty-three of those hearts were pink. One was red, meant for the bachelor who'd made the strongest impression during the group date. Whoever received the Red Heart during elimination night automatically won the chance for a private date of their choosing with the bachelorette for the next episode.

Sophia picked the Red Heart up first, blushing as she did.

Despite himself, Obiora felt his heart begin to race. Being one of the tallest men here, he was stationed at the back row. Ejiro was there too, two men from his right, and had his gaze carefully facing forward. Obiora felt something akin to shame curl up in his chest. He looked away.

"I've had a wonderful time tonight," Sophia began, sounding so natural Obiora was sure she was going off script. It would make sense, since Ameri Shae kept repeating to them how natural she wanted the show to be. It was becoming her mantra on set. "Unfortunately, six of you gentlemen will be going home tonight. One of you, however"—her blushing increased exponentially, revealing the slight dimples on her cheeks—"made quite the impression on me."

She eyed each bachelor in turn, making some of them squirm, and Obiora's already racing heart skip.

"Chris Wu?" The name dripped from her lips with a strange familiarity, a sweet intimacy.

One of the men at the front sucked in a sharp breath. Obiora's eyes, along with those of the other bachelors, narrowed in on the gentleman in question. He was tall, handsome, and slender, with smooth pale brown skin and a beauty mark on the top corner of his upper lip. His mop of dark brown hair went almost all the way down to his shoulders in thick, loose waves, parted neatly in the middle to frame his face.

Obiora couldn't recall meeting him. Perhaps the man had been with Sophia when he'd been getting to know the other bachelors.

"Cupid's calling," Sophia said with a wink. Some of the bachelors snorted. "Would you do me the honour of accepting this heart?"

Chris's smile was a mile wide. "Yes. I accept."

He walked down the step and toward her, holding himself open so she could attach the heart to the magnet hidden behind his breast pocket.

When they stared at each other, Obiora could feel the sparks all the way from where he stood. Chris said something to her, his voice pitched low only for her and the cameras to hear.

Obiora couldn't help it, he felt a keen disappointment, his fists clenching subtly by his sides. He'd been so sure that the move he'd pulled there with the shoes would have cemented him as Sophia's favourite bachelor of the night, and the competitor in him felt sorely bitter at losing. He wondered what Chris could have done to warrant getting the Red Heart.

He barely paid attention to the next few bachelors, managing to accept his Pink Heart with a rogue grin when his name was called.

"How're the feet?" he asked, smiling to emphasise the dimple in his cheek as Sophia attached the heart to his chest.

"Much better, thanks to you." She grinned, holding a leg out through the long slit of her dress, revealing that she was now wearing flat white sandals with straps that criss-crossed all the way up to her thigh. Glamorous and fucking sexy, even without the heels.

"I'm glad."

Eventually, all twenty-four safe bachelors had received their hearts—Ejiro included, Obiora had noticed with a weird mix of relief and dismay—and the other six were immediately sent home, cameras following them as they went back into the mansion to get their already packed bags.

A limo—white instead of black, like the ones that had brought the bachelors to the mansion—drove up the long driveway at Ameri's cue, just as the last evicted bachelor disappeared.

"I'm really looking forward to getting to know the rest of you," Sophia said as the car stopped, and the driver walked out to open the door for her. "Chris." There it was again, that shy familiarity when she said her favourite bachelor of the night's name. "I can't wait to go on our date next week. I'm excited to see what you have planned for us."

"You're going to love it," Chris replied with utmost confidence, his grin playful and boyish.

"I better." She winked.

Then she was gone, the limo disappearing down the long driveway.

"And—cut!"

Obiora relaxed. He hadn't even known he'd been tense.

"Please proceed to the back of the house immediately!"

The bachelors complied, herded impatiently by Ameri, which meant they had no time to chat as they walked. Obiora spotted Ejiro up ahead, his long legs and quick strides almost making it look like he was gliding across the floor. His quick steps might've seemed to be as a result of Ameri's urgency, but Obiora had a feeling Ejiro was running from the rest of the men.

After Obiora had—*like a bush goat*, his mother would've scolded—told Ejiro—to his *face*—that the rest of the bachelors had written him off from the competition because he'd been antisocial, only for Obiora to then sweep in to Sophia's rescue from behind Ejiro's back like a freaking *snake*, Ejiro must be feeling very singled out right now.

And whose fault is that?

Fuck. Damn. Shit.

He was going to have to apologise, wasn't he?

When they were gathered in front of the pool, Ameri made a signal for the cameras to keep rolling then began to speak.

"Congratulations, everyone, for making it past night one!" There was some applause and hollers from the staff, which made some of the bachelors smile proudly. "In a minute, I will be showing you around the mansion where you will be spending most of your time for the duration of the filming. For now"—she nodded at someone behind them, and one of the staff walked forward, handing each bachelor a sealed, thin brown A4 envelope—"the other producers and I have taken the liberty of making a small fact sheet containing pertinent information regarding our bachelorette. Obviously, you have the choice *not* to use the fact sheet, and instead get to know her yourselves as the filming commences. But if you want a leg over for what we have planned for the rest of the filming, go on ahead and give it a read."

Obiora took the envelope. When he looked around him, most of the bachelors wore the same thoughtful frown on their faces. Should they risk not reading the fact sheet—because it *was* a risk, assuming they wouldn't be eliminated next—or should they go in blind and get to know the bachelorette authentically during the group dates?

"For a little bit of incentive, the bachelorette will also be given fact sheets on all the bachelors present here tonight, though whether she will read them or not, we will not reveal. Do with that information what you will." Ameri smiled deviously, then her expression turned serious. "Now, since you all are absolutely cut off from the rest of the world, the other producers and I thought it would be vital to provide you all with a space within the mansion for whenever you feel stressed out and either need some time alone, or simply need a space to vent.

"Please remember, this is still a reality television series, so while this room is absolutely meant for your mental health and privacy, there are still cameras installed within. Only Diana"—she nodded at one of the other producers, who waved at them when they looked—"and I will have access to the feed of this room. If you feel you've revealed something personal you absolutely do not want anyone else to see, please come see us and let us know, and we'll delete the footage immediately."

Her expression turned sly. "You are, of course, highly encouraged to use this room to trash talk your competitors behind their backs, and share some gossip the viewers otherwise may not have seen while the cameras were rolling. For example, if a bachelor is sweet and lovely during the filming but an absolute bastard when y'all are inside the house? Please spill the motherfucking tea."

They all burst out laughing. Ameri grinned wide, all teeth and gums.

"That's all for now. Since it's already quite late today, I'll see you all bright and early in the morning, eight AM sharp! We'll be using the day to film your confessionals while the night is still fresh in your minds. Make sure you have a good rest up until then. Goodnight, everyone."

THE MANSION HAD SIX BIG rooms, each with four beds to one wall and wardrobes on the other. Their luggage hadn't been moved up until after the elimination, meaning the six bachelors to go home tonight hadn't even been able to spend a single night within the mansion's walls. Obiora grimaced as he thought about it. That was really fucking unlucky—making it all the way here only to be booted off on night one.

There were four bathrooms, two upstairs and two downstairs, and the men dutifully agreed to split the use of the bathrooms equally between the number of rooms—three rooms and twelve people to two bathrooms—to prevent any mishaps.

And that was about as far as they'd made it in regards to decisions about the house before most of the men signed off stating exhaustion. They'd deal with how to share the rest of their amenities in the morning.

Their things had been brought up by the staff, so it was a matter of finding their luggage to indicate who roomed where.

Obiora felt a faint sense of dread at the thought that he might be rooming with Ejiro, but let out a sigh of barely concealed relief when his fourth and final roommate finally appeared and it wasn't the man he'd slighted.

"Yo," the guy greeted. He was white, medium height, medium build, with dark moles spotted all over his pale face. His auburn hair was cut short to his scalp. "I'm Ricky. What's up?"

"Jin," the first guy to the room said, already settled in bed, glasses perched on his nose and a book in his lap. Obiora had already met him during the group date. He was Korean-British, his skin brown, eyes dark, hair a perfect golden blonde, with an accent so posh Obiora felt like a slug next to him. The man was wearing actual *silk* pyjamas, with his initials neatly embroidered in gold thread onto the breast pocket.

"Obiora."

"Tyler," the final guy said, looking up from where he'd been rifling through his luggage by the wardrobe beside the door. He was also white—paler, skinnier, and shorter than Ricky, with straight, inky dark hair going all the way down to his hips. His nails were painted with gleaming dark polish.

"Obiora?" Ricky repeated, his grin widening. He walked up to him, holding out a friendly fist. "What you did down there? Class act, man." He laughed.

Obiora grinned a little uncomfortably, and bumped fists with him. "Thanks."

"You think so?" Jin said from his bed, his tone tinged with disapproval. Though they had practically nothing in common—apart from the glasses and the general studiousness—Obiora was suddenly reminded of his eldest brother. It felt like Obinna was here, arms crossed over his chest, lips pursed as he shook his head with disapproval.

Ricky bristled. So did Tyler. The poshness of Jin's accent had made his question come off as slightly condescending

"Yeah?" Ricky said, looking ready to fight. He had a Yorkshire accent, which thickened in his distaste. "And what's it to you? Obi here was just playing the game. Am I right?" He turned to Obiora with a smarmy grin. "No one said we aren't allowed to play dirty."

"One would expect a sense of decorum in delicate matters such as this, competition or not," Jin said crisply. "The gentlemanly thing to do would have been to wait his turn."

"And who shoved a stick up your arse?"

Obiora grimaced. "I mean, I *should* have waited. I'd probably have gotten the same effect either way," he interjected before the argument could escalate.

Jin awarded him with a slight smile and a nod. "Precisely."

"I have to agree, to be honest," Tyler added. His voice was soft, fitting his small frame.

"Oh please." Ricky scoffed. "If you want to be on the bird's mind twenty-four seven, then you have to do what you have to do."

Obiora winced inwardly at Sophia being referred to as a "bird."

"Right," Jin drawled, rolling his eyes and snapping his book shut. His bed was closest to the window, so he propped the book up on the sill, along with his glasses. "That's bedtime for me. Goodnight."

"Don't listen to him," Ricky turned to Obiora to say, sneering in Jin's direction. Jin adamantly ignored him, pulling the covers up to his chin. "I only wish I had thought about that smooth move. You should have seen the look on the other guy's face when he saw how you'd swooped in. You'd think he'd swallowed a lemon." Ricky laughed, loud and deep. Obiora felt like his insides were shrivelling. "If I were him, it'd have been a confrontation—stealing my time with my girl? Like fuck I'd let you get away with that. He's got an eel for a spine, he has. Not gonna last long in the competition, that one."

Obiora smiled tightly at Ricky to show he was listening. Tyler was done with whatever he'd been doing with his luggage, and was now on the bed closest to the door, in nothing but boxers and a worn t-shirt, a notebook in his hands where he was scribbling furiously.

Obiora quickly changed into his night things, uncaring of the other men in the room. When he was dressed similarly to Tyler, except he had shorts on instead of just his underwear, he slipped into his bed, in the middle of Jin and Ricky.

While he could admit his actions had been ... ungentlemanly, he also had to admit Ricky was right as well. If Ejiro had really been bothered, he should've confronted Obiora about it, instead of disappearing into thin air. Obiora had no idea why Sophia had given him a heart.

So far, Ejiro had proved to be everything Obiora and the other bachelors had suspected he was during the evening: average looking, and antisocial to the point of dullness.

He might have made it past night one, but Obiora could bet it wouldn't be long before Sophia sent Ejiro packing his bags.

And if that was a little mean of him, that was just the way of the game.

The official website for the CUPID CALLING series.

Cupid Calling

ABOUT | THE BACHELORETTE | THE BACHELORS | EPISODES | CONTACT | BECOME A CUPID

Episode 1: Breaking the Ice

Episode Summary: The bachelors arrive in limos and greet the bachelorette at the entrance to the mansion. Ejiro gives Sophia a portrait of her he'd hand painted; Obiora spins her around like a princess; Noah arrives on the scene in ripped sleeves and on a motorbike, and Liam dazzles her with a unique bouquet he'd plucked and pruned from his own personal garden.

But this week's Red Heart was given to Chris Wu, who stole the bachelorette's attention with the soft trills of a guitar and the beautiful lyrics of a self-composed song.

CUPID CALLING

Later on in the night, Chad attempted to throw Sophia into the pool, causing a brief disruption that was quickly resolved.

At the end of the night, he, Seamus, Neville, Michael, Rasheed, and Adam were eliminated.

Click here to watch the full episode on Netflicks!

COMMENTS

WATTREBOTTRE

CHRIS WU GOT THE RED HEART AS HE SHOULD (side note: anyone else feel like perhaps Sophia and Chris know each other from before this? I could be reaching, but the way they reacted to each other, y'all ... I'm just )

♥ 10101   💬 3211

DEEKDEEK

im so glad Chad got eliminated like without even looking at the pool bullshit, my guy literally tried to kiss her the second he met her??? that's not a red flag anymore, it's a fucking red billboard

♥ 9045   💬 3029

MOOD247

I know a lot of people are angry at what Obiora did behind Ejiro's back, but tbh I feel like you have to do what you have to do to get the bachelorette's attention. It *is* a competition after all. That's just my opinion ¯_(ツ)_/¯

♥ 8977   💬 2997

 **STFUPAYME**

nah the other bachelors were right. Obiora should have waited his turn. If he can do something shady as that at the very start of the season, imagine what he's actually capable of??

♥ 8712   💬 2952

 ERIC23456

anyone got a link to Chris Wu's song on itunes? 👀 🎵

♥ 8533   💬 4509

LOAD MORE COMMENTS ⌄

SEVEN

EJIRO'S HAND FLEW ACROSS HIS sketchpad almost furiously, a pencil clutched between his fingers. Ameri hadn't let him bring his drawing tablet because he had some social media apps installed on the device and she hadn't wanted to risk it, straightforward promises or no. When he'd bought the sketchpad and drawing materials, he'd been certain it would be difficult—alien—to go back to pencil and paper after he'd spent so long perfecting his skills digitally.

He'd thought wrong. And he had his anger to thank for that.

Ejiro hadn't slept well. He usually didn't when he was in an unfamiliar place, but his shame and self-disgust at the way he'd run and hid after the stunt Obiora had pulled last night had left him too wound up to sleep. It had been a miracle Sophia had given him a heart; her eyes had been alight with a hopeful sort of fondness, like she honestly couldn't wait to get to know him better over the coming weeks.

Well, Ejiro wasn't about to let her down. The regret he usually felt when he walked away from a confrontation rather than face it felt insurmountable in the morning after. God, he wished he could've just—he should've just—

He sighed, scrubbing his hands over his face. There was no use crying over spilt milk; what's done was done. All he could do now was make sure that—no matter what challenges he faced henceforth—he didn't run away again.

He wondered, not for the first time, if he should say a word to Obiora, and felt his pulse race with anxiety at the thought.

He shook his head. What would be the point? What would he say? "Screw you for your lack of sportsmanship"? "Please don't do that again?"? "Next time wait your turn"? It all sounded juvenile.

No, Ejiro was going to let it go. The only way to look better in the light of last night's events was to *do* better in the coming group dates.

He glanced down at his sketchpad and let out a silent chuckle despite himself. Then he started laughing, though quietly, because his three roommates were still asleep.

When he'd found that he couldn't sleep, he'd spent most of his awake hours doodling increasingly vile caricatures of Obiora's face. The images would make for a good villain, if he ever decided to write Sophia as a goddess in a fantasy comic, which he still felt inclined to do. The previous pages were filled with sketches of her dressed like an African deity; with gold hoops around her long throat, her hair in afro curls to her shoulders glinting with polished cowrie beads, and her form covered in the bright, colourful patterns of Ankara wrappers.

Where she was a goddess, perhaps Obiora could be the opposite. A devil. A troll. Sentient pond scum.

He snickered. He slid his sketch materials underneath his pillows and stood up to stretch, his eyes sliding toward his roommates.

Damien, the first of his roommates he'd met, was on the bed next to his, snoring like a generator. The sound weirdly reminded him of Ajiri—she tended to snore sometimes, especially if she was really exhausted. He smiled at the thought, suddenly missing her and Blessing something fierce. He couldn't remember the last time they'd been separated for this long. He tried not to think too hard about it.

Damien was also Black, and owned his own small but slowly growing grocery store in London. On the bed next to him was Alistair, one of the white blondes. He was an underwear model, and he slept naked. Ejiro quickly looked away from where a bit of muscled butt cheek was poking out of the sheets twisted haphazardly around his form.

His last roommate in the bed closest to the door was Chris Wu, the lucky Chinese-Brit who'd been given the Red Heart of the first group date. He was a primary school teacher, and was playful and sweet. When he grinned, with that damn beauty mark above his lip, Ejiro could somewhat understand why Sophia had been taken by him.

According to Chris Wu, there was another Chris on the show: Chris Payne. Ameri had dutifully said they'd be referring to both of them with their full names to avoid any confusion.

As Sophia had given him the Red Heart last night, Ejiro had wondered desperately if Chris Wu had made a grand gesture when he'd first met the bachelorette. He hadn't asked him outright because he'd felt it'd be too childish.

The question nagged, though. Surely Sophia hadn't given him the heart based on looks alone? Chris Wu was handsome enough, but nearly *all* of the bachelors were handsome. It had to be something more—something he said or did.

Ejiro was about to work himself up thinking about it at this point, so he forced himself to stop.

The clock in the room said it was nearing five AM. Perfect time for a quick morning jog.

Blessing had brought exercise and a more balanced diet into his and Ajiri's lives. They'd complained at first, Ajiri most especially— she could be a bit of a slob, he thought fondly—but they'd eventually given in. When the three of them had gotten their house, five AM jogs became a semi-regular thing, at least on Ajiri's part.

Ejiro had kept to a schedule; he always jogged on the mornings of the days he had to be in at *Ewoma's*.

Now, with a slightly more irregular schedule to keep—at least according to Ameri, who said it was likely all of them wouldn't have to film something every single day, but they shouldn't bet on it—Ejiro was going to get his morning jog on any days he could, just in case.

He'd just finished changing into his jogging suit and putting on his mic—they were required to wear them at all times except when they were asleep—when a figure on one of the beds stirred.

"Morning," Chris Wu greeted with a grin, sitting up and taking off his hairnet so he could run his fingers through his thick, shoulder-length deep brown waves.

"Morning," Ejiro echoed, somehow unsurprised to note that Chris Wu was a morning person. He just seemed the type.

"Heading to the gym, then?" Jesus, how was he already so awake? Ejiro had to set at least three alarms in advance to be able to gain the energy to leave his bed in the mornings.

Chris Wu had slept in nothing but briefs, and didn't seem to care that he had an audience as he stood from his bed and yawned and stretched, his skin smooth and toned and golden all over.

Ejiro had gone to boarding school back in Nigeria, so being around unselfconscious naked people wasn't exactly new to him—but that had been *secondary* school, *eons* ago. He'd grown into such a private person it was a wonder he'd survived that time in his life without spontaneously combusting.

Also, yes, the mansion had a freaking indoor gym.

"Nah," Ejiro answered. "I prefer jogging outside. Clears my head." Ajiri and Blessing preferred the gym. Ejiro hated the gym atmosphere, so he usually jogged outside, and if he needed to do anything more, he did so in the safety of his room, with a yoga mat and his own weights.

"Ah, for sure." Chris gave him a thumbs up. "Think I might head to the pool for a swim myself."

Ejiro nodded. He was glad he was already dressed, because next to Chris's surprisingly toned body—he'd looked slenderer in his suit last night—Ejiro felt like a limp noodle. It was a little crushing how fit all the bachelors—specifically his roommates—were. It did absolute *wonders* for his self-esteem.

"See you later," Ejiro said, heading out of the room.

Chris waved.

The mansion was dark and quiet as Ejiro made his way downstairs. Without the producers and crew, the place almost felt like a holiday destination. If he closed his eyes, he could pretend he was on some romantic getaway at some faraway exotic destination.

With about a million hidden cameras and twenty other men, but still.

Outside, beside the first fountain in front of the mansion, he began to stretch, taking in deep long breaths as he did, keeping his mind clear. It was the last day of June, and still early, so the air was perfectly cool. The summer had only just begun, meaning they hadn't quite yet reached that time in the season where the English heat was oppressive and unbearable, and oftentimes even deadly. It was disgustingly hot in Nigeria, but at least the regular home and business utilised air conditioners. It still stumped him that the regular English home refused to invest in the same.

When his blood finally felt warmed enough, his limbs loose, he straightened, and began to jog.

WHEN OBIORA'S INTERNAL CLOCK HAD woken him up at five AM, his first instinct had been to go to the indoor gym. He'd even begun heading in that direction, when he'd remembered the long stretch of road that was the driveway leading to the house and was suddenly in the mood for a jog. The thought of taking a leisurely run in the slowly brightening light of the morning to clear his head was too appealing to resist.

But then he'd walked outside, and the absolute last person he'd wanted to see was the one standing there at the bottom of the steps beside the fountain, in the middle of a warmup stretch.

For a moment, Obiora wavered. He remembered Ricky's words of last night—*you should have seen the look on the other guy's face when he saw how you'd swooped in. You'd think he'd swallowed a lemon*—and felt a renewed surge of guilt. Then he repeated to himself that while what he'd done had been distasteful, he hadn't actually done anything *wrong*. Fuck his guilt.

In his indecision, Obiora couldn't help but notice Ejiro's lithe form, the smooth and easy way his body changed through practised poses, his breathing deep and even. He must do a lot of yoga, Obiora thought distractedly. It was in the fluid, almost sensual way he moved.

When he bent over to touch his toes, giving Obiora a perfect view of his ass, the muscles of his thighs and calves pulling taut through the thin fabric of his jogging pants, Obiora felt a flash of unwanted heat.

The feeling spurred him into movement, and he was jogging down the steps before he could change his mind.

He would simply jog past Ejiro while he was still stretching and they wouldn't have to talk to each other. Easy peasy.

Except, Ejiro straightened and started moving at the exact same second that Obiora reached his side, which put them right next to each other.

Oh, for fuck's sake.

He carefully didn't look beside him. Ejiro would probably slow down. If last night's events were anything to go by, he seemed to be the type of someone who avoided confrontations at all costs.

But Ejiro didn't slow down. In fact, he seemed to be speeding up, attempting to leave Obiora behind.

And that thought, for some ridiculous ass reason, had Obiora's competitiveness rearing its ugly head.

He increased his own pace.

They glanced at each other. Ejiro's eyes burned with barely concealed irritation. Obiora, too immature to resist, *smirked*.

When they reached the second fountain, turning to head back in the direction of the mansion, Ejiro suddenly bolted into a full run.

"Fuck!" Obiora ran after him.

Their feet pounded down the driveway, the only sound apart from their harsh breaths.

And Obiora suddenly felt fucking ridiculous. What the fuck was he *doing*? Here was a man he'd slighted last night, and instead of apologising like a grown ass adult, he was what ... *racing* him? What the fuck?

He slowed down. Ejiro didn't. Obiora met him at the fountain catching his breath.

Fuck it, fuck it. He was here on *vacation*. He'd made an error in judgement last night and it was his job to fix it. If Ejiro held a grudge, it might inspire the other bachelors who'd disapproved to hold a grudge as well. And what if the sentiment somehow got back to Sophia? It didn't seem like she'd noticed his move last night, and the last thing he wanted right now was for it to be brought to her attention. He couldn't risk getting eliminated yet.

"Look," he began, still breathing heavily, hands on his hips. "I'd like to apologise. I'll admit—what I did yesterday? Yeah, kind of a smarmy move, am I right?" He grinned, inviting Ejiro to laugh.

He didn't. Ejiro straightened, his expression twisted into a sneer. Gone was the shy, anxious man of last night.

"*That's* your apology?" he asked with a scoff of disbelief.

Obiora bristled. "Look, this shit wouldn't even be this much of a big deal if you'd just come up to me last night and *said* something, instead of disappearing into—"

"Don't blame *me* for your actions," Ejiro interrupted derisively, his Nigerian accent—thickened in his irritation—doing nothing to soften the blow.

"I'm *not* blaming you." Obiora rolled his eyes. Talking so heatedly with him was bringing out Obiora's own Nigerian accent, and he didn't bother to switch it. "Sophia looked uncomfortable in her heels, all right? It would've been heartless if I'd just *left* her to stand there—"

"And seducing her behind my back—because, let's be clear, that's exactly what you did—was *so* much better, abi?"

"Ejiro." Obiora scrubbed a hand over his face. "I don't want to argue. It really isn't my aim to start this show off with some silly beef that can easily be resolved. So." He held a hand out. "Truce?"

Ejiro looked at his hand like it was the bottom of his shoe. Then he met Obiora's eyes, his own eyes blazing. "If you didn't aim to start this show off with some "silly" beef, then perhaps you should have thought of that *before* you acted."

Then he turned around and left, jogging up the stairs to the mansion.

Obiora watched him go. He slowly dropped his still outstretched hand.

He only realised then that his pulse was back to racing, as if he'd only just finished running.

How the fuck had he thought that Ejiro was *dull* or *average looking*?

Because standing there right then, as he'd stared Obiora down, his eyes dark and penetrating, all Obiora had been able to think about was whether Ejiro looked this fervent and intense when he fucked.

EIGHT

IT'D BEEN NEARLY TWO DAYS, yet Ejiro was still living off the high from facing Obiora. He couldn't believe he'd done it; he could have placated Obiora after that pathetic attempt at an "apology", which was what he usually did when he found himself in situations like that—nodding and fake-grinning until his cheeks hurt, saying, "No, no, it's okay, it's fine, don't apologise!", all the while he shrivelled slowly on the inside.

But during their jog, when Obiora had turned and freaking *smirked* at him, with that frankly irritating dimple of his flashing, Ejiro had felt an irritation so blinding he'd basically responded to Obiora on autopilot.

And the worst thing Ejiro had imagined happening to him during a confrontation—him spontaneously bursting into frustrated tears—seemed almost ridiculous in hindsight.

Standing up to him had felt so *good*. He wished he could've told Ajiri about it the second after it had happened, but since he couldn't, he'd settled for using the "confession" room at the mansion.

"You should have seen his face," he'd said that morning with an almost manic grin. "He obviously thought I was going to be the "bigger person" and let him off the hook, but something in me was like, not today."

"Something to share with the class?" asked an amused voice.

Ejiro blinked back to the present, realising then that he was grinning from ear to ear.

He blushed, attempting to temper his grin but it was no use. "I'm really excited for the group date today," he said, remembering at the last moment not to answer directly.

The limousine chose that moment to come to a stop.

"You ready?" the staff in the passenger seat asked, still sounding amused.

"I'm ready," Ejiro said.

Sophia was standing in front of what looked to be the edge of a dense forest, a few cameramen and one of the directors standing around her. She was dressed in exercise gear; black yoga pants, a loose white t-shirt and neon green trainers. Her hair, held back with a matching neon green sweatband, was pulled up into a tight ponytail, though a few strands escaped from the do to frame her face and neck.

God, she was so beautiful.

Ejiro was still grinning as he walked up to her. When she noticed his smile, her demeanour seemed to brighten, creating a feedback loop between them until Ejiro was almost giddy with it.

"Hello," Ejiro greeted, a little breathlessly, giving her a quick hug when she held her arms open in invitation.

"Hi, Ejiro! How are you doing?"

"I'm good, I'm good. And you? You look amazing, by the way."

"Really?" She seemed to ask in genuine surprise, glancing down at herself.

"Yes," Ejiro said firmly. "Then again, you could probably wear nothing but a bin bag and I'd still think you were beautiful." He laughed a little shyly.

And then he began to panic a little.

Oh dear God, had that been too cheesy?

But Sophia blushed, thank goodness. "Flatterer," she said slyly, trailing her fingers playfully up his chest. "You don't look so bad yourself."

He blushed as well, ignoring how the intimate flirtation in her touch made his stomach clench in on itself, which he attributed to a mixture of nerves and butterflies.

"Do you know what we're going to do today?"

Sophia dropped her hand, thank God.

"Your guess is as good as mine," she said with a laugh, then gestured behind her. "Just follow the pathway and it'll lead you to a clearing. I'll see you there."

"See you soon, Sophia."

With one last exchanged smile, Ejiro headed down the marked pathway, ignoring the few crew members following behind him.

He cursorily looked around, trying to guess what the second group date with Sophia was going to entail. They'd been instructed to wear exercise gear that was easy to move around in, and that was about it.

Were they going on a hike? A bike ride? Climbing atop a mountain range? How would all that help the bachelorette in getting to know them? It was probably a TV show thing, he reasoned. Something to keep the viewers engaged and entertained.

Or could it be a ploy to test their strength? He wrinkled his nose. Wouldn't that be a little unfair? The other bachelors seemed fit enough; Ejiro just thought it was a little shallow to use fitness as a test for compatibility.

He was the first bachelor to arrive, stopping at a large clearing when a staff in the background indicated to him to stop. He took a deep breath and put his game face on. The first night had ended on a rough note for him, but Ejiro didn't plan on falling behind this time around.

His goal today was to get the Red Heart; he'd accept nothing less to overshadow his failure on night one.

He shoved down the soft, insecure part of himself screaming that he was being a little *too* confident, considering the good looks and prowess of the other men.

With his confrontation with Obiora still buoying his spirits, Ejiro was going to utilise this burst of energy and his renewed confidence in order to outshine everyone else in the group date, and secure himself the Red Heart.

"**WELCOME, EVERYONE, TO EPISODE TWO** of *Cupid Calling*!" Ameri said brightly when Sophia and the bachelors had gathered in the marked clearing. "Today, we have an exciting event planned for all of you." Ameri's expression turned sly, a playful, teasing grin on her lips. "If you'll all just follow me."

She headed deeper into the forest, cameras, the bachelorette, and the contestants following close behind her.

"What do you think it is?" Ricky asked Obiora. He was moving with a lazy swagger, his arms crossed behind his head.

"Hm? I don't know," Obiora replied, a little distractedly. "Guess we're about to see."

Stop.

Fucking.

Staring at him.

Obiora could no longer count how many times he'd said those words to himself since his confrontation with Ejiro two days ago.

After Ejiro had walked away, and Obiora had felt the strong stirrings of attraction, he'd written it off as the heat of the moment, only for Ejiro to appear in his dreams that same night in an even more heated re-enactment of their argument, except this time, it had ended with a desperate, passionate kiss. The kiss had immediately evolved, as dreams often did, to them suddenly naked in his bed back in his flat in Sheffield, Ejiro's eyes blazing, his hands holding Obiora's wrists flat to the mattress as he rode Obiora like he fucking loathed him.

Obiora had woken up hard and desperate, the dream so vivid that for a moment he couldn't remember what was real and what wasn't. He'd managed to stumble to the shower after he'd realised where he was, still clinging to that half-asleep state, and had jerked off rough and quick with the faux-memory of the touch of that full mouth, the sting of sharp teeth—all that bare brown skin, flushed with sweat—still clinging to the forefront of his mind.

When he'd come back to his senses, Obiora had consequently spent the hours following avoiding the fuck out of Ejiro, spending most of his free time in his room like a fucking hermit, or outside by the pool when he was sure Ejiro himself was in his room, or heading downstairs to the sitting room if Ejiro was nowhere else in the house to be found.

Now, back in forced proximity, despite the setting and the fact that they weren't the only ones here—far from it—Obiora couldn't take his eyes off him.

Like most of the men, as Ameri had ordered them the night before, Ejiro was dressed for outdoor exercise in black tights covered by loose black exercise shorts, a fitting short-sleeved white spandex t-shirt, and plain grey trainers. Compared to most of the other men, whose chests, arms and thighs strained against their clothing, Ejiro looked almost unassuming with his own slight frame. Yet, something about his demeanour today had Obiora's pulse racing, his blood rushing like he'd taken a shot of pure euphoria.

Layers of the tense, antisocial man of night one had been peeled off, revealing something peeking underneath that Obiora found himself almost desperate to fully unmask.

His eyes unwittingly dropped to Ejiro's ass, which was sadly hidden underneath his loose shorts.

God. What the fuck would Obiora have done if Ejiro had decided to forgo the shorts? The memory of Ejiro bending over flashed through his mind's eye.

Fuck. Best not to think too hard about it.

"Whoa."

The collective sounds of surprise, amusement and excitement forced Obiora to look away and take in their new surroundings.

His eyes widened when he spotted what looked to be an obstacle course lined up ahead of them.

There were monkey bars, a short wall with grooves, what looked to be thick pipes, tires forming a pathway, and a wide net made with thick rope nailed about a foot off the forest floor.

"You got it, folks!" Ameri said, sounding entirely too pleased with herself. "For this week's group date, you all are going to be competing via this obstacle course for a chance to go on a personal date of your choosing with our bachelorette!"

At a cue from the background staff, the bachelors began to cheer and wolf whistle and applaud, some of them looking genuinely excited.

"In four teams of six, you will all be required to complete the entirety of the obstacle course. The winners from each team—that's right, *each* team—will be immediately qualified to take our beautiful bachelorette on a private date of their choosing. That means *four* of you will have the opportunity to wine and dine Sophia without the rest of these interlopers trying to steal the spotlight. I'm looking at you, Obiora."

"Ooooooh," some of the bachelors sing-songed, while others laughed.

Obiora deliberately didn't look in Ejiro's direction as he said, "Don't worry, I won't be pulling any smooth moves—" He paused to wink at the camera, "—*this* time."

Sophia, along with some of the men, laughed out loud. Obiora grinned.

After a moment, he couldn't help it, he glanced in Ejiro's direction. Though he'd looked away from Ejiro earlier as Ameri had been speaking, Obiora's body seemed attuned to Ejiro's presence, and his gaze instantly zeroed in on him like he had some kind of Ejiro-radar.

If he'd noticed Ameri's playful comment, Ejiro didn't show it. In fact, he was in the middle of a whispered conversation with Chris Wu, one of his roommates, Obiora had found out, and the winner of the first night's Red Heart.

His smile, what little of it that curled his lips, small and carefree, was the most gorgeous thing Obiora had ever seen. It still held a trace of reservation, which, for some reason, made it all the more attractive.

Obiora was so fucking *fucked*.

"Before you all get *too* excited," Ameri continued, "there's a catch." The bachelors fell silent. Ameri's grin was wide and predatory. "Here it is: you all aren't only going to compete for a date with the bachelorette, the *bachelorette* will also be competing for a date *with you*."

"What?"

"Oh boy, here we go."

"Oh?"

Sophia waved and blew them kisses, making some of the men pretend to swoon dramatically. She laughed with delight.

"That's right," Ameri continued gleefully. "The bachelorette is also going to compete in the obstacle course. Here's the breakdown: each person to go through the obstacle course will be timed, the bachelorette included. Whoever sets the fastest time within their group will get to go on a date with the bachelorette. However, if the bachelorette's time happens to be faster than that of the winner in a group, *she* gets to pick *whoever* she wants—winner or not—from the losing team to go on a date of her choice."

Obiora could practically feel the wheels in the bachelors' brains turning.

Did the men want to risk losing on the off-chance Sophia *might* pick them? Or did they want to go all out and win the date with her one hundred percent?

Obiora didn't know about the rest, but he was counting on the latter. From the way the men's shoulders were straightening, Obiora assumed they'd chosen similarly.

Ameri clapped her hands delightfully. "Now, before we divide you into your groups, Sophia will run through the obstacle course. Are you ready to cheer her on, gentlemen?"

There was a chorus of yeses.

"Are you all ready to lose disgracefully?" Sophia said, waggling her eyebrows.

Some of the men laughed, some of them booed at her playfully.

"Are you ready, Sophia?"

Sophia began to jog on the spot. "I'm ready. I'm good. Let's do this."

They led the men to the finish line, while Sophia was led to the starting point.

Ameri picked up a megaphone. "On your mark—set—ready?—go!"

The bachelors exploded into a cacophony of sound, screaming encouragement at Sophia as she made her way through the obstacle course, her pretty lips twisted into a moue of concentration.

She did it all smoothly. The bachelors hollered and applauded after she crossed the finish line, sweaty and a little muddy, but still as beautiful as ever.

"Four minutes and thirty-two seconds!" Ameri announced when she made it to their side of the obstacle course. "Can our bachelors beat our bachelorette and win a private date with her? Let's find out!"

Nerves hit Obiora as Ameri led them all to the starting line. He eyed the obstacle course nervously, already trying to pre-predict his movements. On the other side, the staff were buzzing around Sophia, wiping her sweat and handing her a cold bottle of water.

"As I said before," Ameri began in a normal tone, "each team will be a group of six, decided by which number you pick out of our draw." As she spoke, a member of the staff walked toward Ameri, holding out a small fishbowl with plain white cards folded in half mixed within its depths. "So, team one will be from numbers one to six, team two from numbers seven to twelve, and so on. Now that you understand the rules, contestants, please come forward and pick a number. Do not open your cards until I say so."

One by one, the bachelors moved forward, taking a card until the fish bowl was empty.

"Open your cards."

Twenty, Obiora read. He was going to be in the last group. A good thing and a bad thing; if he did really well, he'd make a better impression because he was one of the last, but if he did really bad, that would be what the bachelorette would take away from this. Fuck.

"Bachelors number one to six, please step up to the starting line."

Obiora looked up, his heart in his throat.

Chris Wu—what Obiora was considering to be his biggest competition—was among the first six.

Ejiro was not.

Obiora didn't know if he felt relieved or alarmed. Remembering their jog of two days ago, the way Ejiro had bolted into a run at the end there—obviously he had a lot of stamina.

Fuck, fuck, fuck.

He glanced at him.

Big mistake.

Ejiro had *that* look on his face—eyebrows furrowed, lips slightly pursed, eyes intense. He didn't look worried at all, just simply ... *focused*.

Obiora sucked in a sharp breath, quickly tearing his gaze away before anyone could notice.

Shit buggering bloody fuck Ejiro was so fucking hot when he looked like that what the fuck.

"On your marks—set—ready?—go!"

Chris Wu ended up winning the first round, beating Sophia's time with twenty seconds to spare. She gave him a congratulatory hug.

On the second team, Damien won, beating Sophia's time with twelve seconds to spare. He also received a congratulatory hug.

On the third team, however, the winning bachelor, Eddie, another Chinese-Brit, lost to Sophia with only point nine seconds. She ended up picking Liam, the third to cross the finish line, as her third private date for the week. Ricky seemed to make some kind of offhand remark at that, but Obiora wasn't really paying attention.

His team was next.

And Ejiro was still here.

Standing directly beside him.

Obiora felt like he was floating somewhere above his body. He refused to look at Ejiro, even though he could feel his presence keenly, like a sizzle of electricity on the surface of his skin.

"On your marks!"

Get your head in the fucking game, Obiora!

"Set!"

He focused on the obstacles in front of him, trying to catalogue his movements. He had to win this—he had to stay in Sophia's good graces if he wanted to make it further in the competition. He had to remember why he was here.

He had to snuff out this ridiculous attraction to Ejiro.

"Ready?"

Like his last thought had commanded it, like a moth to a flame, his eyes darted in Ejiro's direction.

At the exact same moment, Ejiro did something that short-circuited Obiora's entire mainframe—he glanced at Obiora, his eyes glinting predatorily, and *smirked*.

"Go!"

And Ejiro was off like a shot, leaving the rest of the men behind, eating his dust.

His speed seemed to affect the other men, for they faltered for a second, Obiora included, before regaining their bearings and following quickly.

But they were no match at all. Not even close.

"Three minutes and forty-nine seconds!" Ameri screamed when they'd all passed the finish line, Ejiro first, Obiora third. "That's the fastest time today, and the only time set at lower than four minutes!"

"Ejiro!" Sophia exclaimed with delight, rushing in his direction.

Obiora's chest twisted with something sweet and painful as, like the sun peeking out from behind the clouds, Ejiro's face opened up into a dazzling grin, wrinkling his eyes and softening his mouth.

He caught Sophia in his arms, blushing furiously. "I'm so sweaty right now," he said self-consciously, though the elated smile didn't falter from his lips.

"I don't care!" Sophia laughed. "Did you all see that?" she asked, finally pulling away from Ejiro's embrace. "He was like—like—freaking Usain Bolt!"

"I'm not really," Ejiro protested, but the man was chuffed, the boost in his confidence making his aura shine brighter, the pull of it like a magnet Obiora had to try furiously to resist.

TO ABSOLUTELY NO ONE'S SURPRISE, later that night, during the Heart slash elimination ceremony, Ejiro was given the Red best-impression Heart.

As Sophia faux-pinned the heart to Ejiro's suit pocket, Ejiro was beaming. His dark eyes danced like he held a secret you desperately wanted him to share—you wanted him to *look* at you, and only you.

Obiora felt the mad, desperate urge to shed the tiny bit of self-consciousness still clinging to the edges of that smile; he wanted to see what Ejiro would look like when *all* his walls and defences were down—how it would feel to be the centre of Ejiro's undivided attention, to be the cause of his unbridled joy.

This, he realised. This was why Sophia had given Ejiro a heart on night one.

She'd gotten a mere *glimpse* of the passion that lurked underneath that unassuming façade, and like Obiora, it had left her practically starving for *everything*.

The official website for the CUPID CALLING series.

Cupid Calling

ABOUT | THE BACHELORETTE | THE BACHELORS | EPISODES | CONTACT | BECOME A CUPID

Episode 2: The Contestants Show Their Prowess
Part One: Brawn

Episode Summary: The Bachelors are invited to compete—in four teams of six—in an obstacle course for the chance to win a private date with the bachelorette. The catch? The bachelorette will be competing with them, and if her time is higher than that of the bachelor's of a winning team, she gets to pick who she wants for a private date from that team.

Chris Wu wins in the first team, and Damien wins in the second. On the third team, Sophia beats the winning bachelor, and ends up picking Liam as her date from that team. This causes contestant Ricky obvious displeasure, which he chooses to voice in the form of barely-concealed misogynistic comments.

For the final team, Ejiro steals the spotlight by having the fastest time set for the day, which earns him the Red Heart of the night.

Ricky, Fred, Sunil, and Cornelius were eliminated.

Click here to watch the full episode on Netflicks!

COMMENTS

 **THISDAY2332**

EJIRO!!!!! YES!!!!

 11221   4033

 BTSBONER

Ejiro?!?!? Skskdjfksjfkd now who tf saw that coming 😱 edit: I'm just saying y'all, apart from his painting, he kind of blended into the bg in ep 1, pls stop attacking me 😱 😱 😱

 10478   3986

 **LOVEMYSELF007**

ngl I had a bad feeling about Ricky from episode one. I'm glad he revealed his true colours this early on in the competition. Good riddance.

 9426   3620

 **MARYANNE__**

You guys were right; I did some digging online and Sophia and Chris Wu apparently went to the same college for their A levels. Not sure how well they knew each other, if they were good friends or not, but there you have it :)

 8812   💬 3049

 HOWWEROLL11

Sophia beating Ricky and him whining like a lil baby? The highlight of this episode nothing makes me feel more alive than the tears of undeserving men

♥ 8423   💬 2771

[LOAD MORE COMMENTS ⌄]

NINE

WHEN EJIRO WOKE UP, HE did so with a smile. He stretched, the taut pain-pleasure pull of his muscles reminding him of the game of the day before, which made his mood lift higher. He'd set a goal for himself—winning the Red Heart—and he'd freaking *done* it.

After the congratulations from some of the bachelors last night, Ejiro had gone straight to the confession room to squeal like a teenager. He'd pretended—and this was probably going to become a constant as the show went on— that the cameras in the room were Ajiri and Blessing.

"Their faces," he'd said, so giddy he could shout. "None of them saw it coming, which made it all the more exciting when I won. I just need to keep this momentum going until the end of the competition. I could ..." He'd paused, looking directly at the camera mounted in front of him, his expression a little stunned, but a lot hopeful and excited. "I could win this. I could actually *win* this."

Ejiro tried to imagine winning the competition, introducing Sophia to his family after everything was said and done, but he couldn't quite picture it. Not yet. But that was fine. He didn't know Sophia all that well just yet, and even though he liked her so far, he had to get to *really* know her to feel more comfortable picturing them having a future.

And now he had that opportunity in the form of a private date. The thought filled him with equal parts excitement and anxiety.

They were going to film their cutaways to yesterday's episode later today, then Ejiro was going to tell Ameri what his plans were for his date with Sophia. Since he'd won on the obstacle course *and* also gotten the Red Heart, he got to have the chance to spend a *full* day wooing the bachelorette, while the other bachelors who'd won during the game only had parts of the day to pick: either the morning, the afternoon, or the evening.

Ejiro had given the date much thought, but he still felt extremely nervous at the thought that he was going to be spending time alone with Sophia. With cameras of course, but still. It would technically be them alone.

Butterflies took flight in his stomach. His heart flew up into his throat.

Oh dear God.

He shook his head lightly, and forced down his nervous excitement. He still had another day until the date, so there was no point in freaking out right now.

Ejiro's eyes had adjusted to the darkness as he'd laid there thinking, so he was able to see the clock clearly when he glanced at it. Almost five AM. Inwardly thanking his inner alarm for waking him up on time, he slid out of bed, stretching again.

He moved to his wardrobe, reaching for his jogging outfit, then paused. The obstacle course might have felt quick as it had happened, but it had been such a workout in the end. He didn't feel too much like jogging this morning. Perhaps a swim?

He glanced at his roommates to make sure they were still asleep—so far, he hadn't been naked around them and had strived not to see them naked in return, even though they didn't seem to care—and when he was certain they were still asleep, he quickly changed out of his pyjamas into his swimming trunks. He had a towel he used specifically for times when he went to the pool, so he pulled that out of his luggage as well. Good thing Ajiri had made him pack it.

The mansion was quiet, the men still asleep. Since he'd arrived at the mansion, apart from night one, Ejiro really hadn't spent a lot of time at the pool. He stared out at the backyard, gently sliding the door closed behind him, eyes slightly wide.

Had it always looked this ... grand?

He stood on the wide, wooden back porch. A veranda stretched out on his right, with low, comfortable-looking white chairs and equally small glass tables, an extended roof and a railing making the space look cosy and inviting.

Down the porch steps, embedded around the grassy floor of the backyard, was a standard rectangular pool with straight white lines running through its length at the bottom, as if whoever had wanted it built wished to do a race at some point. The second pool was off to the right and shaped a little bit like a peanut. There was a concrete floor bracketing both pools on the extreme left and right side of the backyard, holding deep grey pool chairs lined across their lengths, along with a fire pit in front for campfire-style barbecues and whatnot.

On the other side of the pools opposite Ejiro, up some wooden steps and enclosed in glass on all sides was a decently sized hot tub, though if one asked Ejiro what a "decent sized" hot tub was, he'd have no idea how to explain it. It looked big and the design was lovely and modern ... but not so much as to be extravagant?

Surrounding the hot tub, against three of the glass walls, were white seats in the shapes of cubes, pressed up against each other to look seamless. It almost made it seem voyeuristic, Ejiro thought with amusement. Imagine using the hot tub and being surrounded by the men in the house?

On the left, beside the glass room for the hot tub, was the greenhouse. On the right was a set of outdoor showers to rinse off before or after a swim.

The backyard was closed off with a thick fence of greenery, making the space seem like a little hidden getaway. With the sun not yet up, and the backyard lights on and bathing the place in hues of white and gold, the effect of it all was startlingly romantic.

Ejiro imagined vacationing here, just him and his future girlfriend, and felt a flush climb his cheeks at the thought. The place shone with an aura of sensuality, seducing his senses and making him *want*.

Shaking off the desire, he padded over to the pool chairs by the left of the first pool, and placed his towel on top.

After a brief hesitation, he decided to do his pre-jogging stretches, even though he wasn't planning on using the pool to exercise. He felt more in the mood for a leisurely swim this morning.

He was in the last bout of stretching when he heard the sliding door of the mansion come open, quiet as it was. Ejiro's heartbeat stuttered with nerves at the thought of trying to make conversation this early morning with one of the bachelors. He'd hoped to have this space to himself for at least a little while.

"Of course you're here."

Ejiro sighed. Of course whoever *would* disturb his peace would be Obiora. *Of course* it would. He stood up slowly from his last stretch, raising an eyebrow.

Like Ejiro, Obiora was in just his swim trunks—a ridiculous pair of shorts that clung to his muscular thighs like a second skin. And of course the rest of his body was just as ridiculously attractive as his face; all deep, warm brown skin and broad chest, his abs toned and flat. His skin was a gorgeous deep, warm shade of brown all over.

Ejiro resisted the urge to cross his arms over his own skinny chest, suddenly hyperconscious of the fact that he had an outie belly button. Ajiri called his belly button cute—*it's an actual* button, *Ejiro! A cute, perfectly round button!*—but right now, in the face of Obiora's, well, everything, "cute" wasn't precisely what he wanted to go for.

"Shouldn't I be the one saying that?" The question came out sounding a little amused, despite his irritation. "I did get here first, after all."

Obiora grinned, flashing the dimple on his cheek. He raised both his arms in mock-surrender. "Don't mind me."

"Not at all."

Obiora dropped the towel in his hands almost distractedly on one of the pool chairs, and headed in the direction of the pool showers. Ejiro had already finished his stretching. He'd look like a confused baby deer if he just *stood* there, so he followed after Obiora, praying they wouldn't have to talk.

He left a shower space between them.

It was awkward. Jesus Christ, it was freaking *awkward*.

He stayed longer, deliberately, just so Obiora would head to the pool first. He did, switching off his shower and making his way to the rectangular Olympic pool. Ejiro wondered if it would be too obvious if he decided to go to the other pool just to avoid him.

You won the Red Heart last night, Ejiro, the devil on his left shoulder growled, spitting flames. *Don't let him intimidate you!*

Ejiro straightened his shoulders. The little devil was right. Right now, the rest of the bachelors should be seeing Ejiro as they all obviously saw Chris Wu: as their biggest competition.

With that thought, he headed for the Olympic pool, a new confidence in his stride.

Obiora was just finishing a lap.

Ejiro dived in just as Obiora came up for air. He did a casual freestyle down the length of the pool, closing his eyes and letting the slightly cool water wash over him in soothing waves. He thought about the last time he'd gone swimming—Christ, it must've been months now, perhaps since last summer? He'd have to get Ajiri, Blessing, and his other friends on a weekend out to chill at the pool when this was all over.

When he finished the lap and came up for air, Obiora was there, staring at him, seemingly waiting for him, a challenging glint in his eye.

Old-Ejiro would have pretended not to notice and looked away, desperate to avoid any sort of confrontation, good or bad.

But *New*-Ejiro felt bolstered by his win last night; New-Ejiro couldn't help but read the challenge in Obiora's eyes and *react*. There was something about Obiora that made Ejiro feel like he was a teenager back in secondary school, desperate to beat his "rival" at every little thing.

He raised a questioning eyebrow.

Obiora jerked his head in the direction of the pool, his dark brown eyes dancing with mischief.

It took a moment for Ejiro to get it.

"Are you serious?" he said out loud, even as his heart started to pound.

"What? Are you scared?" Obiora wiggled his eyebrows.

"Don't be childish." Ejiro scoffed. "And stop doing that. You look ridiculous."

Obiora laughed. "Come on. What's the harm, Usain Bolt?"

Ejiro blushed. "Don't call me that." But he was moving to the starting position. The need to wipe that smirk off Obiora's face had him blurting, "You sure you want to do this? I'd hate to embarrass you a second time."

"Oh, it's on," Obiora growled, though the tone was still playful. "On your marks, set, go!"

He dived in before Ejiro could react.

The freaking snake!

Ejiro followed quickly. His world narrowed down as it usually did when he was in a race, his focus on getting to the finish line, completely ignoring his opponent.

He shot out of the water first, Obiora a split second behind him.

"*Ha!*" he cried triumphantly. "Cheaters never win," he couldn't help but crow, panting a little.

Obiora laughed breathlessly.

"Is cheating in your blood or something?" Ejiro asked, the question coming out playful despite himself. "Can you just not resist?"

Obiora laughed again, using both hands to push his wet curls back from his face, squeezing the water out down his neck. "Oh jeez. Please no. I am *not* a cheater."

"*Right*," Ejiro drawled.

"Okay, I know all evidence points to the contrary, but I'm really not. I'm serious. Trust me."

"That remains to be seen, but whatever you say, Obiora."

Obiora laughed again. "Are you, like, a pro-athlete or something? Is the whole chef slash artist thing just a cover up?"

"That's *exactly* it," Ejiro said, eyes dramatically wide. "You've done it. You've uncovered my nefarious plan."

"Fuck off," Obiora said, laughing again.

Ejiro felt stirrings of pleasure in his lower belly at how easily he seemed to be making Obiora laugh. Whatever was left of the grudge he'd still been holding against him for his slight on night one finally dissipated.

"So," Obiora began lowly, like they were sharing a secret. "You won the Red Heart last night."

Old-Ejiro would have turned bashful and waved him off or changed the subject.

New-Ejiro smirked.

"I did," he said, a little cockily.

Obiora's eyes seemed to darken. The sight of it made Ejiro feel weird, his stomach flip-flopping all over itself. He looked away, strangely nervous.

"As much as I hate to admit it, it was well earned."

"That must've hurt."

"Fuck off." Obiora laughed. "You thought about where you'll be taking Sophia for your date?"

"I have." He glanced at Obiora, and relaxed when he saw that whatever that look was of earlier, it was gone now.

Obiora raised both eyebrows, nodding his head as if to say, *and*?

Ejiro grinned, a slightly devilish thing. "This is a competition, Obiora. Of course I'm not going to tell you where I'm taking her."

Obiora stared at him, his eyes intense. He was still smiling, but it was a small, barely-there thing. Ejiro suddenly felt put on display.

"You're not at all what I expected," he said quietly.

"And what *did* you expect?" Ejiro asked, rolling his eyes. "What was it you called me? Boring?"

"Evasive," Obiora corrected. "Clearly, I was wrong. You're just full of surprises."

"That's me. Shrek."

Obiora's laugh seemed startled out of him. "*What*?" he said, chortling. "*Shrek*?"

Ejiro blushed furiously. "I just mean—the onions thing—"

"Onions?" Obiora sputtered.

Ejiro blushed harder. "The *layers*—"

"*Layers*?" Obiora said, his voice pitched even higher.

"The metaphor!" Ejiro almost yelled. "Haven't you watched *Shrek*? The bit where he was explaining to Donkey about how he had layers like ..." He trailed off when he realised Obiora was clearly messing with him, Obiora nearly wheezing with how hard he was laughing. "Oh, screw you," Ejiro said, but he was laughing too, splashing water at Obiora and making him yelp and dart away. "You are such a—a *dick*."

"That must've hurt."

Ejiro splashed him again. How had Obiora noticed he didn't usually curse? Obiora laughed and splashed him back.

The sliding door of the mansion came open noisily, startling them out of their little bubble. Ejiro hadn't even noticed when the sky had lightened, dark purple giving way to pale blue.

Chris Wu waved at them as he came down the steps, cheerful as always. "Good morning! How's the water?" He was dressed for a swim as well, a towel thrown around his shoulders.

"Morning," he and Obiora echoed.

"Water's great," Obiora answered, a matching grin on his face.

"Fantastic." The Chinese-British man headed in the direction of the showers.

Obiora lowered his voice to whisper, "I'm pretty sure Chris Wu is like ... ten puppies stacked on top of each other in a human flesh coat. Surely *no one* can be that happy all the fucking time."

Ejiro snorted, even as he wrinkled his nose at the imagery. "A human flesh coat? That sounds disgusting."

"You know what I mean." Obiora splashed water at him.

Ejiro splashed him back. "You need to learn to stop judging people."

"I'm *not*—" Obiora began indignantly.

Ejiro raised an eyebrow.

Obiora sighed, rolling his eyes. "I'm just making an observation."

"Like you and the other bachelors did to me on night one?"

Obiora paused. Ejiro had meant it as a joke, but when he saw the look on Obiora's face, he realised that no, he wasn't joking at all. Like, fine, it was a competition and whatnot, he *shouldn't* take it too personally, but the quickness with which the other men had written him off had honestly hurt, not to mention Obiora's sly move behind his back.

"I'm heading out," Ejiro clipped, wading until he was at the railing and climbing out of the pool. They'd been having a good time; Ejiro didn't want Obiora to think he was being childish or whatever. It was a *competition*. The other men weren't here to play nice. And that was *fine*.

"Ejiro," Obiora called just as he climbed out.

He turned around, aiming for nonchalant and probably failing. "Yeah?"

"I really am sorry about going behind your back like that. It was a rotten thing to do." He seemed sincere.

"You're forgiven," Ejiro replied, a bit of the playfulness of earlier returning into his voice.

"Good." Obiora smiled, relieved, the sight of it making Ejiro feel even better.

"Heading off?" Chris Wu asked, approaching.

Ejiro nodded, smiling at him. "Gonna shower and get some breakfast."

"Big day today, huh?" Chris teased. "What with you telling Ameri about your date with Sophia and all."

"Don't remind me," Ejiro groaned, making Obiora laugh.

"Good luck," he said, and dived into the pool.

Ejiro nodded. His heart jolted when he saw that Obiora was still watching him. Obiora waved the tips of his fingers, a slow grin spreading across his lips.

Ejiro rolled his eyes and turned away.

Obiora's answering laugh had him smiling all the way to the shower.

TEN

"EYYYY!" THE BACHELORS IN THE dining slash kitchen hollered when Ejiro walked in the next morning, dressed up and ready for his date with Sophia.

The kitchen and dining area boasted large windows to let in natural light, and so much space one could skate across the floor if they so wished without bumping into anything. From the entrance of the corridor leading to the rest of the house, the kitchen lay on the right, with sinks, a dishwasher, oven, and cooking hobs lined up against the right wall. Above, below, and around those were pure white cupboards.

Against the adjacent wall were two big aluminium fridges with touch screens on their double doors. To their left were sliding glass doors which led to the backyard. An island separated the cooking space from the dining space, the latter of which held a long table fit for a king. The left wall was made entirely of glass from top to bottom, and looked out onto a small porch on the side of the house.

"Oh my God," Ejiro responded to the bachelors' hollers, blushing furiously, avoiding looking at any of the other men directly. He'd come to get a banana and some water to help tide him over before

Ameri and the filming crew arrived to take him on his date, but sorely regretted the decision now. He'd hoped the kitchen would be empty. "What are you guys even doing?"

He'd already been feeling self-conscious and a little bit insecure as he'd gotten dressed, but now, with the unexpected audience, it was a nearly tangible thing. He resisted the urge to turn back around and walk, and then keep walking until he'd walked right out of the mansion.

"Looking good, Ejiro," Obiora said from where he was standing by the sink, rinsing out a bowl. His dark eyes trailed Ejiro's form from head to toe, making Ejiro blush at the unabashed attention.

Ejiro was wearing a simple, white collared short-sleeved button up shirt with flowers drawn in intricate black line patterned onto the surface. His legs were covered in stylishly ripped black jeans, his feet in black vans with white laces.

"Thanks, I try," he quipped a tad sarcastically, dismissing the compliment without having to do so outright.

From the way both of Obiora's eyebrows rose to his forehead, his lips twisted with amusement, he knew what Ejiro was doing but didn't call him out on it. Which was good, because if there was one thing Ejiro couldn't stand, it was insincere praise.

"And where will you be taking the lucky lady?" Liam asked from where he was sitting on the dining table, along with Damien, Chris Payne, and Chris Wu, all of them at different stages of eating their breakfasts.

"I'm so jealous you get to spend an *entire* day with her," Damien complained, though his tone was light. He had skin as dark as Ejiro's and was just as tall, except he was stunningly handsome with a thick body Ejiro knew Ajiri would have referred to as a "dad bod". He was also one of the winners of last week's obstacle course, and had picked dinner for his date with Sophia. Chris Wu had gone with lunch, and Liam, the last bachelor that Sophia had handpicked herself, had chosen breakfast. The three of them would be filming their dates tomorrow, which seemed to increase the competitiveness between them since they'd all have to impress Sophia within the span of approximately twelve hours.

Ejiro figured since it was already the day of his own date, he could safely tell the rest of the men where he was taking Sophia without the risk of them stealing or copying the idea. Well, he supposed they *could* still copy it if they wished, but it wouldn't look as thoughtful since he was the first.

He headed for the fridge. "I'm taking her to breakfast first, then the *Modern Art Oxford* gallery, then dinner."

Chris Wu wolf whistled. "Museum, huh? She's going to love that." He grinned.

"Yeah?" Ejiro asked, relaxing a little. He'd recalled Ameri mentioning that Sophia was an art aficionado during the filming for his highlight reel, so he'd crossed his fingers and hoped for the best.

"Oh yeah, definitely." Chris Wu stood, taking his dishes to the sink. Obiora was resting against the counter, arms crossed over his chest, that small smile of amusement still on his lips. "Trust me, she's going to love it. Museums and art galleries are Sophia's thing."

"How do you know so much about her?" Damien asked with narrowed eyes.

Chris Wu turned to wink at him. "Trade secret."

"Boo!" Chris Payne said.

Chris Wu laughed.

Ejiro shook his head with a smile. The fridge and pantry were stocked with a variety of foods, from fresh produce to frozen meals, most at the request of the bachelors. Ameri apparently wanted their experience to be as smooth and as enjoyable as possible, so, apart from any late requests, they'd been given two phones—both completely so ancient that they couldn't download any apps on them— with Ameri's and the other director's name as they only contacts in case of emergencies.

Ejiro took out one banana, closing the fridge door and glancing at the clock as he did. He had about ten minutes before Ameri and the crew arrived. The thought made his heart start racing, his palms start sweating.

He closed his eyes as he took in a deep breath, held it, and let it out slowly.

"Nervous?"

He opened his eyes. Obiora was looking at him with that smirk somehow permanently etched onto his lips.

Ejiro's nerves were too shot to tolerate any jokes at his expense, so he said, a little waspishly, "I don't know. What do you think?"

To his indignation—and lack of surprise, if he were being honest—Obiora laughed, though the sound wasn't mocking.

"You've got nothing to worry about," Obiora said, grinning and moving away from the counter. He walked backward in the direction of the corridor leading to the main rooms. "After all, you're *Shrek*." He winked and threw up finger guns.

"Oh dear God," Ejiro groaned, face palming, even though, strangely, Obiora's teasing seemed to reduce some of his anxiety.

Obiora laughed, this time at Ejiro's expense, he was sure, not apologetic in the least as he left the room. Ejiro resisted the urge to flip him off as he disappeared.

Ejiro briefly closed his eyes, wondering why on earth he'd made that awkward reference yesterday. He'd just felt so comfortable in Obiora's presence that for a moment there, he'd forgotten that they weren't actually friends.

He quickly finished up his banana and had barely poured himself a glass of water when Ameri and the crew arrived.

Just like that, his anxiety was back and raging a storm within his chest, his heartbeat a wild drumbeat.

He inhaled and exhaled again, for what little good it did, and braced himself.

"Hope you have a nice time!" Chris Wu said cheerily as he began to leave.

He managed a tight smile. "Thanks."
Let's hope I don't mess this up.

EJIRO TOOK SOPHIA TO A small, cosy waffle house called *G & D's*, where they had their breakfast. The bachelorette looked gorgeous in a light pink summer dress and wooden wedge sandals, her hair left free to frame her face and shoulders.

Ejiro hadn't dated anyone since he and his ex-girlfriend had broken up over two years ago. He'd actually been pretty close to proposing to Samantha, until she'd made him realise—with badly dropped clues instead of just outright telling him—that marriage—specifically marriage *to him*—was not in the cards for her. The breakup had messed him up so badly he'd shied away from the dating scene for a while. By the time he'd felt ready to get back on the saddle, so to speak, he felt slightly terrified of initiating anything new.

This meant that while on the surface, his date with Sophia was going well, it was also kind of a disaster underneath it all.

With Sophia's beauty, wit, and charm, Ejiro found himself donning his "extrovert" mask, the persona he wore whenever he was outside of his comfort zone, where he pretended to be ten times more confident than he was, while maintaining an equal level of self-deprecation.

Sophia was just so lovely and sweet and wonderful that Ejiro couldn't help but pretend to be more than he was, while he squashed the real bits of himself smaller and smaller until there was nothing but the mask left.

It's okay, he tried to tell himself. He just wasn't comfortable with Sophia just yet, and that was the point of the date. Surely, over time, he'd trust her enough to let her see the real him.

Besides, he wasn't pretending *throughout*. When they'd left the waffle house and decided to walk in the direction of the museum since it was close by, the backs of their hands had brushed, and Ejiro hadn't resisted the urge to hold her hand. She'd glanced at him with a shy but pleased smile, and Ejiro's heart had soared.

It all came tumbling down in the museum when Sophia tried to kiss him.

They'd been having a frankly wonderful time, discussing the art pieces they enjoyed, and whispering sly remarks about the ones they found obnoxious. Ejiro had finally begun relaxing a little, all the layers he'd built up—he smiled with a bit of embarrassed amusement as he remembered his conversation with Obiora—to hide his vulnerable self slowly peeling away, when he'd glanced at Sophia mid-conversation to find her staring intensely at his mouth, her face slowly, but obviously drawing close.

Ejiro had casually looked away, as though he hadn't noticed her intention, while his heart had leapt to his throat. At that moment, for some odd reason, he'd felt the strange urge to run—run as fast as he could and never look back. Underneath the urge was also a little bit of irritation, which made him feel deeply ashamed. There was nothing wrong with her wanting to kiss him—in fact, he should feel flattered that she even wanted to in the first place, right? But that thought did nothing to rid him of his discomfort.

Sophia didn't attempt to lean in again, and if her laughter was a tad higher and more strained afterwards, he pretended not to notice it.

Things smoothed over during dinner, then tumbled again after.

For some reason, Ejiro hadn't pictured what would happen at the end of the date, but when Sophia followed him out of the limo and toward the mansion doors, it suddenly hit him that he was going to have to kiss her.

Oh God. Nerves hit him with the force and speed of a highway truck.

If someone asked him later what they'd talked about as they'd walked up to those damning doors, Ejiro would have absolutely nothing to say; it felt like he was in a state of mild dissociation.

When they stood in front of the doors facing each other, Ejiro could see that Sophia was practically *begging* to be kissed; she was standing too close, playing with her hair, biting her lower lip, staring at him so intensely he felt like he was a bug underneath a microscope.

As they chattered about random nonsense, prolonging their goodbye, Ejiro tried to bring himself to do it. He kept glancing at her mouth, trying to imagine it—pulling her close by her hips, or her shoulders, or just cupping her face, but all his muscles refused to obey his commands.

He wanted to kiss her. Didn't he? He was *supposed* to want to kiss her, and he did. He did. A little. Maybe. She had really nice lips, full and pink and lush, her lipstick since faded after their meal and from how often she licked them.

The cameras felt too huge. The lights were too bright. There were too many people.

Sweat built up on his lip, on his palms, and under his arms. His heart pounded in his temples, his throat, and his ears.

"I had a really nice time tonight, Ejiro," Sophia whispered when they'd run out of inane topics to prolong the inevitable, her voice low with obvious desire. Her body was loose and tilted toward him, an open invitation. "I really hope we can do it again."

"Me too," Ejiro said, his own voice hoarse with nerves. "Um." He swallowed. He glanced at her mouth again.

Just do it, Ejiro. You like her, don't you? You had a nice time. You're supposed to kiss your date at the end of the night. It's romantic! And besides, she clearly wants you to!

Screw it.

He leaned in quickly, closing his eyes and bracing himself for the touch of her mouth.

He missed it by a mile, and ended up kissing the corner of her lips instead.

Her eyes widened, pupils blown wide, and her breath hitched softly.

His throat felt clogged. His hands trembled.

"Goodnight, Sophia," he said, then he was practically running out of there, disappearing into the mansion before she could do so much as respond.

Ameri had warned him that she wanted a brief footage of the aftermath of the date—some small clips to boost his cutaway scenes later—so Ejiro was hyperaware of the cameras as they followed him into the mansion.

He waited for Ameri to yell cut, for Sophia to run in after him, but none of that happened. The other director or producers were probably busy filming Sophia's own aftermath of the date, the thought of which made him have a little panic, so he shoved it away.

He headed to one of the main sitting rooms almost on autopilot, the largest one where most of the bachelors spent their free time playing board games or just hanging around, his heart still beating too loud.

Lo and behold, some of the bachelors were there. They must've been prodded into position by the handlers beforehand, because they were all dressed appropriately and behaving themselves.

"There he is!" Chris Wu said, grinning. "How was your date, Ejiro?"

And somehow, though he wasn't sure how because he was still thinking about his botched kiss with Sophia, he managed to reply honestly, if a little shyly, grinning as he said, "It was all right."

"All right, he says," Jin teased with an amused eyebrow raise. "Look at that smile. You look positively chuffed."

Ejiro grew even more embarrassed. "I'm going to change."

The men's playful jeers followed him out of the room. He made it all the way up the stairs before Ameri yelled, "Cut!"

Ejiro nearly sank to the floor like a puppet whose strings had been cut. He hadn't realised how tense he'd been until the filming had ended.

As Ameri gave him a rundown of what to expect for filming his cutaways tomorrow, Ejiro found himself nodding and responding when he was expected. But his mind was stuck on the kiss he'd given Sophia, despite how hard he was trying not to think about it.

He didn't know how he felt. His stomach churned—with butterflies? Probably. Yes. Obviously butterflies. He tried to remember the touch of her lips, the darkening of her eyes, and felt his heart give a sickening jolt.

Yes. Definitely butterflies.

ELEVEN

"WELCOME BACK, EVERYONE, TO ANOTHER episode of *Cupid Calling*!" Ameri Shae announced to the sound of thunderous applause. "We're here on episode three with a *live* studio audience—say hi to the folks at home everyone!—where our bachelorette is going to get to know our bachelors a little better during a blind date style Q & A."

On cue, the audience "oohed".

"Our bachelors will be divided into four groups of five, and will be hidden from the bachelorette via a thin panel. The bachelors' voices will also be altered, so our bachelorette won't be biased when picking her winners. Sorry, Chris Wu!" The audience laughed. "Speaking of winners, for each set of five, the winning bachelor will of course get the grand prize of having the opportunity to take our bachelorette on a private date!" Another "oooh" from the audience. "Now, without further ado, let's welcome our bachelorette, Sophia Bailey!"

Cheers rose.

From backstage, despite the staff rushing back and forth, finishing up the last touches of makeup for the bachelors, and the general air of anxiety hovering about, Obiora found that he wasn't nervous at all.

Part of that was due to the fact that over the past few days, he had come to realise that his attraction to Ejiro—which he had since stopped denying—had built him some immunity to the beauty and charm of the bachelorette. And since Ejiro was most likely straight as a pole, Obiora wasn't in danger of having his interest returned.

He was a grown ass man. Just because he found Ejiro deeply compelling and at times disarmingly sexy—even more so because Ejiro didn't even seem to be aware of his own appeal—it didn't mean Obiora had to *act* on it.

So, with his interest in Ejiro doing anything but waning, he could coast along during the competition without the risk of putting his heart on the line, take advantage of the free days for his vacation, then do something to get himself eliminated when he was done resting. It was almost so easy it made him want to laugh.

"Come on, gentlemen! Time to pick a number; you know the drill."

The bachelors, all dressed sharply in suits as Ameri had required, walked up to where Diana, Ameri's right hand and second director slash producer, was standing, holding a familiar fish bowl.

Obiora picked number six. He would be in the second group.

"Bachelors one to five, please wait here for your cue. The rest of you, please follow me."

Obiora instinctively looked for Ejiro. When Ejiro followed after Diana, he didn't know whether to feel relieved or not. As usual, Ejiro was beside Chris Wu and they were chatting amicably; it seemed, amongst all the bachelors, that Ejiro had made quick friends with the Chinese-Brit. Hell, it seemed Ejiro was only close to his roommates, treating the other men civilly but more like acquaintances. With how shy he was, Obiora didn't find that too surprising. The only other person apart from his roommates that he didn't treat so civilly was Obiora himself, though he tried not to let it get to his head.

It was probably because of their rocky start; something about their semi-rivalry at the beginning of the show, and then Obiora apologising and forming a truce had removed most of the masks Ejiro held in place for the other bachelors. That did not make Obiora special in any way.

Nope. It didn't. Not special. Not at all.

If he kept repeating it, perhaps his delusional head would eventually believe it.

Obiora looked at him again, unable to help it. Ejiro cleaned up really fucking nicely, wearing a deep burgundy suit that brought out the warmth underneath his dark brown skin. Unlike the other men, he'd gone with a matching bowtie rather than a necktie. Obiora couldn't help but imagine tugging that bowtie loose, and using the straps to reel him into a kiss.

Ugh, Obiora. Pull yourself together.

"Please welcome our non-competing bachelors!"

At Ameri's cue, Diana led the bachelors onto a section of the stage to the sound of the live audience's applause.

Ameri must've made them sign some really tough non-disclosure agreements because that was *a lot* of people. There had to be at least a hundred of them minus the cast and crew.

As Obiora took his seat, he saw that the non-competing bachelors were positioned in such a way that they could not see or be seen by the bachelorette, which made sense given the blind date theme. Instead, they could see and be seen by the audience and the competing bachelors, their five empty seats waiting ahead in the centre of the stage. A partition blocked off the rest of the stage, where the bachelorette was hidden from view except to the audience.

"Now please join me in welcoming our first competing bachelors!"

The first section of the show passed relatively quickly. Sophia fired off questions that each of the bachelors answered equally as quickly; some were flirty, some downright silly, and others serious. Obiora would have memorised the questions, but he had a feeling they'd probably change with each set of bachelors.

And he was proven right. Sophia had picked Noah, or bachelor number three, as her favourite bachelor from the first group, and the segment ended with the man in question walking past the partition to reveal himself.

After some hugs and applause, and Ameri reminding the audience that Noah had officially scored a private date with the bachelorette, Diana yelled *cut* and led the first group of bachelors from the stage.

"Bachelors six to ten, with me, please! Bachelors one to five, please take their vacated seats."

Obiora's heart skipped a beat when he stood and noticed Ejiro standing as well. Ejiro looked around, possibly to check out the group as well, and noticed Obiora looking. He smiled, raising one single eyebrow in challenge.

Obiora's heart skipped again. He wanted to kiss that smile off his fucking face.

He returned the eyebrow raise, his lips curving into a confident smirk he did not feel, and Ejiro grinned, his eyes dancing with mischief, every inch of him screaming *it's on*.

Despite his brain screaming at him to stay away, Obiora moved until they were walking next to each other.

"Really?" Ejiro asked under his breath, amusement in his voice. "Are we *really* doing this? You do know there are other people competing for Sophia's heart, not just me, right?"

"Yeah, but, I mean, seeing as you won the last challenge—out of nowhere, if I might add—you'll forgive me if I want to keep you in my sights at all times."

Ejiro laughed, and it was a *real* laugh—nothing like the small, shy, and slightly stifled things he gave the other bachelors when they teased him.

This one was full; *genuine*.

Fuck, Obiora had to be careful here. He might not be in danger of losing his heart to Sophia, but that didn't mean it was safe from Ejiro, either.

"I'm flattered, honestly." The words were teasing, said with the hint of a laugh, but Obiora could tell Ejiro was being honest. Then the smile was wiped off his face, and Ejiro's eyes turned dark, expression intense. *Jesus fucking Christ fuck me.* "Third time's the charm, eh, Obiora?"

"Oh, it's definitely on," Obiora growled. Ejiro laughed just as Diana hurried them up onto the stage.

"May the best man win," Ejiro said, a playful grin on his lips. He was moving down to his seat before Obiora could respond.

They were seated according to the numbers they'd pulled from the fish bowl, which had Obiora on the seat closest to the partition hiding the bachelorette, while Ejiro sat on the other edge, the three remaining bachelors between them.

Diana had the staff fit them all with small microphones pinned to the front of their suits, the microphone packs taped hidden to their backs. Make-up and costuming checked them one more time, then they quickly left the stage.

"And we're going live in five—" Diana held up five fingers, dropping one consecutively as she counted "—four, three ..." *two, one.*

"Hello, and welcome back to episode three of *Cupid Calling*!" Ameri said brightly, standing on a platform between the audience and competitors, cameras in her face. "We're back with our bachelorette, Miss Sophia Bailey!" Applause followed the introduction on cue. "Sophia will be asking our second set of bachelors a series of questions, and whoever she vibes with the most will win the chance of a private date. Now, without further ado, off to you, Sophia!"

"Thank you, Ameri." Sophia's voice rang through the small studio space thanks to her microphone, loud and clear. From the sound of her voice, Obiora could tell she was smiling, genuinely excited. "For my first question, do you believe in love at first sight?" The audience "oohed". "Bachelor number one."

Obiora almost forgot he was the first bachelor.

"Love at first sight?" he repeated to buy himself some time. He managed to hide his flinch when his voice came out slightly distorted; warped and deeper to hide his identity from Sophia. "To be honest? I'll have to say no. Now, *lust* at first sight? That I definitely believe."

The audience laughed, along with Sophia.

"Of course," she said, sounding highly amused. "Bachelor number two?"

"I'm going to have to agree with bachelor number one," he said, confident as you please. With short dark hair, pale skin, and a buff build, he was one of the more attractive bunch of the bachelors. His suit was pinstripe—which Obiora thought was obnoxious, but honestly, Obiora just hated the guy because he let the homophobic f-slur drop from his lips way too easily and frequently. He'd gotten aggressive when Obiora had tried to shut that shit down, and Obiora wasn't in the mood to fight, so he'd let it be and decided to avoid him altogether. "Lust at first sight is just more believable."

"Bachelor number three?"

"I agree as well." Ronald was bachelor number three, another white man. He had short brown hair and tanned skin, and what seemed to be permanently bitten fingernails, despite costuming's numerous attempts to make him TV-ready. "Can the attraction be so intense it can be *mistaken* for love? Absolutely. But that means it's *still* lust at first sight underneath the surface, not love."

"An interesting take. Bachelor number four?"

"Actually, I disagree." The audience "oohed". Bachelor number four was Liam, the florist Sophia had handpicked on the second group date when she'd beat his now eliminated group winner on the obstacle course. "I do believe in love at first sight. Perhaps it's a different, even lesser kind of love, but it's still love. That's what I believe."

The audience "awwed."

"That's really sweet. Bachelor number five?"

Obiora tried not to show how much he was suddenly paying attention.

"I agree with bachelor number four," Ejiro said, his voice silky smooth. "Though I don't necessarily agree that it's a lesser kind of love. What is love, anyway? How can one quantify it? When I was about eight years old, I remember walking home from school with my sister when we spotted an abandoned puppy on the side of the road. What I felt at that moment—my chest felt like it couldn't possibly contain the emotion welling in my heart. That, I believe to this day, was—to me—love at first sight. I wanted to take that puppy home and nurse it back to health, to keep it; watch it grow a long and happy life until it died, safe and loved. Alas, my mother was not receptive to the idea." Some of the audience members chuckled. "What makes that love any different from, say, a romantic love that has grown over a period of time of getting to know someone? Or a familial love? I still think of that puppy, brief as our interaction was, and despite the fact that I never saw it again, to this day. So, yes, I *do* believe in love at first sight."

There was a brief silence, then the audience broke into applause.

"Well." Sophia sounded a little breathless. "Thank you for that insightful response, bachelor number five. For my next question, what is your favourite season, and why? Bachelor number one."

"Definitely summer," Obiora answered, clearing his throat when his voice came out breathless. He couldn't stop thinking of Ejiro's answer, the ache in his voice as he'd spoken about an abandoned puppy. Jesus Christ he was jealous of a fucking *puppy*. "There's just something inherently joyful about the season that I love a lot."

"Winter," Ejiro answered when it was his turn, a little shyly, which was too fucking endearing for Obiora's heart to bear. "I'm an introvert, so cold days where I have to stay indoors all warm and snug with a mug of hot chocolate and thick socks are my jam."

The audience "awwed" on cue.

Obiora hated how vividly he could picture it—Ejiro in a thick oversized sweater, sweatpants, and thick socks, cradling a mug of hot chocolate with melting marshmallows as he curled up underneath some blankets and watched TV on a lazy Sunday afternoon.

"Question number three, and this is a slightly serious one, what ended your last relationship? Bachelor number one."

For a brief moment, Obiora froze. The room seemed to expand around him, while contracting at the same time, making the space feel simultaneously too big and too small. He couldn't breathe, yet there was too much air.

Someone cleared their throat.

"My last relationship ended because ..." He swallowed. Tried to put on his cocky, confident persona. "Well, when I was twenty-one, my girlfriend was involved in a car accident. She died."

Surprised and pitying gasps echoed through the audience.

Obiora forced himself to continue, still with that carefree smile on his face, knowing that if he acted like Ada's death still bothered him to this day, the audience wouldn't know how to deal with it. People always felt uncomfortable in the presence of someone expressing their grief, so Obiora had learned how to hide it so *they* could be more comfortable plying him with empty platitudes until they could eventually change the subject without seeming dismissive or rude.

"A few years later, I met someone new, but I guess I wasn't entirely as over Ada—that was her name—as I thought I was. My boyfriend at the time felt—rightly, might I add—I was still too attached to her, so he decided to walk. But I'm good—I'm here, after all." He winked at the audience, and there was laughter—fleeting, but there, lifting the sombre mood.

"I'm so sorry to hear that, bachelor number one," Sophia said, her voice soft and kind. "And thank you so much for sharing that with us today. Bachelor number two?"

Obiora didn't pay attention to Hunter's, Ronald's, and Liam's responses, only tuning in when it was Ejiro's turn. He was painfully curious about Ejiro's answer. Then again, what was new?

"I've actually only ever been in one serious relationship," Ejiro began, a little nervously. "And I thought we were so in love we'd eventually get married, but I was wrong. She didn't feel the same, and that was the end of that. Hoping I can change that now."

The audience "awwed". There was a blush in Sophia's voice when she responded, though Obiora wasn't listening. He was too busy thinking about this imaginary woman and how he wanted to strangle her. He couldn't imagine Ejiro loving someone and them *not* loving him back. What in the actual fuck? With how reserved Ejiro was, every smile Obiora managed to pull from him felt like a *gift*—if he saw you fit enough to open up and give you his *entire* heart—

Obiora forcefully stopped that train of thought before it could take flight, his pulse galloping away at the base of his throat.

"Speaking of ex-boyfriends …" Sophia's voice was sly. Obiora suddenly realised he'd essentially come out on national TV. Whoops? "How do you feel about the queer community? Bachelor number one."

Obiora grinned lazily. "Well, I'm bisexual, so, I'm in full support of people deserving basic human respect no matter their orientation or presentation."

"Period," Sophia said, which made the audience laugh and burst into brief applause. "Bachelor number two?"

"I disagree." The room went silent. Obiora stiffened, even though he wasn't entirely shocked by the answer. "I'm sorry, but this is just my belief, but I think it's unnatural. That's just my belief. Like, I respect that they're living their truth or whatever, but God did not make man and man to lie with each other. That's it."

The silence grew.

"That's unfortunate." Sophia's voice was hard. "I think you might as well just pack your things right now and leave, bachelor number two. Thank you for your participation."

There was a pause.

Hunter laughed awkwardly. "I'm sorry?"

"I said please pack your things and leave. You're going home right now, bachelor number two. I don't tolerate homophobes."

"Are you kidding me?" Hunter said, his voice rising. "Just because I have a different opinion—"

"Homophobia is *far* from a difference in opinion," Sophia interrupted sharply.

"I am *not* a homophobe," he growled. "As long as y'all keep that shit away from me, I don't care. I just personally believe—"

The audience booed loudly, cutting off his rant.

"Can someone please get him out of here?" Sophia said, sounding bored.

Security was already waiting at the entrance leading backstage. They came onto the platform, but Hunter shoved them off when they tried to escort him out, stomping out of the place by himself. He called Sophia a bitch as he did so, the audience gasping with shock as he did.

Ameri looked like she wanted to stop the filming and deal with him, but Sophia said smoothly, "I'm so sorry about that. Let's get back to it. Bachelor number three?"

Liam and Ronald stated that they were definitely pro-LGBT, though after that surprising elimination, Obiora wouldn't be surprised if either of them were lying.

"My twin is a lesbian," Ejiro said when it was his turn, and Obiora's eyes widened slightly when he heard the "twin" bit. "Her relationship with her girlfriend is the entire reason why I'm here—I want a love like theirs, and that's why I auditioned for *Cupid Calling*. Or rather, why I let them trick me into auditioning for *Cupid Calling*," he added dryly, to the sound of muted laughter. "So, yes, as bachelor number one so eloquently put it, I'm in favour of people being treated with basic human decency, no matter their sexual orientation or gender identity."

"Lovely."

The questions were lighter after that, gently erasing the tense atmosphere after Hunter's abrupt elimination. When it was all over, Obiora wasn't surprised when Sophia picked bachelor number five as her winner.

For a brief moment, Ejiro looked like a deer caught in headlights, then he quickly replaced the expression with a shy smile, growing shyer and more self-conscious when the audience's applause rose as he walked over the partition to reveal himself to Sophia.

After Sophia's excited squeals at the reveal, and Ameri's summary of the events, the bachelors were led off the stage, Ejiro following close behind. He grinned when Liam and Ronald congratulated him, but the smile didn't reach his eyes. In fact, he looked slightly dazed; confused.

Strangely, it reminded Obiora of the night Ejiro had come back from his first date with Sophia, when he'd walked into the main sitting room where some of the bachelors had been instructed to wait and they'd begun teasing him about the date.

He'd had that same deer-in-headlights look about him then, even as he'd smiled and blushed and waved off their teasing.

He wanted to ask if Ejiro was okay, but Ejiro was turning to look at him at that exact moment, smiling at him so brightly, so teasingly that all of Obiora's thoughts were immediately obliterated.

"I guess the third time *isn't* the charm, then?" He raised an eyebrow, a teasing grin on his lips.

Obiora laughed. "Fuck right off."

Ejiro laughed too, and Obiora completely forgot about everything else.

The official website for the CUPID CALLING series.

Cupid Calling

ABOUT | THE BACHELORETTE | THE BACHELORS | EPISODES | CONTACT | BECOME A CUPID

Episode 3 – Blind Date with the Bachelorette

Episode Summary: Sophia goes on her dates with the winners of last week's obstacle course, sharing a steamy kiss with Liam and Damien during their dates, a tender kiss with Ejiro after his, and a lingering hug with Chris Wu.

For this week's group date, the contestants are taken on a Blind Date style Q & A with the bachelorette: in four groups of five, hidden from the bachelorette behind a partition and their voices rendered unrecognisable thanks to scrambled mics, the bachelorette has to pick her winners based on their answers to her questions alone.

Noah's smooth, sexy, savvy and at times vulnerable responses makes Sophia swoon and wins him the Red Heart of the night, Ejiro's shy responses endear him to Sophia, Dean nearly makes her fall off her seat laughing with his charm, and Chris Wu's charisma practically leaps through the barrier.

Hunter is the first bachelor to be eliminated during a date for being a homophobe. Chris Payne, Muhammed, and Leo are also eliminated.

Click here to watch the full episode on Netflicks!

COMMENTS

 LIFEGOESON777

The swiftness with which Sophia eliminated Hunter? That was too sexy of her I think.

 11890   4121

 SOPHIAS_STAN

This was probably my favourite episode so far! I just loved getting to know the bachelors a little bit more, plus the set up??? Reminds me of all those old dating shows lol

♥ 11036   💬 3991

🐱 COOTI3BUNNI3

Awww, Obiora omg T_T You can tell he was being cocky on purpose to hide how much his ex-girlfriend's death must've affected him T_T

 10855   3757

 **AMAKATHEESTALLION**

Sophia's chemistry with Chris Wu on their date? Jesus Christ, they didn't even kiss but the flirting/staring contest they did at the end there felt like pure sex
Edit: why are you booing me I'm right

 9312   4721

 **GOOGOOGAAGAA**

Okay, you can't tell me Ejiro didn't notice Sophia wanted to kiss him 😑 Plus he looked reluctant to kiss her at the end of their date. Maybe he's just shy but idk Edit: I literally said maybe he's shy, enough with the death threats please

 8950   4209

LOAD MORE COMMENTS ⌄

TWELVE

GRIEF WAS A FUNNY THING. Sometimes, to Obiora, it felt like nothing but a trickle, an awareness in the back of his mind that was easily acknowledged and then put aside. Other times, it felt like the tide on a full moon, powerful and violent, yanking him off his foundations and dragging him into its dark, desolate depths until he was left floundering and scrambling to find the surface.

As the years had passed from Ada's death, the times where he'd be overwhelmed with his grief grew fewer and further between. Sometimes he could even predict when it would affect him most—on days like her birthday, the day of the accident, or her funeral—but other times, times like today, the grief came out of nowhere, like someone bludgeoning him in the back of the head.

Though perhaps that wasn't the right metaphor. It had snuck up on him today like a thief in the night. He'd barely paid attention to the other bachelors' surprise and jealousy when Sophia had handed Noah—the tall, Black, tattooed biker with long, luscious locs—the Red Heart of the night. Hell, even when Sophia had handed Obiora his Pink Heart, he had no fucking idea what the fuck he'd said to her as she'd pinned it to his chest, vaguely recalling she'd at least laughed.

Now he sat on his bed, the chain of a locket curled around his fist. Ada had been sentimental like that. She loved things like friendship bracelets, favourite pictures of hers she'd get freaking *laminated* just so she could store them safely in the zipper of her bags and purses without risk of them fraying too soon, along with playful collage photos people took in tiny mall photo booths. He didn't wear the locket anymore, content to have it close in his bag or wallet, but when he was feeling down like today, it felt important to him to grieve while he remembered her face—her dazzling grin and her big, brown eyes, rich with life.

Obiora remembered how nervous he'd been when they were seventeen, the first time he'd looked at her and seen *her*; a young, brilliant, beautiful Black girl who just so happened to be his best friend, except, then, he'd suddenly realised how badly he wanted to kiss her—to sweep her off her feet, and have her look at him the same way.

His opportunity had come in the form of their prom; he'd gone all out that year, making the most elaborate promposal he could think of because he'd known, on some level, she would have loved it, romantic or not. Luckily for him, it had been the former.

She'd taken one look at him, standing nervously in the middle of the school hallway surrounded by red, heart-shaped balloons, rose petals, streamers, and an impromptu choir made up of some of their mates standing behind him, and for the first time, she'd *seen* him—her best friend, but also a young Black boy who'd fallen head over heels for her.

She'd walked up to him, taken the bouquet of roses from his hands with a shy, whispered thanks, then she'd kissed him right there, blushing and ignoring their friends' exclamations of "*finally!*", their hoots and jeers and laughter, while Obiora had felt his whole world shift on its axis.

They'd gone to the same university, shared a flat with their friends. After they'd both graduated, they'd moved from Sheffield to

London, fresh-faced and eager to start life in the city rife with opportunities. God, they hadn't even finished emptying all their boxes before the accident. They'd been tentatively planning out their futures, basking in the few days of freedom afforded to them after their graduation—gorging down on takeaways, piling little knickknacks to decorate their place, not worrying too much about careers and marriage, content at the moment with their service jobs and the privilege of having families more than willing to pitch in to aid their dreams—

And then she was gone. Just like that.

"Do you need the light?"

Obiora looked up. It was Tyler. Jin had already gone to bed, lying on his back with his hands crossed serenely over his chest, like a fucking vampire. The last bed lay empty, since Ricky had been eliminated on week two.

"Nah," Obiora said, slipping out of his bed. "I don't feel tired just yet. Gonna chill a bit in the sitting room."

"All right, man. Goodnight."

The light went off as he exited the room. On his way to the sitting room, he noticed Ejiro's room light was also on, their room door open. A quick glance showed him the man in question on his bed by the window, his sketchpad and pencils in his lap. Obiora's heart dutifully skipped a beat, before he looked away, curling his hand tighter around the locket until it bit into the tender flesh of his palm, as if to punish himself for feeling something for someone else when he was currently feeling raw about Ada.

The sitting room proved not to be conductive for his frame of mind, housing some of the other bachelors who were laughing and talking. So he headed toward the dining and pool. The first option was another no go, with Alistair and Eddie cooking something spicy on the stove. The scent of it, delicious as it was, made Obiora's stomach turn.

The pool was no better; Noah was taking a leisurely swim. Obiora really didn't feel like talking to anyone right now.

He was about to give up, turn around and head back to his room to lay in bed and stare at the ceiling until morning, knowing sleep wouldn't be coming easy tonight, when his eyes caught on the veranda extending from the back porch and surrounding the right side of the house.

The very end of the veranda had some chest-high plants entwined with the railing, essentially blocking the seating there from view of the pool and the house, creating a soft, cosy nook.

Obiora ducked there before Noah could notice him. The chair there was a specially made unit that fit the entire nook in the shape of an "n". It was a soft creamy colour with comfortable cushions, and had a small black coffee table in its centre. The plants blocking it off from view surrounded it on all three sides.

Obiora sank into the far right corner of the chair against the side of the house with a soft sigh.

Then he quietly flicked the locket open, and let himself drown.

EJIRO HAD WON ANOTHER DATE with Sophia. He should've been happy, excited even, but all he could feel was a strange nervousness. The botched kiss of their previous date filled his thoughts; what if she wanted a kiss again? She'd *definitely* want a kiss again, and Ejiro *should* want to kiss her—she was beautiful and sweet and lovely and he *liked* her, so why did the thought of kissing her fill him with slight panic? Why did it make him feel like running as far away as possible?

Maybe he was just nervous, he told himself, though the conclusion didn't feel completely accurate. He did feel nervous, yes, almost extremely so, but there was something else, something he couldn't quite name.

His thoughts wouldn't stop churning until he was grabbing his sketchbook from underneath his pillow and losing himself to the movement of his pencils.

At first, he drew aimlessly, letting his hand flow freely across the page. Eventually, his mind went to the group date, and he found himself drawing some of the other bachelors, the emotive, animated expressions on their faces as they'd answered Sophia's questions, before drawing some sketches of the bachelorette herself.

Soon, his thoughts narrowed in on Obiora. Ejiro had once thought Obiora to be nothing but a cocky, obnoxious pain in his butt. Even though their relationship had started thawing ever since their banter in the pool a few days ago, Ejiro still hadn't been able to picture anything else underneath the surface.

Until today. When Obiora had been talking about his late girlfriend ...

Ejiro bit his lip, his eyebrows furrowing with concentration as he tried to recreate the vulnerable look in Obiora's eyes on the page.

Obiora had tried to hide it, of course, and perhaps if you weren't looking for it, you wouldn't even notice, but Ejiro had seen it in his eyes; his love for her, his grief. It had humanised him so much in that moment that Ejiro had wanted badly to give him a hug.

"Hey," Chris Wu said sleepily from his bed. "I'm sorry, buddy, but do you mind—" He gestured at the lights.

"Oh!" Ejiro blushed, slamming his sketchbook closed. He glanced at the clock and winced. It was nearing midnight already. How long had he been drawing? "Sorry about that, I'll—"

He stood, indecisive for a brief moment. He didn't feel like sleeping just yet.

He headed toward the door, switching off the lights as he did.

"Thank you."

"No problem. Goodnight." He gently closed the door behind him, and headed in the direction of the kitchen.

He waved at Eddie and Alistair, who were busy chatting on the dining table, dirty plates, cups, and a half-finished bottle of wine in front of them. It seemed like they'd cooked a meal, the countertop and sinks a mess. Ejiro wrinkled his nose. They had a cleaning service come in a few times a week, but Ejiro still didn't think that meant they should leave the place looking like a gutter.

Outside, someone who Ejiro vaguely recognised as Noah was doing laps in the pool. Noah didn't notice him, so Ejiro didn't feel too bad not saying hi as he headed straight for the little secluded nook at the end of the veranda.

Not unlike when he was with Sophia, so far, Ejiro still hadn't felt comfortable enough to completely relax around the other men, wearing his "extrovert" mask whenever he was in their orbit. It was—pardon his language—*bloody* exhausting pretending to be cool and interesting and funny, laughing with the other men when one of them teased him or cracked a joke, even if he didn't find it funny. He knew that if he was his usual quiet and reserved self, the other men would think him weird or dull or whatever, and he'd rather not face that kind of ostracism when he didn't have Ajiri or Blessing or the rest of his support network here to have his back.

When he'd discovered the nook at the end of the veranda a few days ago, apart from the "confession" room, it had become his secret place of solace when he wanted to essentially hide away from the other bachelors and recharge.

His heart dropped to his feet with painful disappointment when he realised someone was already there. The person was seated facing him, their knees pulled up to their chest, so he couldn't just turn around and leave without seeming like he was specifically avoiding them.

"Sorry," he said quietly. "I didn't know someone was here. Do you ..." He paused with surprise when he registered that the person was Obiora. "Sorry," he said again, nervous for reasons he couldn't quite discern. The sketchbook in his hands, filled with small but elaborate sketches of Obiora's facial features, burned damnably. "Uh, I'll leave you—"

"No, it's fine," Obiora said. He smiled, a soft, honeyed thing so unlike his usual grins and smirks that Ejiro felt his heart pound. "Plenty of space for both of us."

Ejiro hesitated. "If you're sure."

"I'm sure."

"All right." Ejiro echoed his smile, moving until he was perched on the opposite corner of the "n" shaped sofa.

Obiora was playing with something in his hands, uncharacteristically quiet. Ejiro was so used to him constantly teasing and grinning that seeing this greyed out version of him was a little worrying.

"Um ... are you ... okay?"

Obiora blinked, like he'd been far away for a moment, then his eyes cleared. "Hm? Oh. Yeah. I'm just ... thinking." He seemed to brace himself, before waving what was in his hands—a locket with a chain—and saying, "Just reminiscing. The game today has me going down memory lane."

It took a moment before Ejiro understood. "Oh. *Oh.*" His heart twisted with empathy as he remembered the vulnerability Obiora had tried desperately to hide. Ejiro clutched his sketchbook, preparing to stand. "I—are you sure you don't want to be alone? I completely understand if you do." And even if it meant losing his alone, recharge time, he honestly meant it. Obiora seemed to need it more.

"Sit down, Ejiro. Seriously. Don't worry about it. I like your company."

For some reason, the last sentence made Ejiro feel flustered. "Oh, okay. All right. If you're sure."

Obiora looked amused. "I'm sure."

Ejiro decided to focus studiously on his sketching. The vulnerability clung visibly to Obiora like a tangible aura, making

Ejiro feel strangely untethered. He opened the page to where he'd left off, where he'd been trying to capture Obiora's eyes, their intensity when ...

Oh.

He glanced up surreptitiously. Was it wrong to do this? To draw him when he was sitting right there, drowning in memories, obviously upset? It felt almost voyeuristic.

"I'm sorry for your loss."

Ejiro startled so hard he nearly dropped his sketchbook. "What?" he gasped, voice high with surprise and confusion.

Obiora laughed. "I'm sorry for your loss," he repeated. Ejiro didn't think he'd missed seeing that awful smirk on Obiora's lips until he saw it returned, even though it was just a shadow of his usual cocky quirk. "I know you're thinking it, so I just helped you out. Get it out of the way and all that."

Ejiro could feel a flush heat up his neck. "What? No. I didn't—I mean, yes, I *am* sorry for your loss, but I'm not—I mean—"

Obiora laughed again. "It's all right, Ejiro. Stop panicking. It's honestly been years; I don't mind."

"That doesn't mean it might not still hurt," he retorted, looking away.

Obiora was quiet for a moment. "You're right," he whispered.

He flicked open the locket in his hands, the sound drawing Ejiro's attention. For a moment, Ejiro felt painfully curious. What did she look like, this person that Obiora had so—and in so many ways *still*—obviously loved?

He felt like the question might be rude or too invasive, so he swallowed it down and focused back on the drawing in front of him.

His hand itched. He glanced up at Obiora again from underneath his lashes, and his heart skipped a beat when he saw *that* look on Obiora's face, something gentle and loving and achingly sorrowful it made Ejiro feel—just ... *feel*.

Before he could tell himself what a bad idea it was, his hand was moving across the page, sketching furiously. The tight curls of Obiora's afro; his firm, defined jaw; the barely-there dimple in his cheek, hidden underneath an artful layer of stubble; his thick, almost bushy eyebrows; his eyes, so dark and intense—deep unfathomable depths Ejiro felt he could get lost in. He kept going back to them, a frown furrowing his forehead as he tried to get the intensity in those eyes just *right*.

He tried to be covert each time he glanced up at Obiora so he wouldn't notice, and from the unchanging look on his face, it seemed he didn't.

Then his lips curled up slightly at the corners, and he didn't look in Ejiro's direction when he said, "Are you drawing me?"

Ejiro wanted the ground to open up and swallow him whole. He swallowed the guilty lump in his throat, his hand frozen mid-sketch. "No?" he squeaked.

Obiora laughed. He finally looked at Ejiro, his eyes dark. "Go ahead. I don't mind."

Ejiro gripped his pencil. "Sorry," he said, voice thick. He cleared his throat. "For ... I mean, I should have asked."

"It's okay. Now you have my permission. Knock yourself out. I could even pose if you want?" Obiora winked.

Ejiro snorted, though the wink made him feel strange. Fluttery.

God, Obiora was so obnoxious.

"That won't be necessary."

"If you say so." He grinned.

Their eyes locked. Ejiro's heartbeat stuttered. His eyes, almost without his control, dropped to Obiora's lips, which he hadn't noticed were surprisingly full, soft-looking and the palest of pinks—

The sound of the back door sliding shut startled him into looking away. That had to be Noah, turning in for the night. Ejiro shook his head with a confuddled frown, clutching his sketchbook like it'd reorient his suddenly disorganised feelings.

"So, you've won another date with the bachelorette." Obiora's voice was teasing.

Ejiro felt like he'd been doused with cold water. The mask he hadn't even realised he'd taken off instantly sprung back into place in the form of a smile so fake his face could have cracked with it.

"Yup," he said with false cheer. "I can't wait."

"Is that right." Obiora raised an eyebrow. Ejiro panicked, wondering if Obiora could see the mask for what it was.

"Mhm," he echoed, carefully not meeting Obiora's eyes.

He was excited. He *was*. Mostly nervous, yes, but still a little excited. Just a bit.

"We're friends, right?"

Ejiro's heart began to race again. "Huh?"

Obiora was smiling, flashing that irritating dimple, some of the life back in his expression. "Cause if we're not," he continued, like Ejiro hadn't responded, "I'd like to be."

"Oh." Ejiro suddenly felt shy. When last had someone actually *asked* to be his friend? It felt ... surprisingly good. "Yes. Right. I suppose we could be."

Obiora laughed at the stilted, overly formal response. "Thank you for the ringing endorsement."

"Oh shut up." Ejiro blushed.

Obiora laughed again, stretching out on the sofa, his bare feet nearly brushing against Ejiro's socked ones. The almost-contact, for some odd reason, had Ejiro's breath hitching in his throat.

"Come on, Ejiro," Obiora teased, waggling his eyebrows. "Draw me like one of your French girls."

"Oh my God." Ejiro groaned, rolling his eyes. "You piss me off."

Obiora laughed again. He raised a challenging eyebrow. Ejiro responded to the action with another roll of his eyes, but dutifully flicked his sketchbook onto a new page.

Friends, he thought, a pleased smile curling his lips.

Yeah, Ejiro would like that a lot.

THIRTEEN

IT WAS BARELY LUNCHTIME, BUT for Ejiro, today was already turning out to be a really good day. He propped his sketching materials against the door, then sank into the comfortable seats opposite the camera in the "confession" room, exhaling giddily and running his sweaty hands down his thighs. His cheeks hurt from how hard he was grinning, yet he couldn't bring himself to stop.

"First off, I miss you both so, so much," he said. "And … I have good news!"

He'd just come back from his second date with Sophia, and whatever qualms he'd had the first time they'd gone out together had been completely eradicated by today's date. Since Noah had won the Red Heart, the tattooed biker was given the opportunity to have Sophia to himself for an entire day. The other three bachelors—Ejiro, Dean, and Chris Wu—only had breakfast, lunch, and dinner to choose from.

Ejiro had chosen breakfast, feeling it would be safer than lunch or dinner due to the expectations for a kiss being lessened, even as the thought had had him immediately feeling weird and guilty.

Now though, he wasn't even sure what he'd been so nervous

about. After the initial awkwardness of waiting for their meals and fielding away small talk, something simply just *loosened* between them, and they were suddenly relaxed, laughing and cracking jokes with each other. Ejiro still didn't feel completely himself just yet with Sophia—he still donned his "extrovert" mask in a desperate attempt to make her laugh—but little by little, as the date had progressed, he'd felt the mask grow looser and looser.

By the end of the date—he'd been warned beforehand that he would be returning to the mansion alone—he'd felt confident enough to take Sophia's hand in his and press a tender kiss to the tips of her knuckles, hoping it would please her. The way she'd shivered and her eyes had lit up had made the action worth it, leaving Ejiro feeling thrilled all the way back to the mansion.

The giddiness made him re-evaluate their first date; perhaps he'd only been uncomfortable then because he'd felt she was moving too fast. When she'd tried to kiss him, he'd recoiled because he hadn't felt ready, for whatever reason, to kiss *her*.

"I think I might just be the kind of person who likes to take it slow," he reasoned after he'd finished explaining the date to the camera. "To be honest, I'd always been uncomfortable with how fast things had gone with Sam, so perhaps I was still harbouring some apprehension from that relationship when I came here? I don't know, this date just felt so *good*—no expectations, you know? Just two people hanging out and getting to know each other. I loved it. If our relationship continues to progress like this ... slow and sweet and steady, then I really can see myself falling in love with her."

He covered his face to hide his blush from the camera, then, feeling a little silly, he outright left the room, biting his cheek to reduce his grin. He didn't want the other bachelors asking any questions of him just yet.

He must not have succeeded, because when he entered the kitchen, sketching stuff in one hand, intending to head to the little nook outside, he stumbled upon Obiora making French toast. Ejiro beamed, shoulders relaxing when he saw that Obiora was the only one currently in the kitchen, and headed straight for him.

At Ejiro's expression, something flashed through Obiora's face so quickly Ejiro missed it, before it settled on amusement.

"Someone have a good date today?" Obiora teased, waggling his eyebrows.

"Abeg, leave me alone," Ejiro said, but he was blushing, coming to stand beside Obiora as he inhaled the sweet, delicious scent of frying cinnamon, butter, and brown sugar.

Obiora laughed. "It's like that, abi?"

"Yes, it's like that," Ejiro said, grinning. He inhaled again, groaning slightly. "God, that smells so good."

"Did you not eat on your date?" Obiora asked with amusement.

"Shut up," Ejiro said, eying a plate set with an already fried stack of the French toast greedily. He glanced at Obiora slyly, playfully, nudging Obiora's hip with his own. Warmth filled his chest at the easy intimacy of the act, at the way Obiora echoed the movement, nudging him back like they did this every day.

Obiora snorted when he noticed Ejiro's puppy eyes. "Fine. Go ahead and take one, before you end up absorbing the plate with your eyeballs."

"Shut up," Ejiro repeated, laughing. He made sure to take the fattest slice with a perfect golden-brown burn, the edges crisp from the pan. He took a bite and moaned as he chewed. "God, so good. I can't remember when last I had French toast." He sucked the sweet, excess butter and sugar from his fingers one by one.

Obiora sounded strangely hoarse when he responded, "And you call yourself a chef?"

"*Assistant* chef," Ejiro argued weakly. It was becoming a mantra between them now.

Obiora smirked. "Sure."

Ejiro glared at him, but it held no heat. "Keep smirking like that and you'll end up wrinkling asymmetrically."

"I'll WHAT?"

Ejiro laughed so hard he snorted. He finished up his slice and swiped another one, dodging out of the way before Obiora could smack him with the spatula in reprimand.

"Thanks for the toast," he said, waving.

"The second one isn't free. You owe me."

"Ahn ahn, Obiora, seriously? That's so petty."

"Petty is the hand that feeds."

"Petty is the hand that WHAT?"

Obiora choked on air, and Ejiro laughed, feeling lighter than air.

"Hey!" Obiora called before he could leave.

Ejiro paused, a smile still on his lips. "Yeah?"

"I'm glad your date went well." Obiora smiled.

"Oh." Ejiro felt flustered. "Um. Thank you. You need to step up your game, you know," he said to get the attention off him. "You can't just coast along the competition with your charm and good looks alone; soon enough, Sophia's going to get bored."

"You think I'm charming and good looking?" Obiora leered.

Ejiro blushed furiously. "Goodbye."

Obiora's laughter echoed behind him as he left the kitchen.

Most of the bachelors seemed to be in the pool area—it looked like they were barbecuing—but Ejiro managed to go unseen as he headed straight for the nook on the veranda. He fell onto the chair with a happy sigh, finishing up his stolen slice of toast with a fullness in stomach, and in his heart. He licked his fingers clean, and then flipped open his sketchbook, his fingers itching to draw; his thoughts revolved around the crinkle in Sophia's eyes when she laughed, and the dimple in Obiora's cheek when he smirked.

Yeah, today was a really good day.

OBIORA WAS BEGINNING TO REALISE that when he'd made the decision to befriend Ejiro, he might've made a grave mistake. At first, Ejiro was still shy and didn't seem to believe that Obiora was serious, so Obiora had taken it upon himself to prove that he was.

He'd done that by dragging Ejiro out of his room the day after their heart to heart, pulling him to the kitchen with a challenging grin. Ejiro had been reserved, if a little wary, but Obiora paid it no mind.

"So, you're a chef."

Ejiro's eyes had narrowed. "*Assistant* chef," he'd argued weakly. Then he'd glanced at the food items Obiora had meticulously arranged on the kitchen counter, and raised both eyebrows. "Jollof rice?"

"As a fellow Nigerian, I believe Jollof is the best way to test if a chef actually has any cooking skills to speak of."

"Yeah, I'm not doing this." Ejiro had turned to leave.

"Oh, yes you are." Obiora had dragged him back by the arm, grabbing an apron and artfully tying it around his hips before he could blink.

Ejiro had stood there and stared, looking a little dazed, but Obiora had spotted amusement dancing in his eyes, in the slight quirk of his lips.

Ejiro let out a disbelieving laugh, and Obiora could see the moment he consciously chose not to go back to his room to "draw", which, while he *did* draw, Obiora had noticed Ejiro had begun using "drawing" as an excuse not to socialise. Yeah, not on his watch.

"Fine, then." Ejiro made a show of retying the apron around his hips. "Just watch. I'm going to have you singing *Iya Basira* by the time I'm done."

It took a moment for Obiora to remember the song, then he burst out laughing. It was an old classic by Style Plus, one of the most successful bands to come out of Nigeria, and was about a woman who ran a roadside restaurant; her food was apparently so good, it had all the men literally enchanted and unable to consume the food of anyone else but hers.

Ejiro glanced at him, looking terribly pleased. Obiora's heart skipped a beat.

"That song is so *old*," Obiora said, shaking his head.

"Still a classic, though."

"And like hell you're that good." Obiora snorted, though the words came out challengingly.

"Is everything with you a competition?" Ejiro asked dryly, bringing out some pots and pans and extra ingredients from the cupboards.

"Yes," Obiora deadpanned.

Ejiro laughed.

It shouldn't have been arousing, watching Ejiro as he began to prepare the food. The way his hands deftly moved across the chopping board was nothing short of artful. He genuinely seemed to get lost in his own world, not feeling the need to fill in the silence.

For some odd reason, Obiora felt something thick build up in the back of his throat—pure, aching longing rising inside him like the tide. The silence between them already felt full, sweet and easy, like they did this all the time. He remembered how Ejiro had just ... sat with him the previous night and let him grieve; no comments or judgements or questions—no forced cheer or toxic positivity. Obiora subtly clenched his hands into fists, tried to shove the longing down and away—pretend it didn't exist.

When Ejiro began preparing the chicken, he added chopped onions, a sprinkle of salt, two cubes of Knorr, and a dash of mild curry powder.

Obiora's eyebrows flew up.

Ejiro glanced at him. "Secret ingredient," he said, miming a shushing motion.

"Your secret's safe with me," Obiora said, pretending to zip his mouth shut.

Ejiro laughed softly.

Fuck, Obiora felt warm all over, his pulse slightly faster than normal. Ejiro got back into the zone, while Obiora watched him, entranced, like Ejiro was some kind of siren and Obiora was caught in his thrall.

By the time he was done, it was the best Jollof rice Obiora had ever eaten, but he would take that truth with him to his grave. Though something about the smug curve of Ejiro's lips as he'd watched Obiora eat told him he already knew how good he was anyway. Which was all kinds of hot.

Since that moment, something within Ejiro had loosened, and the walls he kept up for the other bachelors completely disappeared when he was with Obiora.

Now, instead of hanging out with Chris Wu and his other roommates, when Obiora was within the vicinity, the two men found themselves gravitating toward each other; Ejiro because he probably saw Obiora as his only genuine friend amongst the bachelors, and Obiora because his attraction was quickly blooming into a little crush.

Okay, a huge crush.

A massive fucking crush.

He was so fucking fucked.

FOURTEEN

"**WELCOME BACK, EVERYONE, TO A** brand-new episode of Cupid Calling!" Ameri Shae said brightly, her focus on the camera mounted directly in front of her. She had her back to the bachelors, who were lined up behind her. "Today is going to be a game of wit—a game of puzzles, and speed, and teamwork, but most importantly, it will be a game to test how well our bachelors know our bachelorette and vice versa. Some of you must've already guessed it, so I won't leave y'all hanging—today's challenge is an Escape Room!"

She paused while the bachelors applauded and made excited noises on cue. "That's right. Our bachelors will be divided into four teams of four; the members of whatever team that makes it out of their room first will all have the chance to take the bachelorette on a private date! The catch is, the bachelorette will also be participating in an escape room. If she ends up coming out before the bachelors, then she gets to pick her four winners from any of the teams, regardless of when and with whom they finish."

The bachelors made noises of dissent, some of them loudly talking about how unfair it was because Sophia would definitely be biased in picking her winners.

"Exactly." Sophia smirked at them. "If you don't want me playing favourites, then I guess all you'll have to do is win."

The men *oohed*, to the sound of Ameri's laughter.

"And there you have it, folks! Without further ado, let the games begin!"

Diana was already waiting with the numbered cards in the fishbowl.

Beside Obiora, Ejiro was vibrating with energy. "I've always wanted to do an escape room," he said, voice high with excitement. "I've just never had the time."

"I've done it once," Obiora said, looking for all who saw like he wasn't internally losing his shit. Ejiro did that to him a lot, when he spoke to Obiora like this; in a private whisper while in the midst of the other bachelors, like Obiora was the only person in the room that mattered. "That is, if my mother turning our house into one counts."

Ejiro laughed. "I'd say it counts."

Obiora glanced at his full mouth, his infectious smile, then quickly looked away, cursing himself for his weakness. He'd promised himself to act natural; the day had barely begun and he'd already fucking failed.

Ejiro picked his number first, then Obiora picked his. They moved away for the rest of the bachelors to pick theirs.

"Two," Ejiro read aloud. "What number are you?" he asked, his voice filled with hope. And then, like he wasn't already endearing enough, the bastard crossed his fingers.

Obiora's heart donned chaps and a guitar, and started to write a serenade.

Did he want to be on the same team as Ejiro? Or did he not? Fucking hell.

He opened his card.

There was a God. And there was also a Devil.

"Four," he said.

"Yes," Ejiro hissed, then quickly wiped the excitement from his face, though it didn't completely work. He cleared his throat. "This could go wrong so easily, if you're paired with people you're incompatible with."

He thinks we're compatible! Obiora's crush-sick heart screamed.

"That's true," Obiora said, calmly. "I mean, I adore my best friend, but I don't think we'd last long if we were locked together in a room for any amount of time." With Obiora's competitive streak and Esther's constant need to be right about everything, they'd probably end up in a fistfight.

Ejiro laughed. God, every time he laughed, Obiora had to resist the urge to sway forward into his space, like Ejiro's laughter was the sound from the Pied Piper's flute, and Obiora was the ensnared.

"Now!" Ameri clapped her hands to get their attention. "As you might have noticed, there are only two escape rooms here today: one for the bachelorette, and one for the contestants."

Ameri went on to explain that she wanted the bachelors to watch and react to Sophia while she tried to escape her room, and vice versa. But for the latter to happen, the bachelors would have to go in team by team, with the non-competing teams waiting outside the building to prevent cheating.

"So, bachelors one to four, please step forward! Bachelors five to sixteen, please follow Diana out of the room and wait until your cue."

Obiora looked around. His and Ejiro's other two teammates turned out to be Jin and Noah. A good balance, Obiora thought, since he and Jin had yet to win a private date with the bachelorette, while Noah and Ejiro had both managed to win Red Hearts. Since the bachelorette would be watching them, he wondered what criteria she'd be looking for to pick this week's Red Heart. Co-operation? Intuition?

"Wonderful," Ameri said when the other bachelors had disappeared and only four of them, Sophia, the other directors, and some of the staff were left. "Are you ready, bachelors? Please proceed into the room."

"Good luck!" Sophia called, beaming and waving.

"Thank you," Ejiro said shyly.

"Won't need it, but I appreciate the thought," Noah said cockily.

"Okay! I see you," Sophia hollered, making them laugh.

"Thank you," Jin said flirtily, bowing a little as he did. Not for the first time, Obiora wondered if Jin was secretly royalty. With that posh accent and that full mouth, Obiora could see Sophia literally trying not to swoon.

Ejiro's words about him coasting along in the competition came back to haunt him, and Obiora found himself blurting, "Can I have a good luck kiss on the cheek?" his usual smirk curling his lips.

"Oh?" Sophia blushed. "Well. I don't see why not."

Obiora grinned, heading to her. She leaned up and brushed her lips against his cheek, lingering a little.

Obiora winked at her as he pulled away. "Thank you, gorgeous."

"Stop it." She blushed. "Off with you, now."

Obiora laughed. In the background, Ameri was giving him two thumbs up, no doubt because his little stunt was going to look great on TV.

When he turned around, Ejiro's smile had faltered, and he looked deeply uncomfortable. But when their eyes met, Ejiro quickly wiped away the expression, grinning widely instead. Obiora's heart gave a traitorous skip. Had that been jealousy he'd seen? Then his stomach plummeted, because if Ejiro *had* been jealous, he would've been jealous *of* Obiora.

The memory of how happy Ejiro had looked after his second date with Sophia flashed through his mind's eye, and it was like being doused with icy water.

Ejiro didn't want him. He would *never* want him. Attraction was all well and good; Obiora saw it as relatively harmless. But a crush? Crushes spoke of longing and hoping; wishing—be it conscious or subconscious—that the object of your desires would one day return your attention. For Obiora, that way lay heartache.

He needed to squash down this ridiculous crush by any means possible.

"Are you ready, bachelors?" came a tinny voice from overhead when the bachelors were locked inside the room. "Your time starts ... now!"

The space mimicked that of a bedroom, with a bed, dresser, reading desk and chair, bookshelf, wardrobe, and a door that led to a bathroom.

"I suppose our exit is a hidden passageway of some sort," Jin commented, mostly to himself. "It wouldn't do to have it be where we'd come in from, after all."

"Right. How do we start?" Ejiro rubbed his hands together excitedly, looking around the room.

Obiora smiled fondly in his direction, then scowled and looked away.

Squash the crush, squash the crush, squash the crush ...

"It's a hostage situation, how cliché," Jin said from where he was standing by the desk. He turned around to show them a note he was holding.

"Well?" Noah asked. "What does it say?"

""To find the Princess, know where to look; a clue awaits in her favourite book.""

Ejiro snorted. "What a cheesy rhyme."

Jin looked up, his lips quirked. "Isn't it?"

Obiora felt a spark of jealousy.

"Obviously, Sophia's the princess," Noah reasoned. "But how on earth are we supposed to know her favourite book?"

"Her favourite book is *Raybearer* by Jordan Ifueko," Jin and Ejiro said at the same time.

The two men glanced at each other, then laughed as they did.

The spark of jealousy turned into a flame.

"Okay, how do you both know that? I mean, I understand how Ejiro might know, considering he's been on two dates with her so far, but Jin, you're in the same boat as me I thought?" Obiora said teasingly, walking until he was standing slightly between Ejiro and Jin.

You're being ridiculous, his brain said, which he dutifully ignored.

"It was in the fact sheets we were given in the first episode," Ejiro said, his smile a tad self-conscious.

"You guys read those?" Noah asked incredulously, making them all laugh. He seemed to remember Sophia was currently watching them right now. "I mean, personally, I thought I'd get to know her on her own terms, you know? A fact sheet feels like cheating."

"Right?" It was a good save, but Obiora agreed, even though the truth was the second he'd put the fact sheet away, he'd promptly forgotten about its existence.

"Well, I mean, I see it more like a summary?" Ejiro explained. "Like, if you went on a dating site and found Sophia's profile, then all the information there would be like a "fact sheet", right?"

"Precisely." Jin nodded. "If it were cheating, then they wouldn't have been provided, though I do understand where you're both coming from."

"All right, come on, we have no time to waste!" Ejiro was already heading to the bookshelf, scanning the titles until he found the right book. He excitedly flipped it open, and another note fell out. His nose wrinkled. "Another cheesy rhyme." He laughed. ""Clue number two she used to hide, but now these hidden things are her pride."" Ejiro looked up at Jin and they said it at the same time, "Romance novels."

Ejiro looked giddy. Obiora wanted to punch something.

"Yeah, but which one?" Noah gestured at the full stack of books on the shelf.

Jin shook his head. He looked smug. "When Sophia was eleven years old, her parents thought she was way too young to be reading

Mills & Boon. So, what did she do?" He headed to the wardrobe and opened it, revealing a messy interior; half the clothes were on the floor, the other half arranged haphazardly in hangers above. "She secretly had her cousin borrow the books from the library, and hid them underneath the clothes at the bottom of her wardrobe."

Jin moved the clothes aside, and lo and behold, there was the next clue.

"Imagine if none of us had read the fact sheet," Ejiro said with mock horror.

"I'm sure at least one of the other groups wouldn't be so fortunate," Jin said with a smirk.

"Can you imagine? I would love to see that. Does that make me a bad person?"

Jin smiled, a reserved thing. "If it does, then I guess I'm just plain awful."

Ejiro laughed.

Obiora silently seethed.

The rest of the time passed like that, with Jin and Ejiro bonding over their insider knowledge of the answers to the clues, while something cloying and bitter thickened in Obiora's throat.

Sometimes even Noah chimed in, since he *had* spent a full day with Sophia. Obiora remained the odd man out. His only opportunities came in the more generic clues, in the simpler riddles and codes—there'd been a map, and thanks to his degree in Architecture and his numerous days of drawing plans, his eyes were sharp enough to pick up the illustrated clue hidden within the map's depths.

By the time all the teams had been through, their team was the winning team with literal seconds to spare.

"We won?" Ejiro asked, vibrating at a speed that could shatter glass. "We won? I can't believe it." Then he turned the full force of his smile on a defenceless Obiora as he leaned over and nudged their shoulders together, whispering, "I guess this means you *can* coast along the competition with your charm and good looks alone, because God knows you weren't much help back there."

"Oh, you can fuck right off," Obiora said, but he was grinning.

Ejiro laughed, waggling his eyebrows.

Obiora wanted to kiss that smile off his mouth. He wanted to hug him—*touch* him, in any fucking capacity. See how it would feel to have Ejiro in his arms, his magnetic warmth sinking into Obiora's skin.

The realisation dawned, sinking like a rock in his stomach.

This crush wasn't going any-fucking-where.

The official website for the CUPID CALLING series.

Cupid Calling

ABOUT | THE BACHELORETTE | THE BACHELORS | EPISODES | CONTACT | BECOME A CUPID

Episode 4 – The Contestants Show Their Prowess Part 2: Brains

Episode Summary: Sophia goes for breakfast with Ejiro, lunch with Dean, and dinner with Chris Wu, the winners of last week's blind date. Ejiro makes Sophia swoon like a lovesick girl when he ends their date with a tender kiss on the back of her hand, Dean curls Sophia's toes with a steamy kiss after their lunch date, and Sophia and Chris Wu almost have to be pulled apart when the man kisses her after their dinner date. But Red Heart winner Noah steals the spotlight when he takes Sophia on an exhilarating ride on his bike, gives her an impromptu tattoo, and ends the day with a quiet picnic dinner in a gazebo strung with fairy lights. He becomes the first contestant to receive the Red Heart during the date.

For the group date, the bachelors are invited—in four teams of four—to break out of an escape room. All members of the team that break out first will win a chance to go on a private date with the bachelorette. However, the bachelorette will ALSO be competing in the escape room, and if her time beats the contestants, she gets to pick her four winners from whatever team she wants, no matter their finishing time.

Jin, Ejiro, Obiora, and Noah end up winning the challenge. Oscar, Ronald, Liam, and Charlie are eliminated.

Click here to watch the full episode on Netflicks!

COMMENTS

🤍 RAGE_ROVER

I'm so glad Ejiro's second date with Sophia went so well! Like Sophia said, I was a little worried when he seemed hesitant to kiss her last time. Perhaps he really is just shy.

❤️ 13090   💬 5611

🤍 DYNANANANA

Noah is so fucking sexy what the fuck

❤️ 12999   💬 5001

 **PLSSUBSCRIBE**

Y'all I googled it and apparently Jin IS some kind of British royalty LMFAO I'M SCREAMING

♥ 11265   💬 4740

 ILIVESOILOVE

I feel so bad for Liam :(He was so sweet and so nice, I was rooting for him, I'm so upset. Edit: Pls stop telling me "but Liam was boring!" I honestly do not care.

♥ 10532   💬 4031

 WANGXIAN

I like how my girl was like "I've always wanted a tattoo!" and Noah was like, "Bet." 😭😭😭

♥ 9964   💬 3882

LOAD MORE COMMENTS ⌄

FIFTEEN

OBIORA SANK INTO THE BUBBLING hot tub with a sigh of pleasure. The small glass room was currently deserted, and Obiora planned to take full advantage of that fact. Some of the other men had barbecued earlier, and Obiora had managed to steal himself some of the meat—a variety of hotdogs, beef and veggies skewered on sticks, and hot ribs. He carefully removed one of the beef skewers from the plate he'd balanced on the flat, wide edge of the hot tub, and took a bite, moaning sinfully at the taste.

This was the life. Right now, Obiora could say with confidence that he was finally fully beginning to enjoy his "vacation." When he eventually went back home, he'd have to make sure to give Esther whatever the fuck she wanted for the foreseeable future, because he couldn't remember when last he'd been so relaxed. If she hadn't convinced him—read: *challenged* him—he'd still have been home, slaving away and stressing himself to death. Then he remembered that when this was all over, he'd have to go back home to said work, which threatened to ruin his mood, so he shoved the thought far back down the back of his mind where it belonged.

There were whispers between the other bachelors that in the

coming days, they were going to be travelling to an exotic destination.

"It's a trope in these kinds of dating shows," Jin had said. "They film in one location for a few episodes, then there's a surprise trip about halfway through. There might even be celebrity visits at some point, I'll bet."

Obiora had inwardly snorted. What the fuck would they gain from a celebrity visit? The thought of travelling to some exotic destination greatly appealed though.

Yesterday, he'd gone on his first private date with Sophia, which had ended successfully, if the lingering hug he'd given her at the end had been anything to go by, which meant he was safe from elimination for at least another week. He'd felt a smidgen of guilt for leading the bachelorette on, considering his growing feelings for Ejiro, but he'd told himself nothing was going to happen with either of them in the end, so it didn't really matter. The thought made him feel a pang, which he studiously ignored.

With this rumoured trip supposedly coming up, it would be the perfect conclusion to his vacation time. He wondered where they'd end up. Some place in England? Or out of it? Paris, maybe? Edinburgh? Amsterdam? The possibilities seemed endless, and with Ameri Shae's flair for the extravagant, it could be the freaking South Pole for all he knew.

His goal now was to make it to whatever exotic destination it was. Even though being in the mansion felt like a holiday, there was still this feeling of being too close to home, because outside these walls, *everything* felt familiar. It would help immensely if he left the country —really make it *feel* like a vacation. After that, he'd plan his graceful exit from the competition, and get home feeling hopefully refreshed.

The thought of leaving filled Obiora with slight panic—it meant he probably wouldn't see Ejiro again—which was exactly *why* he had to leave, and soon.

"Fuck," he whispered, dumping his now empty skewer back on

his plate, before sinking into the depths of the hot water for a quick second. When he came back out, inhaling deeply, he didn't feel any better. "Fuck," he repeated, with more feeling.

He'd been avoiding thinking about it, but eventually, he was going to leave or be eliminated or whatever. Ejiro would probably carry on to the final episodes, seeing as he was literally right now on his third date with Sophia; it'd been quite a few hours since Ejiro had left for the date, which made Obiora assume the date was probably going really well. Out of all the bachelors, the likely top three candidates so far were Noah, Chris Wu, and Ejiro.

Obiora had managed to see Ejiro before he'd left for the dinner date, which had been a huge mistake. Ejiro had been dressed in a lovely cream suit that emphasised his slight build, complementing the width of his chest and shoulders, while making his already ridiculously long legs look even longer. God, those fucking *legs*. He'd seemed shy but genuinely excited for his date, which had made Obiora feel like punching the nearest fucking wall.

This was why he had to leave. His feelings were getting way too intense, and he couldn't even fucking *stop* it. Every moment he spent with Ejiro felt like falling off the edge of a cliff with no end in sight.

He grabbed another skewer off his plate and bit into a chunk of fried meat and chopped vegetables like it'd distract him from his thoughts. He'd just finished and dropped the empty skewer down when he heard the sliding door behind him come open.

He twisted around to look, and felt his heart skip and his stomach twist all over itself when he saw that it was Ejiro, clad in nothing but swim trunks and a towel. It had to be nearing nine PM right now, which meant Ejiro had spent nearly three hours with Sophia.

"Hey, you're back," Obiora said with an automatic grin, excited to see him even as his stomach roiled at the thought of where exactly he was coming from.

"Hey!" Ejiro said, almost too brightly. "I'm going to have to interrupt your solitude. Sorry not sorry." He grinned, his eyes wide and slightly manic, before he turned away to drop his towel on one of the leather cushioned square-stools surrounding the tub.

"Uh. Right." Obiora stared at him, a little flummoxed. Was he okay? "How was your date?"

"Oh, it was fine, it was lovely." Ejiro was entering the tub, not meeting his eyes. He moaned as he sank into the hot water, the sound sinful. "God, that's good."

Obiora tried to reroute the blood back into his head. "You sure you're okay? You just seem a little ..."

"Of course. I'm okay. I'm good. I'm fine. What have you got there? Did you guys barbecue without me?" Ejiro teased, leaning over and grabbing one of the skewers from Obiora's plate. He promptly shoved one of the meats into his mouth before Obiora could say anything, effectively cutting off all means of communication between them. "Mm," he moaned as he chewed. "So good."

Something was clearly wrong, but Obiora decided perhaps it was best not to push.

Since their only topic was the date, which Ejiro clearly did not want to talk about, there was a slight awkward silence. Ejiro was chewing vigorously and looking anywhere but at him, which didn't help at all. Obiora's concern grew.

"So," Obiora began playfully, wanting to diffuse the tension, "that's an extra slice of French toast, eight pieces of plantain, an extra piece of chicken, and now one skewer of barbecued beef."

Ejiro nearly choked on his food. Obiora's chest swelled.

"Oh my God," Ejiro said when he'd finally finished, still laughing. "Are you serious? Are you *really* keeping a tally?"

"Of course I'm keeping a tally," Obiora scoffed, mock-seriously. "A man's food is his pride, after all."

"You're ridiculous. You actually don't care when I steal your food, stop pretending."

Obiora didn't mind at all. In fact, he kind of loved the almost-distracted but comfortable intimacy of the act, but that wasn't the point. "It's the principle of the thing."

Ejiro burst out laughing again. "The principle of the thing," he mocked, not maliciously. "You're so obnoxious."

"Obnoxious is my middle name."

"Oh my *God*."

Obiora grinned, relaxing further into the tub and closing his eyes. There was a brief, comfortable silence.

Then Ejiro blurted, "I fucked up."

Obiora startled so hard at the curse word water sloshed around them. He sat up, eyes zeroed on Ejiro.

All traces of comfort and amusement were gone from Ejiro's frame, replaced with the manic look he'd had when he'd first come into the room. His shoulders were hunched up to his ears, like he was waiting for an attack. The skewer had been replaced on the plate.

"What's wrong?" Obiora asked gently, moving a little closer, but not too close to stifle him. "What happened? Are you okay?"

Ejiro got out of the water abruptly, perching instead on the edge of the hot tub so only his legs were in the water, propped up on the seats. He held onto the edge of the tub, his grip so tight his knuckles paled.

"Sophia kissed me."

Obiora felt a quick rush of emotions he didn't bother to interpret, focusing instead on the foremost of them: confusion.

"Okay …" he said slowly, waiting for the punchline.

Ejiro abruptly shoved his hands through his hair. He looked so fucking distressed, almost on the verge of tears. It made Obiora alarmed.

Obiora quickly stood from the water, reaching over the side so he could switch the bubbles off. The silence afterward was loud.

He sat on the edge of the tub adjacent to Ejiro, trying to exude calm.

"It's okay," he said, as sincerely as he could. "Just talk to me. She kissed you. Then what happened? Did you tell her she was a bad kisser?" he tried to tease.

Ejiro snorted, then made a pained noise and hid his face behind his hands.

Fucking hell.

Fuck it, Obiora thought, moving to sit beside Ejiro, not too close that their bodies touched, but close enough that Ejiro knew he was *here*. Ejiro's tense shoulders tensed up even further for a moment, before relaxing completely. Obiora bit back an exhale of relief.

Ejiro dropped his hands. He took a deep breath. "We were—we had just finished eating, right? And we were talking, and then—she just—out of nowhere, she *kissed* me. And ... I wasn't expecting it, and I kind of froze—oh God, she's going to eliminate me—"

"Hey, hey now. Ejiro, slow down. Breathe."

Ejiro obeyed, though his breaths were harsh. "I still—I kissed her back, all right? But I still *hesitated*—God, I feel like fucking *shit*, right now. I feel so *awful*. Why was I so surprised? She's going to think I—that I'm—*fuck*! Fuck. Fuck. Fuck."

Christ, Obiora had never seen Ejiro so upset. "Hey, it's okay, no one's going to eliminate you. You said you kissed her back, right? You're fine. You were just surprised, right?"

"But that's the thing." Ejiro moved away slightly, like he needed the space to protect himself. Obiora felt the loss at his side keenly. "That's the thing—I didn't *want* to kiss her. Oh God."

"Oh," Obiora said, while Ejiro silently hyperventilated.

"I like her, I really do, but I didn't—I *couldn't*—"

"Hey, hey, it's okay, calm down—"

"How is it *okay*? How could I *not* want—"

"Ejiro. Stop." Obiora's voice was harsh. Ejiro's mouth clicked shut. His eyes were wide. Obiora continued, "You said you didn't want to kiss her; do you know why? Was it something she did?"

Ejiro started shaking his head. "I don't know—I don't *know*. I just—I didn't *want* to. I know how—I know that must sound—"

"Did you tell her that?" Obiora interrupted.

Ejiro stared at him like he'd grown two heads. "Did I *tell* her that? Are you being serious right now? I know this might just be a—a game to you, but Sophia and I—we're dating. Technically, we're dating. It doesn't make sense that I—and on live TV! I can't, I can't."

"Yes, you can," Obiora said evenly. "You said it yourself, you and her are technically dating. And Sophia's a lovely person, Ejiro. I'm sure if you'd explained, she would have understood."

Ejiro's lower lip trembled. Obiora's heart fucking broke.

"How can I explain myself when I barely understand?" Ejiro whispered. He looked away, wiping his eyes. "Ugh. Fuck. Ugh. I like her a lot, I do, but ..." Abruptly, he seemed to go from upset to angry as he spat, "I felt so fucking *disgusted* when I kissed her. I hated every moment of it. How could I *explain* that?"

"You said you didn't want to," Obiora said gently. "You didn't want to, but you did anyway, just to make her feel better. Of course you'd feel disgusted about that. Look." Obiora adjusted himself so he was facing him. "Ejiro. I want to ask you something, and I want you to answer me honestly."

Ejiro swallowed, then nodded.

"You like Sophia, right?"

"I do," Ejiro admitted, almost desperately. "I like her. So much."

Obiora ignored the painful twist of jealousy. "And you're interested in her romantically, yeah?"

Ejiro rolled his eyes. "Obviously."

Obiora grinned. "All right. But are you *attracted* to her? *Sexually* attracted to her, I mean."

Ejiro stared at him incredulously. When he realised Obiora was serious, he scoffed. "What? What kind of question is that?"

"I'm serious. I want you to think about it."

"I think she's freaking gorgeous; of course I'm attracted to her."

"And I'm sure you think at least one of the other bachelors are *freaking* handsome, but that doesn't necessarily mean that you're sexually attracted to them," Obiora retorted.

"I—" For the second time that evening, Ejiro's mouth clicked shut. His eyes were wide.

"Maybe you're just not attracted to Sophia like that—at least, not enough to want to kiss her just yet," Obiora finished, hoping he sounded reassuring. "Or, I don't know, have you ever considered you might be asexual? Or at least demisexual."

EJIRO JOLTED. ALL THOSE MONTHS he'd spent questioning his sexuality seemed to come back full force, making his breath come quick and harsh. Was he really asexual? Demisexual? He inwardly shook his head, almost in denial. He couldn't be—because—what about—?

"I—I've—I mean ..." He blushed furiously and lowered his voice. "I've had sex, and I've enjoyed it, and I'd very much like to have it again." God, if his skin weren't so beautifully dark, he'd probably be as red as a ripe tomato. "If that's what you're—"

Obiora laughed, but the sound was kind. "Sexual attraction and sexual desire are two completely different things." Was Ejiro imagining it, or was Obiora's voice growing a little deeper as he explained? "Are you going to say that every single time you might have felt desire in your life, it was solely because of someone?"

"No." Ejiro immediately snorted.

Obiora laughed. "Exactly. Sometimes man's just horny, am I right?"

Ejiro snorted again, though the word made him blush harder.

"And you're right to question it; some ace-spec folks only feel sexual desire *after* they've felt sexual attraction, and they often only feel sexual attraction after an emotional bond has been formed first,"

Obiora explained. "Choosing to have sex or, in your case, to kiss someone"—Ejiro's belly swooped when Obiora's voice lowered on those last three words—"doesn't *need* to have anything to do with your attraction to said person, if that makes sense. Though, of course, most of the time, it does."

"Right." Ejiro already knew this. He'd spent what must've been *months* agonising over it. He'd felt sexual attraction before, he was sure. With Sam. He wouldn't have had such an intimate relationship with her that he eventually wanted to marry her otherwise, right?

But this time, instead of immediately using that as proof to dismiss his feelings like he always did in the past—instead of shoving away the oftentimes invasive, uncomfortable questioning, he forced himself to think now. *Really* think.

He forced himself to examine the first time Sam had kissed him, and remembered how he'd just ... let her, because ... well, because he'd liked her, and she'd liked him, and he'd thought that was what he was supposed to do, even though he'd felt strangely passive about it at the time—which just about summed up the totality of their relationship. His breaths started to come fast.

But there were times when Ejiro had been the one to initiate things —

Again, Ejiro had to force himself to think—had those moments ever really been about his attraction to her? Had he ever wanted her because he specifically found *her* so completely irresistible—

Ejiro felt his nose wrinkling automatically because that just sounded unrealistic—come on, who wanted *anyone* that much, right?

Oh.

Oh.

Oh no.

Oh God. Had he *ever* been sexually attracted to her? To anyone?

He searched frantically through his past relationships and encounters, and froze when he remembered one; the memory practically leapt out at him, like he'd been staring into a pond and a frog had suddenly burst through the water to land on his forehead.

He was seventeen. The night of his prom. He'd asked Amaka to go with him because they were friends and didn't really want to make the night a big deal. They'd spent all night talking, gossiping and laughing, and Ejiro vividly remembered at some point wanting desperately to kiss her, and feeling panicked at the thought. Amaka was his *friend*, why was he feeling this way?

He'd been aware of her beauty before, but only abstractly, yet in that moment, as she'd laughed at something he'd said, he'd suddenly noticed how the lights reflected over her eyeshadow and lip gloss; his hands had begun to sweat when he'd taken notice of the curvy shape of her hips defined by her tight, short, prom dress, her thighs thick, her legs long and shapely.

Ejiro had spent the rest of the night with his heart racing and his head confused, wondering where on earth these feelings were coming from.

When he'd hugged Amaka goodnight later, lingering a little as he did, he'd felt a strange heat in his lower belly at the feel of her body in his arms, the smell of her sweet perfume. It had taken a herculean effort to keep his hands respectfully at the middle of her back, when they'd so desperately wanted to feel the curve of those full hips in his palms.

He'd eventually written his feelings off to being high off the euphoria of the night, and had promptly forgotten all about it.

"Ejiro? Still with me?"

Ejiro blushed furiously, shaking himself out of it. "What? Yes. Good. I'm fine."

Obiora looked amused, one eyebrow raised. "Didn't mean to send you off on a crisis there."

"Will you keep quiet."

Obiora laughed, then sobered. "Look, I might be wrong, yeah? I'm sorry for immediately jumping to try and explain away your feelings. It's probably not that deep. As you said, you just didn't want to kiss Sophia at that moment, and that's perfectly okay. It literally doesn't need any more explanation than that. If you still feel uncomfortable, on your next date with her—which is inevitable at this point," Obiora added a little bitterly.

Ejiro laughed, nudging their shoulders together, grasping at the levity with both hands. "Don't be jealous, now. It's your own fault for not doing better."

"Yeah, yeah." Obiora grinned. "As I was saying, when next you go out, just tell her the truth; you weren't ready to be kissed. Also, you should tell her that the next time she wants a kiss, she needs to ask you first." That last part was said darkly.

"Right," Ejiro said mockingly, "because that's sexy."

Obiora wasn't smiling anymore. In fact, he seemed a little angry. "It's not about sexiness, it's about *consent*. You came here feeling, as you put it, like *shit*, because, intentionally or not, Sophia had violated your boundaries. That's not a joke, Ejiro."

Ejiro swallowed, feeling strangely flustered, his chest full. He looked away from Obiora, unable to bear the intensity of his gaze.

"Right. Yes. I mean ... you're right."

"Of course I'm right," Obiora said lightly, trying to lighten the mood once more. "And believe it or not, asking for consent *is* fucking sexy."

Obiora winked but didn't wait for a response, splashing back into the hot tub and wading to the side for the buttons. The bubbles and steam resumed with a low hum.

Ejiro let himself slip back into the water, blaming the heat for the strange flush in his cheeks.

"Thank you," he blurted, grateful all of a sudden. "For just ... I mean—"

"Ejiro," Obiora interrupted, his gentle tone making Ejiro feel all kinds of strange. "Seriously. What are friends for?"

Ejiro ducked his head, but he was grinning.

CUPID CALLING

SIXTEEN

"**YOU'RE TALKING ABOUT WHAT IT** feels like to grow up with a twin, while Sophia comments on how it feels to be a single child," Ameri Shae said to Ejiro from where she was seated across from him in the greenhouse, where they filmed all the cutaways. "Then Sophia leans in to kiss you and you hesitate, briefly, before eventually kissing her back. Go."

Ejiro clenched his hands in his lap to keep them from trembling. He'd almost asked Obiora to escort him to the filming for his cutaways, but he'd bitten back the request because he didn't think having an outside audience—even if it *were* Obiora—would be helpful right now.

"Tell the truth," Obiora had told him when Ejiro had expressed his worry about the cutaways. "You didn't want to kiss her, but you did, because you felt like you had to."

Ejiro had winced at the phrasing.

Obiora's eyes had darkened. "I get that this is TV or whatever, and that it might look bad if it looks like you don't want her, but that doesn't mean you shouldn't have boundaries, Ejiro."

"But ... I mean, we're technically here *for* her." And Ejiro didn't want to hurt her feelings, no matter how small, but he didn't say that out loud because he knew it might anger Obiora even further.

"That doesn't mean she gets to bulldoze you into doing anything she wants, especially when you're not ready," Obiora said, exasperated. "A relationship is a partnership, isn't it? You *both* have to be on the same page. If you want a future with Sophia, you can't build it based solely on what *she* wants."

The words had hit somewhere close to Ejiro's chest. For some reason, they'd made him think about Sam, how his ex had—as Obiora put it—*bulldozed* him into a relationship, even though, looking back, he'd *felt* like he'd been ready. At the time, whenever he'd hesitated or expressed his worry at how fast things were moving, Sam would kiss him to shut him up and tell him how cute it was that he was so shy and insecure; "Don't you like me?" she'd ask, and Ejiro would say yes, even as his stomach squirmed uncomfortably at the admission. "Don't you want to be with me?" she'd follow up, and again, Ejiro would admit the affirmative. "You're just … you're really shy, Ejiro. If I didn't get you to do things, you wouldn't do *anything*. I don't think we'd even be dating right now." She'd laugh, and Ejiro would laugh, too, and internalise her words, all the while shoving down how he really felt. She was right, he'd thought, maybe he *was* just shy and insecure; if she hadn't asked him out, Ejiro wasn't sure *he'd* have ever asked her, and then where would they be?

Back in the present, with the cameras in his face and the directors staring him down, he could feel sweat building up in his armpits.

Obiora was right. If Ejiro intended to have a future with Sophia, then he had to be honest. Yes, it might make him look bad, but what really mattered was his potential future with her. If he lied, or let things go, what if Sophia pushed for *more* than a kiss, next time? The thought made him feel vaguely ill.

"The truth is …" He stopped, almost forgetting he was supposed to talk like the action was still happening. There was the sound of clicking and snapping as someone off to the side took a mountain load of pictures. Normally, being in the greenhouse, no matter how brief, filled Ejiro with a sense of excitement and calm. Now, though, all the flowery scents and the low buzz of insects were doing nothing but giving him a headache. Ejiro swallowed. Cleared his throat. "So, uh, Sophia and I are having a good time, right? We're talking, getting to know each other better. She's really interested in knowing how it feels to be a twin, so I'm sharing some of my experiences when, suddenly, she leans in and kisses me."

Ejiro wanted to close his eyes. He wanted to curse. Instead, he imagined a tiny Obiora with pompoms sitting on his shoulder cheering him on. The image made his lips twitch. He subconsciously straightened his spine.

"And I'm ... surprised. I hesitate because, well, truthfully, I don't want to kiss her." He panicked at how terrible that sounded, and added quickly, "I mean, I'm not *ready* to kiss her. At least, not at that moment, and I kind of panic because of all the cameras. I don't want her to feel embarrassed or hurt, so I kiss her back. She looks pleased, afterwards, which just makes me ... upset. I'm upset. Really upset."

Ameri looked slightly alarmed. She quickly wiped the expression from her face.

"I don't want to kiss her," Ejiro continues, struggling to keep his eyes on the camera, "and it makes me feel awful that I do it anyway. I know I should say something in the moment, I should tell her how I feel, but I'm so overwhelmed—it's all happening so fast. Before I know it, the date is over, and I'm back at the mansion."

There was a brief silence, but Ameri took over effortlessly, smoothly wrapping things up.

Ejiro heaved a sigh of relief when it was over. He felt unusually drained by today's cutaway and just wanted to go to his room and have a little lie down.

"Ejiro, sorry, hold on. Can I see you for a sec?" Ameri called before he could make his escape.

He briefly tilted his face up to the heavens, before turning to face

Ameri, a small smile on his lips. "Yes, of course."

Ameri led him out toward the smaller pool, away from the rest of the crew. None of the bachelors were outside, thank God.

Ejiro resisted the urge to hug himself.

"Are you okay?" Ameri asked, her expression and tone serious.

Ejiro's eyes widened in surprise before he quickly concealed it. "What? No. I mean, yes. I'm fine. Why?"

"While this is reality TV, the last thing I want is for any of you to be uncomfortable. You said just now that you didn't want to kiss Sophia, but you did anyway, because of the cameras."

Ejiro swallowed. "I—that's not—"

"No, look," Ameri interrupted, "You should know that at any point during the filming, if you feel uncomfortable, at all, even the slightest bit, you can make a signal at either me or any of the other directors, and we can stop the filming immediately. You don't have to do anything just because the cameras are rolling. Do you get me?"

Ejiro felt a little choked up. "Oh," he whispered.

"Jesus," Ameri said, patting her locs the same way Blessing did when her scalp was itchy but she didn't want to mess up her hairdo. "This is my fault. I'll make an announcement later to the other bachelors. Don't feel pressured by the cameras to do anything. Jesus. I'm not mad at you, I'm mad at myself. The whole point of reality TV —for me, personally—is the *real* part. I don't care if other producers allow icky stuff to slide just because it looks good on TV; do not, under any circumstances, do something you do not want just because you feel it might look better on TV."

"I understand," Ejiro said, a little sheepishly. "Obiora said the same thing."

"Smart man." Ameri grinned. "All right, then, love? Good. I'll be coming in to talk to the other bachelors in a bit anyways. I won't mention you, don't worry," she added when she noticed Ejiro's slight look of panic.

Ejiro blushed. "Thank you."

"Right. I'll see y'all in a bit. Thank you for talking to me."

"Thank *you*," Ejiro responded.

Ameri waved him off, then went back to the crew. With a small smile on his face, Ejiro headed back toward the mansion. He was the last to film his cutaways for the day, so none of the other bachelors were waiting on the back patio as he climbed up to the back doors.

The second he closed the sliding doors behind him, the smell of something delicious and familiar wafted into his nose.

"Just in time," Obiora said from where he was just turning off the stove.

Ejiro inhaled again, deeply. "Is that ...?"

"Goat meat pepper soup? Why yes. Yes, it is," Obiora said smugly. He untied the apron from around his waist, and removed the hairnet from his hair, ruffling his curls after.

Ejiro swallowed. "How ...?"

"I may or may not have ordered some goat meat from Ameri last night. She had one of the staff bring it this morning while you were preoccupied."

Ejiro felt an intense rush of emotions.

Homesickness. Relief. Elation.

"Obiora ..." he whispered, voice thick. When Obiora had asked him last night what his comfort food was, he'd thought they'd just been making conversation. When he'd shyly said, "goat meat pepper soup", Obiora's eyes had lit up and he'd exclaimed, "Really? Same here!" Ejiro had laughed and added, "My mother thinks it's the remedy to every ailment in the world, be it physical, emotional, or mental." "You sure we don't have the same mother?" Obiora had teased, making Ejiro laugh again.

Now ... this.

"Look," Obiora began, washing his hands. "I thought it might be a little upsetting for you to relive what happened between you and Sophia while you filmed your cutaways this afternoon, so I just ... I don't know, I wanted to do something to make you feel better, just in case. I'm sorry if I overstepped."

Strangely, at that last sentence, Obiora's head ducked, his blush obvious in the helpless curve of his lips and downturned lashes, the sight of it making Ejiro feel strangely warm all over. It was the first time Ejiro had ever seen Obiora look shy.

Ejiro wanted to move closer. Hold Obiora's hand, maybe. Give it a little squeeze. Or hug him. Just a bit. But maybe that would be weird.

"Thank you," he said instead, voice thick. "This was really thoughtful of you, Obiora."

"Yeah, yeah," Obiora waved him off, still blushing. "Let's eat before it gets cold."

They dished for themselves, then headed to the dining table, automatically seating opposite each other, the table between them.

Obiora cooked his pepper soup with yam diced within its depths, thickening it a bit. Ejiro's mother—and Ejiro after her—usually made the yam on the side, to go with a spicy tomato, onion, and chilli sauce. Or palm oil and sugar, if they were feeling fancy.

But this was perfect, because Ejiro didn't want to think of his mother right now.

The first mouthful had him groaning and closing his eyes, savouring the flavour. It was just the right amount of hot, burning his lips with the chilli, while being intensely flavourful. A bite of yam balanced out the richness of the soup, creating a small party in his mouth.

"God," he groaned when he was done chewing. "So good."

"Yeah? I'm glad."

Something in Obiora's voice had Ejiro's eyes snapping open, meeting the ones of the man sitting across from him.

Obiora's pupils were wide and dark with something that filled Ejiro with an odd awareness, his lower belly turning molten with unfamiliar heat. His pulse began to race, and his breaths came fast. He quickly looked away, frowning, wondering if it was the heat from the soup that was making him feel so strange.

"Drink?" Obiora asked, his voice still in that husky timbre.

Ejiro squirmed in his seat, his pulse pounding harder. "Yes, please," he said, fighting to hide his inner turmoil. He spooned another bit of soup and yam into his mouth to distract himself.

"Sprite, yeah?" Obiora asked, already taking a can of it out of the fridge, while taking a malt for himself.

For some reason, Obiora knowing his favourite drink—Ejiro was sure he'd never mentioned it—made him blush, a little pleased that he'd noticed.

"Thank you," he said, taking the chilled can from him.

"You're welcome." Obiora smiled, flashing his dimple.

Ejiro blushed and looked away.

"How *was* the filming, by the way? I forgot to ask."

"Oh." Ejiro looked up. "Honestly? It was excruciating."

Obiora snorted. "That bad?"

"Yes," Ejiro deadpanned. "I hope I never have to do that ever again."

Obiora laughed. "Aww, I'm proud of you." The words were said teasingly, but Ejiro could tell Obiora meant it. "I know it must've been hard."

Ejiro blushed. "Leave me alone, abeg," he said to Obiora's answering laughter, while on the inside he glowed with pleasure. In the moment, he'd just wanted it done and over with, but looking back, in the face of all those cameras, Old Ejiro would have panicked and diminished his own feelings and lied. New Ejiro had handled it as well as he could without having to sacrifice his dignity.

So yeah, perhaps Ejiro was a little proud of himself, too.

They ate in a companionable silence, Obiora's words along with the soup working their magic and pumping Ejiro full of happy and content endorphins. They were only just finishing up when Ameri finally came into the house, the crew following behind her.

"Hey, y'all," she greeted. "Oh, that smells amazing. What's that?

Pepper soup?"

"Yup," Obiora said, grinning.

"Great, now I've got a craving," she said. Obiora laughed. She grinned. "Any chance one of you could get the other bachelors down here for me?"

"I'll do it," Obiora volunteered.

Ejiro smiled at him gratefully. Obiora winked. Ejiro's heart skipped. Obiora was gone before Ejiro could properly process his feelings.

He'd just rinsed off and dumped the dishes in the dishwasher when the bachelors came trooping into the kitchen slash dining area.

"Good evening everyone," Ameri greeted, nodding briefly when the men echoed her greeting. Most of them remained standing. "I won't take up much of your time. First off, we will be filming within the mansion at some point this evening, so this is your warning. No, I will not be telling you why. Don't groan at me." Some of them laughed. "Secondly, I just want to remind you all that while this is reality TV, you absolutely still should not do something you're uncomfortable with just because you think it'll look good on TV. If the other men, or the bachelorette, or heck, even the staff, are making you feel some kind of way, please say something to either me or one of the other directors and we'll rectify the problem immediately. That's all. The staff will be setting up the cameras; please ignore them for the time being. See you all at seven." She winked mysteriously as she left.

The bachelors burst into a cacophony of sound.

"What do you think they're filming for?"

"A message from Sophia?"

"Ah, yes. Probably."

"I'm telling you"—Jin crossed his arms—"it's the announcement for the exotic trip."

Some of the men groaned.

"Don't get my hopes up, please," Obiora said, which made some of them laugh.

It was a little past five PM, meaning they had less than two hours to look camera ready. The men began to leave, one by one.

Ejiro and Obiora found themselves beside each other, as usual.

"See you in a bit," Obiora said when they got to Ejiro's room.

For some reason, Ejiro blushed, even though it wasn't the first time Obiora had said those words to him.

"Right, yeah," Ejiro said, not meeting his eyes, disappearing into his room.

By some general unspoken consensus, after the makeup and costuming team had approved of their chosen fits and touched up their faces, the bachelors ended up in one of the larger sitting rooms upstairs, the walls lined with bookcases filled with books and games. The cameras and lighting had already been set up, and the men were so used to being filmed at this point that they completely ignored the staff, sitting around and acting normal.

Not for the first time, Ejiro and Obiora sat beside each other. But, for some reason, Ejiro suddenly found himself hyperaware of the places their bodies touched—the side of their arms and thighs—and found himself struggling to focus. Had Obiora's body always been so invitingly warm?

"How can you not know how to play chess?" Noah was saying. "You're so posh!"

Jin sniffed. "I don't know why you think my family line has anything to do with my ability to play chess. It's such a boring game."

Tyler made an awful noise. He was apparently a chess aficionado. The other men laughed.

"I don't know," Noah said, but he was grinning. "I guess there's something just so ... elitist about it all."

Tyler made another noise.

"Excuse me?" Jin's eyes narrowed. "Are you calling me elitist?"

Ejiro snickered. Obiora grinned, nudging their shoulders

together. Ejiro blushed furiously and looked away. His pulse hadn't slowed since Obiora had sauntered into the room and sat down next to him, no invitation needed.

Noah blanched. "No! I just meant a lot of people who play the game are elitist and ableist, seeing as most of them believe that if you can't play it, then you're automatically "stupid"."

"And now you're implying that I'm also ableist," Jin drawled.

The sound of a doorbell saved Noah from further embarrassing himself.

"Saved by the bell," Tyler grumbled, and they laughed.

The times they'd heard the bell were far and few; sometimes the bachelorette sent a message to the house before a private date with her winning bachelors, always in the form of a cheesy poem, or a request on how they should dress for the date and so on. Sometimes Ameri was the one sending a message on how the bachelors should dress for their next group date, while giving a small clue on what the group date would be. The messages were always announced with the bell, and the men were always filmed a little beforehand, during, and after.

Since the winning bachelors had all gone on their dates with Sophia and filmed their cutaways, the men couldn't be blamed for their curiosity. Usually, Ameri waited until the next day to send a message about the dress code for the next group date.

"What do you think it is?" Damien mused.

"Let's go on ahead and find out," Chris Wu said.

There was a wide, flat-screen TV mounted in the foyer of the mansion, and once all the bachelors had gathered in front of it, the cameras focused on them, the TV came on, revealing the bachelorette.

Sophia's smile was wide and playful. "There are blossoms in the air, and water in the streets; I hope you're ready boys, we're going to Venice!"

There were hollers of excitement—some a bit exaggerated for the cameras—as the screen turned dark. It took a second for Ejiro to process the poem.

"Did she—did she say we're going to *Venice*?"

"Yup," Obiora said from beside him, looking just as excited as the other men, but more contained.

"Oh my God," Ejiro gasped, bouncing on his feet. "Venice?"

"I take it you're excited," Obiora teased.

"Are you *joking*?" Ejiro said. "I've literally only been to two places; Nigeria doesn't count because I was born and raised there, and I'm definitely not counting England because I only came here for school."

Obiora was laughing. He threw an arm over Ejiro's shoulders, dragging him close against his side and squeezing him companionably as he said, "You're so fucking adorable."

At the touch, as Obiora's woodsy scent wafted into his nose, Ejiro froze, and his heartbeat went into overdrive, pounding furiously like an African drum. Warmth encompassed him from head to toe, and his cheeks felt hot with a self-conscious blush.

"Gentlemen, shall we celebrate?" Chris Wu called from the head of the group, walking backwards in the direction of the kitchen. "We've got wine and beer in the fridge."

"Yes!" the men chorused.

"Let's do it. Come on, then," Obiora said to Ejiro, leading him in the direction of the kitchen with his arm still casually flung around his shoulders.

Ejiro didn't know why he felt so weird. Obiora's arm, thick with muscle, felt slightly heavy on his shoulders, but instead of making him feel overcrowded, he felt more ... grounded.

He wanted Obiora to stop touching him. He wanted Obiora to *never* stop.

When they reached the kitchen, Obiora dropped his arm, heading for the fridge. "Sprite?" he asked, a grin on his lips.

"You already know," Ejiro said, managing to smile back.

He hugged his arms around himself, rubbing his shoulders, missing Obiora's touch. When he realised what he was doing, he abruptly dropped his hands.

What was wrong with him today? He glanced at Obiora from the corner of his eye. The need to be held again wasn't dissipating; in fact, now that he knew what it felt to be in Obiora's embrace, even in such a casual, friendly way, he realised how badly he wanted more.

Perhaps he was just missing Ajiri and Blessing. He and his twin were tactile, always lying haphazardly on top of each other when they were in the same vicinity, Blessing soon joining in when she'd come into the picture. It'd been so long since Ejiro had been touched, perhaps that was all it was.

When Obiora handed him his drink, their fingers brushed, making Ejiro's heart skip.

"Let's go," Obiora said, leading them toward the backyard, where most of the other men had already headed.

Obiora brushed by him, his body heat pulling at Ejiro like a siren song. He walked ahead, and Ejiro used the opportunity to unabashedly take in the breadth of Obiora's wide shoulders, the thickness of his arms. He could easily imagine himself being enfolded within Obiora's embrace; Obiora looked like he was *made* for warm hugs and cosy snuggling. The thought of it made Ejiro's entire body practically burn with longing.

Yeah, he was most definitely just starved for touch. That was all.

SEVENTEEN

FILMING BEGAN ALMOST THE SECOND the bachelors and crew arrived in Venice. They used a water taxi to get to their accommodation, a lovely place located away from the hustle and bustle of the city centre, but still within a reasonable walking distance.

Most of the men had slept on the journey from Oxford. They'd been so excited about the trip they'd ended up staying up all night talking, drinking, and eating junk food, that after waking up at ass-o'clock in the morning to get to the airport, they'd all promptly passed out on the flight, Obiora included.

Now, though, despite still not getting nearly enough sleep, the men were completely wide awake, taking in the sights and sounds on their journey to their accommodation, which ended up being two first floor flats connected by a long terrace.

"I'll let y'all decide your sleeping arrangements," Ameri said after Ragna, the muscular, towering white, blonde woman who happened to be their host and the building's owner, had shown them to the place, and Ameri had filmed their reactions and entrance into the house. "Remember; myself, the other directors, and the staff, are situated just a three-minute walk from here; you've got your emergency phone, but you can call Ragna if you need anything else. Best use the rest of today to catch up on sleep, because filming resumes bright and early tomorrow. Welcome to Venice, y'all!"

The men hooted and hollered in response. Ameri grinned and waved, and then she and the crew were gone. There were no cameras installed within their accommodation in Venice, which had the men exhaling slightly and letting out a tension they probably hadn't realised they'd held. Ameri, the other producers and crew, would instead come in in the mornings and evenings to film before and after their group and personal dates with the bachelorette.

"Okay, so, we have six bedrooms in this house and four in the next one," Chris Wu started, getting right to business.

"That means seven people in the bigger house, and five in the smaller." Noah crossed his arms over his chest. "Which means some of us are going to have to share."

"There are two bedrooms that have two single beds instead of a double, one in each house. Who doesn't mind sharing?"

"I don't mind," Ejiro said quickly. His eyes darted in Obiora's direction for a quick second before darting away. Obiora's heart skipped a traitorous beat.

"I can share with Ejiro," Obiora said, trying to look casual and like every inch of him wasn't screaming *what the fuck are you doing*?

"Alistair," Eddie said, walking over to the underwear model and throwing an arm over his shoulders. "Wanna share with me?"

Alistair shrugged. "Sure."

"Great." Jin clapped his hands primly. Obiora didn't even know one *could* clap their hands primly. "First come first served on the other bedrooms, then?"

"Deal."

The men dispersed quickly, eager to pick the best bedrooms for themselves.

Obiora and Ejiro ended up in the smaller house, as Alistair and

Eddie managed to call dibs on the unit in the larger flat.

The place was absolutely stunning. The connecting terrace was a marbled walkway, covered entirely with a curving metal frame that had vines and other plants and flowers interspersed through its hexagonal holes, creating a magical, portal-like corridor. On the ground floor on the right was an alleyway and some private housing, while on the left, the terrace looked into a small private garden. The big house had a generous veranda with elegant outdoor seating that could take everyone from both houses. Obiora could already see the nights the men were going to spend there socialising.

When he and Ejiro finally got to their assigned room—their other housemates ended up being Jin, Tyler, and Jack; the more introverted of all the bachelors—Obiora's traitorous heart did something funny when he spotted the two "single" beds. They were placed ridiculously close to each other in the middle of the wall opposite the door, with literally only a sliver of space between them. Heck, neither he nor Ejiro would be able to fit a hand between their bedframes, that was how close they were.

Ejiro didn't seem to notice anything awry as he dumped his luggage in a corner, kicked his shoes off and collapsed onto the bed nearer the window with a long, drawn-out sigh.

"I'm in Venice," he said, staring with wide eyes at the ceiling. "Obiora"—fucking hell, did it feel all kinds of simultaneously amazing and devastating every time Ejiro said his name—"we're in *Venice*. Oh my God." He laughed, covering his mouth with his hand, his giddiness contagious. "You know, I was pretty sure the second we got here I was going to fall into the deepest sleep—I was so exhausted on the plane—but now I'm just too jittery."

"I feel you," Obiora said, tentatively making his way to the other bed.

He perched on the corner of it, and instantly struggled to take in air. Ejiro was so close. So fucking close. Obiora could literally just lean over and he would be able to touch Ejiro's hip with his fingertips.

Jesus. Fucking hell.

Unaware of Obiora's inner turmoil, Ejiro twisted around on the bed to face him, balancing himself on one arm. "We've only been here for, what? Two hours at most? But I just know Ajiri and Blessing would *love* it here. God, I wish they were here."

It was something in Ejiro's eyes, the openness of his expression, the genuine excitement in his voice that had Obiora admitting, "Ada would have loved it here, too." He looked away, casually, as if what he'd said didn't matter, as if the last time he'd spoken about her like this it hadn't been about his grief—never about *her*. "She had a bucket list, you know?" he continued, unable to stop, some part of him suddenly desperate to share the bits of her he was afraid he was losing, because he couldn't talk about them to anyone else back home without them looking at him with either pity—Esther and his brothers—or concern—his parents. "Things she wanted to do, and places she wanted to visit. I remember her literally googling the top twenty most romantic cities in the world so she could put them all on the list."

He laughed a little at the memory, the sound bittersweet. He'd taken to calling it her "barrel list" because of how fucking long it was, while she'd rolled her eyes and told him he made no freaking sense considering that the word "bucket" came from the phrase "to kick the bucket"—it wasn't a *literal* bucket. Obiora had, of course, ignored her, to her fond annoyance.

His shoulders were tense as he waited for Ejiro's response, braced for pity, or empty platitudes, or Ejiro's discomfort and changing of the subject.

They never came.

"Aww," Ejiro crooned, his voice tender. "She sounds absolutely lovely. I'm so sorry she couldn't be here to see it."

And Obiora's heart cracked neatly in two.

"Yeah," he said, his voice coming out hoarse. He cleared his throat. "Me too."

He slid his shoes off and laid down on his bed next to Ejiro, staring carefully at the ceiling even though he could feel Ejiro's gaze burning into him.

God, he missed Ada. He missed *talking* about her. He wanted to say more, lots more, but it seemed that now he had the opportunity to finally talk about her—without being made to feel guilty about it—everything he wanted to say had slipped right out of his head. He wanted to lovingly recount all the memories they'd shared *without* the pity and judgement of his friends and family weighing him down, their fear that him showing his undying love for her meant that he would never be able to "move on"; they saw his love for her as something being *wrong* with him, like he was *broken*—a wounded man desperately clinging onto his grief as an excuse to keep himself from ever loving another again.

They'd been so happy when he'd met Nick. They'd seen it as proof that he'd "healed". Oh, how wrong they were. Ada was part of him, a part of his being. She may not be here, and he may not think about her as much as he used to, but she would *always* be a part of him. Nicholas hadn't been able to accept that, and it was fine, Obiora couldn't blame him—he should've been honest about it from the start. But he knew it now like he knew how to breathe: Ada had been the love of his life, and that was never going to change. The thought was almost devastating.

Maybe his family was right.

Maybe he *was* broken.

"I used to want to have a bucket list, when I was younger," Ejiro said, his voice pulling Obiora from his thoughts. Obiora couldn't help but look at him. His breath stuttered at the closeness. God, how could he love and miss Ada the way he did, yet want Ejiro just as desperately at the same time? "But now the thought just makes me panic."

He registered Ejiro's words and frowned. "Why on earth would the thought make you panic?"

Ejiro's expression dimmed. He looked down at his bed, fingers fiddling with the folded corner of his duvet. "Well, the plan was always that after I finished my bachelor's, I would go back to Naija and use my Business Management degree to start up my own business or what have you. I wanted to go back because of my mother." He smiled, though it was a little strained. "I didn't want to leave her alone."

Obiora's chest warmed, even as a part of him panicked at the thought of Ejiro permanently leaving England. "That sounds like a good thing," he said with a raised eyebrow, wondering at Ejiro's self-deprecating tone.

Ejiro laughed. "Yeah, well, it's been three years since I graduated and I'm still here. I even have a freaking citizenship. Not the signs of someone who's eager to leave." He sounded bitter.

"Do you ... not want to leave, then?" Obiora asked, trying to mask the hope in his voice.

He must've been unsuccessful, because Ejiro looked up at him with a little knowing smile. Obiora's heartbeat stuttered.

Ejiro sighed. "This is one of the arguments Ajiri and I never seem to win." It felt nice, Obiora thought, that they could talk to each other about their families so easily; so unguardedly. It spoke of a closeness, an emotional trust that made him ache with want. "She knows—even though I will never admit it—Ajiri *knows* I don't want to go back home. I'm only doing it because I feel like I owe my mother."

"And do you?"

"What?" Ejiro frowned, though he'd clearly understood the question.

"Do you owe your mother?" Obiora clarified anyway.

"I—what? I mean, she's my mother," Ejiro said weakly.

"That doesn't answer the question," Obiora replied gently.

Ejiro shook his head. "It doesn't matter. Anyway, what was I even saying? Right, I feel like if I go back to Nigeria, my mother would probably monopolise all my time, so having a bucket list just isn't realistic."

There was a story there—it was in the slightly desolate way Ejiro mentioned his mother monopolising his time, like it wasn't something he wanted, but it was going to happen anyway, whether he liked it or not. Obiora wanted to ask about it, but Ejiro didn't seem like he would be receptive to Obiora pushing, so he didn't.

"I mean, you could still make a bucket list specifically for Nigeria," Obiora teased, trying to lighten the mood.

Ejiro thankfully laughed, then groaned, covering his face with his hands. "I don't know. I guess. Maybe. What about you?" he said quickly, obviously desperate to change the subject. He looked up, smiling at Obiora. Obiora blinked, a little dazed. "Did you ever have a bucket list?"

"Nah." Obiora shook his head. "Trust me, Ada's list was *more* than enough for the both of us."

Ejiro laughed.

Obiora loved his laugh. He wished, for the briefest second, that he could just be in this moment forever.

The silence that followed was the kind of silence everyone probably craved; when you're in the presence of someone you're so comfortable with, that silence didn't feel like silence at all.

Obiora felt so calm, so safe, that he was about to fall asleep when Ejiro spoke, his voice a soft, shaky whisper, "Obiora? I think I might be demisexual."

Obiora was immediately wide awake. His eyes met Ejiro's and held. The moment felt tense but fragile, like a butterfly had landed on Obiora's forehead, and he didn't dare breathe for fear of scaring it away.

"Yeah?" he said, his voice barely a whisper.

"Yeah," Ejiro echoed, his voice just as light.

"That's wonderful, Ejiro. That you're figuring things out,"

Obiora said, giving him a small encouraging smile. "Thank you for trusting me. It means a lot."

Ejiro blushed, tearing his eyes away, back to focusing on the sheets, obviously self-conscious. "I mean, I don't know. What if—?" His breath hitched slightly. His voice lowered even more, so Obiora had to strain to hear him. "What if I'm just faking it? What if I'm just —God, I don't know." He flopped onto his back, hiding his face behind his hands.

Obiora's heart felt so fucking tender. "Don't worry yourself, Ejiro. You feeling like this? At this point, I'm pretty sure constantly doubting yourself and your right to belong is almost like a queer rite of passage."

Ejiro dropped his hands, laughing. "Are you serious?"

"I'm serious." Obiora grinned. "Like, trust me on this. I'm sure everyone who's ever suspected they were queer went through a stage of thinking that they're just "faking it", that they're not valid or something along those lines—not like those "*real*" queers with their "*real*" trauma and "*real*" experiences, or some such bullshit." Ejiro laughed, even as he looked a bit guilty, and Obiora had to resist the urge to lean forward and kiss his forehead. "I think that sort of thinking stems from this desperate need to belong. We want to fit in, you know? But we're afraid of rejection, so we give ourselves some arbitrary criteria to meet—like, am I *really* bisexual if I'm attracted to women a hundred percent of the time, but other people like, only once in a blue moon? The answer is yes. Yes, I am. Not to say that having this fear isn't valid; with how vilified the LGBT+ community is, some of us queer folk can get really defensive about who belongs and who doesn't. But personally, I believe that as long as you aren't hurting anyone and you aren't like, a fucking paedophile, then you're okay.

"Look at me, Ejiro." He waited until Ejiro shyly met his eyes. "You're valid, do you hear me? You're absolutely valid, and the most important seal of approval you really need is your own."

"Yeah. Okay." Ejiro nodded, his voice thick with emotion, but Obiora could tell he didn't really believe him, at least not yet.

Fuck. Obiora wished he could instil in Ejiro the confidence he himself already had in his sexuality, but he knew all he could do was support him. Ejiro unfortunately had to do the work for himself.

"Thank you, Obiora," he said. A tiny smile curved his lips. "You know, I've been thinking about it, like, every single moment I've had to myself, ever since you said I might be—I've thought about it. What really cemented it for me, I think, is that I don't know what sexual attraction even *is*? Like, you see someone and you can just, what, picture having sex with them?" He wrinkled his nose in faint disgust. "Sounds fake, but okay."

Obiora laughed. Ejiro looked at him, pleased.

"Sexual attraction is a spectrum," Obiora said, still grinning. "I mean, in general, *all* attraction is a spectrum, but I'll focus on sexual attraction for now. Sometimes you see someone, and you absolutely can and do picture how they'd look naked." Obiora leered, which made Ejiro roll his eyes.

"Be serious, abeg."

Obiora laughed, then sobered up. "Sometimes, you can imagine—and often desire—what it might feel like to have their naked body pressed against yours." Obiora's voice, completely without his control, went deeper, gravelly. It could be a trick of the light, but Ejiro's eyes were unusually dark, his full lips slightly parted. "Sometimes—*most* times, I think—sexual attraction is all about the ability to recognise, appreciate, and *respond* to someone's inherent sexual appeal; to see a person as a sexual being, and find yourself helplessly drawn in reaction to it."

"Right." Ejiro's voice was hoarse. "That ..." He swallowed visibly. "That makes sense. A helpless response when you recognise someone's sexual appeal. Got it."

His eyes dropped to Obiora's lips.

And Obiora *saw* it, the moment Ejiro—for the fastest second—

stopped seeing Obiora as merely a walking flesh bag, but instead considered him as a *sexual* being. His eyes drank in Obiora's mouth, his chest, his arms, his legs. The perusal was lightning quick, but it lit Obiora up like a match.

And then came the response. The slight quickening of Ejiro's breath, the restless shifting of his legs; his eyebrows were furrowed, his eyes dark and intense, his tongue darting out to wet the seam of his parted lips.

Obiora felt like he was going to spontaneously combust.

"So, what ..." Jesus *fucking* Christ, his voice was so fucking *deep*, scraping through his throat smooth yet raspy, like whiskey through rocks. Obiora felt his dick begin to thicken between his legs. "What about when ... when you want to be close to someone?" Ejiro whispered. Obiora didn't think Ejiro noticed he was leaning closer as he asked the question. "Like, when you find yourself desiring to be—to like, hold their hand, or be in their arms but like, not in a completely sexual way. What ... is that also ...?"

"Sensual attraction," Obiora answered, his voice just as hoarse. Ejiro shivered visibly at the sound, his eyelashes fluttering. Obiora was going to die. "The desire to be close, right? Like, holding hands, cuddling, maybe even kissing, but in a non-sexual way ..."

"Right. Kissing." Fucking hell, did Ejiro even know? Was he aware how—how *naked* his desire was? "Yes. Exactly."

"Yes. That's sensual attraction."

"Sensual attraction. Right. Um."

Ejiro was staring at his mouth again. The only word Obiora could think of to describe his expression was *hungry*.

Obiora made a tiny, frantic noise.

It startled Ejiro out of his trance. He abruptly shot out of his bed. "I'm just—" He jerked his thumb in the direction of the ensuite. "I need to—freshen up. I'll ... see you." He grabbed one of his bags from the floor and disappeared into the bathroom like the hounds of hell were on his heels, locking the door behind him.

Obiora waited a beat. He shoved a hand between his legs after the sound of the shower came on, biting his lower lip hard.

Was Ejiro going to jerk off? To thoughts of him? Of *them*? Together? In this bed, maybe?

"Fuck, fuck, fuck." Obiora squeezed his dick—once, twice, helplessly thrusting into the pressure, then dropped his hand away, breathing heavily.

This was bad. This was fucking bad. Because it was all well and good when the attraction was one sided.

But having the possibility of *Ejiro* being attracted to *him*?

Obiora was so fucking *fucked*.

EIGHTEEN

EJIRO PRESSED HIS BACK AGAINST the bathroom door, clenching his eyes shut, his hands fisted at his sides, like if he stood still for long enough, the hot ache between his legs would disappear.

Instead, the stillness seemed to make him more aware of his arousal, and without his conscious control or permission, he began to roll his hips, biting his lip, his dick desperate for friction.

Obiora, he thought, shaking, his desire burning hotter at the mere *thought* of his name alone.

Fuck. Obiora. *Obiora*.

He could—just a little—just to take the edge off—

With a furious growl, he ripped himself away from the door and headed to the bath to switch on the shower. It came out hot within a second, steam rising from the surface, then he began to take off his clothes.

"Oh." His gasp was soft, barely there, as he tried to get his jeans off without further stimulating his throbbing dick. "Uhn. Christ. Fuck. God."

Then he was in bath and underneath the water, closing his eyes and tilting his face up into the spray, trying to think of anything, absolutely anything but Obiora talking about sexual and sensual attraction with a voice that sounded like sex itself.

He managed to pretend he *wasn't* going to touch himself for one minute, at most, before his hand was wrapped around his stiff length and he was stroking furiously, thinking about Obiora's thick lips, his broad chest, his deep *fucking* voice, and his big *hands*—oh God, oh God, oh God.

He curled in on himself, biting back his gasps, slowing down his strokes until he was shuddering with every pull of his hand. His dick felt extremely sensitive—he hadn't touched himself in so long—and the desire in his gut felt like the hottest flames from hell. Each slow stroke had him whining and curling his toes, shaking with a pleasure so intense it was indescribable.

No one had ever looked at him the way Obiora had looked at him. His dark eyes had practically *burned*, like Ejiro was the *sexiest* thing he'd ever seen; like Ejiro was a delicious piece of dessert and Obiora wanted to devour him *whole*.

"Ah," Ejiro gasped, his strokes speeding up again. He had to come. He *needed* to come.

His thoughts raced as he imagined what would have happened if he'd kissed Obiora the way he'd been dying to—the way he was *still* dying to—if Obiora would have kissed him back just as desperately. He imagined those big hands on his hips, pulling him until he was on top of Obiora, their bodies pressed close, every inch from head to toe.

What would it feel like to just—*grind* against him until he came? To have those thick thighs wrapped around his hips? Oh Jesus. Oh God. What would Obiora sound like in the throes of passion? What would he *look* like? Would he bite his sexy lips, head tilted back, throat vulnerably bared? Would he groan in that deep, sexy voice?

Ejiro lifted his free hand, tentatively, to pinch one of his stiff, sensitive nipples, imagining Obiora taking the dark bud into his mouth, nipping it lightly with his teeth, and that was it.

He came with a strangled grunt, pumping and squeezing his dick until he was whining and oversensitive and had to force himself to stop. He nearly slipped when he was done, the orgasm so intense it left his legs feeling like jelly. He collapsed against the tiled wall, trembling all over, trying to catch his breath.

"Fuck," he gasped, panting. "Jesus Christ."

His language filter always slipped when he was overly emotional or aroused, which never failed to make him blush after he'd calmed down.

He covered his face with his hands, heat blooming underneath his skin. "Oh dear God. Oh Jesus." Embarrassment at what he'd just done washed over him in a tidal wave. When last had he touched himself to the erotic imaginings of another person? He literally couldn't remember. Whenever Ejiro jerked off, he did so to the imaginings of fictional people in arousing situations; rarely had his fantasies ever involved himself. Or anyone *real*, for that matter.

It was as if, when Obiora had described what it was to feel sexual attraction—when he'd specifically mentioned it being about "seeing and responding to people as sexual beings"—a switch in Ejiro had flipped, just like that.

He'd blinked, and Obiora wasn't just "Obiora" anymore; he was "Obiora, a *sexual* being". The thought had made Ejiro's brain short-circuit, and then he hadn't been able to *stop* thinking about it. Obiora practically exuded sex appeal like it was a freaking cologne, it was a miracle Ejiro had never really noticed. Well, not a miracle; apparently just his sexuality. The suddenness of Ejiro's attraction had been so intense it had taken everything in him to keep from jumping Obiora's bones right then and there.

"Oh dear God," Ejiro repeated again.

He shook his head and reached for the soap, determined to put all thoughts of Obiora's apparent sex appeal to the back of his mind. Some part of him felt like he should be freaking out more about this—did this mean he was apparently attracted to men? Was he bisexual as well as demisexual? *Could* he be both or would he have to choose? Perhaps there was even a specific term for a bisexual demisexual, what the heck did he know?

God, he didn't want to think about any of it right now. It all felt too overwhelming.

After he finished his shower and was appropriately dressed, hair damp and his bag at his feet, it was time to go back into the room.

He began to have a little panic. Just a little.

He was going to have to face him, sooner or later. And maybe Obiora hadn't noticed Ejiro's sudden attraction. Probably. Hopefully.

In fact, it was highly likely this attraction thing was even a fluke. I mean, who *wouldn't* be aroused when someone as devastatingly handsome as Obiora started talking about sexual attraction with his voice all deep and gravelly like sin. Right?

Before all this, when Ejiro had been pondering his sexuality, he could have counted on both hands the number of people he felt he'd been sexually attracted to in his entire life. After Obiora's explanation, however, that number had dwindled down to one hand. It turned out a lot of the feelings Ejiro had attributed to sexual attraction might just have been *sensual* attraction; his desire to be physically close to someone, but not specifically in a sexual way.

So, yeah. Maybe this whole thing with Obiora was him getting confused because of the topic, that was all. Yes. That made sense.

Squaring his shoulders, Ejiro opened the bathroom door and pulled his bag out, focusing intently on it instead of anything else inside the room. From the corner of his eye, he could see that Obiora was still lying reclined on his bed where Ejiro had left him.

"All done," Ejiro said, wincing inwardly when his voice came out way too bright. He resolutely did not look in Obiora's direction, instead pulling his boxes toward the wardrobes on the other side of the room.

"Good shower?"

Ejiro jolted, his eyes flying up to meet Obiora's. "What?" he squeaked. Did he know? Had he heard? And holy *hell* had Obiora always been that *fucking* handsome?

Obiora grinned slowly, the curve of those full lips transforming his features from merely attractive to downright sinful, the dimple in his cheek flashing, begging to be kissed.

Obiora raised an eyebrow, the move so effortlessly sexy Ejiro didn't know how he was still standing.

"The shower," Obiora drawled. "Was it good?" Ejiro tried frantically not to stare at his mouth.

"What?" His heart slammed against his ribs. "Oh. Yes. Fine. It was fine. Pressure's good. Hot water seems endless. You know. It's good." *Oh God, Ejiro, shut up, shut up, shut the heck up.*

"Great." Obiora stood from the bed and stretched. "Think I'll have a shower myself."

Ejiro's eyes snapped down to where Obiora's shirt rode up as he stretched, hungrily taking in a revealed strip of beautiful, deep golden-brown skin and a trail of dark, coily hair.

Obiora moved, and Ejiro looked away quickly, cheeks on fire. He didn't look up again until he heard the bathroom door click shut. He waited for the sound of the lock, but it didn't come. He waited some more. His eyes grew wide and his hands clenched into fists when he heard the sound of the shower come on.

Obiora hadn't locked the door—the freaking *heathen*.

Ejiro began to furiously unpack, ignoring the way his heartbeat fluttered and heat flooded his body. Why had Obiora left the door unlocked? Had he done it on purpose? And why the heck did Ejiro even care?

He groaned, dunking his head into his open bag.

So. His attraction to Obiora apparently wasn't a fluke.

Fan-*freaking*-tastic.

"THIS WEEK'S EPISODE IS GOING to be a little different," Ameri said early the next morning, when all the men had gathered in the empty ground floor of the bigger house, the entrance to the entire accommodation. Sophia was there, too, looking bright and excited, dressed in a pretty peach knee-length sundress, pale pink sunglasses and a wide straw hat on her head, her feet in cute flat white sandals. "Here's the challenge: you will all—yes *all*—be going on a private date with the bachelorette." All the bachelors whooped and hollered, especially those who hadn't yet been on a private date with Sophia.

Sophia winked and blew kisses at them, grinning flirtatiously.

"Before y'all get too excited, there's a catch," Ameri continued with amusement.

"Of course there is," Noah deadpanned. Some of the men laughed.

"You'll each have a time limit of one hour only, and you can only take her to one of the places written on the list we've handed to you this morning. We'll be going on a private scheduled tour by water taxi to visit all the places written down on the list; your assignment is to check them out to make sure the spot you pick is perfect to impress our bachelorette. Now, are we ready men?"

There were enthusiastic responses in the affirmative.

"Then let's go!" Sophia said, her grin wide. Her excitement seemed to rile up the men; they were practically vibrating with the need to get started.

The bachelorette left the building first. The men all chatted to themselves as they walked the short distance to the water-filled streets.

"Ameri's smart to do this, don't you think?" Obiora leaned over to whisper.

Ejiro tried not to stiffen at the closeness, as a gentle breeze blew Obiora's scent right into his nostrils. God, Obiora smelled *amazing*, heady and woodsy. Ejiro wanted to bury his face in the point that joined Obiora's neck with his shoulder, and inhale his scent like a vampire.

He cleared his throat. "What do you mean?"

Obiora smirked. "You know how Eddie was complaining about feeling cooped up—"

"Ah, right." Ejiro laughed. "You think she's giving us a tour of Venice so we don't complain that we came all the way here, yet we aren't really seeing any of it?" Just like back in Oxford, they weren't allowed to leave their accommodation under any circumstances. It was a part of their contract.

"Exactly." Obiora winked.

Ejiro felt that wink all the way down to his toes. He looked away, heart racing.

Sophia was the first to get into her private taxi, one of the directors, two cameras, plus three members of staff following after her. The remaining four water taxis were shared between the twelve men and remaining staff; it ended up with four men in a taxi with three camera crew. The directors took their own taxi, following after the men at the back.

The taxi was actually quite spacious, but despite this, Ejiro could feel the heat of Obiora's body like it was a brand. He'd barely been able to sleep last night, unable to stop thinking about how close their beds were, how easy it would be to cross the little boundary between them. Only his panic at his new found feelings kept him rooted right to his bed, because with the way Obiora had started looking at him, Ejiro was afraid Obiora knew exactly how he felt, and worse, he felt the same way, too. Ejiro didn't know what the heck to do with that information, so he chose to pretend he didn't notice.

Eventually, Ejiro was soon taken in by the sights and sounds, nearly leaning over the side of the boat in his awe. He felt slightly upset that he'd left his sketching materials behind, because his fingers itched to draw everything. The men weren't even allowed cameras, so Ejiro couldn't even take reference pictures for later. He'd much prefer drawing the real thing, obviously, but pictures he'd taken himself would have sufficed.

The voice of the tour guide slash driver faded to the background as Ejiro practically gobbled up the scenery with his eyes, wishing fiercely that he could've experienced this with Ajiri and Blessing. Heck, even his mother. The woman deserved a break.

At one point, he'd glanced at Obiora to show him something, trembling with excitement, and found Obiora already watching him, his eyes soft with a terrible fondness.

Ejiro's stomach had swooped, and he'd found it hard to breathe. He'd shown Obiora what he'd been pointing at, then focused resolutely on the sights outside of the taxi for the rest of the trip, though his heart didn't stop racing, his cheeks hot with a self-conscious blush.

The list of attractions Ameri wanted them to see wasn't long, and were located vaguely close to each other around the canal, so the tour only took thirty minutes.

Afterward, they were taken back to the house.

"Right, I'll be giving y'all the next thirty minutes to pick your locations. Your dates with Sophia will start exactly at twelve PM—so about three and a half hours from now—and will end at eight PM, with time for her to move between dates. Six people will be taking Sophia out today, and six tomorrow to give her time to breathe. I'll let y'all toss a coin on who can go first." She winked. "I'll see y'all in a bit. Good luck!"

Ameri faded back into the crew. The cameras followed them as they headed into the house, so they had to be on their best behaviours. When they arrived in the veranda of the big house, settling around the chairs laid out around a wide, round table, they didn't waste time in picking who would go when.

Ejiro ended up with today. Obiora ended up with tomorrow.

At the thought that he was going to go on a date with Sophia, Ejiro *really* began to panic. The second Ameri returned to know their locations and left to prepare the crew, Ejiro disappeared, finding his way to the private garden. The terrace extended out of the house and was held up with thick, baroque pillars, creating a small nook at the edge of the garden that he could successfully hide and panic in.

The last time he'd gone out with Sophia, she'd ended up kissing him when he hadn't wanted to be kissed. With everything happening with his feelings with Obiora and all, he'd completely forgotten he'd have to tell her about it if he wanted a future with her.

Did he still want a future with her? He didn't know anymore. No. Yes. Yes, he did. *Of course* he did. Right? So what if he was attracted to Obiora? He could be attracted to him without it having to *mean* anything, right?

Except—

The way Obiora had looked at him on the boat during the tour, like Ejiro was the centre of his universe.

He shook his head. No. He was probably reading into things. Besides, he was here for Sophia. He was technically dating her; his feelings for Obiora would have to be pushed to the side.

The bachelorette had to come first.

EJIRO ENDED UP BEING THE last bachelor to take Sophia out for the day. Since it was going to be in the evening, he'd picked one of the canal-side restaurants to take Sophia on his own date. He'd initially wanted to take her to one of the famous museums since she loved them so much, but literally all the other men had had the same idea, so Ejiro at least had some originality going for him.

"Ejiro!" Sophia exclaimed happily.

He was waiting for her outside her accommodation. Ejiro grinned. "Hey, Sophia."

She jogged lightly up to him and jumped, throwing her arms around him.

Ejiro stiffened automatically in surprise, then forced himself to relax, hugging her back. When she pulled back slowly, tilting her face up, obviously aiming for a kiss, Ejiro pretended not to notice, taking her hand instead and a careful step back.

"Are you ready?" he asked with a smile to distract her from his withdrawal.

Her eyes dimmed for a moment—crap, she'd noticed—then brightened again. "Let's go. I am starving."

There was no escaping it. They were going to have to talk about it. But not right now.

Venice seemed to follow England when it came to sunset times in the summer, because it was nearing seven in the evening but the sun was only just beginning to show hints of lowering in the sky.

They took a water taxi to the restaurant, talking all the while. On the surface, their conversation seemed smooth and easy, but Ejiro could feel a tension in the air. Or maybe that was just his fear of the painful conversation they needed to have.

When they got to the restaurant and were led to their table, located right on the edge of the canal, Ejiro almost had to take a pause at the breath-taking beauty of it. The sunset and the bright lights of the restaurant behind rendered the scene like a painting.

"Oh Ejiro. Isn't it gorgeous?" Sophia sighed from beside him.

"Yeah," Ejiro breathed, wishing desperately again that he could just ... sit down and paint the scenery. He could literally get lost drawing this place for hours, it was so beautiful.

The meal was lovely. They'd already built up a good rapport thanks to their previous dates, so everything went smoothly.

Just as it was about to end, Sophia blurted, "Do you want to go for a stroll? I'm not ready for the day to end just yet." She looked at him shyly.

Ejiro's heart thumped at the look, though it wasn't exactly the same feeling he got when Obiora looked at him.

Fuck. *Stop thinking about Obiora.*

"That sounds lovely," Ejiro said. He stood and held a hand out to her, helping her out of her seat.

"Thank you," she breathed, eyeing him from underneath her eyelashes.

Ejiro's heart thumped again. He felt weird. Uncomfortable.

They strolled down the canal—the directors, cameras, and crew following after them—talking about random nonsense.

When they reached a small bridge without too many tourists and a stunning view of the sunset, Sophia paused.

For a moment, Ejiro was rendered frozen by her sheer beauty. The deep orange glow of the sunset kissed her dark brown skin like that of a lovers', bringing out the richness of the russet tones underneath. Her brown eyes shone like melted honey, the light framing her body like a soft, golden halo.

Ejiro couldn't believe she was here, with him, holding his hand.

Then, for some reason, Obiora's words of yesterday popped into his head, and he blinked, his brain immediately trying to see Sophia not just as *Sophia*, beauty and grace extraordinaire, but as *Sophia*, a *sexual* being.

He found himself noticing things he hadn't paid attention to before; like how her dress had the tiniest straps, baring her shoulders, collar bones, and the lush curves of her breasts. The material clung to the dips and curves of her body almost invitingly. Her makeup was minimal, but the lipstick she wore made her lips seem poutier, more kissable.

He shouldn't have been surprised to acknowledge that Sophia was ridiculously *sexy*.

But, even with the realisation stunning him, he felt ... nothing. Not a single stirring of heat or interest. Not a single response. Nothing like the way Obiora had lit him up from the inside out yesterday with nothing but the gravel in his voice, and the searing heat of a single look.

Sophia misinterpreted his perusal as an invitation because she stepped closer, right into his space, tilting her face up yet eyeing him coyly.

"I had a really lovely time tonight, Ejiro," she began, and Ejiro already knew where this was going.

The meal. The stroll. The sunset.

It was a perfect setup. If he'd actually wanted her, he'd have been swooning.

"Sophia ..." he began, swallowing nervously.

Either she didn't pick up on his nerves, or she interpreted it entirely wrong, because her voice was seductively breathy when she answered, "Yes?"

Ejiro wanted to drop her hand and take a step back, but this was already excruciating enough without it looking like he was dumping her on reality TV, so he stayed put where he was.

He was breathing too fast. He felt a little lightheaded. Where the fuck was New Ejiro and his seemingly endless bouts of confidence and bravery when Old Ejiro needed him?

He looked away, at the reflection of gold on the surface of the water below them.

Do it, he told himself, his inner voice sounding suspiciously like Obiora. *Just tell her.*

He swallowed again. "Remember when you kissed me? On our last date?"

"Yeah." She giggled, her voice still low, seductive.

"Well"—*oh fuck, oh God*—"Well, I didn't actually want to be kissed." There. It was done. Fuck. Fuck. Fuck. Fuck.

Sophia stared at him. Slowly, she detangled their hands. She looked horrified.

Instantly, Ejiro felt sick to his stomach. He felt like he was going to throw up. "It's not you," he began desperately, "you're lovely; you're great, actually. I just—I'm—I think I'm—" *Demisexual*. The word hooked in his throat. Refused to come out. Why had it been the easiest thing to admit it to Obiora, but not to her? "I just like to take things slow," he amended, knowing it probably sounded weak, a ridiculous defence, but it was all he had. "I wasn't ready, and—"

"But you kissed me back," she said, almost desperately.

Ejiro winced. He couldn't look at her. "I-I felt pressured. I didn't want to hurt you."

"Jesus, Ejiro, I'm so sorry."

"Oh," Ejiro said, surprised that she'd apologised.

"Ejiro," she said, anguished, once more taking his hands in hers, encouraging him to face her. "I'm *sorry*. I would never want to do anything someone doesn't want—or, or to make anyone feel pressured. And that I did—it's inexcusable. I really like you, Ejiro. And I assumed you were just shy, that you might want me to take the lead—but I was wrong, obviously. And arrogant. I shouldn't have assumed something like that. I'm really sorry, Ejiro. Do you—shall we head back?"

"Right. Yeah. Okay."

She gave his hand a squeeze. "Okay?" She looked so distressed, but she was trying to hide it, probably so he wouldn't feel coerced.

This time he genuinely relaxed. "Yes. Let's go."

"Okay."

The walk back was silent and a bit strained. The cameras felt oppressive around them, and Ejiro tried to ignore their presence with difficulty. He wished this conversation didn't have to happen on camera. Even if Ameri had talked about wanting it to be all "real" and "natural", there was still something voyeuristic about it all.

Ejiro walked Sophia up to her door. She immediately took a step away, giving him space.

"God, Ejiro, I'm so sorry. How are you feeling? Are you upset with me?" She couldn't quite meet his eyes.

To be honest, Ejiro had been expecting her to get defensive, to even blame him for saying anything—it's what Sam would have done—so her apologising and accepting that she'd fucked up? It was everything.

"No," he said, smiling a little. "I'm not mad."

"All right." She looked nervous, off kilter. "Um. Can I have a hug? Only if you're comfortable."

"A hug sounds nice." Ejiro held out his arms.

She walked into his embrace, hugging him tightly. They stood there for a few moments, just holding each other. It felt ... nice. Good. Lovely. But just ... nice. Like hugging Ajiri.

Sophia pulled away eventually. "I'm so sorry. Are we going to be okay? Is there anything I can do to fix this?"

"Everything's fine." Ejiro was quick to reassure her. "I promise. I honestly just wanted you to listen."

"Of course." She nodded, smiling tentatively. "Thank you for telling me. And I'm sorry again."

They said their goodnights. Some of the cameras split, some following after Sophia, the others trailing after Ejiro as he headed back to the house.

"You good there, Ejiro?" Ameri asked when she'd finally yelled cut.

Ejiro grinned. "Yeah. Yeah, I'm good."

Ejiro waved off the inquiries from the men with generic responses until he got to the room he shared with Obiora. He hadn't spotted him on the way here, so Obiora was probably inside.

He reached for the door handle and hesitated.

He took a deep breath.

And another.

And another.

He opened the door.

Obiora was sitting cross-legged on his bed and reading a comic, wearing a worn, plain white t-shirt and loose, grey knee-length cotton shorts. Ejiro had seen him dressed like this *tens* of times.

But Jesus Christ, his legs. His *thighs*. His coily locks were messy on his head, and his smile was bright and genuine when he noticed Ejiro at the door.

"How was your date?" He waggled his eyebrows.

Ejiro felt attraction slam into him with the weight of a two-ton boulder.

So. Still not a fluke then.

Fan-*freaking*-tastic.

NINETEEN

OBIORA WAS GOING TO HELL. Had he deliberately taken his shirt off after Ejiro had returned from his date last night, and then gone to bed like that, knowing he was in full view of the other man? Perhaps. Had he come out of the shower this morning with nothing but one of the accommodation's tiny ass white towels wrapped around his hips, steam bellowing around him as he'd told Ejiro the shower was free? Maybe.

And now, here he was again, playing with fire. Since he'd noticed Ejiro's attraction to him, Obiora just couldn't *help* himself.

His shoulders tensed imperceptibly when he heard the sound of Ejiro's voice out in the dining area, where Jin was having his breakfast. They exchanged good mornings. Obiora listened to Ejiro's footsteps as he approached the kitchen.

His lips curved into the tiniest smirk, which he immediately wiped off his face when he heard Ejiro's sharp intake of breath as he walked into the kitchen.

"Oh," Ejiro said in surprise, his voice low and breathy.

Obiora looked over his shoulder, casual as you please, and like he wasn't currently half naked, dressed in nothing but loose white cotton shorts, sliders, and a bright smile. The sliding doors leading to the balcony were open, letting out a stream of the morning's sunlight, which Obiora was sure was bathing the skin of his toned brown chest in stunning shades of bronze and gold.

"Hey, shower okay?" It took everything to keep the smirk out of his voice.

"Hey, yes, hello, hi." Ejiro was trying so hard not to stare that he walked right into the kitchen island. "Ow! Jesus Christ." Embarrassment spilled from him in waves.

"You okay?" Obiora had to bite his lip to keep himself from laughing.

"Fine. I'm fine." Ejiro spun away, heading straight for the fridge. He opened the door and abruptly shoved his face inside. "What are you making?" he asked, voice a little strangled.

"Scrambled eggs, Naija style." Obiora was enjoying himself far too much. "Want some? I took the liberty of making enough for two."

"Oh? I'd love some, thank you. That's very considerate of you." Ejiro's head remained in the fridge.

Obiora felt amusement mixed with a sweetly excruciating fondness. He was just about done with the eggs, so he turned off the flames and moved the pan to a cooler burner.

Then, crossing his fingers and praying he still had this right, he quietly made his way to the fridge until he was standing directly behind Ejiro.

Ejiro noticed his steady approach and froze, but his tenseness felt … anticipatory, rather than wary. Obiora's heartbeat sped up.

His voice was unintentionally pitched low when he leaned further, over Ejiro's shoulder in pretence of looking into the fridge as he murmured, "What are you looking for?"

Ejiro seemed to sway a bit where he stood, as though he didn't know if he wanted to get away from Obiora or lean into him. His obvious desire was like a flame to the fuel of Obiora's own need.

"Um. Orange juice." Ejiro's voice came out just as husky. He didn't seem to even notice it, the way he subtly tilted his head to the side, baring his throat where Obiora's face was, as if silently begging him to place a kiss on the smooth skin that joined his neck and shoulder.

Jesus Christ.

Obiora had forgotten the question he'd even asked. He leaned even closer, over Ejiro's shoulder, making sure his chest brushed against Ejiro's back. Ejiro shivered, but he didn't move away. In fact, his body seemed to melt a little, shoulders loosening, like he'd let out a breath he'd been holding in.

Obiora wanted to do something reckless. His eyes dropped to Ejiro's bared throat; it would be so easy to kiss him there, just a slight brush of lips—so slight Ejiro might wonder if he'd imagined the contact. But even if Ejiro's *body* might want him, Obiora didn't want to take that as consent; he wanted explicit words of desire from Ejiro's mouth.

He wanted Ejiro to *beg* to be touched, the way he so clearly, desperately wanted to be.

The sound of cutlery tinkling on ceramic from the dining area yanked Obiora back to earth. There was a brief silence, then the sound of flip flops slapping gently against the tiled floors, coming in the direction of the kitchen.

"Pulp is on the bottom shelf, on the door," Obiora said at a normal volume, though his voice was still throaty. "Pulp-free's in the middle."

Then he walked away, toward the cupboards holding the plates just as Jin came into the kitchen with his dirty dishes, heading for the sink.

"Oh, that smells amazing. What is it?" He peered into the pan on the stove.

Ejiro seemed to shake himself out of his trance, grabbing the pulp-free orange juice and closing the fridge door. Even with his dark skin, Obiora could tell he was a little flushed. His dark eyes were even darker—dazed, deep pools of black desire.

"Scrambled eggs," Obiora answered, barely able to tear his eyes away from Ejiro, despite how obvious he knew it must make him look.

"With tomatoes and onions?" Jin asked, wrinkling his nose a little. He seemed to be completely oblivious of the tension in the air.

Obiora laughed. "And hot peppers. Some call it egg sauce. It's a Nigerian recipe."

"Well. It smells absolutely delicious. I would ask for some, but I'm stuffed."

"I can make it again if you like?"

"Oh, would you? That would be lovely. Thank you. I really want to taste it."

"It's no problem at all."

"Um." Ejiro cleared his throat. "Obiora, can I have the bread please? I'm going to make some toast."

"Oh, I apologise," Jin said, in the middle of washing his dishes. "I made French toast and forgot to return the bread to the right counter. Do pardon me."

"It's all right," Ejiro said, a small smile on his face.

Obiora found the loaf of bread beside the stove. He picked it up and reached over the island to hand it to Ejiro.

Ejiro took it from him, deliberately or not-so-deliberately brushing their fingers together as he did. With how quickly he turned around to face the toaster, Obiora was betting on it being the former. God, he was so fucking endearing.

"Ejiro?"

"Yeah?" Ejiro hesitated, before glancing at him.

"Four slices for me, thank you." Obiora punctuated his sentence with a wink.

Ejiro literally stumbled backward over thin air. He spun around in embarrassment to face the toaster, reaching for the bread like it'd save him. Obiora wanted to walk right up to him and kiss him so badly it was like a physical ache.

"See you both later." Jin returned the hand towel he'd used for his hands back to the hook attached to the wall. "And enjoy your date with Sophia today, Obiora."

"Will do. Later, Jin."

"Later," Ejiro echoed.

Obiora, grinning like a maniac, set the plates and served up the eggs between them. Then he carried the dishes over to where Ejiro was standing by the toaster just as the first two slices popped up, perfectly golden brown.

As usual, Ejiro stiffened for a moment at the proximity, before relaxing completely. He set the slices on the nearest plate, placed fresh ones in the toaster, and pressed the button.

Obiora nudged their shoulders together after a moment of comfortable silence, feeling ridiculously giddy.

Ejiro nudged him back automatically, glancing at him with a small, amused smile on his lips. "What?"

"Nothing." Obiora nudged him again.

Ejiro nudged him back. "Go away."

"I like it fine right here, thank you."

The toast popped out. Ejiro used it as an excuse not to look at him, though Obiora could see the blush in his expression. He set two fresh slices in the toaster and pushed the button.

"Are you really going to stand here and watch me make the toast?" Ejiro mock glared at him.

"Yes." Obiora leered.

Ejiro blushed and looked away, then seemed to steel himself and looked back once more. "You're so annoying. And why on earth aren't you wearing a shirt?" The last sentence seemed to come out almost without Ejiro's will, quickly and almost shrilly. His eyes darted down to said chest, a quick onceover that made Obiora feel like he was on fire.

"I just felt like it." He shrugged, voice a little deep. "Why? Is it distracting?" He waggled his eyebrows.

"What? No." Ejiro looked away quickly. "Why would it even—?" He growled. "You know what—"

Obiora laughed, dodging out of the way when Ejiro tried to smack him.

The toast popped out before Ejiro could chase him around the kitchen like a child. He grabbed his two slices and placed them on his plate.

"Abeg leave the road, jor," Ejiro said, using his hip to playfully butt Obiora out of the way.

Obiora felt his chest expand to painful proportions, like his heart had grown ten times its size. He picked up his own plate, following Ejiro out of the kitchen and to the dining table.

They sat opposite each other. Obiora stretched his legs out until the insides of his feet were bracketing the outsides of Ejiro's.

Ejiro sucked in a sharp breath. He looked up quickly, but Obiora was focused intently on his food, pretending like he hadn't done anything wrong.

He waited for Ejiro to react—to remove his feet or make a playful but pointed comment about the surprise contact. Or hell, he waited for Ejiro to panic and decide he didn't want to eat next to Obiora anymore.

Ejiro didn't do any of that. Instead, he focused on his own food, his breathing slightly faster than usual, the only sign he was affected at all. Obiora could've imagined it, but he could've sworn Ejiro's feet moved slightly, nudging against his own.

God, Obiora wanted him so fucking *fiercely*. It felt like he'd been in a constant state of minor arousal, because teasing Ejiro meant teasing himself. But Obiora loved the sweet torture of it all.

Yeah. He was definitely going to hell.

"**I JUST DON'T THINK IT'S** fair," Obiora was saying later that evening on his date with Sophia. He was the last bachelor for the day. "I mean, the tour was nice and all, but it's just not the same as an *actual* holiday, you know?"

"Well, I don't know about you, but I'm personally having a great time," Sophia said, leering at him.

Obiora laughed, then pretended to clutch at his chest. "Seriously? Are you *really* rubbing it in my face right now that you're going on romantic dates around Venice with other men?"

"I mean, I'm just saying." Sophia shrugged, grinning, completely unapologetic. "It's not my fault the show is catered to my desires."

"*Ouch.*" Obiora laughed again, even as he felt a pang. He was sure at this moment, now that he'd gone on two private dates with the bachelorette, that if he hadn't already been invested in Ejiro, he could easily see himself falling for Sophia. She was smart and sexy and witty, and they got along extremely well.

It was too bad that even though they were having a great time—he'd chosen to take her on a stroll around the winding Venice streets, with the aim of ending with a light dessert at the canal—all Obiora could think about was Ejiro. How it would have felt if it were just the two of them here, on holiday, together.

God, he was really getting in too deep. As he and Sophia explored the ancient parts of the city, getting lost, forgetting about the cameras, all Obiora could think about was how Ejiro would react to everything.

Ejiro had practically almost fallen off the water taxi during the tour yesterday. He'd done that thing with his hands that he usually did when he was itching to draw—cracking his knuckles, squeezing his hands together against his chest, sometimes even mock sketching the scenery in the air, distracted and completely unaware, his eyes glazed as he tried to picture putting whatever was in his head on paper.

It made Obiora try to see how the world looked through Ejiro's artistic eyes, and it really was fucking beautiful. Their dessert at a small ice-cream and bakery by the canal was the icing on the cake; the view, the sights and sounds, Obiora wished desperately that he could somehow capture the image for Ejiro.

There had to be a way they could capture it. They had to. When this was all over, what would Obiora have to remember these moments? Because he knew it now like he knew how to breathe—when he and Ejiro eventually went their separate ways, there was no way Obiora was going to be able to ever forget about him.

OBIORA WAS GOING TO DO something reckless.

After his date with Sophia, when he returned to the house, he did so to find most of the men chilling on the spacious veranda of the big house, eating finger foods, drinking, and just chatting in general. The only people missing in the gathering were Jin, Tyler, and Ejiro.

Ejiro wasn't in their shared room, and neither was he in the dining nor living areas. Obiora went to the kitchen and saw the sliding door leading to the balcony slightly open, letting in a soft, cool evening breeze.

As if on cue, his heart began to race as he approached the doors, sliding them fully open and stepping out. The balcony was a small thing that stretched out to meet the fence that separated their accommodation from the house next to theirs. On the left, it held a small, round, black wooden table with four chairs, potted plants sitting at the four corners, spilling vines of green through the metal railings.

Ejiro was in the seat that backed the house, a furrow in his eyebrow as he sketched furiously onto his notepad. He didn't notice Obiora's presence at all. From where he stood by the sliding door,

Obiora could vaguely make out what looked to be the canal taking shape on the paper.

Then Ejiro made a frustrated sound and slammed his sketchbook shut, dumping it on the table along with his pencil so carelessly both items slid across the smooth surface and nearly landed on the floor, only hanging onto the edge by sheer miracle.

"Ahn, ahn, what did the poor sketchbook do to you?"

Ejiro startled at the sound of his voice, turning to look at him and smiling automatically when he noticed it was Obiora. That smile made Obiora feel like he was flying.

"Let me not even get into it," Ejiro replied with a groan. His smile faltered a little, then falsely brightened as he asked, "How was your date?"

Obiora shrugged. "It was all right." He didn't want to talk about Sophia; he didn't want Ejiro thinking he had even an inkling of interest in the bachelorette. "What were you working on that's got you so frustrated?" he asked, taking the seat next to him.

"Oh, you know." Ejiro tried to wave him off. Obiora waited him out. Ejiro sighed. "It was the canal. It was—during the sunset yesterday, it was so beautiful. I just really wanted to capture it on paper. But my imagination—the one time I absolutely need it to work—is being uncooperative. Like, I understand the risk, but I wish Ameri would at least let us take pictures."

Obiora felt a pang.

And then he made his decision.

Maybe it was the melancholy feeling of getting to see a mere glimpse of Venice but not really experience it. Maybe it was the wistfulness in Ejiro's voice when he'd admitted the day they'd arrived, how much his twin and her girlfriend would have loved it here. Maybe it was the fact that what was waiting for Ejiro after all this was a confrontation with his mother about going back to Nigeria. Perhaps it was because *Obiora* himself was going to have to go back to work for his father, when he really, *desperately*, didn't want to.

It was something in the air, the tension and growing attraction between them.

It was the dreadful fact that their time together was quickly running out.

It was all that and more, that had Obiora blurting, "Let's do it."

"Let's do what?" Ejiro asked incredulously. "Take pictures?" He laughed, like Obiora was joking.

Obiora stood. "No. Well, yes. Something like that. Grab your sketchbook, come on. We probably have about an hour before the sun completely sets."

Ejiro's eyes were widening. "What—what are you talking about?"

Obiora grinned, wide and devilish. He grabbed the railing and neatly swung himself over it until he was standing on the fence separating the two buildings. The concrete was just wide enough for him to balance comfortably.

"Obiora!" Ejiro gasped, stumbling out of his seat. "Are you mad?"

Obiora laughed a little. He didn't think his heart had ever raced this fast. "Maybe. Come on, Ejiro. We'll be there and back in the blink of an eye. None of the guys are going to miss us."

"No." Ejiro shook his head. "What? You must be joking. Get back here right now."

"Ejiro." There must've been something desperate in his voice, because Ejiro paused and looked at him, his eyes so, so bright, yet so terrified.

Obiora held a hand out. "Come *on*. When next are you going to come back here? Be honest with yourself. Don't you want something— something more than what we're confined to?"

Ejiro looked outward, toward the sky. He looked back at Obiora. The desperation Obiora felt in his chest was mirrored in Ejiro's eyes.

Then Ejiro nodded. Thank fucking God, he *nodded*.

He grabbed his sketchbook and pencil, then took Obiora's hand.

Obiora felt the contact from the tips of his hair all the way down to his toes.

It felt like coming home.

"**OH MY GOD, OH MY** God, oh my God," Ejiro repeated over and over as they walked quickly through the winding streets. His eyes darted wildly around, like he expected Ameri to materialise out of the crowds and grab them. "I can't believe we're doing this."

"Honestly? Me neither."

"This was your idea!" Ejiro exclaimed, but he was laughing.

The sound of his carefree laughter, his pure uncontained joy, made Obiora laugh as well, giddy with it. He felt like a child on Christmas day, his stomach doing literal somersaults. It didn't help that after they'd jumped the fence and made it onto the street, Ejiro had hooked his arm through Obiora's, blushing as he'd said, "We need to stay close so we don't lose each other."

Obiora had gladly taken the excuse to sidle closer, so their bodies were practically glued together, side by side.

Now, here they were, walking with their arms linked, like a Victorian couple. By some silent mutual agreement, they wound through the streets aimlessly instead of heading straight for the canal, as though they wanted to soak in their stolen moment of freedom for as long as possible. If he did so hard enough, Obiora could pretend that they actually *were* on holiday together, just the two of them.

He felt the loss keenly when they finally got to one of the bridges overlooking the canal in full view of the sunset, and Ejiro let go of him, rushing to the edge of the bridge and pulling out his sketchbook.

Ejiro laughed breathlessly, giddily, his eyes taking it all in, as if he was unsure where to start.

He glanced back at Obiora, his dark eyes shining, reflecting the golden light of the sunset. "Thank you for dragging me out here."

Obiora moved up until they were pressed together, side by side, the crowd of tourists around them fading to a distant hum.

"No problem. Now, go on; take your picture."

Ejiro grinned, and did just that. It took him a few moments, just taking in the scenery, his hand poised on his sketchbook, waiting for inspiration to strike. He was stiff at first, like he was hyperaware of his audience, of the fact that they weren't alone on the bridge, people taking photos, laughing and talking.

Which was why it was obvious the moment he finally found his zone.

His shoulders relaxed, his breaths slowed. His lips pursed, eyebrows furrowed into a cute little frown of concentration. The world seemed to disappear around him when he began to draw.

Obiora could feel his chest expanding again, his ribs too small to contain his heart. He remained quiet, unobtrusive as Ejiro's hand flew across the page.

Obiora didn't know how long they stood there, Ejiro lost in his world, and Obiora lost in him. The sun had set completely, and the crowds had fluctuated, thinning, then thickening, then thinning again.

Finally, Ejiro heaved a heavenly sigh and slid his sketchbook shut.

"Yeah?" Obiora said, voice pitched low for only Ejiro to hear. He nudged their shoulders together.

Ejiro pressed against his side, his smile a soft, beautiful thing. "Yeah," he echoed.

His hands clenched around his sketchbook for a second, before he spun abruptly and flung his arms around Obiora, hugging him tightly.

Obiora's arms immediately went around him. He buried his face in Ejiro's throat, inhaling the sweet, buttery scent of the shampoo in his hair.

"Thank you," Ejiro whispered. "I'll never forget this."

Obiora swallowed with difficulty, holding him tighter. "It was my pleasure, honestly."

They pulled apart slowly, so slowly it was excruciating. Their cheeks brushed. Obiora felt the touch like he'd been struck by lightning.

Their faces were so close they were practically breathing the same air. Ejiro was staring at his mouth. Obiora's own eyes dropped to Ejiro's lips, his stomach turning molten when those sweet peach lips parted slightly in invitation.

"Hello! Excuse me!"

They jumped apart like guilty schoolchildren. Obiora's heart raced.

The woman who'd called after them watched them with amusement. "I'm terribly sorry, but would you mind taking a picture for us?" She held out her phone. Behind her stood what Obiora assumed were her entire extended family, who also wore amused looks on their faces.

Obiora could feel himself blushing. Ejiro looked just as flustered.

"Um, sure," Ejiro said, clearing his throat when his voice came out hoarse.

He took several photos until the woman was satisfied.

"Thank you. I'll leave you both to it." She winked, then turned back to her family.

"Oh my God." Ejiro hid his face behind his hands.

Obiora burst out laughing.

"Stop laughing!" Ejiro managed to smack him in the arm before he could dodge.

"Come on," Obiora said with a grin. "Let's head back."

Without looking at him, Ejiro walked up and linked their arms again, his fingers pressing gently against the inside of Obiora's elbow. Obiora was on cloud nine with no way of ever coming back down.

The walk back was much slower, all the urgency gone. Obiora trembled with want; he didn't want this moment—this day to end.

It felt like it took too long and yet not long enough, when they finally made it back to their accommodation.

There was slight muffled laughter when Ejiro had to give Obiora a boost up the fence, then Obiora had to reach down to pull him up.

They landed on the balcony, no worse for wear. The kitchen was dark, the sliding door closed. Tyler, Jin, and Jack had probably gone to bed already.

They snuck inside, hearts beating in tandem, and heaved sighs of relief when they made it to their room unnoticed.

Obiora flipped on the light. Ejiro collapsed onto his bed, clutching his sketchbook to his chest.

"That was exhilarating," he said breathlessly, laughing a little. He sat up, looking at Obiora, pinning him there with the earnestness in his gaze. "This was hands down one of the best days of my life."

The words shook Obiora down to his marrows, every inch of him wishing he could stay in this moment forever.

"Yeah," he said softly. "Same here."

The official website for the CUPID CALLING series.

Cupid Calling

ABOUT | THE BACHELORETTE | THE BACHELORS | EPISODES | CONTACT | BECOME A CUPID

Episode 5 – The World's Most Romantic City

Episode Summary: Noah, the winner of last week's Red Heart, takes Sophia on a stroll through the University of Oxford's botanical gardens, then a dinner snack from a roadside kebab truck, ending the date with a spicy and passionate kiss. Ejiro takes Sophia to a fancy restaurant for dinner, and Sophia plants one on him that he seems to reciprocate, but later admits he did not want. Jin takes Sophia for a romantic riverside picnic, then punting down the river itself; he kisses the back of her hand after the date, which makes Sophia swoon. Obiora takes Sophia to lunch, ending his date with a lingering hug.

For this week's group date, the bachelors and bachelorette are taken on a surprise trip to Venice. The men are given a list of places they tour upon arrival, and are told to pick one place to take the bachelorette on a private date, with a time limit of one hour each. During their date, Sophia apologises to Ejiro for kissing him without consent. Jin is the second bachelor to win the Red Heart during his date; he takes Sophia on a private picnic in a water taxi circling the canal, and reads her a romantic poem he wrote about her. They end up kissing for most of the rest of the date.

Eddie, George, Tyler, and Jack are eliminated.

Click here to watch the full episode on Netflicks!

COMMENTS

PARAMORE_11

F*cking hell I feel so bad for Ejiro. Do you know how hard it must've been for him to admit (IN FRONT OF THE CAMERAS???? TWICE?????) that he didn't want to be kissed? Like, I've been the recipient of a non-consensual kiss, and let me tell you, it is NOT fun. Edit: to everyone trying to make this about how Sophia is so "mature" for "at least" apologising (which is the BARE F*CKING MINIMUM), FUCK YOU :)

 15790   8032

 **STEALURGIRL**

LOL I think it's hilarious how Ejiro and Obiora were like, enemies in the first few episodes, yet now they seem really close? 👀 Like they're always standing or sitting next to each other plus the water taxi tour?? Did y'all catch the way they were looking at each other, especially Obiora? Or am I reaching?? 👀

 13101   5539

ARCTICBOOB

TYLER WAS ELIMINATED NOOOOOOOOOOOOOOOOO Edit: WHY IS EVERYONE SAYING THEY HAD NO CHEMISTRY LMFAO YOU'RE SO MEAN

 12000   5107

 **YRSNYRS__**

Jin can punt my lake any time xD Edit: I am sorry

 11901   7538

REDTEMPTS

Okay, we're halfway through the season, who's your top three so far?👀 I'm thinking Noah, Chris Wu, and maybe Ejiro (though after this episode, Jin is a high contender as well for me lol) Edit: I said Ejiro because of the amount of times he's been given the Red Heart, plus I personally feel after the kiss thing and Sophia apologising, it seems like their relationship has strengthened, but that's just my opinion.

 10066   4893

LOAD MORE COMMENTS ⌄

TWENTY

DESPITE THE FACT THAT OBIORA knew they were going to be filming bright and early today, he and Ejiro hadn't slept until the wee hours of the morning. After their illicit impromptu visit to the canal, Obiora hadn't wanted the night to end, and Ejiro seemed to have felt the same way, because they'd spent the rest of the night talking.

Obiora didn't think he'd ever felt so vulnerable, two of them with the lights off, eyes bright in the darkness, lying on their sides and facing each other, with only an arm's length of space between them.

The bonding from their time at the canal plus the darkness had felt comforting somehow, which had led to them talking about things Obiora was sure they would never have spoken about in the light of day.

"I've never said this out loud before," Ejiro whispered, "but each time I think about how I don't want to go back home—each time I so much as *think* of telling my mum—I end up feeling so—so *guilty* that I just freeze up."

Obiora had felt a little alarmed. "Is she—?" he began, then stopped, not knowing how to phrase himself. He didn't want to be indelicate.

Ejiro seemed to understand where he was coming from, because he shook his head almost violently. "Don't—I know how it seems—but it's not—she's not abusive or anything. That's not why I—I mean, she's never hit us, not once."

Obiora could feel his heart breaking. "Abuse doesn't have to be physical, Ejiro."

Ejiro didn't seem ready to hear it. "I just don't want to abandon her. That's it."

"Why do you think not going home means you're abandoning her?" Obiora prodded gently. "You can always visit—or she can come visit you."

Ejiro had looked down at the space between them. "You don't understand. All her life, she's done everything alone. Ever since my father died, despite being completely shut out from her family, despite all the obstacles she faced—a single mother in Nigeria—she did her best for me and Ajiri. Without her ... I don't know where I'd be." The words sounded slightly stilted, rehearsed—like Ejiro had said those exact words to himself over and over again until they became a mantra. "This is the one thing she's asked of me. *One* thing. Surely I can do just one thing?"

Even that didn't sound like Ejiro talking—it sounded like his mother talking *through* him.

It sounded very much like emotional manipulation. But Obiora didn't know enough about the situation to make a judgement.

Instead, he tried again to be delicate. "I understand where you're coming from, Ejiro. But all those things she did, she did *for* you. Those are the things our parents are supposed to do; want the best for us. Love us. Care for us." Ejiro was shaking his head, like he'd heard it all before. From his twin, most likely, since he'd mentioned arguing about this exact topic with her before. Obiora switched tactics. "Do you think she'd be happy if she knew you were only doing this out of some misplaced sense of guilt?"

Ejiro had paused, then remained quiet. Obiora had let him. He probably needed some time for it to sink in.

Obiora ended up reflecting on his own words, and felt them smack him in the face like running face-first into a brick wall.

Christ. Obiora was a fucking hypocrite. When it seemed like Ejiro wasn't going to say anything further, he decided to speak.

"Know what *I've* never said out loud before?" he whispered, his heartbeat racing madly in his chest. "Since we're being honest and all."

Ejiro rolled his eyes, but his expression was fond. He looked grateful that the focus was no longer on him. "What?"

"I want to leave my job." The words came out in a rush. Obiora couldn't quite meet Ejiro's eyes. Even then, millions of miles away from home and his father's ears, Obiora felt flooded with guilt at the admission. Fuck. Maybe he could understand Ejiro a little better. "It's not ... horrible, per se." Obiora exhaled aggressively. "Okay, that's a lie."

Ejiro laughed a little, a soft intimate sound in the darkness. "So, why don't you? Leave, I mean."

Obiora had to swallow a few times to get the words out. He was suddenly grateful for the faux intimacy of the darkness, because—even though his and Ejiro's eyes had adjusted already, and they could see each other clearly—he could pretend he was alone when he spoke again.

"When Ada died," he began thickly, "I was ... lost. My father was the one who brought me out of the worst of my depression and self-imposed isolation. He gave me a job at his firm. Going through the motions, obeying his orders, being the best—it became like therapy to me. Because of him, I was able to find myself again."

"Aw, Obiora," Ejiro cooed, the empathy in his voice making Obiora feel warm all over. "Let me guess," he continued, sweetly amused. "You feel like you'll be betraying his kindness—or something along those lines—if you decide to just up and leave."

"Got it in one." Obiora laughed, some of the heaviness leaving his chest. "Like, my guy is already writing the future of the company with me and my brothers' names on it. Woe betide me if I end up breaking his heart."

Ejiro laughed lightly. "Well. Now you see where I'm coming from," he said smugly.

"I guess," Obiora hedged.

Ejiro hit him with one of the pillows. Obiora laughed.

"I don't think your dad would want you to feel guilty, Obiora," Ejiro said softly. "He did this—he gave you the job because he cared about you, not because he wanted you to owe him for it."

Obiora raised a pointed eyebrow. "You're preaching to the choir, Ejiro."

Ejiro blushed guiltily. "Yeah, yeah. Okay. I hear you. What would you do, then?" he asked, smoothly changing the subject. "If you quit your job today, what would you do?"

"Oh," Obiora said, pulse suddenly fluttering. "Yet another thing I've never admitted out loud."

"Oh? I must be special then, eh?" Ejiro waggled his eyebrows.

Obiora's heart did something devastating. Who was this suddenly flirtatious Ejiro, and where had he been hiding? "I will slap you."

Ejiro laughed. Obiora wanted him so badly it felt like heartache.

"I'm sorry," Ejiro said between laughs. "I'm sorry." He cleared his throat. "Please continue."

Obiora sighed, shaking his head, but he was smiling. "I want to be a personal trainer."

"Yeah?" Ejiro encouraged, sounding genuinely interested. "Like Esther?"

Obiora felt the usual warmth at hearing his best friend's name in Ejiro's mouth. It made Obiora's feelings for him intensify—made this thing between them feel that more tangible.

"Yup," Obiora admitted. "While working for my father helped a lot to distract me from my grief, there were still the long nights and even longer weekends to account for. I didn't want to bother my family any more than I already had, so I took to walking."

It had been mid-June, probably, about three months after Ada's funeral, after his father had managed to finally pull him out of his self-imposed isolation. His family had gone all the way down to London to help him move out of the house he'd shared so briefly with his late girlfriend, and when he'd refused to move back into his parents' house—he'd been terrified he'd never be able to leave again if he did—they'd helped him sign the rental agreement for a flat in Sheffield.

But the place had felt so fucking alien and so fucking empty. Working all day at his father's office had helped, but the evenings and the nights and the weekends had been awful. Not wanting his family to worry, Obiora had practically taken to running out of the building almost on autopilot every single day after work, wandering the hilly Sheffield streets until he was so exhausted he collapsed the moment he headed back home. It was on one of those days he'd stumbled, entirely by accident, on the small, private gym that was *Isi Fitness*, hidden as it was within a small, residential area off the main streets.

He'd spotted the poster on the outside wall beside the single, glass door holding the image of a punching bag, and remembered thinking, *yeah, actually, I'd really fucking like to punch something*. Esther had met him like that—her family owned the gym, but she'd only just gotten her own licence back then—and she'd taught him how to use the gym to channel his grief in a healthier way, instead of using it as something self-destructive. After that, the gym had kind of become his second home.

"It wasn't like I always wanted to be a personal trainer or whatever; the desire kind of snuck up on me. I noticed a lot of folks struggling during my time at the gym, and found myself going over to help them out. Then they kept coming back to me for advice, or updating me on their progress. Then they referred me to their friends." Obiora shook his head a little, smiling as he recalled when Mrs. Rhysand, one of the regulars, had come back with her sister-in-law, touting loudly about how sweet and patient Obiora was, the best personal trainer she'd ever had. The mix of embarrassment and pride he'd felt at that moment—he'd never forget it. "Some of them had apparently thought I worked there." Ejiro laughed. Obiora grinned. "Esther, naturally, took advantage of that."

"Of course," Ejiro said, amused.

Obiora grinned wider. "She pretended to come late for her classes, which usually left me in charge. And I—well, when I began to do it for real, without pretending I was just being a nice neighbour—well. I love it. I absolutely adore it. At this point, Esther's just waiting for me to give her the greenlight, so I can have my own class."

Ejiro's eyes were bright, shining. He was staring at Obiora like he'd hung the moon.

Overwhelmed—afraid, suddenly, Obiora abruptly flung his hand out between them. "Let's make a pact."

The movement startled Ejiro out of whatever he was feeling, and he blinked, looked away, a little self-conscious.

When he met Obiora's eyes once more, his emotions were gone, carefully shuttered away. Obiora felt a pang of painful regret.

"A pact?" Ejiro repeated, raising both eyebrows.

"Yup." Obiora wiggled his fingers.

Ejiro reached out and joined their hands.

Obiora sucked in a sharp breath at the lack of hesitation, the complete trust in the gesture. He took a moment to compose himself.

"Let's promise," he began, "that when this is all over—when we get back home, we'll tell our parents how we really feel."

Ejiro swallowed visibly. His hand squeezed around Obiora's reflexively, subconsciously. "I—"

He was afraid. Terrified, even. It was in his eyes.

Obiora knew exactly how he felt. The thought of telling his father he wanted to leave—and to become a personal trainer, as well—felt like he was shoving the man's kindness back up his own ass. But that was just his fears—that was just him projecting.

He gave Ejiro's hand an encouraging squeeze.

"Continuing like this isn't stable," Obiora whispered. "For either of us. Something's got to give. If our parents get upset, then that's okay. They won't be upset forever. But if we keep on like this? That's our *lives* we're talking about, Ejiro. Our happiness." His voice grew stronger with conviction the more he spoke.

Ejiro took in a shuddering breath. He closed his eyes, but he nodded.

"Okay," he said hoarsely, eyes still closed. "Okay. I will. I'll tell her. I promise."

"I promise," Obiora echoed.

He gave Ejiro's hand another squeeze. Ejiro squeezed back. Ejiro didn't let go immediately afterward, instead holding Obiora's hand for a few heart stopping moments, before slowly sliding his hand out of Obiora's grasp. Obiora missed the touch instantly.

Ejiro's eyelids fluttered open. "We should probably go to sleep," he whispered.

"Yeah," Obiora said, ignoring the desperate pounding of his heart.

Ejiro smiled tentatively. "Goodnight, Obiora."

"Goodnight, Ejiro."

They'd watched each other, eyes locked, breaths in sync, until they'd fallen asleep. Obiora didn't even know if he'd fallen asleep first, or if it had been Ejiro. All he knew was that something had passed between them, something so sweet and so fragile, that when Obiora had woken up the next morning, the universe at large felt bigger, *brighter*.

They were in the big house now, outside on the veranda where the round dining table could take all seven of them. Dean was the only one missing, currently in the small house with Ameri and the crew, filming his cutaways for the previous date.

"This is beginning to feel real, isn't it?" Jin murmured during a lull in conversation.

"What, it didn't feel real before?" Noah teased lightly.

Jin limply waved a hand. "You know what I mean. There's only eight of us left—it'll be down to six after the next episode. Soon, we're going to go back to our real lives. It's a little ... jarring, isn't it?"

Noah nodded. "Yeah, yeah. I understand what you're saying."

Ejiro was different when he was in the company of the other men, Obiora had noticed. He'd gotten so used to seeing Ejiro relaxed and teasing and carefree, that seeing him behave more subdued when he was around the other men suddenly reminded Obiora that Ejiro was actually quite a reserved person.

Until you got to know him, that is. The thought filled him with an indescribable heat, something almost possessive. That Obiora had seen sides to Ejiro *none* of the other men had, had Obiora's chest feeling too small to contain his heart.

Ejiro noticed him staring and smiled shyly, tentatively, before looking away, his blush obvious in the helpless curve of his mouth, the slow, hypnotic sweep of his eyelashes. Obiora's entire *being* trembled with want.

Ejiro glanced at him again, like he couldn't help it, his blush deepening when he found Obiora still watching him.

And Obiora knew it then, viscerally, though some part of him must've known it all along, subconsciously, that it was inevitable.

He'd gone ahead and fallen in love.

ONE THING THAT HAD BEEN awful at the start, but the men had eventually gotten used to, was making sure most—if not all—of their things remained packed at all times, because one never knew when they would be eliminated. One of them had already been eliminated during a date, after all, and the Heart ceremony wasn't a safe bet either.

Take now, for example.

"Jesus," Damien muttered, standing, when Alistair appeared with his luggage, followed by one of the cameramen.

Alistair was grinning, seemingly unbothered. "Guess my time here is up, boys."

"It was a good run," Jin said, also standing up.

The rest of the men followed, Ejiro included.

"Gonna give us a hint about what's going on out there?" Dean asked with a teasing glint in his eyes.

Alistair laughed. "Sorry. My lips are sealed. Ameri'll be coming in a bit for the next of you, so prepare yourselves." He winked.

He gave them all brief hugs, then he was gone, just like that.

"Jesus," Damien repeated.

Only one of the bachelors had been eliminated during a date—homophobic Hunter from episode three—but it hadn't felt like this. They hadn't actually *seen* Hunter leave with his bags; by the time the filming was up and they'd gone back to the mansion, he was already gone, and when the other men were eliminated, it was during a Heart ceremony, which was just as abrupt, but less jarring because it was expected.

"Now what the fuck do you suppose is going on out there?" Dean asked again. He glanced at Chris Wu, Jin, Noah, and Damien, who'd already filmed their part of the episode earlier in the day.

"Apologies," Jin said, sounding truly apologetic. "We were instructed not to talk about it."

"What he said," Chris Wu added with a nod and a carefree grin. "Don't worry your heads too much. It isn't *completely* awful."

"That doesn't help at all," Dean groaned, making some of them laugh.

Ameri had said this week's episode was a surprise. She'd had the men dress semi-formally, and that was about all the hint they'd been given before they were essentially confined to the sitting room of the bigger house, with explicit instructions not to go anywhere but the bathroom or kitchen.

Ameri and crew had then taken over the long veranda outside that connected the two houses, using the dining area outside for the filming. It was a beautiful spot, Ejiro had to admit, with the domed metal frame covering the space, along with the vines and flowers crawling through the covering. It almost felt like the greenhouse back in the mansion in Oxford.

The men were taken one by one to film with Sophia. Ejiro tried and failed to picture what the episode could be about. They'd all had one on one dates with the bachelorette at this point, so it couldn't just be an ordinary date. Since they were all filming in the same location, that meant there had to be a specific theme to the "dates".

"Any ideas?"

Ejiro nearly jumped at the sound of the voice in his ear. He glanced at Obiora, unable to help it, and felt his stomach do cartwheels when their eyes met.

"Nope. None at all," he said, looking away quickly, grateful his dark skin hid the blush burning his cheeks.

Ever since the night of the canal, since he and Obiora had spent all night talking, something between them seemed to have shifted. There was the heady attraction, of course—which, to Ejiro's dismay, seemed to be reciprocated—but there were other things even more dangerous, at least to Ejiro.

He found that afterward, whenever he met Obiora's eyes, even when they were standing right next to each other as they were now, he felt this inexplicable need to be *closer*, to somehow merge their bodies so closely that he didn't know where he began and Obiora ended. It was like Obiora was his centre of gravity, and Ejiro was exhausted from trying to resist the pull.

Sensual attraction, Obiora had called it. It led to him trying to avoid Obiora, and failing because he ultimately ended up missing him. Ejiro just didn't share the same intimate, carefree rapport with any of the other men, which served to make his growing feelings for Obiora seem starker in contrast.

"Ejiro." That was Ameri, her heels muffled on the carpeted floor as she walked into the room. There was a tiny smile on her lips. "You're up."

"Here we go," Ejiro muttered under his breath.

His nerves must've shown, because Obiora reached out and gave his shoulder a friendly squeeze. "I'm sure it'll be fine."

Ejiro was blushing again, unable to meet his eyes. "Right, thank you." The part of his shoulder that Obiora touched burned—in fact, every *inch* of him burned, desperate to be within Obiora's embrace.

"Come on, chop chop!" Ameri clapped her hands.

Ejiro couldn't help but glance at Obiora as he made his way out, and found Obiora already watching him, something soft in his expression.

Oh.

Ejiro was in so much trouble.

TURNED OUT, THIS WEEK'S SURPRISE episode was a visit from Sasha Pierce, a famous celebrity counsellor slash therapist. She was known for "fixing" failing celebrity relationships, getting celebs into and out of rehab, and even handling the aftermath of the occasional celebrity divorce.

"Do you think the reason you don't want to share anything more intimate with Sophia, is because of what Sam put you through?" Sasha had asked after she'd practically torn the story of Ejiro's past relationship from his lips.

Even now, hearing the echo of her voice in his head made Ejiro feel like punching something. Sasha had apparently been filming with them right from the start, but she'd kind of blended into the background with the rest of the multitude of staff they normally had on set, so no one had noticed. She'd been following all their interactions with Sophia closely, so she could dissect them for this episode.

Ejiro didn't know how to feel. On the one hand, he could understand why Ameri had wanted this to be a surprise—so the men wouldn't mentally form shields or pretend during the filming or whatever when it came to their turn. On the other hand, he felt completely blindsided, and it left him feeling awful, like Sasha had violently ripped his skin back to see what was underneath.

It had helped only a little that Sasha didn't focus entirely on him during the filming; she focused on Sophia as well, on how the bachelorette had handled the relationship between her and Ejiro so far, and what they could *both* do to make it better.

The whole thing left Ejiro feeling scraped raw. Which was why he'd disobeyed Ameri's orders to stay in the big house after his filming, and had ended up in the garden instead. Noticing his discomfiture—and probably thinking it might look good for the cameras if some of the men disappeared—Ameri had let him go.

There was some seating underneath the roofed extension of the terrace from the house, held up with pretty baroque pillars, which was where Ejiro found himself.

Sasha hadn't directly called him names, but she'd implied a lot of things. That Ejiro was still harbouring hurt from his last relationship, which was why he was reluctant to form anything more intimate with Sophia. That he wasn't shy but insecure, and projecting a lot of his issues with Sam onto Sophia.

No, it's because I'm demisexual, and I see Sophia as nothing but a friend.

He was still tentative about labelling himself out loud, but the words had rung, sure and true in his head.

He knew the second he came out, so to speak, Sophia would be sending him home. At this point in the competition, he wasn't supposed to *still* be feeling platonically about her. They were literally three episodes away from the finale, and most of the other men seemed half in love—if not fully in love—with Sophia already.

But Ejiro had finally accepted it to himself that his feelings for her were always going to remain platonic.

Things might've been different if it hadn't been for that awful kiss. After it, Ejiro just couldn't feel comfortable around her anymore, at least, not enough to see or want her sexually or romantically. Though he couldn't say he hadn't tried.

There was also the matter of Obiora. *Fuck*, Obiora. Ejiro scrubbed his hands over his face.

He was in trouble. So much trouble.

Like his thoughts had summoned him, there Obiora was, stalking down the steps that led to the garden. He must've finished filming already. So quickly? Christ, how long had Ejiro been down here?

Obiora didn't spot Ejiro at first, pacing around the twisting cobblestones, only stopping abruptly when he noticed him.

Then Ejiro properly took in the tortured look on his face. His heart dropped into his stomach.

"Obiora?" he gasped, shoving out of his seat and closing the distance between them. "What's wrong? Are you okay? What happened?"

"Fucking *Sasha Pierce*, that's what," Obiora growled, and continued pacing. "Telling me I've built barriers around myself because of Ada's death." Ejiro's heart cracked into tiny little pieces at the pure anguish in his voice. "I mean, nothing she said was a lie, I knew it already, but fuck her. *Fuck* her." He laughed, almost maniacally. "I'm probably going to be eliminated after this. And I don't even fucking care."

Panic encompassed Ejiro's being at the thought of Obiora leaving. They hadn't even had a chance to figure things out between them—

if there *were* things to figure out.

But that wasn't important right now. Ejiro's need to heal whatever hurt Obiora was feeling took precedence.

"Obiora," he said, soft but firm. "What do you need?"

Anything, Ejiro thought desperately. *Absolutely anything, and I'll give it to you.*

"I still celebrate her birthday, did you know that?" Obiora said abruptly. He stalked to the roofed edge of the garden before Ejiro could respond, like he was suddenly in need of cover. "Ada," he clarified when Ejiro followed after him. This corner of the garden did feel more private, and Ejiro was glad to notice Obiora's harsh breathing had slowed down. "I do it secretly, and I do it on my own, because I don't want my family to worry. I don't want them to see that I'm broken."

"Obiora," Ejiro whispered, choked. The admission hurt, like an arrow to Ejiro's heart, the thought of Obiora mourning his lost love by himself, and because of what?

"I mourn during our anniversaries. I cry for what could have been. The wound hasn't healed; I just learned to fucking live with it. I miss her *every* fucking day. And I know that I will *never* stop loving her. But if I ever want to be with someone new? Then I'll have to let her go." He bit back an anguished sob. Ejiro's own eyes burned. "Trust me, I've *been* there. I met someone new. I thought I was in love. But how could I say, with utmost confidence, that I was in love with him, when I still ached so much for her? How was it fair to my new partner, that I still celebrate my anniversaries with a dead girl"—he spat the words viciously, but they didn't sound like his own—"that I refuse to overwrite my history with her, because I don't want to lose even a tiny bit of her? He proposed to me, on the anniversary of her accident." Ejiro sucked in a sharp, furious breath. He *what*? "He wanted to overwrite my history with her with something new, something happy and positive. And I went *ballistic*." Obiora laughed again. "How dare my new boyfriend want all my love and attention for himself, right?" he said mockingly. "And I thought—God, I thought—" He shook his head violently. "More fool me. I've always known he was right, and fucking Sasha Pierce is right; I can't let her go, which means it's impossible for me to truly love someone new."

He stared at Ejiro as he said those last words, like they were a confession. Ejiro's chest went tight and hot. He was shaking.

"That's bullshit."

Obiora blinked in surprise at the vehemence in his tone.

Good.

"Do you hear me? That's fucking *bullshit*. You have to let her go? That's fucking bullshit, Obiora."

"I—" Obiora was staring at him, eyes wide and wet.

"She was a huge part of your life—she still *is* a huge part of your life," Ejiro said harshly, wanting furiously to imprint the words on Obiora's brain. "Do you think your emotionally manipulative ex—or fucking *Sasha Pierce*, would say the same thing if it was one of your parents that died? Or your brothers? Or even Esther? If you celebrated *their* birthdays and *their* anniversaries, or mourned on the days you lost them, they'd *understand*, because they know how those people shaped your life. If someone proposed to me on the anniversary of Ajiri's death, *God forbid*, I'd stab them in the fucking face. The fucking *disrespect*, Obiora. It's the exact same thing with Ada, I promise you. You grew up with her. You fell in love. And before you could start your life together, the world snatched her away from you. Of course you still love her." Fuck, Ejiro was crying. "Why? Is it because it's romantic, that it's suddenly different? *Why*?"

"Ejiro," Obiora whispered. Tears glinted on his cheeks, silent and heart wrenching. "Ejiro."

Ejiro stepped closer, hands clenched into fists to stop their trembling. "Obiora, you are more than capable of loving her while *still* loving someone else—in fact, you clearly already *have* loved someone else, though he didn't deserve it." Ejiro's eyes flashed with pure hatred at the thought of Obiora's ex. The monopolising self-centred *bastard*. "I don't care what anyone else says or thinks, but grief is grief, love is love. And you don't—" He took a shaky breath. "You *don't* have to choose."

"Oh, fuck." Obiora shook. "Ejiro. Ejiro." His name fell from Obiora's lips like a prayer; a plea.

"Yes? Yes?" Ejiro answered just as passionately, stepping even closer. Their eyes were locked. Electricity crackled between them like lightning. "Anything. *Anything.*"

"*Please,*" Obiora begged brokenly. "Kiss me."

Ejiro sucked in a trembling breath. Then he flew forward, crashing into Obiora's arms, joining their lips desperately. Obiora yanked him closer, pressing their bodies together more fully, making Ejiro shudder with pleasure and desire.

Obiora's lips were soft and plush, the feel of them seriously short-circuiting Ejiro's brain. Ejiro hadn't even realised just how badly he'd wanted Obiora's kiss until their lips met, and it felt like Ejiro's entire world came to an abrupt halt, his universe exploding with a multitude of bright stars.

His hands fisted at the back of Obiora's shirt, and his heart raced like a rabbit's, his breaths short and frantic. Obiora had one hand at the small of Ejiro's back with his palm spread wide and flat, like he wanted to touch as much of Ejiro as he could, while his other hand was on Ejiro's upper back, holding him steady. Ejiro *needed* to be steadied; it felt like his legs were slowly turning to jelly.

Their mouths moulded furiously as they hungrily explored the shape and feel of each other's lips, Ejiro gasping when Obiora pulled his bottom lip between his teeth and *tugged*. Ejiro let out a truly embarrassing sound, his hips jolting.

Obiora licked away the sting, then the hand on his upper back moved up, cupping the back of Ejiro's head and angling it slightly so Obiora could lick *into* Ejiro's mouth, his tongue sliding in hot and wet. Ejiro just about died on the spot, electrocuted from head to toe by the illicit sensation. He pressed impossibly closer, instinctively sucking Obiora's tongue deeper into his mouth and licking *back*, tangling their tongues, making Obiora shake and groan.

Obiora tasted like salt from their tears; he tasted like heat and passion and desire. His hands moved to grip Ejiro's hips, anchoring him as he slid one of his powerful thighs between Ejiro's legs. Ejiro made another embarrassing sobbing sound, instinctively rocking his hips, his nails clawing at Obiora's back.

God, please. Fuck. Yes. More, *please—don't stop, don't stop, don't stop.*

"Obiora? Are you down here?"

They jumped apart, panting.

Ameri's heels clacked loudly as she made her way down the stone steps.

Ejiro quickly sat on one of the chairs and tried to control his breathing. Fuck, he was shaking. His mouth was still wet; *swollen*, tingling. He quickly wiped his eyes, where he could feel his tears drying rapidly on his cheeks. Obiora did the same, then scrubbed a hand roughly over his mouth. God, that fucking devastating mouth.

"Oh," Ameri said when she noticed Obiora wasn't alone. "You guys all right?"

"Fine," Obiora clipped, his voice hoarse. He looked flushed, his mouth devastatingly pink, but it could be blamed on something else. Probably, hopefully.

"Good, good," Ejiro echoed. He didn't look directly at either of them. *Couldn't* look directly at either of them, sure his desire for Obiora still burned, obvious in every tense inch of him.

"Obiora, can I talk to you for a moment? Ejiro, could you excuse us, please?"

Ejiro met Obiora's gaze. Obiora nodded slightly.

At the confirmation, Ejiro stood. "Right, then."

He turned and walked away, even though he wanted to touch Obiora's arm, or his shoulder—*anything* to reassure him. But he was too afraid that Ameri might read into the touch, so he didn't.

As he walked away, he felt an inexplicable pull to the man behind him, made even worse now that Ejiro had tasted the pure blazing passion that was his kiss.

TWENTY-ONE

"**ARE YOU ALL RIGHT?**" **AMERI** asked after Ejiro left, her voice unusually tentative. "You seemed upset after your talk with Sophia. I thought I should check on you."

No, I'm not all right.

"I'm fine," he said.

He couldn't quite meet her eyes, and knew the way he was clenching and unclenching his fists contradicted his words, but he didn't want to talk to her about his feelings right now.

All he could think about was the burning heat in Ejiro's eyes, the intimate press of their bodies together, the feel of Ejiro's tongue shyly but passionately licking into his mouth, and the way the movement had set Obiora on fire. The vehement way Ejiro had defended Obiora's right to mourn his lost love—his belief that Obiora didn't—*shouldn't* have to choose.

Fuck, fuck, fuck. Obiora loved him. He fucking *loved* him.

"Look, I thought maybe I should apologise," Ameri continued, straightening her shoulders. "Sasha might be a therapist, but she's still a celebrity." Ameri smiled wryly. "It's highly likely she might've deliberately pushed you and Sophia in order to get a reaction."

"Right. No, I get it."

Sasha Pierce had nailed Obiora's relationship with Sophia right on the head: "You two have *amazing* chemistry, don't get me wrong, but I feel like both of you are—for some reason—unwilling to cross that final bridge—really *cement* things between you, you know?"

Yeah, because I'm not in love with Sophia.

But Obiora obviously wasn't going to admit that on live TV, not if he wanted to remain in the competition—and he did, desperately. His motivation for staying now had completely changed; he wanted to spend as much time as he could with Ejiro before the real world came knocking.

After Sasha's mild accusation, Sophia had admitted she put up walls with Obiora because she'd dated guys like him before—cocky, sexy, and self-assured—and men like that had always hurt her in the end.

Obiora had in turn used Ada as a shield, even as guilt had swamped him the second he had. He'd talked about Ada the way he usually did, briefly and flippantly, like he didn't hurt anymore. But Sasha wasn't famous in her field for nothing, and she'd cracked him open like an egg.

"I don't know, Obiora. It feels to me like you're not over her," she'd said, point blank. Obiora's mouth had clicked shut. As the silence had stretched, she'd used the opportunity to continue, "I just feel that like Sophia, you've built barriers around your heart because of your ex-girlfriend's death."

His first instinct had been to placate, to deny, to change the subject. But for some reason, Ejiro's face had flashed in his mind's eye—the gentle, respectful way he always spoke about Ada, treating her death with the gravity Obiora had forgotten she'd deserved—and years of his grief being smothered and discarded and treated like trash built up in that microsecond until something within Obiora had snapped.

"She's not my *ex-girlfriend*." He'd sneered, startling both Sasha and Sophia with his venom. Everyone always used "ex-girlfriend" to diminish the impact Ada's death had had on his life. And Obiora was fucking done. "She was my *girlfriend*, and then she *died*."

Their matching looks of shock—though they'd instantly tried to mask it—had immediately made him panic. He'd taken a breath and apologised for his outburst, but it was too late. Sasha had taken his defensiveness as an admission of guilt, and had used it to put him on the spot.

"I don't mean to be indelicate, Obiora, I really don't—but please understand where I'm coming from. How can you expect to fully commit yourself to Sophia when, by all accounts, you're literally in love with someone else?"

Obiora hadn't known how to respond, because she was right, wasn't she? And the fact that she was right had filled him with a weird mixture of rage and grief, because just a day ago, he'd thought he'd fallen in love with Ejiro. But could he truly love Ejiro while he still loved Ada?

After her question—which was obviously rhetorical—Obiora had gone quiet, letting Sophia do all the talking until their time with the therapist ended. Then he'd immediately walked away.

Sophia, bless her fucking heart, had rushed after him, both of them ignoring the cameras and crew that quickly trailed after them.

"Are you okay?" she'd asked, obviously genuinely worried. At the question, Obiora wished they could be friends when this all was over, though he knew that probably wouldn't happen. "That was kind of intense, wasn't it?" she added playfully, trying to lighten the mood.

Obiora didn't even *consider* being vulnerable with her. All his walls had built themselves up instead, reinforcing themselves with steel.

He'd grinned, wide and forcefully carefree, opening his arms so she could give him a hug. "I'm good, don't worry. Sasha means business, doesn't she? Jeez."

Sophia had laughed, none the wiser. "Right? Fucking hell, I

thought I was being cross-examined for like—murder or something. Therapy is pretty invasive, isn't it? But I guess that's the point."

"Mhm."

"You know I don't care, right?" she'd said suddenly, pulling out of his arms, looking him in the eye. "I don't care if you're still—I mean, if you—that is, what matters to me, is how you feel about *me*, if you get me?"

At first, he'd frowned with confusion. Then with a surprising amount of disappointment, Obiora understood.

He was allowed to be sad, or even love Ada a little, but Sophia had to *always* come first. Which was understandable. But her dancing around the subject—her hesitation to actually *name* what it was that Obiora was feeling—to not even mention Ada by name at all, had Obiora's fury and irritation building once more.

"Yeah, I get you," he'd said, forcing a smile.

Sophia had heaved a sigh of relief, oblivious. "Good. That's good. I'll see you later?"

After that, Obiora had walked off. He'd been too antsy to go back into the house, so he'd ended up in the garden.

And one look from Ejiro, one heart-shattering question from his lips—*Obiora, what do you need?*—and all of Obiora's walls had simply crumbled to dust.

And *God*. Ejiro was right. The world *did* expect Obiora to move on just because his relationship with Ada had been romantic. They treated Ada's death like—like it was some kind of *breakup*—and a pretty insignificant one at that—I mean, Sasha had called Ada his *ex-girlfriend* for fuck's sake—instead of treating it like something monumental—something so devastating it had changed the shape of his heart irreparably.

"Still." Ameri's voice brought Obiora back to the present. "If Sasha brought up any bad memories, or made you feel some type of way, I apologise. I just thought—"

"Look, it's fine," Obiora interrupted. "I promise. I'm good. I'm okay."

Ameri didn't look convinced. "If you're sure."

"I'm sure."

Ameri sighed. "Then I won't push. I'm sorry, either way. We'll be reconvening in the big sitting room in a few minutes if you still need some time to collect yourself."

"Got it."

"See you in a bit, then."

Ameri turned around and walked away.

Obiora waited a beat. Then a few more. It didn't seem like Ejiro was going to return, which made Obiora feel equal parts relieved and disappointed.

Relieved because he didn't know what the fuck he would do—or say—if he saw Ejiro right now, and disappointed because, well, Obiora wanted to kiss him again. Badly. It had been so long since anything in Obiora's life had felt as right—as fucking *perfect*—as that kiss had.

You don't have to choose.

"Fuck." Obiora scrubbed his hands over his face, said hands trembling slightly.

Behind his ribs, his heart felt so fucking *big*.

AS EJIRO LEFT THE GARDEN, he didn't go back to the room he shared with Obiora, too shaken after that earth-shattering kiss, too afraid of what he'd do if he ended up there and Obiora followed him and they ended up alone. *Together.* The thought filled him with unbearable heat—a scorching desire he was in no way ready to deal with.

He could still feel the press of Obiora's soft mouth on his own, the scrape of Obiora's barely-there stubble against his chin and cheeks, the sensual wet heat of Obiora's tongue inside his mouth—Obiora's thick thigh between his legs—

Oh dear God.

He frantically shoved the memories down, increasing his pace, like he could run from the lingering taste of Obiora in his mouth.

When he got to the sitting room of the big house, the rest of the men were there. The air was slightly heavy, probably due to the fact that the men now knew what the episode was about, but by some kind of silent agreement, none of them were talking about it.

On his way here, through the terrace that connected the two houses and led to the garden, Ejiro had seen that a majority of the crew were still on the veranda of the big house. Ameri and Sophia were in a far corner at the very end of the terrace, talking lowly, while the crew seemed to be on a break, chatting amongst each other and checking their equipment.

"Ejiro, you all right?" Jin asked when there was a lull in their conversation.

Ejiro startled, realising he was just standing there by the door leading into the sitting room like a cow, lost in thought.

He shook himself and walked in further, taking a seat on one of the free armchairs. "No. I mean, yeah. Yes. I'm fine. I'm all right. How are you guys doing?"

There were echoes of assent from the men.

"We were just saying," Jin said, "we highly suspect Alistair might not have been very receptive to Sasha Pierce, hence his sudden elimination this afternoon."

"Right." Ejiro nodded. "That makes sense."

"And is completely understandable," Jin said with slight amusement. "Honestly? I don't feel Ameri went about this the right way at all. It takes a lot in people to even *consider* therapy on a normal day; it is such a personal decision. So, springing one on us, just like that? Not a good look, in my opinion."

"Yeah, I get it." Ejiro hummed neutrally. He inwardly agreed with Jin, but he felt guilty if he said it out loud. He was realising that he'd unfortunately put Ameri on a pedestal, and it felt awful to imagine that she wasn't actually perfect. Of course she wasn't, she was only human. But he couldn't help how he felt.

Obiora appeared at that moment, stepping in through the open veranda doors. Ejiro's heart stopped beating at the sight of him, and then resumed at a frantic pace.

Obiora met his eyes for a brief second. Ejiro's breath caught in his throat.

"You okay, Obiora?" Dean asked, making Obiora look away, thank God. "It seems like you and Ejiro took today's filming a lot harder than the rest of us, seeing as you both disappeared after."

Obiora waved him off. "Nah, I'm fine. I did need a breather, you're right about that, but it isn't anything to worry about."

Oh, Obiora, Ejiro thought, his chest twisting painfully. Did he always do this? Downplay his feelings, especially when it came to Ada? It made Ejiro want to bundle him in a nest of blankets and hide him away from the world.

You don't need to hide from me. Never.

Like he could hear the words, Obiora glanced at him again. His dark eyes burned with all the things left untouched and unsaid between them, and Ejiro trembled with it.

"Hey, y'all!"

Ameri's voice broke them out of their stare down, nearly making Ejiro fly out of his skin, his heart racing now for a different reason.

Sophia followed in behind the director slash producer, and Ejiro felt his stomach plummet.

The bachelorette's eyes and nose were a little puffy and red. The other men seemed to notice how she looked at the same time, because they all stood up in alarm. Behind them, coming in from the veranda, some of the crew had their cameras on, red lights blinking.

At the sight of the bachelorette, Ejiro felt a swamp of guilt. It didn't matter that he felt platonically for her, it still wasn't fair of him to kiss someone else behind her back, especially when she was hoping for something solid to form between them.

Oh God. He couldn't look in Obiora's direction.

"Sophia, are you okay?" Noah asked before the rest of them could.

"I'm fine, I'm fine." Sophia tried to wave them off. Her voice was hoarse. She stood off to the side, away from the men, hugging her arms around her chest. "Ameri has something to say."

It hit Ejiro suddenly, that if the therapy sessions had hit the men hard, how bad must it have been for Sophia, who'd had to go through it *eight* times?

"I owe you all an apology," Ameri said before the men could press further. "This episode was supposed to be a bonding episode between you and the bachelorette. Sasha was meant to reveal what wasn't working between y'all and Sophia, and give advice on how you could make it better. But instead … it turned into this. I'm very sorry."

The men were silent for a moment.

"It's all right." Jin finally spoke. "I appreciate the apology. It would have been better that we were warned so we could mentally prepare, rather than it being a surprise, that's all."

"You're absolutely right." Ameri nodded. "Anyone else have anything to say?"

Ejiro couldn't help but glance at Obiora. Obiora wasn't looking at Ameri, or anyone else, his eyes instead focused on the wall. Ejiro bit his lip.

It seemed Jin had said everything.

"All right." Ameri clapped her hands. "I'll let y'all say goodnight to Sophia."

"Goodnight hugs, then?" Noah asked, smiling a little.

"Yeah."

"Sounds good."

More sounds of agreement echoed around the room.

"Sophia?" Chris Wu prodded gently.

Sophia sniffed, then shrugged, smiling a little. "Yeah, sure, all right."

The men grinned, walking up to her one by one to give her a hug. Noah and Chris Wu kissed her cheek, Jin kissed her forehead. The rest gave her different degrees of lingering hugs, gently rubbing her back.

By the time they were done, Sophia was teary-eyed again.

"Thank you," she said, voice thick. "Goodnight."

"Goodnight," the men chorused.

The cameras followed her out of the house.

"So," Dean began when they were alone, hands on his hips. "Anyone who wants to get completely smashed right now, say I."

"I!" the guys yelled, making themselves laugh.

Ejiro's eyes met Obiora's. He blushed furiously, and looked away. Dean had already headed to the kitchen presumably to get the drinks, followed by Noah and Chris Wu. The rest of the men were heading to the veranda.

Clearing his throat, Ejiro headed in the latter direction, feeling his breath seize when Obiora moved at the exact same moment, ending up with them walking side by side.

Ejiro could feel his body heat like it was a furnace. His lips tingled with vivid memory. He couldn't look at him.

When they got outside, Obiora headed to the other side of the wide table, but not before brushing the back of his hand against Ejiro's in a not-so-accidental caress.

Ejiro bit back a sound of pure desire. And then he gritted his teeth and forced himself to think of Sophia, who was hoping for a stronger relationship with him—with *all* of the men.

He and Obiora couldn't carry on like this behind her back; it wasn't fair to lead her on. But the thought of making the decision to either tell Sophia what was going on, or pull out of the competition entirely, was completely terrifying.

So, even though New Ejiro was screaming at him to just go for what he wanted, no matter how daunting it was, Old Ejiro resurfaced and chose the easiest option.

To pretend the problem didn't exist at all.

OBIORA WAS PLAYING WITH FIRE.

He could tell, after their goodnights to Sophia, something within Ejiro seemed to have shuttered. He refused to meet Obiora's eyes as the night progressed—in fact, he seemed to be trying really hard to pretend that Obiora didn't exist at all.

But Obiora *refused* to let Ejiro ruin this thing building between them. He refused to let Ejiro grow scared and pull away. He wouldn't let him.

Which was why, even though Ejiro hadn't taken a single drop of alcohol all night, he was breathing a little fast and looked slightly flushed, because Obiora currently had their legs tangled underneath the table.

During short intervals, Obiora would sensually run his foot up Ejiro's calf, making Ejiro give a small, nearly-imperceptible shiver that burned Obiora all the way down to his soul.

Despite his daring, Ejiro didn't once acknowledge him, but neither did he pull away or adjust his stance. He just sat there, his eyes half-lidded and full lips slightly parted, trying to contain his obvious desire, which made Obiora burn even hotter.

"Is there a reason you don't drink, Ejiro?" Chris Wu asked when the conversation lulled.

Ejiro startled slightly at the mention of his name. His eyes darted to Obiora's for a fast second, like he couldn't *help* it, and Obiora wanted him so fucking badly it hurt.

"Just personal preference," Ejiro said, though he looked just a bit uncomfortable at the question. He'd probably been asked about it a lot and was tired of answering.

"Are you saying you've never had alcohol in your life?" Dean asked with surprise. "Like, *never*? Not even a sip?"

Ejiro shook his head. His next word came out almost strangled, because Obiora had used that exact moment to run the side of his foot up his calf again. "Nope," he squeaked. He cleared his throat.

"Sure you don't want at least a sip?" Noah asked, waggling his eyebrows playfully, swishing the golden whiskey in his tumbler around. "I'm sure Jin makes a mean piña colada."

"Please don't drag me into this," Jin groaned. They laughed.

"I'm sure," Ejiro replied. "I'm literally just not interested, all right?"

"All right, all right." Noah held his hands up placatingly.

Obiora wanted Ejiro's attention back on him. He wanted to break down Ejiro's barriers again; he wanted Ejiro to look at him the way he'd looked at him back in the garden, like Obiora was the only thing that mattered in his entire world.

Obiora slid his leg up higher, up to the inside of Ejiro's knee.

Obiora expected Ejiro to make another noise again, or flush, or shiver—any one of the reactions he'd come to expect so far.

And he did all that; he flushed, he shivered, his peach lips parted, a soft gush of air escaping his mouth.

But he did all this while looking *directly* at Obiora. His eyes were inky black, on fire with lust.

Oh *fuck*.

Obiora stood up abruptly. He was breathing too fast. He took a deep breath, tried to slow down. The men looked at him curiously.

"Think I'm going to head to bed," he said.

Ejiro stood as well. He didn't take his eyes off Obiora. "Yeah, me too."

Oh fuck, oh fuck, oh fuck.

"Goodnight, boys!"

"Goodnight."

"The rest of us should probably call it a night, huh?" Jin was saying, but Obiora was no longer listening.

He was heading down the terrace to the smaller house, Ejiro's footsteps echoing behind him. Anticipation danced through his blood like the alcohol he'd just drank, making him feel warm and slightly dizzy.

They didn't bother to switch on the lights when they entered the room, shutting and locking the door behind them.

In a blink, they were standing in front of each other, but like they'd shared some kind of unspoken agreement, they didn't touch—hovering instead, barely an inch of space between their bodies.

"Ejiro," Obiora whispered, his voice so fucking deep, shot to hell.

"Obiora." Ejiro's voice was just as thick, hoarse with need.

Obiora leaned closer, brushing the sides of their noses together.

"Oh God. Obiora. We shouldn't," Ejiro moaned, even as his body said otherwise, swaying closer instead of away. His lips were parted in sweet invitation.

And suddenly, it was on the tip of Obiora's tongue—to tell Ejiro that they should just pack their things and leave. Or explain to Sophia during the filming of the next episode that they were attracted to each other and wanted to try things out in the "real" world. What did they have to lose?

But fear and insecurity chose that moment to rear their ugly heads.

What if, when it came down to it, Ejiro *didn't* choose him? What if this whole thing was just the heightened emotions of the day? Ejiro had spent more time going on dates with Sophia—hell, he and Ejiro hadn't even *liked* each other at one point, why would Ejiro choose to leave with him after everything he'd invested into his relationship with the bachelorette?

What if Ejiro only wanted him in here, and didn't want him *out there*?

The thought was excruciating. And Obiora was still too raw from Sasha's talk, from his kiss with Ejiro earlier—a rejection right now would literally destroy him. He couldn't risk it.

So he swallowed down his longing, and whispered hoarsely, "All right."

"All right," Ejiro echoed. Obiora didn't know if Ejiro sounded relieved or disappointed—or both.

Unable to resist, desperate for some kind of confirmation that this thing between them wasn't one-sided, Obiora leaned in closer and brushed his lips gently against Ejiro's cheek.

A small, sweet sigh of pleasure escaped Ejiro's lips, filling Obiora with equal parts hunger and relief.

"Goodnight, then," he whispered.

Ejiro swallowed loudly. "Goodnight, Obiora."

The official website for the CUPID CALLING series.

Cupid Calling

ABOUT | THE BACHELORETTE | THE BACHELORS | EPISODES | CONTACT | BECOME A CUPID

Episode 6 – A Talk With Sasha

Episode Summary: This week, the men are paid a surprise visit by celebrity therapist Sasha Pierce. Unknown to the cast, Sasha has been a part of the filming from day one, observing their interactions with the bachelorette in order to offer her advice for this episode.

The surprise session brings out a vulnerable side to Jin that endears him to Sophia, earning him this week's Red Heart. The bachelorette's relationship with the other men also seems to have strengthened after their sessions, especially those with Chris Wu and Noah.

Alistair refused to take his own session seriously, which frustrated Sophia. He was eliminated during the session. Sophia felt like out of the remaining bachelors, Dean was the one she unfortunately connected with the least, and he was the second bachelor to be eliminated.

Click here to watch the full episode on Netflicks!

COMMENTS

 ELDORADO1_

Words cannot describe how much I hated this episode.

 16001   10233

 EBELEBOS

God this episode was awful. You could tell most of the men (hell, even the bachelorette) were extremely uncomfortable with the set-up. I didn't like that it was a "surprise". Imagine you're eating dinner and then BAM, a friggin' clown pops out in front of you 😭 that's honestly how it felt Edit: whoa thank you for the top comment lololol also, I didn't know so many people actually liked clowns? lmfao I sincerely apologise to the clown community 😭

 13985   6076

 SUGA_MP3

Tbh I completely understand why Alistair was uncooperative. These men didn't come to the competition to be psychoanalyzed 😐

 13246   5831

 GRANSHIN_I

Idk why so many people are angry with this episode, like the ENTIRE point was for Sasha to point out what wasn't working between them so they could work on it and therefore make their relationship with the bachelorette stronger? Wtf is wrong with that? And of course it felt invasive asf, it's f*cking therapy, not a friendly chat with your best friend Beyonce Edit: Yeah, ok, maybe the "surprise" of it all wasn't great, but I still stand by my opinion. This episode brought out all of the strengths and weaknesses in Sophia's relationship with each of the men, which should help them in the long run.

 12908   8018

 ROSEYPOSEY

Aww who knew there was such a soft side to Jin?

 11873   5194

LOAD MORE COMMENTS

TWENTY-TWO

TOMORROW, WAS WHAT OBIORA HAD told himself the night after his kiss with Ejiro, when Ejiro had told him in a hoarse, frantic voice that they *shouldn't*. *Tomorrow*, Obiora had thought, as they'd watched each other in the darkness until they'd fallen asleep, their hands stretched out across their beds, stopping short of the small space that separated their mattresses. *I'll talk to him properly tomorrow, and figure out where we stand.*

That had been nearly three days ago. Now, here Obiora was, his heart in his throat, and his stomach molten with a desire so intense and so unwavering it was practically becoming a part of him.

Ejiro sat on the other end of the n-shaped sofa, his legs stretched out along the length of it, where Obiora's own legs were perched. Their legs were subtly intertwined, with one of Ejiro's calves between Obiora's and vice versa, but both men were pretending like nothing was amiss—like the very air between them wasn't rife with a tension so thick Obiora could have cut into it with a knife.

The men's too-brief visit to Venice had finally ended, and they were back at the mansion in Oxford. Since there were only six of them left—Dean had been eliminated during the heart giving ceremony of last week's episode—the mansion felt infinitely larger. The men had decided to share the six rooms between themselves, leaving each man to a single room. After the intimacy of their shared room in Venice, Obiora's chosen room at the mansion felt painfully big.

For what felt like the millionth time—Obiora didn't even know how long they'd been out here—an hour? Three?—Ejiro pretended to adjust himself where he sat, and Obiora bit back a sound of pure torture when their legs "accidentally" brushed, lightning bolting up his legs and to his groin, to his heart and his throat, at the contact.

They were outside on the veranda, in the partially hidden corner Obiora had begun to inwardly refer to as their private nook. The rest of the men were inside the house; Jin, Noah, and Damien were sleeping off the jet lag, while Chris Wu was in the kitchen, whipping himself a sweet snack that permeated the air with the smell of dark chocolate and hot strawberries.

The surroundings plus the scent did nothing to help with the already heady atmosphere between him and Ejiro.

Ejiro licked his lips, his eyes intensely focused on the sketchbook balanced on the pillows he had piled into a makeshift desk on his lap. His hand clutched a charcoal pencil, etching with confidence across the page. He was pretending to be completely engrossed in his task, but Ejiro wasn't a very good actor.

His eyes flicked up, as they'd done every other minute, and Obiora looked away, pretending like he hadn't been staring, like he hadn't been struggling to take his eyes off Ejiro for even a second.

This was how it had been for the past three days since Ejiro had stopped Obiora that night. They still hung out together—in fact, their being together was almost *constant*—but they ignored the tension that hung thick around them like it was a foreboding cloud.

"After the disaster of last week, I wonder what this week's episode is going to be about," Obiora said, desperately trying to reduce the tension between them before he did something reckless. Like jump across the sofa and pin Ejiro to the cushions, and capture his lips in a furious, desperate kiss.

His mouth longed to trace a path along the long arch of Ejiro's throat, his teeth to sink into the flesh that joined his neck and shoulder. He imagined sliding his hand between their bodies, slipping it into the waistband of Ejiro's bottoms and wanking him off like that until he came, arching into Obiora, a soft cry of passion escaping his kiss-swollen lips. Fuck, Obiora couldn't count how many times he'd had to jerk off over the past three days, wound so tight it felt like his fucking teeth were vibrating.

"Mm," Ejiro hummed, eyes on his sketchbook, eyebrows furrowed, teeth sunk into his plush lower lip.

Ejiro was lost in his thoughts, his hand poised frozen over the sketchbook, gaze faraway, despite his eyes being on the page in front of him. The sun was just setting, lending some warmth to his cool, dark brown skin, making it glint like it was burnished. The thick coils of his hair had grown a little longer from day one, still shorter on the sides, but longer on top, enough that Obiora could imagine sinking his fingers into it and pulling. Ejiro had changed from the more formal clothes he'd used on the journey back to England, and was now in a plain t-shirt and his yoga pants, his feet covered in thin, white ankle socks.

Fuck. How could one person be a combination of both hot and adorable at the same damn time?

Like he'd been doing since he'd realised Ejiro was attracted to him, Obiora couldn't help playing with fire.

THERE WAS NO ONE EJIRO could blame but himself. Ever since that fateful kiss—since that fateful night Ejiro had stopped

Obiora from deepening things between them, he and Obiora had been left in some kind of limbo. Ejiro was desperate, almost frantic with the need to just—*be* with Obiora. To kiss him, to freaking *claim* him, but some unnameable fear held him back. The emotions were so intense they left him trembling sometimes; of course Ejiro was terrified.

And Obiora—God, *Obiora*—respected Ejiro's indirect request for space; it was almost annoying really. Ejiro wanted Obiora to say screw it and jump his bones, but of course Obiora—the freaking gentleman—wasn't going to do that. Ejiro felt that since he'd been the one to grind things to a halt, the ball was now in his court if he wanted things to go further.

And he did. God, he really *fucking* did. He'd never wanted anyone so badly, never felt this deeply for anyone in his life before.

The desire built up in him like lava, a volcano threatening to erupt. He was so full of it he had no choice but to pour his desire onto the page or risk exploding. He'd almost filled his sketchbook with nothing but Obiora, but the therapy didn't seem to be working. In fact, the longer he put his desires onto paper, the more intense said desires became.

It wasn't enough. Ejiro just wanted *him*. But how could he tell Obiora that, while they were still here, waiting to go on their next date with Sophia? It felt wrong.

But Ejiro was too scared to just up and leave, so here they were. Stuck.

"You drawing me again, Ejiro?"

Obiora's sexy drawl brought him crashing back down to earth. He felt himself go still. His eyes registered the sketch he'd been drawing, and he felt heat crawl up his cheeks at how obvious his feelings were, splashed on the page like this for all to see.

He swallowed. "I don't know. Maybe."

Obiora let out a soft laugh that Ejiro felt all the way down to his marrow.

"Am I ever going to see these alleged drawings?" he teased huskily. He shifted a little as he spoke, making their legs brush again. Ejiro shivered visibly at the contact.

The question registered, and Ejiro's head snapped up, his eyes wide, his heartbeat rabbiting at the thought of Obiora seeing—

He pulled the sketchbook to his chest almost protectively. "I—um."

Obiora laughed lightly. "You don't have to if you don't want to. I'm just curious." That seemed to be an understatement. The look in Obiora's eyes was hungry; if curiosity were rain, then Obiora was a thunderstorm.

Ejiro looked away, his hands tightening around the charcoal pencil and the sketchbook.

Ejiro wasn't going to make a move. He knew it, and Obiora probably knew it. The thought made him feel slightly ashamed, like he was leading Obiora on. But he wasn't—he *wasn't*. He was just terrified. If he admitted his feelings, if he let either of them so much as *voice* what was growing between them, then it would feel too real.

They'd have to leave the competition—it wouldn't be fair to Sophia otherwise—which would mean going back into the "real" world, which meant possibly *dating* Obiora, which meant eventually coming out to Ajiri, to Blessing—to his *mother*. Oh dear God.

Yet, despite the terror clogging his veins, Ejiro knew they couldn't remain like this. Obiora deserved to know how Ejiro felt. He deserved more than this—more than Ejiro jerking him around.

So, if Ejiro couldn't make a move, maybe he could do this.

"HERE," EJIRO SAID ROUGHLY.

OH. Obiora's heartbeat kicked into overdrive, jumping up from behind his ribs to lodge somewhere in his throat. He tried not to look too nervous or eager as he took the sketchbook from Ejiro's outstretched hand.

"I'm going to the bathroom."

Ejiro headed to the house, walking quickly like the hounds of hell were on his heels. Obiora felt a smidgen of concern, but it was quickly overridden by his curiosity.

His eyes dropped to the sketchbook, open to the page Ejiro's hands had transformed just moments ago.

Obiora's lips parted on a soft exhale when he saw the man depicted onto the page.

Fucking hell, that couldn't be him. The drawing was in simple line and shade, yet it was filled with such vibrant life that Obiora was sure the real him had to pale in comparison.

"Ejiro," he whispered, so full of love he ached with it.

He glanced up quickly, feeling like a thief in the night. Ejiro was nowhere in sight. He glanced back down at the sketchbook, his pulse thumping harder at the base of his throat.

Had Ejiro meant him to see—? Was that why he'd left so abruptly? The way he'd handed the sketchbook to Obiora had felt pointed, somehow. Or was Obiora reading into things? He didn't know.

Taking a deep breath, Obiora made a decision. If he was about to overstep, then he'd apologise. But he chose to believe Ejiro had left the sketchbook with him for a reason.

Quickly, he began to flip through the pages.

His eyes widened. He had to slow down immediately, go back to the beginning.

It was him. Every single page was *him*. His eyes, the curve of his mouth, the bridge of his nose—his hands, his thighs, his legs, his feet. His curls, his smiles, his dimple—his naked back and chest, drawn with such detail Obiora found he was struggling to breathe.

He slowly flipped through the pages, his throat thick, feeling weirdly choked up, eyes burning. Some were of him just sitting on his own, reading one of the books from the mansion's library. Other times he was eating, or talking, or laughing. There was one—the one on that first night how many days ago—when he and Ejiro had sat here for the first time, and Obiora had been mourning his lost love.

Ejiro had captured the depth of heartbreak in his eyes, in his frame, the gentle way he'd clutched at the locket Ada had given him. He'd drawn Obiora with deference, with a melancholy sort of longing that left him aching.

"Fuck," Obiora whispered, shaking.

Did Ejiro know? Was he aware how *naked* his feelings were in these pages—how vulnerably he'd bared his heart?

Obiora was composed when Ejiro returned. Ejiro took the now closed sketchbook from him, not meeting his eyes, folding himself into his corner of the sofa.

"Ejiro." He waited until Ejiro met his eyes.

When he did, Obiora knew, instantly, that he'd been meant to see. Ejiro had *wanted* him to see. A kernel of something lodged itself behind Obiora's ribs and took root.

"Yeah?" God, he looked so sweet, so soft, braced as if for rejection.

"As my mother would say, your hands were touched by God."

Ejiro ducked his head, laughing and blushing furiously. "Shut up. That's so cheesy."

Obiora laughed, all the while his heart thumped with love.

SOPHIA VISITED THE MANSION THE next day as a "surprise"— the men had been prepared beforehand and had pretended they weren't awaiting her arrival.

Since last night, after the way Ejiro had laid bare his heart, Obiora had been filled with restless energy. He wanted desperately to *do* something, but with Ejiro still acting so skittish—with Ejiro still so tentative, Obiora didn't want to push and end up scaring him away.

The sketchbook was proof that Ejiro wanted him just as much as he wanted Ejiro. The question now was what were they going to do about it?

After Sophia had exchanged some light banter with the men, she asked what in their minds was their idea of *the* perfect date.

Obiora hadn't thought too much of the question, tuning in and smiling fondly when Ejiro bashfully said, "Bungee jumping. I've always wanted to do it. Nothing like a near-death experience to make you truly bond with your partner, am I right?" he'd teased, making them laugh.

Obiora's heart skipped at the gender-neutral mode of address. Ejiro glanced at him shyly, before glancing away. Oh God.

On his turn, Obiora mentioned a picnic inside a hot air balloon. It had actually been one of the many items on Ada's bucket list, and had been one of the first things they'd wanted to tick off after they'd started their life together. Obiora still planned to do it at some point, but he'd imagined he'd probably have to do it alone because there was no way he could do it with someone else without them knowing what it had meant to him and his lost love. And once they knew what it meant, they probably wouldn't like it.

But when his eyes met Ejiro's across the room, he could picture it easily, suddenly—so easily he could almost taste wine on his lips, feel the breeze in his hair, hear Ejiro's voice as he said a toast to honour Ada and Obiora's past, then, more importantly, a toast to honour *them* and their future.

And Obiora *burned*.

So, when Sophia said, in that bright mischievous voice of hers, that, "What if I told you, that every single scenario you've mentioned today, Ameri is going to make come true for us?", Obiora had felt himself crash back down to earth.

"Yup!" Sophia laughed, delighted at the stunned look on the men's faces. She clapped her hands with glee. "After last week, I thought it would be nice if we all did something a little extravagant this time around, but still light-hearted and fun—something that would *actually* strengthen the bonds I have with each of you that isn't as traumatising as surprise therapy."

The men laughed. Obiora tried to, but he knew he probably looked constipated instead.

When Sophia left, Ameri had remained behind to plan their "perfect" dates with more detail, and they'd used the opportunity to film their cutaways for the day. Ejiro had eyed Obiora with concern, but Obiora had forced a smile and waved him off, even though the small kernel that had taken root in his chest had burst into a weed.

THE WEED GREW AND GREW until his date with Sophia arrived, and Obiora had to laugh and tease and pretend to be having the time of his life, because if he didn't, he'd get eliminated, and if he was eliminated, then that would be the end of him and Ejiro.

Or would it?

"Okay, I've had it."

Obiora blinked. The date was over, and they were standing in front of the mansion, after having strolled down the long driveway, their path lit with the bright lights lining the road, and those of the cameras surrounding them.

Sophia had her hands on her hips, a frown on her face. "Obiora, what's going on? This was supposed to be a date to make us finally connect, but you've been spaced out all day. Are you all right?"

The weed in his chest grew into a forest, and Obiora realised he couldn't do this anymore.

He wanted Ejiro so fucking badly. He loved him so fucking *fiercely*. He *couldn't* do this anymore.

"Sophia," he began, his voice heavy with finality.

"What?" She looked wary.

The words spilled from his mouth like vomit. "When Sasha said I was holding back from making a deeper connection with you, she was right, she just wasn't right about *why*. It isn't because of my late girlfriend, though I will *never* stop loving her. It's because—"

The lights from the cameras suddenly felt too bright. The microphone pack taped to his back, under his shirt, felt hot and heavy, a damning weight.

"I—" He swallowed. "I've fallen in love with one of the bachelors." For a brief moment, Obiora was filled with euphoria—that he'd finally been able to say it out loud seemed to release something in him that had been coiled tight.

Then the sudden hush brought him back to earth.

Obiora expected Ameri to yell cut, expected Sophia to slap him, *something*—instead, the world went deadly quiet.

"I'm sorry," Obiora began profusely when the silence stretched on for too long, even though he really, truly wasn't. "I'm so sorry, Sophia. I didn't mean for this to happen. I didn't mean to hurt you, or lead you on—"

"Who is it?" Sophia asked, sounding just a little bit excited.

Obiora felt his heartbeat start to race. Was she serious? Was she really not disappointed?

Slowly, he shook his head. "I can't say."

At that moment, like a dart landing right on his forehead, it hit Obiora.

What if Ejiro's hesitance had nothing to do with Sophia or the competition at all? What if his hesitance was because all this was probably new for him, and he felt a little overwhelmed?

If Obiora made them leave the competition, or tell Sophia the truth, then that would mean Ejiro coming out when he probably wasn't ready; hell, Ejiro probably hadn't even had the time nor the space to even *address* his feelings, yet Obiora had wanted him make a decision, just like that.

For the first time since Ejiro had stopped things between them on that fateful night in Venice, Obiora felt his shoulders relax, and his chest filled with warmth. *Oh, Ejiro.*

Sophia laughed a little, though it didn't hold any malice.

"Are you really not upset with me?" Obiora asked, raising an eyebrow.

"Obiora," Sophia said, still giggling. "I'm going to be honest with you, I'm a little relieved."

Obiora couldn't help but smile, her giddiness affecting him. "Are you now."

She laughed again. "Obiora, not gonna lie, I was literally going to eliminate you tonight," she deadpanned.

She laughed even harder at his gobsmacked expression. "I'm sorry, I'm sorry, but come on! You're a great guy, don't get me wrong, but right from the beginning, I could tell you haven't been *here*. I felt like—like you've been playing a part all this time, and today, I felt—well, it doesn't matter. This bachelor." She leered. "Does he know how you feel?"

Obiora could feel himself blushing. "No," he lied. Well, it wasn't really a lie. Ejiro knew Obiora wanted him, but he probably didn't know the depth of Obiora's feelings.

Sophia shook her head, an amused curl to her lips. "Well, this has been an interesting turn of events. I have *nothing* against you falling for someone else, by the way. We can't exactly help who we love, can we? But you know you're going to have to leave the competition, right? Probably like, right now. It doesn't make sense to have you stay on when we both know where we stand now."

Obiora slowly began to panic. "Right, no, I understand."

Sophia smiled. "I'm glad. Come here, give me a hug."

Obiora did as she asked.

She pulled away after a moment. "You're not the only one at fault here. I really like you, Obiora, but Sasha was right on my end; you really do remind me too much of my asshole exes, and even though I'm madly attracted to you, I've also been holding back a part of myself as well. I guess, right from the start, this just wasn't meant to be, huh?"

Obiora laughed a little. "I guess not."

"Glad we could have this talk, and thank you for being honest with me."

"Of course, no problem."

"I guess this is goodbye."

Fuck. "Yeah."

They hugged again, saying their goodbyes, then one of the directors and some of the cameras followed Sophia as she made her way away from the mansion.

"Cut!" Ameri yelled when Sophia was gone. "Well," she said, watching Obiora with curious amusement. "That was a plot twist I did not expect, but I'm sure the fans are going to love. Were you being serious or was it an excuse for you to nobly end your time here? Just between us, don't worry." She winked.

Obiora turned to face her, sure his eyes were wild. "I know I'm going to have to leave in a second, but I need a moment, Ameri, *please*." His voice broke on the last word.

"Oh." Ameri's eyes widened. "You were serious, then."

"*Ameri*."

She rolled her eyes. "Fine. But hurry, we're going to have to film you leaving *and* film the rest of your cutaways tonight, so—"

But Obiora was already turning and rushing into the house, his heart beating so hard he could feel it in his ears.

If Ejiro still needed time, then Obiora was going to give him all the time he needed. And even though he could hardly breathe for the fact that he was leaving—*leaving Ejiro*, his heart wailed dramatically—Obiora knew he'd made the right decision.

TWENTY-THREE

EJIRO WASN'T JEALOUS, HE THOUGHT furiously, his hand slashing across the page on his sketchbook. He absolutely wasn't thinking about the way Obiora had watched him with his eyes dark with desire and longing when he'd mentioned his perfect date idea, like he was already imagining taking Ejiro on said date. Ejiro had begun to imagine it, too: the two of them alone, miles above the earth with a picnic spread out before them, nothing but an ocean of sky to see around them.

He'd also imagined Obiora when he'd mentioned his own dream date—bungee jumping—how exhilarating it'd be to share that experience with him. And with the way Obiora had been looking at him as he'd mentioned it, he was sure Obiora desperately wanted it, too.

Then Sophia had quickly burst their bubble, saying that actually, Ameri *would* be bringing their date ideas to life, but they'd be taking *her*. Which was ... *fine*, obviously. If they wanted to remain in the competition, then they had to do what they had to do.

Except, Ejiro wasn't sure he wanted them to remain in the competition anymore. Especially now that Obiora was on his date with Sophia, the thought making Ejiro clutch harder at his pencil, his throat thick with bitterness. Ejiro's own date was still two days away, which felt like plain torture. If he felt this awful about Obiora being on a date with Sophia, how was he going to feel when he went on his own date with her, and left Obiora behind at the mansion? How was he going to keep up this game of pretence when the very thought of Obiora out there right now, enjoying a picnic in a hot air balloon with someone that *wasn't him* made Ejiro feel like screaming and smashing something.

But the thought of leaving this place, of having Obiora *out there*, in the real world, no pretences, was so—so *fucking* scary Ejiro didn't know how to handle it. But if he wanted Obiora, *truly* wanted him, then shouldn't it be worth it?

Old Ejiro wasn't brave. Old Ejiro clung to his comfort zone with the zeal of a koala refusing to let go of the security of its tree.

But Ejiro didn't want to be Old Ejiro anymore.

He wanted to be brave. He wanted Obiora, period.

After this episode, he told himself resolutely, with a confidence he couldn't yet feel. But fake it till you make it and all that, right? *After this, I'll tell him how I feel, and we'll figure out how we can gracefully bow out of the competition.*

Then I can be with him for real.

The thought made his stomach bubble with nerves and anticipation, and a yearning so fervent it left him short of breath.

He noticed a presence in his periphery and looked up. When he spotted Obiora watching him with a soft, fond smile on his lips, Ejiro's heart skipped several beats. His body lit up like sparks, his lips stretching into a wide grin.

"Obiora!" he exclaimed happily.

Then he realised he was probably being a little too obvious, and quickly tempered his reaction. He snapped his sketchbook shut, placed it on the bench and stood quickly, sliding his feet into his outdoor slippers. He was blushing, grateful his dark skin hid the flush in his cheeks.

"You're back," he said, calmer this time. Then he suddenly remembered *what* Obiora was coming back from, and felt his stomach sour like curdled milk. "How was your date?" he asked with false brightness.

Please don't tell me, please don't tell me, please don't tell me—

Hearing about Obiora taking Sophia on his "dream" date would literally rip Ejiro's heart to shreds, even if it was just pretend.

"That's what I'm here to talk about," Obiora said, a little solemnly.

"Oh?" Ejiro said, caught off guard by the tone.

Obiora seemed to inhale deeply for strength. Then he walked up to Ejiro, and took both of his hands gently in his.

Ejiro's pulse jumped. He stared at Obiora, eyes wide. For some reason, the easy, intimate act of Obiora holding his hands like this made Ejiro feel like Obiora was holding his very heart. His lips parted slightly, and Ejiro swayed forward almost helplessly, a piece of metal drawn to magnet.

Obiora's eyes darkened. He pulled Ejiro down to the bench so they were sitting beside each other, knees pressed close, still holding hands, resting on their knees between them. When Obiora gave Ejiro's hands a squeeze, Ejiro dutifully squeezed back, the action making Obiora's eyes darken impossibly further. God, Ejiro wanted him.

"Ejiro," Obiora began, his words hoarse. He took another breath to fortify himself. "I'm leaving."

Ejiro felt his world come to a violent stop. "What?"

"Sophia eliminated me after our date," Obiora clarified, his voice still thick. "I have to leave in a few minutes."

"What?" Ejiro repeated. Oh God, he couldn't breathe. "Why is she eliminating you? What happened?" His voice kept rising in pitch after each question, his panic palpable.

He tried to pull his hands away, but Obiora tightened his grip, refusing to let him run. Refusing to let him hide.

"I told her the truth," Obiora said.

"The truth?" Ejiro was barely listening. Obiora was leaving. He was *leaving*. The fact repeated itself over and over again in his head and heart, blocking his lungs so he could barely take in air, spots dancing in front of his eyes.

Obiora *couldn't* leave—Oh God, he couldn't—not yet—not *now*—Ejiro hadn't even told him now he felt—he wasn't ready—

"Ejiro," Obiora said firmly, giving his hands a grounding squeeze. "Come back to me."

Ejiro blinked. He was breathing too hard. "I'm here," he said, a little desperately. "I'm here."

"I told her the truth," Obiora repeated, staring deeply into his eyes. "I told her that I couldn't in good faith continue on, because I was—" Obiora hesitated. "I told her I was in love with someone else."

Oh. Ejiro sucked in a sharp breath. The grip he had on Obiora's hands tightened to the point of pain. "With someone ... else," he repeated, his voice too high, his heartbeat too loud.

Obiora blushed. He lifted one of his hands to tenderly cup Ejiro's cheek, his thumb stroking his skin.

"You," Obiora confessed, a little shyly. "I'm in love with you."

"Oh," Ejiro gasped. His pupils blew wide. He was trembling. It felt like he was flying. "Obiora," he said desperately, clutching his other hand like it was a lifeline. The hand Obiora had on his cheek burned like a brand.

"You don't have to say anything," Obiora reassured quickly, his thumb still stroking. "I just—going out with Sophia today just really cemented it for me; I don't want to go on any more dates with people unless they're with you."

Ejiro felt himself flush from his head to his toes. He felt like he was floating high above the clouds, so high he didn't ever want to come back down.

It was time to be brave.

"If you're leaving, then I'm leaving, too," he blurted, heart pounding.

"Ejiro—" Obiora began, a little worriedly, even though his eyes were bright with joy.

"No," Ejiro interrupted, letting Obiora's obvious happiness spur him on. He tried to shift closer, but there was nowhere to go unless he twisted his body away, and he didn't want to take his eyes off Obiora's for one second. He settled for squeezing Obiora's hand instead, using his other hand to cup over Obiora's hand on his cheek, curling his fingers possessively over it. "If you aren't here, then I don't have any reason to stay either. For some time now, probably since Venice—or even longer than that—" He laughed a little self-consciously. "I've only been here because of you."

"Fuck," Obiora whispered. He was staring at Ejiro's mouth, his eyes burning. Ejiro automatically licked his lips, biting back a sound of lust when Obiora's eyes followed the movement, his own tongue darting out to mimic it.

Obiora sounded hoarse, distracted as he muttered, "Wait—we have to—we have to think about this." He blinked, shook his head, and tore his eyes away from Ejiro's mouth and back to his eyes. "I didn't tell them who you were. If you decide to quit out of the blue right now, then everyone is going to put two and two together. Is that what you want?"

Ejiro's first instinct was to say yes, but Obiora shook his head, stopping him.

"Think about it, Ejiro. Even if the episodes won't come out for a few months after this, it'll still be on National TV—on *Netflicks*, for that matter. You'll essentially be coming out to the world. Are you … are you okay with that?"

Ejiro froze. The thought filled him with bone-chilling fear. He hadn't even thought about coming out to Ajiri and Blessing, to his friends at home—oh God, his *mum*.

But *some* part of him must've known—why else would he have

wanted him and Obiora to stay in the competition for as long as possible? Some part of him must've subconsciously realised that going back to the real world didn't just mean admitting his feelings for Obiora, it also meant coming out to his friends and family. And he was far from ready for that.

"Oh God," he repeated. His eyes burned, and his hands began to tremble. His heart broke to pieces when he realised couldn't do it—he *couldn't*. He wanted to be brave, he wanted to be with Obiora, but he couldn't—he wasn't—

"Ejiro." Obiora pressed their foreheads together. He freed his second hand so he had Ejiro's face cupped in his hands, both his thumbs stroking in rhythm across his cheeks. "Baby, breathe for me."

Ejiro sucked in a sharp breath, the endearment, falling sweet like honey from Obiora's lips, managing to immediately push down his panic.

"Yeah. That's it," Obiora encouraged, his voice gentle, his eyes closed.

Ejiro stared at Obiora's eyelashes, his nose and mouth, the dimple in his cheek. He basked in the heat in his cheeks from the warmth of Obiora's hands on his face, and felt like he was freefalling.

"You okay, baby?" Obiora asked softly, his eyelids fluttering open, dark eyes locking with his.

It hit Ejiro like a punch to the stomach.

He was falling in love.

"Yes," Ejiro managed to say when he registered Obiora's question, his voice barely wobbling, as if his world hadn't just been rocked down to its foundations by his revelation. "I'm good. I'm okay. I'm ... wonderful." The last word came out a sigh.

Obiora pulled back a bit, only a little, so their faces were still intimately close. "Yeah?" he said, a little playfully. His eyes kept darting to Ejiro's mouth.

Ejiro's own eyes dropped to Obiora's lips. "Mhm."

"You don't have to do anything, you know?" Obiora said, his

voice husky. "You can just play along until Sophia eliminates you, then —"

"But I want you," Ejiro interrupted, hoarse with need. "I don't want to wait anymore."

"Oh God. I love you."

Ejiro shivered. "Obiora," he whispered, too afraid to return the words; they still felt too new, too raw.

Obiora didn't seem to mind. "Baby, I don't want you to force yourself out of the closet when you're obviously not ready. Your feelings come first, Ejiro."

"But—but I—" *I wanted to be brave.*

Obiora seemed to see the words on his face, because he softened as he said, "Taking your time with your sexuality doesn't make you afraid or a coward or an imposter or whatever. And neither does it mean your feelings for me aren't real."

Ejiro swallowed with difficulty. Then he nodded. "Okay." Then, a little shyly, unable to meet Obiora's eyes—"Will you wait for me?"

Obiora's breath caught in his throat. "Yes," he said fervently. "Yes, baby. Of course I will. I'll wait for you."

"Kiss me," Ejiro pleaded, and had barely finished the sentence when Obiora's mouth was covering his.

Ejiro moaned, a sound of pure carnal lust—a sound of such quivering need it made him feel slightly ashamed, before the sound of Obiora echoing his desire with his own agonised groan blew Ejiro's self-consciousness away.

Obiora immediately slid his tongue between Ejiro's slightly parted lips, thrusting it hungrily into his mouth, like he'd been positively *dying* to taste him again. Ejiro eagerly opened up for him, trembling when Obiora's tongue slid along the sensitive roof of his mouth, exploring, making Ejiro shake. He pulled his tongue out so he could nip at the fleshy part of Ejiro's lower lip with his teeth, then sucked the flesh into his mouth. Ejiro groaned, reduced to putty.

Obiora kissed him like it was the first and the last thing he'd ever do, taking apart Ejiro's mouth with a deft skill that had Ejiro shaking, his toes curling in his socks.

Obiora eventually pulled away reluctantly, and Ejiro whined in need and distress.

"No," he said, pouting, managing to capture Obiora's lips in another kiss.

Obiora laughed into his mouth, kissing him again before pulling away. "I know, baby. But I have to go. Ameri is waiting for me."

Ejiro began to tremble again. He didn't want Obiora to leave, not without him, but he knew why they couldn't leave together, and it *hurt*.

"Can I?" Obiora nodded in the direction of Ejiro's sketchbook, which was lying between them.

Ejiro nodded, though he wasn't sure what Obiora wanted.

Obiora flipped the book onto a new page. Ejiro's heart began to race for a different reason when he saw what Obiora was writing. He handed the sketchbook back to Ejiro, and Ejiro's eyes immediately tried to devour the eleven digits that made up Obiora's phone number.

Obiora cupped his cheek, tilting his face up. He was blushing again.

"Call me?"

Ejiro kissed him hard in answer.

"The second I get out of here," he said breathlessly when the kiss broke. "I promise."

"All right." Obiora kissed him again. "Okay." Another kiss. Another. Ejiro was melting into the bench. Obiora licked and sucked at his lips, moulding their lips together like a man starved.

"Fuck. Okay," Obiora said for the final time, pulling away and standing abruptly. "Okay."

Ejiro stood, too. "You'll wait for me?" he couldn't help but confirm, a little desperately.

Obiora looked so, so soft. "Yes, baby. Forever if I have to." He winked.

Ejiro managed a small laugh, cheeks flushing at the flirtation. "It won't be that long. I promise."

They stood, staring at each other for a moment, before they were kissing again, frantically, arms wrapped tightly around each other, their bodies pressed so close it hurt.

And Ejiro decided he *had* to leave the competition this week, no matter what it took.

The official website for the CUPID CALLING series.

ABOUT | THE BACHELORETTE | THE BACHELORS | EPISODES | CONTACT | BECOME A CUPID

Episode 7 – The Perfect Date

Episode Summary: The men return to Oxford, and Sophia pays them a surprise visit at the mansion. In what is seemingly an innocent question, she asks the men what their ideas of a "perfect" date are, before revealing that Ameri plans on bringing their perfect dates to life.

Chris Wu and Sophia go to Port Gaverne in North Cornwall specifically for their beautiful cliffs. They fulfil Chris Wu's idea of a perfect date: skinny dipping at sunset after diving off a cliff. They end up talking and making out for hours, before having a picnic by the beachside to end the night. Both separately admit during their cutaways to being in love.

Damien has always wanted to go on a long road trip with his significant other, so he and Sophia get into a car and explore the scenic beach towns of Norfolk, falling in love with the sights, and also seemingly with each other.

Jin takes Sophia for a relaxing date at the Bath Hot Springs, his idea of the perfect date being to pamper and be pampered. They are both even more vulnerable with each other in a way that hasn't been seen in the season so far. Jin kisses her for the first time on their date, and in a cutaway, Sophia admits she might be falling in love with him. Jin admits in his own cutaway that "[Sophia] is everything."

Obiora takes Sophia on a hot air balloon date across Oxford. In a shocking turn of events, after Sophia confronts him of being aloof during their date, Obiora confesses to being in love with one of the other bachelors. Sophia takes it in stride, but Obiora is immediately eliminated.

Noah takes Sophia mountain biking down Coed Y Brenin in North Wales, and then they go stargazing along Pembrokeshire's wild coastline. Their connection deepens as they gaze at the stars, and after their goodnight kiss, Sophia leaves on cloud nine.

Ejiro takes Sophia bungee jumping in Manchester, after which they have an intimate dinner at a high-end restaurant. During a cutaway, Ejiro reveals his connection with Sophia has been affected by Sophia's ill-advised kiss, and is not sure he can continue on in the competition.

On the night of the Heart Ceremony, Sophia seems to echo his feelings, and Ejiro is then eliminated.

CUPID CALLING

Click here to watch the full episode on Netflicks!

COMMENTS

 **MILKY_WAY**

OKAY SO I WENT BACK AND WATCHED ALL THE EPISODES AGAIN SO YOU WOULDN'T HAVE TO AND I'M PRETTY SURE THE BACHELOR OBIORA IS IN LOVE WITH IS EJIRO SHHSSKSDFKSHD LIKE THE EPISODES FOCUS SO MUCH ON THE DATES AND THE OTHER BACHELORS' DRAMA THAT OBIORA AND EJIRO'S INTERACTIONS KIND OF FADE INTO THE BG, BUT THERE'S SOMETHING THERE Y'ALL, YOU CAN'T TELL ME OTHERWISE. THINK I'M DELUSIONAL? REWATCH EPISODE FIVE: WHEN THEY'RE DOING THE VENICE TOURS ON THE BOATS AT EXACTLY 55 MINS IN AND 23 SECONDS LOOK IN THE BACKGROUND THERE WAS A "LOOK" THEY SHARED LIKE OBIORA WAS LOOKING AT HIM WITH LEGIT HEART EYES AND EJIRO F*CKING BLUSHED BITHDSAHSFKD;AHF. THAT'S IT. THAT'S THE COMMENT. EDIT: MY COMMENT IS IN ALL CAPS BC F*CK YOU THAT'S WHY

 20345   18954

STICKSNBONES

Not CUPID CALLING trending at number one on twitter for nearly six hours just because of Obiora's confession 😭 some people are saying it's a marketing gimmick, though 🤔 Edit: So, I rewatched episode five as suggested and I stand corrected 😄 It happens in the background sorta but Ejiro's reaction when he found Obiora staring at him like *that* just seemed too genuine to be faked 🫠

💜 18067   10432

 MIRIAM111

Me going through all the comments theorising who Obiora is in love with: has anyone tried the chicken? XD edit: omg thank you for the top comment O.O

 17894   8866

😊 OMELETTEDUFROMAGE

Ejiro said the whole kiss thing with Sophia was what destroyed any chances of them having a fulfilling relationship, but what if he's lying and the truth is that he's really in love with Obiora 👀 Edit: I'm sorry for calling it a "kiss thing". I didn't mean to downplay the fact that it was non-consensual or how much it affected him afterwards. I didn't mean to invalidate his experience as well and make it all about Obiora. I'm sorry.

 14597   12246

😊 PEOPLE_MP3

THIS EPISODE AFJKSAJFKJSDJ JS GAYS, HOW DOES IT FEEL TO WIN? Edit: not the homophobes in my replies crying NoT eVeRyThIng iS aBoUT gAy PeOplE tHis ShOw iS suPpoSeD tO Be aBouT SopHiA adlkfjdlsfkj SORRY B*TCHES THIS SHOW IS FOR THE GAYS NOW 👻

 12043   11099

LOAD MORE COMMENTS ⌄

TWENTY-FOUR

OBIORA MISSED EJIRO SO BADLY it felt like he had heartache. He literally had a fist pressed to his chest like a brokenhearted rake in a historical romance, and even though his heart *wasn't* broken, it sure felt like it. He'd forgotten, after so many years since Ada, and then Nicholas, how love could be so intense, so overpowering it sometimes felt like pain.

Before everything that had transpired over the last few weeks, Obiora had thought he'd be leaving the competition hopefully refreshed and no worse for wear, ready to come back to Sheffield and tackle the job his father had gifted him with a new sense of purpose. Those first few days, he *had* missed home; he'd felt extremely homesick, especially in the nights when he was left alone to his thoughts.

Now, he wondered when his idea of "home" had changed from a place to a person, and how he'd missed it. Because right now, as a cab drove him from his flat to his parents' place, he should be feeling warm and excited and grounded, but all he could think about was Ejiro. As he'd left the mansion, it felt like he'd left a part of himself behind. That sense of something missing, of displacement, had him feeling strangely untethered.

"That'll be fourteen pound twenty," the cabbie said, bringing Obiora out of his thoughts.

His heart began to race. "Great, thanks." When he'd left the mansion and the hazy fantasy of it all, one of the first decisions he'd made was to come clean to his parents about where he'd been. He hadn't done it in the first place because he hadn't wanted them getting their hopes up about him "finally moving on" from Ada, or whatever other misguided notion they had because they loved him and couldn't stand to see him hurting. But there was no way Obiora was going to be able to look them in the eye and not tell them about Ejiro, the man he loved.

He exited the cab after paying the driver, and made his way up the driveway to the front door of his parents' slightly less than humble abode. They lived away from the hustle and bustle of the city centre and Sheffield's rife student life, settled instead in the cosy residential area closer to the outskirts of the town.

When his mother was the one to answer the door, Obiora knew he was probably the first of his brothers to arrive.

"Obim!" she exclaimed, pulling him into a tight hug. "My son. Ah, I've missed you."

"Nne," he greeted, his throat feeling thick. The homesickness seemed to hit him from all angles suddenly, as he smelt her familiar perfume and was surrounded by the warmth of their home.

Ifeoma was also speaking in Igbo, her love language. "Come inside, come inside. Ah, I've missed you. Look at you."

He began to blush as she fussed over him, cupping his cheeks and eyeing him from head to toe.

"Obiora, is that you?" That was his father, also speaking in Igbo. He came down the stairs, a wide grin on his face.

"Nna," Obiora greeted his old man, swallowing to rid the lump in his throat.

"Ah, my son," Osita said warmly. They hugged. "You're looking good," he said when they pulled apart. He gave Obiora the same look his mother had given him, his avid eyes trailing over Obiora's form appraisingly. It made him feel scraped raw.

His old man nodded with approval after his perusal. "You're looking healthy."

"Come, come, sit," his mother said, urging him into the sitting room. The three of them sat, his parents on the sofa, while Obiora took one of the armchairs. "I made goat meat pepper soup and yam. There's also egusi, okra, and Jollof, just in case."

"Mummy," Obiora chided playfully, even as his chest felt so full it could burst. "You know you didn't have to do all that."

"Eh." She scoffed, waving him off, but she was blushing.

"How was your journey?" His father asked. "Did you sleep well? We've missed you."

"My journey was fine. I slept fine. I missed you, too." He'd arrived last night, and after updating his friends and family that he was back, he'd immediately gone straight to bed. This morning, it was a given that he'd come over to see his parents first thing.

"How was your ..." Ifeoma hesitated, and exchanged a quick glance with Osita. Obiora's heartbeat quickened. "Your retreat?" she finished.

Wait, what? What was that look about? Obiora looked between them, but their faces gave nothing away.

Before he could open his mouth to answer—to tell the truth—the buzzer for the door went off.

"I'll get it," Obiora said.

His mother was already standing up. "No, no, you sit down. You just got back home, for God's sake, you need to rest."

"Mummy," Obiora groaned. "It's just the door."

"Do as I say, young man."

Obiora laughed, but dutifully resumed his seat.

He stood at the sound of his brothers' voices before they came into the sitting room. Their wives were at work, and since it was summer, Obinna's daughter was out of school but currently visiting her other grandparents. Since Obinna and Obioma worked for their father, it was easy to get the day off. The entire extended family planned to reconvene the following night to properly welcome Obiora back home. Obiora's heart felt full at the thought; you'd think he'd been in the hospital or won a prestigious award or something with all the fanfare.

"Brother!" Obioma said, his grin wide and infectious as he practically yanked Obiora into a tight hug, thumping him hard on the back. "I missed you!"

"Leave some hugs for the rest of us," Obinna grumbled. Obiora laughed.

He hugged him as well. Obinna held him at arm's length after the hug, his eyebrows furrowed.

Obiora rolled his eyes, but he was grinning. "Put the parental perusal away, Obinna, I already got a double dose of it when I got here."

"Don't mouth off while I'm here, young man," his mother scolded, making him laugh.

"You look good," Obinna said, completely ignoring Obiora's comment.

Obiora blushed, and pulled away. "Yeah, yeah, okay."

"Yeah, you *do* look good," Obioma said, leering a little, sensing blood in the water.

Obiora blushed harder. "Shut the fuck up."

"Language," Obinna and his parents said at the same time; his brother by rote, while his parents' reprimand was sharper.

"Sorry," Obiora said sheepishly.

"Wait, wait, wait!" Obioma exclaimed, eyes wide with realisation, even as Obiora widened his eyes comically and tried to subtly shake his head. "Does this mean—did you—?"

"Uh—" Obinna tried to interject, sensing Obiora's panic.

"Oh, for God's sake," Ifeoma interrupted. "We know, Obiora."

"Oh." Obioma seemed to realise what he'd done. "Oops?"

Obiora sighed, though he felt a little relieved. "You *told* them?"

"Why are you looking at me?" Obioma said when Obiora narrowed in on him. "It could've been Obinna!"

"But it *was* you," Obiora accused.

Obioma shrugged, a lazy grin stretching his mouth. "Yeah, okay, fine. You caught me. I can't lie to mummy to save my life."

"Oya, oya, all of you should sit down." Even seated, Ifeoma still managed to look intimidating, her hands on her hips as she said, "Well. Obiora. Is there something you'd like to tell us?"

"I'm sorry, mummy, daddy," Obiora began contritely. "I should've told you the truth about where I was going."

Ifeoma immediately softened. "Oh, honey, don't apologise. We understand."

"You ... do?" Obiora asked dubiously. He glanced at his brothers, but of course they were no help, staring back at him blankly. The worms.

"Your brothers explained," his mother continued, and Obiora tried not to panic. What the fuck had they told his parents? He deliberately avoided looking at his father. "We should be the ones apologising." Obiora's head snapped up at that. His mother heaved a sigh. "We shouldn't—that is, your father and I—we shouldn't have put so much pressure on you to find a partner. We just want you to be happy, Obim, but obviously, we went about it the wrong way. If we'd done it correctly, perhaps you could have entrusted us with the truth about going for this, eh, bachelorette competition."

"Did you win, then? Is that why you look so good?" Obioma asked with another leer. Obinna elbowed him violently in the ribs, making him grunt.

Osita glared at them both, but it held no heat.

Obiora instantly wanted to lie to placate his mother—she seemed really upset that he'd kept this from her. He wanted to tell them it was because of the contract that he'd kept it from them—he wanted to smooth over their hurt, but he knew it wouldn't help.

He thought of Ejiro at that moment, and felt his heart twist painfully. His mother was partially right; he hadn't told them mostly because he'd wanted a break from his father's firm, and hadn't known how to ask for it. But he also hadn't wanted them to get their hopes up about him "getting over" Ada.

Which he needed to address. Now. There was no way he was going to be able to tell them about Ejiro, not if they planned to use his feelings for him as proof that he was "moving on". He couldn't let them tarnish his love for Ada any longer.

"Mummy, daddy." He couldn't quite meet their eyes. "I have to say something, and I want the two of you to listen."

"All right, Obim."

"What is it?"

Obiora braced himself. "Brother, you should probably listen, too," he said, referring to both of his siblings. They only ever used the formal mode of address when they were being serious or teasing, there was no in-between.

"Go on," Obinna said, plastering a neutral expression on his face.

Obioma nodded.

Obiora swallowed. He thought of Ejiro again, the passionate strength in his voice when he'd told him *you don't have to choose*. Fuck, he wished Ejiro were here.

"I'm never getting over Ada," he said in a rush.

His mother seemed to swell in her seat. "Obim—" she began worriedly, sternly, about to argue.

"No, mummy, please. Listen."

She pursed her lips reluctantly.

"I'm never getting over Ada," he continued, "because there is nothing *to* get over. I loved her, I was planning to spend the rest of my life with her, and then the world took her from me. We didn't— *break* up, or part ways; she was *taken* from me, do you understand?" He met each of their eyes, silently begging. "Of course I'm never going to stop loving her. But that doesn't mean I'm incapable of loving someone new. I loved Nicholas with my entire heart, but he wanted me to *choose*. When I refused, he decided to choose for me. That's not something I ever want to go through again."

His mother interjected again, stubbornly, "Obim, I get you, I understand what you're saying, but Nick's issue was that you kept making Ada a priority during your relationship—"

"No, I didn't," Obiora said, using a herculean effort not to snap. "What, because I celebrated her birthday or mourned on the anniversary of her funeral? How is that making her a priority?"

"Obim, you need to understand. It must've felt to Nick like he was sharing you—your—your attentions—I mean, celebrating an ex-lover's birthday—"

"*Mummy*," Obiora interrupted, his heart breaking. "You're not listening."

"I'm listening," she said, a little desperately, switching to Igbo. "I hear you, and I loved Ada—I loved her so much, Obim, like she was my own daughter—but you need to understand where Nick was coming from. How would you feel if Nicholas had pictures of his ex all over his house? In his *wallet*, kukuma? Wouldn't you feel somehow?"

"Ada isn't my ex," Obiora said, jaw clenched, hands fisted on his thighs.

"You know what I mean." Ifeoma waved him off.

Obiora felt a sinking sensation in his stomach. He regretted ever bringing this up. He should have taken his mother's apology at face value and left well enough alone. Let them think whatever they wanted to think about Ejiro. Oh God, he felt like he was going to be sick.

"Ah, I think I understand now," his father said. Obiora looked up, feeling his heart swell with painful hope.

"Ify," Osita called his wife by the nickname he solely used for her. "Say, God forbid, I die today, and you meet someone new down the line. Will you stop loving me?"

Ifeoma recoiled. "What? God forbid! How can you even—?"

"No, nne. Please, *listen*. Pay attention to what your son is saying. Will you forget about me? Will you pack all the things we've shared together, all our mementos, and shove them in a box, never to speak of or see the light again?"

Ifeoma looked stricken.

"Did we make you feel like that?" Obioma asked, looking painfully small. "Did we make you feel like you couldn't mourn her?"

"No," Obiora said immediately, hating that he was the one making his brother look like that. Then, "Yes," he admitted hesitantly, because he couldn't coddle them any longer without hurting himself. He didn't want to hurt anymore.

"Nicholas was jealous," Obinna said, seemingly explaining to himself. A smidgen of shame bled into his next sentence. "You did nothing in the course of your relationship to make him feel insecure—heck, I remember you pretending the anniversary of her funeral didn't make you feel like poop, all to coddle a grown man's feelings. And we prioritised his feelings of inadequacy over your need to grieve Ada however you saw fit. She was someone you loved, and she died too soon. Nicholas should've respected that."

Oh, oh God. Obiora was going to cry.

"Oh, obim," his mother said, almost a sob, and that was it.

He looked away, wiping his eyes furiously.

"Come here. Come here, my son." But she'd gotten up, perching herself on the armrest of his chair, pulling him into her bosom like he was still a child. "I'm so sorry, I'm so, so sorry."

Obiora let her baby him, and cried.

"WELL, THAT WAS CATHARTIC," OBIORA said a few hours later when he and his brothers left the house, after being stuffed full. In the end, they'd strayed away from topics of conversation that could've been upsetting.

His parents didn't ask him about the competition again after that, probably thinking perhaps he'd lost. Or maybe they thought he'd *won*, but weren't sure if their excitement for that would be read as them being happy that he was "moving on" or not. Fucking hell, this whole thing was a mess.

"I really missed you, brother." Obioma threw an arm over Obiora's shoulders. After a beat, Obinna echoed the movement on his other side.

Obiora felt warm all over, though he pretended he was irritated instead. "What is it, now?"

"What? We can't just miss you again?"

Obiora couldn't help but laugh, because out of the three of them, Obinna was the one who'd lost the Nigerian accent and mannerisms the fastest, but he'd said that in the thickest Igbo accent he could muster.

"Don't think I didn't notice you not answering the question earlier," Obioma continued. Obinna groaned.

"For God's sake, Obioma, let it rest."

"Just answer the question: did you win or not?"

At that moment, Obiora's phone beeped as the cab he'd ordered pulled up in front of the house.

He slipped from his brothers' clutches, smiling a little as he spun around, walking backward towards his cab.

"No, Obioma, I didn't win."

"Oh." Obioma tried—poorly—to hide his disappointment.

"Couldn't leave well enough alone, could you?" Obinna sighed.

Obiora laughed. He opened the cab door. "That doesn't mean I didn't meet someone, though."

He'd already shut the door before the words could sink in.

"Wait, what?"

"Obiora, you get out of that car right now!"

"Drive!" Obiora told the man, laughing, and the car was off, the driver shaking his head with amusement.

His phone pinged several times after that, and Obiora grinned. Finally. It felt good to be home.

TWENTY-FIVE

THE THREE DAYS IT TOOK for Ejiro to get eliminated from the competition felt like the longest days of his entire life. But when it finally happened, Ejiro felt simultaneously relieved, scared, and melancholic in equal measure. After Sophia had told him he was going home, they'd hugged, and he'd known, as he'd looked into her eyes, that even without his feelings for Obiora, things between them would never have worked out, even if Ejiro had tried. The non-consensual kiss really had ruined everything.

"I'll probably see you at the live show in a few months," she'd said, low enough so their mics wouldn't pick it up.

Ejiro grinned. "Yeah. See you then." He raised his voice a little. "Good luck, Sophia. You've got your choice cut out for you."

"You're telling me," Sophia said, grimacing playfully. He laughed.

And then it was over. The second Ejiro got in the car Ameri hired to take him straight home, Ejiro spared only one last despondent glance back at the mansion, before he was fumbling in the secure little bag that held his devices, bringing out his phone and switching it on. A flood of messages and notifications lit up the screen, which he ignored for now. He'd ripped out the page from his sketchbook that held Obiora's number earlier, and it had been sitting folded in his suit pocket like a brand all evening as they'd filmed the Heart-giving Ceremony.

Ejiro already had the digits memorised—whenever he missed Obiora, he'd stared and thumbed at the paper, like imprinting Obiora's handwriting into his brain would somehow make him miss him less (spoiler alert, it didn't)—but he still double-checked that he had the number right from the piece of paper just in case.

His heart leapt into his throat when he created a new contact and the WhatsApp icon immediately appeared underneath.

"Oh my God," Ejiro whispered, struggling to breathe.

Unable to help it, he clicked on the icon. It redirected him to the messaging app.

Seeing Obiora's face, even if it was just his profile picture on WhatsApp, had Ejiro's heart skipping several beats, his stomach roiling with butterflies. He clicked on the picture to see it better, nearly swallowing his tongue when he saw that Obiora was at the gym. He was sitting with his thighs spread on either side of the weight-lifting bench, dressed in nothing but black gym shorts and a black tank top, thick curls messy, his skin glistening with sweat.

He held a water bottle loosely in one hand, and was smirking and flipping the camera off with the other hand, which told Ejiro that Esther had probably been the one to take the picture.

Warmth pooled in Ejiro's lower belly as he stared at the muscles in Obiora's bared arms, his ridiculously sexy smirk, and his freaking *thighs* Jesus freaking Christ. Ejiro clicked back into the chat, like staring at the empty chat box would rid him of his lust.

This was real. This was *freaking* real.

Obiora's status abruptly changed to "online". Ejiro immediately locked his phone and resisted the urge to throw the device across the seat.

He must've made a distressed noise, because the driver asked, "All right, mate?"

"Huh? What?" He cleared his throat when his voice came out too high. "Yeah. Yes. I'm fine. Thank you."

I'll message him later, Ejiro thought, unlocking his phone and clicking instead onto the chat he shared with Ajiri and Blessing. When he got home tonight, before he went to bed, he'd message Obiora. The thought made him feel like squealing.

"This is real," he repeated out loud in a low whisper. "This is ..." He hesitated, then let the curse fly. "This is *fucking* real."

When Ajiri and Blessing flooded the chat with excited messages and emojis after Ejiro said he was on his way home, Ejiro locked his phone and sat back, closing his eyes.

He tried to take a nap, then when that failed, listen to music on his headphones, but he was just too jittery.

He was home before he was ready, walking down the short path that led to the three-bedroom house he shared with Ajiri and Blessing. Everything still felt dreamy. It almost felt like homesickness, even though he was home.

"EJIRO!" Ajiri screamed, jumping into his arms. She must've heard his key in the lock and rushed to open the door.

Ejiro laughed, stumbling back in surprise but managing to catch her.

"Ejiro!" Blessing echoed, also running at him.

"Oof!" he gasped as she joined in on the hug, the momentum making him take several steps backward.

"Welcome back, welcome back! Oh God, I missed you." Ajiri abruptly turned away to wipe her eyes.

"Ajiri, stop! Don't cry! You'll make *me* cry," Ejiro protested, his eyes already burning.

In the back, Blessing sniffed.

Ejiro laughed, even as the tears slid down his cheeks. "Not you, too!"

The three of them laughed, hugging tightly. Ejiro clenched his eyes shut, breathing in their familiar scents. God, he'd missed them.

He hadn't realised just how much he'd missed them until he was in their arms again.

"Come on," Ajiri said, wiping her eyes again and sniffing.

They helped him with his bags. The buzzer went off a moment later.

"That must be the pizza," Blessing said. "I'll get it!"

"Ah, tell me everything! Any good news to share?" Ajiri waggled her eyebrows, heading to Ejiro's room, which was on the ground floor. Every inch of her was vibrating with excitement.

Ejiro grinned. His pulse raced. "Why don't we wait for Blessing?"

"Ugh, fine. Spoilsport."

Ejiro laughed. He didn't bother unpacking; he and Ajiri dumped his bags in his room before they reconvened to the sitting room, Blessing back with the pizza.

Everything in the house was the same. The drier apparently still wasn't working properly, because their clothing rack at the edge of the sitting room by the windows was filled with Ajiri's and Blessing's latest wash.

Blessing collapsed onto the sofa beside Ajiri after dropping the pizza boxes on the table.

"Drinks!" Ajiri jumped up from her seat and rushed to the kitchen. She came back with two ciders for her and Blessing, and a Sprite for Ejiro. "Now," she said, when she was back in her seat, her drink open, and a slice of pizza in her hand. "Tell us everything!"

"Did you win?" Blessing asked excitedly.

Ejiro's heart began to pound again. Slowly, he shook his head, but he was blushing furiously, unable to help it. He felt nervous, even though he knew Ajiri and Blessing would love him no matter what.

"Oh." Blessing slumped. "Aw, that's okay, though!"

"Wait, but what's that look on your face?" Ajiri asked, shoving forward from her seat. Her eyes were bright. "Why are you blushing?"

Ejiro swallowed. He bit the inside of his cheek to try and stop himself from smiling helplessly, but it didn't work.

"Um, well." He couldn't meet their eyes. His cheeks hurt. "I might not have won, but I did meet someone."

There was a brief silence.

"*What*?" Blessing screeched.

Ejiro winced, his cheeks burning harder. "Not so loud!"

"Ejiro, you sly dog!" Ajiri jumped out of her seat so she could crowd onto him where he'd sat on one of the armchairs. She rubbed his head with her knuckles, and he laughed, shoving her off. "Did you sleep with one of the producers?"

"Or—" Blessing gasped. "One of the *crew*?"

"Ejiro!" Ajiri cried, scandalised.

Ejiro laughed so hard it hurt. "No! Don't be silly! I didn't sleep with anyone. I—" Oh God, if the crew and producers were scandalous, just how scandalous would it be when he said it was one of the other bachelors?

"If it wasn't someone working on the set or one of the producers then how the fuck?" Ajiri asked, her brain working a mile a minute. "Did you manage to meet other people during the filming? What the fuck, Ejiro?"

Ejiro couldn't feel his cheeks. He hid his face behind his hands. "It wasn't a woman," he said, voice muffled.

There was another silence.

"WHAT!" Blessing screeched again.

"One of the *bachelors*?" Ajiri cried. "Ejiro, was it one of the other bachelors?"

Slowly, still hiding behind his hands, he nodded.

"Ejiro!" Ajiri screamed, sounding both proud and scandalised in equal measure. "No you didn't!"

Blessing was laughing hysterically. "Motherfucking plot twist!"

"You tell us everything right now!"

"Yes, ma."

Ajiri pinched him. Ejiro yelped, but he was laughing.

"I think I'm going to need something stronger than a cider," Blessing said, still laughing, standing and heading into the kitchen.

"Just bring the entire bottle of vodka in here, babe!" Ajiri called at her.

Ejiro couldn't stop grinning. God, he loved them, he loved them. It felt good to be home.

"MY GOD," **BLESSING SAID WHEN** he was done, ending his tale with Obiora leaving his number in Ejiro's sketchbook (though he'd glossed over the passionate goodbye kisses they'd shared). She and Ajiri were "buzzing", thanks to the alcohol and the topic of conversation. They sat almost straight-backed on the sofa, their eyes intent on him. "So." Blessing waggled her eyebrows. "Are you in love with him?"

Ejiro blushed furiously. "I-I don't know. Maybe. I don't know. Stop staring at me!"

His twin and her girlfriend laughed.

"Look at how he hasn't stopped smiling," Ajiri said, still laughing. "My guy is fucking *whipped*!"

Ejiro groaned, hiding his face behind his hands again. His cheeks were so, so hot. "Abeg, leave me alone."

"Aw, you must really like him," Blessing cooed playfully.

"So, what does this mean?" Ajiri asked. "No pressure, obviously. But does this mean you're bisexual? If you don't want a label, that's also completely fine."

"Oh, um, I guess I am?" He dropped his hands. "I'm—I'm demisexual."

"Huh," Blessing said. "That makes a lot of sense."

"Wow. Now why does this kind of make me hate Sam a lot

more?"

Ajiri had never liked Ejiro's ex, and now that Ejiro was settling into his newly discovered sexuality, he realised that his relationship with Sam really had been bad. He'd gone through the motions with her because he'd thought they were what he was *meant* to do, not because he'd actually wanted to do them. She'd been pretty and she'd talked to him and Ejiro had mistaken his awe and nervousness at her beauty for sexual attraction.

Looking back at how she'd bulldozed him into a relationship and then dumped him like hot coal when he'd begun to think he was going to marry her, Ejiro had to admit that he hated her a little, too. Sure, he hadn't been aware of his sexuality then, but he'd tried to be good for her. He'd practically tried to mould himself into whatever shape she wanted—after all, he'd thought, wasn't that what a good boyfriend did? But looking back, it was obvious she had known this, and taken advantage of it.

"She was always so grabby, wasn't she?" Blessing said with a wrinkle of her nose. "I thought you were just a no-PDA kinda guy, but you were literally uncomfortable and she—Jesus Christ."

"Let's not talk about that bitch."

"Ajiri!" Ejiro gasped, but he felt warm at her defence.

"So." Ajiri leered, ignoring his scolding. "Have you called him yet?"

Ejiro's phone suddenly felt heavier in his pocket. He swallowed, throat bobbing. "Not yet."

Blessing raised an eyebrow. "*Are* you going to call him?"

"Of course I'm going to call him!" Ejiro scoffed. "Just not when you two are staring at me like that."

Ajiri comically widened her eyes, leaning forward in her seat, not blinking. "Like what?"

Ejiro threw a pillow at her.

She laughed.

"Oh God," she said suddenly, wheezing. "Oh God, I just realised—

mummy's going to flip her shit!" She laughed hysterically, while Ejiro felt his heart drop into his stomach. "Can you imagine? With all her disgusting homophobic talk and now both of us are queer! Ha! I wish I could see the look on her face when you tell her." Ajiri narrowed her eyes when she noticed his strange silence. "You *are* going to tell her, right?"

"Ajiri," Blessing said gently.

"No, I'm serious. Ejiro?"

Ejiro shook his head. "Look, I just got back, can we not? Please?"

"Fine." Ajiri sighed. She grinned. "You know mummy actually called me?"

Ejiro's heart skipped. "Are you serious?"

"Mhm." Ajiri nodded, laughing a little. "She's so desperate. I truly believe she thinks you're ignoring her or something. She called me like—six times, was it, babe?" And in Ajiri's world, six times was a million too many; the only time their mother called her was when she couldn't reach Ejiro for some reason, which only happened once in a blue moon. "And each time it was at a ridiculous time, like, ass o'clock in the morning."

Ejiro decided it was in his best interest not to tell Ajiri that his mother had called him, too, even though his phone had been switched off. He was pretty sure about half of the notifications on his phone were from her.

"It was so awkward," Blessing said, giggling. She tackled Ajiri into the sofa, burying her face between Ajiri's breasts.

Ejiro wrinkled his nose in disgust and rolled his eyes, though he'd unfortunately seen worse. "Still here, Blessing."

"Mm."

"It's really good to have you back, Ejiro. I missed you."

Ejiro smiled tenderly. "I missed you, too."

It didn't take long after that before Ejiro began to yawn, and Ajiri and Blessing drunkenly began to feel each other up, though they were trying—and failing—to be discreet. It was an unfortunate fact he knew; Ajiri and Blessing were horny drunks.

Once upon a time, seeing them like this would have filled Ejiro with a bittersweet mix of jealousy and longing; he still felt the latter, but it was a different kind of yearning, especially now that he knew he had this—that he *could* have this.

Just as soon as he messaged Obiora.

Ejiro stood and stretched, ignoring the way his heart had begun to race. "I'm going to bed."

"Mm. Okay," Ajiri said, her voice husky. "Goodnight."

"Goodnight, Ejiro," Blessing echoed, though she and Ajiri made no move to get up.

Ejiro walked to the sofa and stood next to them, hands crossed over his chest. "Up. Both of you. I'm not letting you have sex on the sofa. Again."

"We've practically christened this entire house, Ejiro, you might as —"

"No!" Ejiro yelled, covering his ears. "La! La! La! I can't hear you!"

The two women laughed, but staggered off the sofa and up the stairs to their room, giggling and kissing as they went. Ejiro shook his head fondly and headed to his room.

As he closed the door behind him, leaning on it, his heartbeat began to go haywire.

Ignoring the heavy presence of his phone in his pocket, he painstakingly began to unpack his bags. When he was done, he brushed his teeth and took a shower. Then he checked up on his notifications, telling his friends he was back, and he'd talk to them properly tomorrow. He checked on his Patreon and Tapas accounts, his heart swelling with love when he noticed the number of patrons and subscribers had actually increased since his hiatus. He'd written and outlined a lot for his comic while he'd been offline, and he couldn't wait to redraw the pages on his tablet and upload them. Perhaps he'd even do a double or triple update, as a surprise and a gift for their trust and patience.

He completely ignored the messages and voice notes left from his mother. The thought of talking to her made him feel like he couldn't breathe. If she asked him anything about where he'd been, he wasn't sure he could lie to her anymore—the thought alone was painfully exhausting. He'd deal with her tomorrow. Or whenever.

Finally, it was time to talk to Obiora.

Ejiro trembled. He switched off all his lights and dived underneath his covers, like the darkness and the sheets would protect him.

Oh God oh God oh God.

What if Obiora had forgotten about him? What if being out of the whole dreamy aura of the filming and the isolation and everything made Obiora realise his feelings weren't true? Surely Obiora could do better.

"Stop it, Ejiro," Ejiro whispered out loud. He gently slapped his cheeks.

Obiora had said he loved him. And Ejiro believed him.

He clicked into a fresh chat with Obiora on WhatsApp. Quickly, before he could chicken out, he sent a "hello" with the "see no evil" monkey emoji.

Then he buried his phone underneath his pillow and closed his eyes, kicking his legs like a child as emotions bubbled through him like champagne.

When Obiora didn't respond immediately, Ejiro felt his stomach sink. Then he inwardly slapped himself. It was really late, almost one AM. Obiora was probably asleep. Ejiro shouldn't get his hopes up. Obiora would reply to him tomorr—

He nearly jumped out of his skin when his phone began to vibrate in his hand.

He yanked it out from underneath his pillows.

Ah! Obiora was *calling*.

Ejiro sat up quickly, fiddling with his hair, his night clothes, then silently cursed himself because it wasn't a video call.

He cleared his throat then answered. "Hello. Hi. Hello," he said shyly, nervously.

"Oh fuck," Obiora murmured, his voice thick yet light with happiness. The sound of it filled Ejiro from head to toe with heat, made his ribs swell and hurt, too small to contain his thumping heart. "I missed you."

Oh, Ejiro felt lighter than air. "Hello," he repeated, like a dork. The butterflies in his stomach were going to make him sick. "I missed you, too. So much."

"Fuck, baby, it's so good to hear your voice."

Ejiro sighed dreamily, like a freaking Disney princess.

Yeah, maybe Blessing had been onto something; Ejiro was definitely in love.

TWENTY-SIX

> Roses are red,
> Violets are blue,
> I don't know how to rhyme,
> But I can't stop thinking about you
> 🖤
> 07:01

> Hello there 🏚️ 07:04 ✓✓

> 🖤🖤🖤 07:04 ✓✓

> oh thank god 07:04

> that wasn't too cringey i take it 😁
> 07:04

CUPID CALLING

> lmfao noooo 🙈 07:04
> I loved it please 07:04
> it was a lovely thing to wake up to 07:05
> 🥺🏠 07:05

🥰 07:05

good morning baby 07:05

how was your night? 07:05

> It was lovely thank you 😊 07:05
> How was yours? 07:05

best sleep I've had in a while thanks to hearing your voice last night 👅 07:05

> oh my god 07:05
> stop it 🙈 07:06

😁 07:06

I love you 07:06

I'm going to start preparing for work now babe 07:06

just wanted to message you first 07:06

🖤 07:06

                                        Thank you baby 07:06 ✓✓

                                                            ♥ 07:06 ✓✓

                        Have a nice day at work 😊 07:06 ✓✓

You too 07:06

I'll call you later, yeah? 07:07

                                                  Okay 🥰 07:07 ✓✓

Hey, I miss you 13:10

                                                     Baby 🥺 13:10 ✓✓

                                      I miss you too 13:10 ✓✓

Are you busy rn? 👀 13:10

I mean, are you in a place where you can listen to a voice note 👀 13:11

                                        No, I'm not busy 13:11 ✓✓

                                        And yes I am 👀 13:11 ✓✓

 13:13

Transcript: "Hey baby, I really wanted to call but I can't right now. You can probably hear the noise in the background—I'm at the pub across from the office; we're on lunch break now—but I really wanted to hear your voice, so maybe send me a voice note, pretty please? *laughs*

CUPID CALLING

▶ ||·|||·|||·|·|||·|||·|||·|· 13:15 ✓✓

Transcript: *shyly* "Hiiii. This is ... my voice. *laughs* Okay bye." *tender laughter again*

Is it just me or do voice recordings always make you sound like straight up garbage 😬   13:15 ✓✓

(talking about myself btw)   13:15 ✓✓

(you sound lovely 🙈)   13:15 ✓✓

I have no idea what you're talking about Ejiro   13:15

I'm literally setting that voice note to be my ringtone as we speak   13:15

LMFAOOO 🙈🙈🙈🙈   13:16 ✓✓

PLEASE   13:16 ✓✓

[Obiora sends a screenrecording of his phone]

you think this is a game?   13:16

if you don't stop   13:16 ✓✓

🙈🙈🙈   13:16 ✓✓

god why are you like this 🙈   13:16 ✓✓

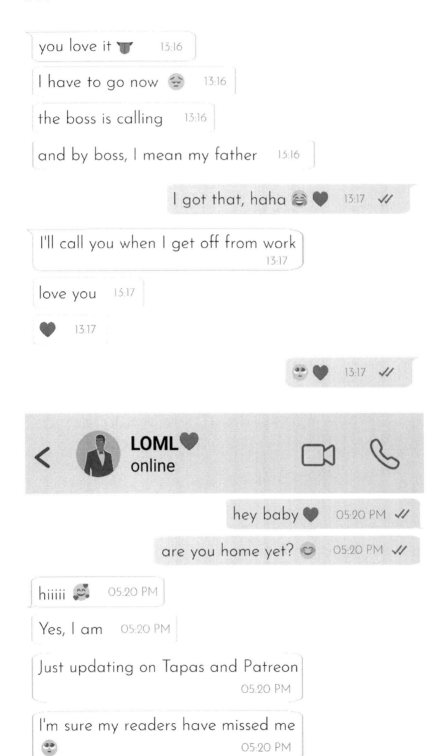

CUPID CALLING

👀 05:20 PM ✓✓

? 👀 05:20 PM

I may or may not have stalked you online and found your website 👁👄👁   05:22 PM ✓✓

LMFAOOO   05:22 PM

I—   05:22 PM

😂😂😂😂 05:22 PM ✓✓

glad you find my stalkerish tendencies amusing 😂   05:22 PM ✓✓

nooooo don't think that way   05:22 PM

this actually means a lot to me   05:22 PM

that you wanted to check out my stuff 🙈   05:22 PM

And now like every creative who finds out their irl friends are seeing their stuff, I'm going to go crawl into a hole and never emerge   05:23 PM

😂😂😂😂 05:23 PM ✓✓

you are too fucking cute   05:23 PM ✓✓

can I call you?   05:23 PM ✓✓

yes please 🥺   05:24 PM

[Obiora sends a picture of a plate of jollof rice]

eating jollof at my parents' rn 07:41 PM

it's not as good as yours, but you won't catch me telling my mum that 👀 07:41 PM

come, guy, why do you like lying 07:43 PM

LMFAO 07:43 PM

I speak nothing but the truth baby 🤭 07:43 PM

Also, the fam says hi 07:43 PM

Hello 🦍 07:44 PM

🖤 07:46 PM

Call you tonight, yeah? 07:46 PM

Yes baby 07:49 PM

🖤 07:49 PM

God I can't wait to see you 🦍 11:08 PM

The days honestly can't go fast enough 11:08 PM

Aw baby 11:08 PM

Me too 11:08 PM

God I miss you 11:08 PM

CUPID CALLING

> I love you 11:08 PM
>
> I'll let you go to bed now 11:08 PM
>
> Can I call you in the morning? 11:08 PM

Yes, please 11:09 PM

I don't care if you wake me up 11:09 PM

Call me anytime 11:09 PM

> Okay, love. I will 11:09 PM

Goodnight baby 11:09 PM

♥ 11:09 PM

> Goodnight 😴 11:09 PM

TWENTY-SEVEN

THE BUTTERFLIES IN OBIORA'S STOMACH had turned into helicopters. Ejiro's train was going to pull into the platform any second now. Obiora was so fucking nervous. People on the platform had been trying—and failing—not to stare at him curiously since he'd arrived, mostly because of the bouquet of flowers he held. He didn't blame them; a lot of people loved to see public romantic gestures.

Obiora couldn't wait to see Ejiro's face because he knew deep down that Ejiro would *adore* the flowers. He had gleaned from their conversations—since they'd started getting to know each other back in Oxford—that Ejiro had never been loved romantically the way he'd so dreamed of; Obiora had read between the lines, understanding that Ejiro's ex had told him, in not so many words, that Ejiro should be *grateful* for her attention. The thought made Obiora see red. He swore to himself he was going to love Ejiro loudly and proudly. It was the least he deserved.

He straightened when the voice over the intercom finally announced that the train from Manchester was arriving. His heart was beating so hard he could barely hear anything else over the roar of it.

The train pulled in, and Obiora tried to control his breathing. His eyes frantically devoured all the seats he could see through the windows, trying to spot his boyfriend. The word filled him with pleasure.

The doors opened, and a crowd spilled out.

Like it was fate, Obiora had ended up standing right where one of the carriages' doors had come open.

And there he was.

It'd been exactly a week since Obiora had last seen him, yet it felt like a lifetime. The slightly dreamy atmosphere of the mansion in Oxford wasn't here anymore, and even though they'd practically been texting and talking on the phone nonstop since Ejiro had left the competition, seeing the man in front of him now was still enough to take Obiora's breath away.

He was wearing a long-sleeved yellow t-shirt and black jeans, and was sporting a fresh fade, his hair cropped close on the sides, but left a little long on the top. The brightness of the shirt made his brown skin positively glimmer, and along with the way he just seemed to *glow* when he spotted Obiora—it was like being punched in the gut.

For one breathless moment, Obiora wanted to say fuck the flowers. He wanted to drag Ejiro into his arms and kiss him within an inch of his life.

Ejiro's expression was already bright when he spotted Obiora, a helpless-looking grin stretching his mouth. When he spotted the flowers though, he literally gasped, his eyes so wide, his hands moving up to cover his mouth like Obiora had just proposed to him.

Yeah. Totally fucking worth it.

"Hey," Obiora said with a grin when they were in front of each other. His voice came out gravelly completely without his control.

"Hi." Ejiro's voice was just as deep, sending shivers dancing up Obiora's spine.

For a moment, they simply stared at each other.

Ejiro smiled a little flirtatiously—he'd started becoming bolder with his emotions the more they'd talked—and each time Obiora thought he couldn't fall in love any harder, there Ejiro went, merely *existing* and proving him wrong.

"Are those for me?" he asked, his voice light and teasing.

"Yes," Obiora said, deciding not to crack a joke instead like he wanted to.

"Oh," Ejiro breathed, probably surprised at the seriousness, but obviously pleased.

Obiora handed over the flowers with a slight bow. "My love."

Though no red showed up on his deep, lovely dark skin, Obiora could tell Ejiro was blushing furiously.

"Stop it," he said, and then shyly, "Thank you."

Obiora held a hand out, his heart skipping a beat when Ejiro didn't hesitate to tangle their fingers. They left the station like that, hand in hand, and like the rest of the world had ceased to exist.

They took one of the cabs waiting outside the station instead of an Uber. They had to detangle their hands to sit, but then immediately reached for each other after Obiora told the driver his address.

They sat there, Ejiro clutching his flowers in one hand, the other gripping Obiora's tightly, while they tried to see into each other's souls through their eyes.

"Journey okay?" Obiora asked, his voice still rough. His eyes dropped to Ejiro's lips.

"Went by in a blink," Ejiro replied, his voice just as rough. They'd texted almost throughout the one-hour train ride it had taken for Ejiro to get here, so Obiora agreed that the time really had gone by in a blink.

Ejiro's own eyes also dropped to Obiora's mouth. They were both tense, trembling.

Obiora's lips parted, and Ejiro's mouth seemed to echo the movement, a soft sigh escaping his sweet lips. God. Fuck. Obiora wanted to kiss him now, but he wasn't sure he would be able to stop. With how hard Ejiro was gripping his hand, it seemed he felt the same.

They couldn't get to Obiora's fast enough. Obiora paid quickly, telling the driver to keep the change as he pulled Ejiro toward the high-rise where his flat was located. For a moment, he hated that he'd chosen not to live in a house, especially after Ada's death—the space would have felt too big, too empty.

Right now, though, the walk to his front door felt like a million fucking miles.

The minute Obiora had the door open, they were crashing into each other's arms and slamming their lips together.

Obiora pushed Ejiro against the closed door, devouring his mouth like a man starved. And from the low-pitched, desperate sounds Ejiro was making, he felt just as fevered.

Obiora trailed his hands all over Ejiro's body, pressing harder against him, trying to imprint Ejiro's heat and hardness into his skin. He wanted Ejiro's heady scent imbued deep into his lungs. Ejiro's hands were in his hair, one leg hooked up around his hip, arching against him—a livewire of raw lust.

"Christ," Obiora groaned, trailing kisses down his jaw, nipping at the sensitive skin with his teeth.

"Obiora," Ejiro moaned, trembling with pleasure, his hands gripping Obiora's hair tightly, as if to prevent Obiora from even thinking about pulling away.

"Your flowers are on the floor," Obiora said hoarsely.

"It's the thought that counts," Ejiro quipped, and Obiora laughed, so in love it fucking hurt.

They kissed again, this time a bit slower, deeper, feeling out the shape of their lips, dipping their tongues in and out, tasting each other's mouths. It did nothing to quench the fire blazing in Obiora's veins—in fact, it seemed to make the flames of his desire burn even hotter.

He slipped his hands down to grab at the taut globes of Ejiro's ass, squeezing gently. "Okay?"

"Yes." Ejiro's voice was a moan.

Obiora lifted him up until Ejiro took the hint and wrapped his legs around Obiora's hips.

"Oh God," Ejiro gasped, throwing his head back, rocking his hips forward. Obiora could feel Ejiro where he was hard, his dick a hot brand through his jeans. Obiora bit back a groan, snapping his own hips forward, grinding their hard lengths together. Jesus *fucking* Christ. "Obiora. *Obiora.*"

Christ, the way he said his name. Obiora sucked hickeys into his throat, each one making Ejiro gasp and tremble and grind, until they were both shaking with the effort it was taking not to just let go and come in their underwear like teenagers.

Sucking on his throat made a different desire rise in Obiora; suddenly, he wanted to get on his knees. He wanted Ejiro's hot, hard length filling his mouth, fucking into the back of his throat. He wanted to know what kind of sounds Ejiro would make when he was losing control, if he'd grip Obiora's hair the way he was grasping it now —if he'd still tremble and shake so fucking sweetly. Obiora's stomach swooped at the thought, his legs threatening to buckle with the strength of his want.

"Ejiro," Obiora whispered hotly, gently tugging his earlobe with his teeth, enjoying his answering shiver. "Baby. I want to suck you off."

"Oh!" Ejiro stiffened, his nails digging into Obiora's scalp. He clenched his eyes shut, his expression twisted with pleasured agony at the thought of it alone.

Obiora buried his face in Ejiro's neck, shaking and trying to breathe through the orgasm threatening to take him over.

"Yes?" Obiora encouraged, nipping at his throat.

"I—" Ejiro hesitated. He swallowed. "Okay," he said finally.

Obiora smiled, kissing his throat again. He took Ejiro's mouth in a tender kiss, gently bringing them down from the high, slowly letting Ejiro's legs drop to the floor.

When he pulled back, Ejiro was flushed, dazed, his lips wet.

"Hi," he said, nonsensically, dreamily. Obiora laughed, and couldn't help but kiss him again.

He took Ejiro's hand, and led him off the small entrance nook—the bathroom was on the right, his bedroom up ahead opposite them, and the second bedroom he'd turned into a workout area in the top right corner of the corridor. The sitting room slash kitchen and dining were through an open entryway on the left.

As Obiora began to lead him there, Ejiro stopped him, gently tugging on his hand.

"Wait." Ejiro licked his lips and sidled closer until he was pressed up against Obiora's side. He couldn't meet Obiora's eyes as he whispered, his voice low and soft, "You said you want—I mean—" God, he couldn't even say the words; he was so fucking endearing.

Obiora cupped his face in his hands, grinning and kissing his forehead. "All the words in the world couldn't even *begin* to describe how badly I want you," he admitted huskily. "But you're obviously not ready."

Ejiro swallowed visibly. "But I—I want it. I want you," he confessed, like it was a secret.

A hot bolt of desire shot up Obiora's legs, which he ignored.

"You can want me and still not exactly be ready, baby," Obiora said, pecking him on his lips. Then he leaned in closer to whisper, "Besides, I like my consent explicit; absolutely zero hesitation."

When he pulled back, Ejiro was staring at him with shining eyes. Obiora didn't need to hear Ejiro say those three words to recognise that they were what were lighting up his expression.

"I love you," Obiora responded to the silent declaration.

Ejiro trembled, his eyes getting shinier.

Obiora's entire being seemed to soften. He stroked the back of Ejiro's palm with his hand. "Food's on the stove"—Ejiro had skipped breakfast, too excited and nervous to eat as he'd told Obiora earlier in the morning before he'd gotten on his train—"but I was wondering if maybe you'd like to cuddle on the sofa for a bit? I've just—I've missed you. And to be honest, I'd also like to compensate for all the times during the competition where I wanted to hold you but I couldn't."

Ejiro laughed, though the shine didn't leave his eyes. "That's probably going to be a lot of cuddles."

"An infinite amount of cuddles, yes," Obiora said, winking.

Ejiro grinned, his happiness sunny and unreserved. "Come on, then. Cuddling sounds perfect."

EJIRO MISSED HIS EVENING TRAIN back to Manchester twice, only forced to get off his butt when it was literally the last train of the night. He'd have stayed over, but Obiora was right, he wasn't ready. God, he loved him.

They'd ended up making out at the station as they'd waited for his train. Ejiro didn't think the simple act of kissing had ever felt so *good*. With Sam, kissing almost always led to sex; she'd never let them just enjoy the intimacy of making out itself, even though most of the time, that was all he might've wanted to do at the moment. Of course, he hadn't *minded* having sex with her when she wanted, but he was beginning to realise there was a difference between "not minding" and—as Obiora had eloquently put it—"explicit consent".

Obiora trying to get himself attuned to Ejiro's body language spoke of how much Obiora cared about him and what he wanted, which made Ejiro love him all the more.

When the train finally arrived, they shared one last heated kiss before they parted, then immediately started texting the moment they were apart, and the train was taking him home.

Can't wait to see you again, Ejiro sent, his blood bubbling like champagne as it did every time they texted each other. He felt like a lovesick teenager as he added a blushing emoji. *Today was so, so lovely.*

All they'd done was eat food and hang out, in the simplest sense of the word; making out, watching TV, taking a nap together, then cuddling and talking about nothing and everything. And even though his mother had called him later in the afternoon, completely oblivious of where he was and *who* he was with, nearly tainting his day as she'd hounded him about when he was coming back "home", it was still the best date Ejiro had ever had.

Miss you already, Obiora replied almost instantly, with the heart-eyed emoji.

Ejiro resisted the urge to hug the phone to his chest.

They texted throughout the train ride, and then the cab ride from the station to Ejiro's house.

He got home feeling like he was walking on air, and headed straight for the sitting room, knowing Ajiri and Blessing would probably still be awake even though it was past midnight.

"Ejiro!" Ajiri called, proving him right, before he'd even entered the room. "How was your date?" He knew his twin was leering without having to see her face.

"It was fine," he said as he entered the room, trying to look and sound casual as he flopped into the armchair.

Blessing squealed when she noticed what he held in his hands. "Aw, he got you flowers? And they're *real*! That's so cute!"

Ejiro blushed furiously, but he was so, so happy. The flowers were probably going to die in like a week because he didn't know squat about taking care of plants, but as Ejiro had said to Obiora earlier, it was the thought that counted.

"Oh?" Ajiri looked impressed. "That's given him some extra brownie points, I'll give him that."

Ejiro laughed. "I'm going to bed." He stood and stretched. "I just wanted you both to know that I had a great time."

"Going to bed, huh," Blessing said, raising an eyebrow.

"Is that what the kids are calling midnight calls these days?" Ajiri waggled her eyebrows.

"Leave me alone," Ejiro complained, but he couldn't stop grinning. "Goodnight!" he called as he left the sitting room.

"Goodnight!" the women echoed.

"I'm glad you had a great time," Ajiri said, twisting around on the sofa to meet his eyes, her own earnest. Sometimes, it felt like Ajiri's happiness at *Ejiro's* happiness was even more than his own.

Ejiro turned bashful. "Thank you."

He entered his room and began to prepare for bed.

He'd changed into his pyjamas and had just finished brushing his teeth when Obiora finally called. Seeing his name light up the screen of his phone set Ejiro's heart alight.

"Hey baby," Ejiro said into the phone, feeling shy as he did. He'd never been one for cliché pet names, but there was just something about how Obiora made him feel that brought the desire out in him.

"Hey," Obiora replied, a grin in his voice. "Got home okay?" he asked, even though they'd texted throughout and he *knew* Ejiro had gotten home okay.

Ejiro loved that he still asked anyway. "Yup. I'm getting in bed now."

"Good, good. Today was awesome, huh?"

"How do you manage to sound both dreamy and cocky at the same time?"

Obiora laughed. "I don't know, babe. It's a skill."

Ejiro laughed. Tomorrow was Sunday and they were both off from work, which meant they could talk for as long as they wanted to.

Ejiro tried to keep his voice and his laughter quiet. He didn't know how two hours passed, just like that.

The house was quiet. Obiora's voice had gone low, gravelly as it always did when he was feeling sleepy. Ejiro had always found it intensely sexy, but he'd ignored the way it made his stomach swoop.

Until tonight.

"Baby," Obiora whispered, words all grit.

"God, you sound so sexy right now," Ejiro confessed in a rush, pulse racing.

There was a slight pause. "Yeah?"

Oh God. Ejiro's dick twitched, then began to thicken. "Yeah," he said, swallowing when his voice came out a tad rougher, thick with desire. "You know I've never—no one's ever—" He swallowed again. Lowered his voice. "I've never gotten a blowjob before," he confessed.

"Jesus," Obiora whispered roughly. "Really?"

Ejiro shook his head, even though Obiora couldn't see him. "Really."

There was another slight pause. "Are your lights off, baby?"

Ejiro was suddenly overwhelmed with an intense rush of love for this man, at how Obiora had read and understood what he wanted so quickly, so easily.

"Yes," he whispered huskily. Oh God.

"Have you got your lube nearby?"

"Yeah." Oh Jesus. He couldn't believe he was doing this. Was he doing this?

"Mm. Are you hard for me, baby?"

"Oh," Ejiro gasped, his dick suddenly straining in his pyjamas. "Yes. Obiora. Please, please—"

"Fucking hell. Get your sheets off, baby. Touch yourself for me."

Ejiro obeyed, kicking the sheets off his legs and reaching for his dick, squeezing. He bit his lip.

Like he could see him, Obiora commanded, "No, baby, don't do that. Let me hear you."

"Oh fuck," Ejiro groaned, his profanity filter shot to hell. "How do I—how do you—?"

"Fuck, baby. You want me to tell you how to touch yourself?"

Ejiro's dick *throbbed* in his grip. "*Yes.*"

"Christ. Okay. Jesus. Can you take your clothes off for me? And get your lube out as well."

"Okay." Ejiro did as he was asked, his hands shaking.

For a moment he felt self-conscious, ridiculous, but when he brought the phone back to his ear, Obiora's first words were, "Fuck, I'm so hard for you right now. You have no idea how much this is turning me on—how much *you* turn me on."

"Obiora," Ejiro whispered, pleading.

"Go on, baby. Get some lube on your hand. Warm it up a little. Then stroke your dick for me; slowly."

Ejiro groaned at how filthy the word sounded coming from Obiora's lips, like sin itself. He had to drop his phone for a bit to get the lube in his hand, but soon he had the device back to his ear and was wrapping a hand around himself and stroking. He hissed through his teeth at the cold.

Obiora laughed a little, the sound like pure sex. "I told you to warm it up, baby."

Ejiro swallowed, still stroking. "I couldn't wait. I want you."

"Fucking hell, Ejiro. I want you, too. So fucking much. Can you hear me, baby? Hear how I'm touching myself, too?"

"Oh," Ejiro gasped. Now that he'd mentioned it, Ejiro could hear slick sounds echoing from the other side of the line. The sound of it, matching with Ejiro's own rhythm, was so fucking hot Ejiro felt like he would spontaneously combust. He moaned, stroking himself faster, *harder*, thrusting his hips, fucking up into his fist.

"Christ," Obiora groaned, automatically speeding up, too, his breaths coming out sharp and quick through the phone. "Those nights in Venice," Obiora began.

"Yes?" Ejiro encouraged, heat spreading through him as he remembered. Looking back, he had no idea how the fuck they'd been able to keep their hands off each other.

"Almost every night," Obiora confessed, "I thought about just—getting into your bed. I thought about waking you up with a kiss, about how you'd probably melt into it, how you'd spread your legs for me."

"Oh God," Ejiro groaned, imagining it and wanting it so badly he could feel the desire in his *teeth*.

"I never locked the door when I showered," Obiora continued in that deep, sexy as sin voice. Ejiro bit back his "I know", wanting to hear the rest. "I stroked myself while you were on the other side of the room. I imagined you saying fuck it and walking in there, climbing into the shower with me, slamming me against the wall and kissing me so hard I wouldn't taste anything but you for days afterward."

"*Obiora.*" Ejiro tried to ease his strokes, his hips lifting and his eyes rolling back at the torture of it. He wanted to come. He *needed* to come. His prick ached with it, throbbing and leaking into his palm. But he wanted to hear more.

"I thought about fucking you on the balcony," Obiora continued coarsely. "Just—bending you over *right* there, your pants around your hips, your hands clutching at the railing, your moans so fucking loud while I fucked you so hard you couldn't see straight."

"*Uhn.*" Ejiro arched, his balls cramping up. He tried to stop, to pull his hand away, but he was so fucking close, his dick so stiff, so sensitive it hurt.

"Obiora," he moaned, his hand flying across his length. "Oh God. I'm gonna come."

"Oh fuck." Obiora's voice was a sob. "Me too, baby. Oh fuck. Christ. *God*!"

They came at the same time, both of them going silent and still, before exhaling in a rush, Ejiro collapsing onto his mattress. He didn't stop stroking himself, milking every drop until he was whimpering and oversensitive and had to yank his hand away.

"Jesus," Obiora whispered, panting, his voice shaky. "Holy shit. Fucking hell."

"Fuck." Ejiro grinned, stretching lazily like the cat who'd gotten the cream. They were silent for a moment while they both caught their breaths.

"Best sex I've ever had," Ejiro said when he was breathing semi-normally, "and it wasn't even sex!"

Obiora laughed. "It's sex if we say it's sex."

"Okay." Ejiro giggled. He fucking *giggled*.

There was a grin in Obiora's voice when he said, "I love you."

"I—" The words nearly slipped past Ejiro's lips; he was so relaxed, his guard completely down, that he'd forgotten he hadn't yet said them out loud.

And he wanted to say them, desperately. But he didn't want to say it for the first time over the phone, and after they'd just had sex.

"I'll let you go to sleep, yeah?" Obiora's voice was soft.

Ejiro loved him so fucking fiercely. "Okay."

"Sleep well, baby."

"I'll call you in the morning."

"Thought *I* was your alarm?" Obiora teased, referring to how his phone calls in the mornings always seemed to be the thing to wake Ejiro up.

"Shut up," Ejiro said, but he was smiling. "So I like waking up to your voice first thing in the morning; sue me."

"Aw, baby. You're so fucking cute."

Ejiro blushed. "I'll wake you up this time; you'll see."

"Sure thing, grandpa."

Ejiro laughed and clutched his chest, trying and failing to stop the warmth spreading underneath his ribs, like his heart was growing. "Goodnight, baby."

"Goodnight."

The bone-deep exhaustion that seemed to come only after an intensely satisfying orgasm hit Ejiro from all corners after the call ended and Ejiro had cleaned himself up and gotten back into bed. When he said this had been the best sex he'd ever had, he meant it.

He still wasn't ready to progress further physically, but he knew there was no rush. Plus, he was still kind of trying to get used to the brand-new desire of wanting someone—specifically wanting *Obiora*—over him—*inside* him. He'd never even spared ... back *there* ... with a single thought before, but after Obiora talked about—about *fucking* him, it was suddenly all he could think about.

How would it feel? He knew his prostate was up there somewhere, and was supposedly sensitive, but still, wouldn't it feel weird? Invasive?

A picture flashed through his mind, of Obiora leaning on his elbows over him, his face taut with pleasure and concentration as he smoothly pumped his hips.

"*Oh*." Ejiro shivered and pressed his thighs together.

Like clockwork, his phone beeped with a text. Even though they said their goodnights during their "midnight calls"—as Ajiri called them—they still texted again afterward before properly going to sleep.

Ajiri was right. He and Obiora were *obsessed* with each other.

And Ejiro didn't hate it one bit.

TWENTY-EIGHT

THIS IS IT, OBIORA THOUGHT, eyes stinging as Jennifer talked passionately to him about her fitness journey. He'd just finished taking over one of Esther's classes—as was becoming his usual for the past month—and Jennifer had stayed behind to talk to him. She was on the bigger side of the people in the class, and from day one, she'd felt self-conscious about it. But Obiora loved these people so fucking much because they'd done their best to make Jennifer feel like she already belonged, regardless of the fact that she was new, and they hadn't once given her reason to feel discomfort.

Soon enough, she'd relaxed and grown bolder, and begun to truly enjoy herself, which was Obiora's goal for what he was becoming to accept were his clients; not Esther's, *his*. Working out and sticking to a routine was hard as fuck, so Obiora tried his best to make his class as fun and engaging as possible to keep them inspired.

"You don't understand," Jennifer was saying, clutching both his hands in hers, her eyes shiny with tears. She was short, pretty, and round, with smooth dark skin and shoulder-length violet braids. "I thought I needed to be skinny to feel better about myself, but I think what I really wanted was community—*this* kind of community—

where I can work out and just ... be me. I wanted to say thank you. You don't know how much this class—how much your training means to me. How much it's helped."

Obiora had to swallow. "You're welcome."

She smiled, gave his hands a gentle squeeze, then she went over to the locker rooms to change.

Obiora watched her go, his throat thick with pride. He'd *done* that. He'd helped put that confidence in her stride, that carefree brightness in her smile.

Each time one of his clients said something along the same lines as Jennifer, Obiora felt like he could fly.

Esther drifted to his side. He hadn't noticed when she'd come in. "Feels good, doesn't it?"

She sounded so smug Obiora couldn't help but laugh.

"I think I'm going to do it," he said after a moment, still staring off into the distance.

Esther knew what he was talking about instantly, without him even having to explain. There was a grin in her voice when she said, "Yeah?"

"Yeah." He finally turned to look at her. "Please wipe that smug grin off your face."

She laughed and punched him playfully in the shoulder. "Fucking finally!"

"Yeah, yeah, yeah," Obiora said, rolling his eyes, but he was grinning.

"The classes are yours whenever you want it, you know that, right?"

Obiora felt bashful. His heart raced at the thought of doing this, for real. "I'm still going to need an actual licence, like, there are a lot of —"

"Semantics," Esther interrupted, waving him off. He grinned. She grinned back. "I prefer doing house calls, anyway. The one on ones. You're really good with the group setting, so I want you to have it, whenever you're ready. They practically already see you as their trainer anyway, so, as I said, the rest is just semantics."

It didn't sink in until he was home and had texted Ejiro, as he usually did. They'd officially been dating for a month since Ejiro had left the competition, and Ejiro had been coming over to his twice a week since then. Whenever Ejiro left his home after a visit, Obiora missed him something painful, but the way they talked to each other literally all the time did its best to soothe the ache.

Hey, babe. Are you home yet? He sent it when he got home, ending the message with the tongue emoji because he knew how the emoji made Ejiro blush.

The reply was instant: *Yeah, I'm home!*, with the kissy face emoji. *How was work, baby?*

Obiora felt the usual mixture of heat and warmth when Ejiro called him "baby". It made him think of their phone call last night, of Ejiro's breathy gasps and throaty moans vibrating in his ear as Ejiro had fingered himself for the first time until he'd come long and hard and explosive. Obiora didn't think he'd ever come so hard himself, and that was saying something, considering ever since the first time about three weeks ago, the passionate, mind-blowing phone sex between them had become an almost nightly occurrence.

Pushing aside the flush of heat at the memories, Obiora replied: *It was great, love. Can I call you?*

Yes, please, Ejiro sent, with a soft smiley emoji.

Ejiro picked up on the first ring. "Hey, baby."

Love and desire began to make a delicious cocktail in Obiora's belly. "Hey, love. I just got home. Going to shower and then head to my parents'. What's in store for you today? You finished working on that new chapter for your Patreon?"

"Yes!" Ejiro said, his voice filled with excitement. "You were right. I actually managed to finish it before I went to work this morning."

"Yeah?" Obiora replied, Ejiro's excitement contagious. "That's great, baby! I'm so proud of you. You see what I said, abi? You need to start listening to me more."

"Okay, okay, okay. I've heard." There was laughter in his voice. "How about you? How was work? Did Esther make you take over her class again today?"

Obiora grinned, almost helplessly. "You already know." Ejiro laughed. Obiora's heart began to race. "That's what I'm calling you about, actually."

"Yeah?" Ejiro encouraged.

Obiora hesitated. Once he said the words out loud, there was no going back. He inhaled, then exhaled explosively.

"I've decided I'm going to talk to my dad about leaving. Tonight."

"Really? Oh, Obiora, that's wonderful!"

Obiora felt shy. "Thank you, babe. Honestly, the truth is I've been procrastinating doing it ever since I got back, because after being away for so long, being back didn't ... feel too bad? If you know what I mean."

"I know exactly what you mean," Ejiro said softly. Things with his mother were still strained; she was still badgering him about going back to Nigeria, and he was still wavering with the guilt of telling her that he didn't want to go.

"I just know that if I go on like this ..." He knew he didn't need to finish the sentence.

Ejiro sighed. "I guess ... I guess this means I have to talk to my mother, too, huh?"

He sounded so reluctant that Obiora couldn't help but say, "Baby, you don't have to do anything you don't want to do. Just because I—"

"I know, I know," Ejiro interrupted. "I know, baby. But firstly, I made a promise to you." Obiora's heart expanded. "And secondly, you've already said it; I can't go on like this."

Obiora ached for him. "You don't have to do it today, babe," he continued stubbornly. "Maybe take some time to think about it. I want you to do it because you're ready, not just because *I'm* doing it, promise or no."

"I don't think I'll ever be ready. And honestly, I'm tired of making excuses and placating her feelings." There was an edge to Ejiro's voice that Obiora hadn't heard before, one that simultaneously made him feel proud and horny. "Maybe it was my being away from her badgering for two months, but I realise that's exactly what it is: *badgering*. I'm only hesitating because I know she'll be hurt and I don't want to hurt her. I don't—" Frustration bled into his voice. "I don't want her to think I'm being cruel or ungrateful."

"Baby," Obiora began.

"I know," Ejiro answered softly.

Obiora smiled. "I love you."

He could practically see Ejiro blush. "So, you'll talk to your dad and I'll talk to my mum, yeah? Then we'll reconvene."

"Yes. They might be upset, but they'll get over it. In fact, I'm pretty sure our relationship will be stronger after this. Honesty and vulnerability go a long way to strengthening bonds."

Ejiro sighed. "I hope you're right."

EJIRO WAS BESIDE HIMSELF WITH with nerves, which was why he'd only replied with a thumbs up emoji when Obiora had texted him "*I'm about to do it, pray for me*", after he'd had finished having dinner with his family.

Ejiro had also finished with dinner as well, which was usually when his mother called; she always called either right after he'd finished work, after he'd had dinner, or when he was going to bed, there was no in-between. Though she didn't call every single day, she did so every *other* day.

It'd been two days now since her last call, which meant he was due for one really soon, possibly today.

As Ejiro had silently panicked, trying to gear himself up for the tough conversation ahead, he'd noticed Ajiri seemed just as agitated as he was. It made it easy for Ejiro to push his own anxiety aside so he could take care of his sister.

"You all right?"

Ajiri startled. They were cleaning the dishes and filling up the dishwasher. Blessing was in the sitting room, spreading out their laundry.

"We really need to do something about the drier," Ajiri muttered.

Ejiro laughed. "We do. But that's not what's really bothering you, is it?"

Ajiri looked away, cleaning off the plate in her hands and dumping it into the dishwasher. Ejiro didn't push.

It didn't take long until the dishwasher was filled and running, its gentle hum filling the kitchen.

Ajiri took a deep breath. She was wiping her hands aggressively with the hand towel, not meeting his eyes. Ejiro felt his heart begin to pound.

"Blessing and I were thinking of getting our own place," Ajiri blurted.

Ejiro heard what she said, but for a moment, his brain refused to compute it.

Ajiri quickly met his eyes. "It's not for a while," she continued in a rush, "at least not for another year or so; we're waiting until after she graduates and my internship is over, but I just—we just thought you should know."

"Right." Ejiro nodded. He was blinking too much. "Right."

"Are you okay?" Ajiri asked desperately.

Ejiro smiled. It was small, but it was genuine. "Come here."

They hugged tightly.

"I'm fine," Ejiro said when they pulled apart. "Seriously," he added at Ajiri's probing look. "It was a long time coming, anyway.

I've always felt like I was somehow ... intruding."

"Ejiro," Ajiri began, upset.

"No, no, I know," Ejiro said. "It's not a slight against you two. I just know how you two feel. You deserve privacy. And besides, we've been together our entire lives." Same classrooms in primary and secondary school, same classes for their Bachelor's—and they'd lived in the same space since they'd moved to the UK; they'd never really been physically apart from each other for too long.

It was Ajiri's turn to say, "Come here."

"I love you," Ejiro whispered into her buzzed afro, swallowing repeatedly.

"I love you, too. Don't cry."

Ejiro laughed, quickly wiping away his tears. Ajiri wiped hers as well.

"Are we okay?"

"Ajiri," Ejiro said, making sure to input all his love for her into the way he said her name. "We're okay," he promised.

"Okay." Her answering smile was wobbly, but her dark eyes were filled with gratitude.

Ejiro took a deep breath, their heart-to-heart finally giving him the confidence to admit, "I've decided I'm going to talk to mummy."

Ajiri looked so fucking proud of him. "Yeah?"

He nodded, bashful. "I don't want to leave the UK. I've *never* wanted to leave. And I hate that she's all alone over there, but I—" He hesitated, because despite the conviction he'd used to talk Obiora earlier on, he *still* felt awful and selfish and guilty as he whispered, "I deserve—"

He was startled by his phone ringing. He glanced at the caller ID, hoping, praying that maybe—

"Oh God."

Ajiri reached out and grabbed his hand, holding it tight. "Go on. Answer it. Whatever happens, I'm here."

"Thank you," he whispered, squeezing her hand hard.

Ajiri nodded just as he answered the call. "Hello, mummy, mingwo."

"Vredo. How are you?"

"I'm fine." Fuck, he couldn't breathe.

"Has your uncle spoken to you yet?"

Ejiro frowned. "No. Spoken to me about what?"

"I spoke to him last night. I've bought you a ticket home for next week."

Ejiro stilled.

"Ejiro?" his mother inquired when he'd been silent for too long. "Did you hear me?"

"Yes, mummy," Ejiro said numbly. "I heard you."

"You were dragging your feet too much so I took matters into my own hands. Shebi you can pay me back when you get here?" She said that last part jokingly, but Ejiro knew it wasn't a joke; he *would* be expected to pay her back, like he'd asked for this, like he'd *wanted*—

Suddenly, his Uncle's weird behaviour today made a lot more sense. While Ejiro had been making the lunch rush at the restaurant, Uncle Reuben had come up to him and placed a hand on his shoulder, and said, cryptically, "You know I'm here for you, Eji-ji? I support and *will* support you in everything you do."

Ejiro remembered smiling distractedly at him, even as warmth had filled his chest. "Yes, I know, Uncle. Thank you."

Uncle Reuben had squeezed his shoulder, then left to continue his own part of the work. Ejiro had thought nothing of it until now.

Tears filled his eyes. His uncle had been such a quiet but steady part of his life that Ejiro had forgotten that apart from Ajiri and Blessing, and now Obiora, he had someone else he could count on if things went south.

It was that thought that made his voice firm when he said, "No."

"No, kini? What does that mean?"

"No," Ejiro repeated. "I'm not coming home next week. In fact, I'm not coming home at all. I didn't want to hurt your feelings, mummy, but the truth is I'm staying in England. I'm making my life here. Nigeria has nothing to offer me."

His mother inhaled sharply. "Ejiro? Is it me you're speaking to like this?"

For a moment, Ejiro felt cowed, but Ajiri squeezed his hand, helping him stand firm.

"I'm sorry, mummy. If you can't get a refund for the ticket I'll reimburse you. But I'm not coming home any time soon. I don't want to go back to Nigeria; there are no opportunities for me there."

"What do you mean no opportunities? My catering company, nko? Or are you saying you can't come home and work for your mother?"

"I don't want to be a caterer for the rest of my life, mummy."

"Jesus Christ, please save me. You're not on about this your cartoons again?" she said derisively. "Ejiro, I expected better from you. How are you going to survive on the paltry salary of an artist? As your mother, it's my job to worry about you and your prospects. I make thousands in naira every month with my catering business; how can you say you have no opportunities? Honestly, Ejiro, I'm so disappointed."

Fury burned, bright and hot in his stomach. "My *cartoons* pay me three times as much as what Uncle Reuben pays me, and even if I was earning a *paltry* salary, it's still what I *want* to do. Besides that, I've made a life here, mummy. I've *planned* my life here."

"Ay! Oghene. Am I hearing this correctly? Ejiro, after everything I've done for you? After I used my blood, sweat, and tears to send you abroad, this is how you repay me?" Oh God, she was crying. She was fucking *crying*. "I did everything for you; I put the clothes on your back and the food in your mouth. I ask you for one thing—one thing, Ejiro, and you can't even do it for me?"

Ejiro couldn't speak. His throat felt like it was filled with rocks.

"I know this is Ajiri's doing. This is her doing. She is so selfish. I've never seen someone so spiteful and ungrateful that she can't just leave me in peace. She's poisoning your mind and trying to—"

"This isn't about Ajiri," Ejiro forced himself to say. "This is all me, mummy. This is what *I* want."

"Don't lie to me!" she snapped. "I may not speak to her anymore, but I know my daughter. I know how vindictive she is. Everything she does, she does it to hurt me, just because I refuse to accept that sinful waywardness she calls a lifestyle. She knows you are my heart, my everything, and now she wants to take you away from me? Tufiakwa. Next thing I'll hear is that you're a gay."

His mother sounded like she was going to pass out when Ejiro didn't immediately deny it. "Ejiro? Ejiro?"

He remained silent. He was biting his lip so hard it was this close to bringing blood.

"Ay!" she cried. "You have killed me, Ejiro!" She was wailing so loudly Ejiro was sure the neighbours could hear. "You have killed me, o! You've finished me. I hope you're happy."

She hung up.

Ejiro burst into tears.

"Oh God, Ejiro, no," Ajiri said, gathering him into her arms.

He hugged her tightly, biting back his sobs, unsure why he was even crying. There was a heavy weight lifted from his shoulders, yet he still felt like literal shit.

"It's okay, Ejiro. I've got you, I've got you."

"What's going on?" Blessing came into the kitchen. She lowered her voice when she noticed Ejiro crying. "What's happening? Is Ejiro okay?"

Ajiri lowered her voice as well. "I'm sure he'll tell you when he's feeling better, babe. Just give us a moment, yeah?"

"All right." She hesitated. "Whatever it is, I'm sorry, Ejiro. And I'm here for you."

Ejiro managed a nod. Blessing left the kitchen.

Ejiro let his twin hold him, and though he felt slightly better, there was one person's arms he specifically wished he could be in right now, if only Obiora weren't so far away.

OBIORA WAS FULL OF JOY and relief. Of course, his father had been disappointed when he'd told him he wanted to leave, but his old man had been deeply supportive.

"Some part of me didn't want to acknowledge it," Osita had said when they'd had their talk in the guest-room-turned-office in his parents' house. "I knew you were struggling, that while you had drive and creativity, you lacked that certain passion and intensity your brothers brought into their own projects. But I thought maybe that was just how you expressed yourself. I see now that it was just wishful thinking."

"I'm sorry, daddy."

His father scoffed, waving his apology away. His other hand held a shot glass filled with Amarula. Obiora had fond memories of his father sneaking him and his brothers a sip of the milky rich alcohol when they were children. The taste of it now felt like happiness and nostalgia.

"Don't you dare apologise," Osita said roughly. "When you graduated and you moved in with Ada, do you remember I offered you a spot at the company?"

Obiora felt bittersweet at the memory. "I remember."

"And do you remember what you said?"

Obiora frowned. That part was a little hazy. "I remember wanting to wait. Me and Ada wanted to take a little break from work and school, just, you know, be with each other for a bit."

Osita smiled, fondly instead of sadly as he might have done in the past, and it helped gentle the ache of loss in Obiora's chest. It felt so good that he could talk about her like this with his family now. It felt freeing.

"You told me," Osita continued, "point blank, that you weren't quite sure yet if Architecture was what you wanted to do, even though you'd just spent three years at University studying it." Obiora laughed. "Or, looking back, perhaps studying it was why you didn't want to do it?"

Obiora laughed again, rubbing the back of his neck. "I said that?"

"Oh yes. But I was desperate. I wanted to help you with your grief, yes, but I was also being selfish."

Obiora bristled at that. "Daddy," he began, his tone placating.

"No, no, let me finish. I was selfish in the sense that I'd had the dream of handing over the company to my three sons. And while I wanted to help you get back on your feet, the means I used to do so was not entirely honest."

"Daddy." Obiora felt choked up. "But you helped. This job—it helped a lot. It was exactly what I needed at that time."

"And now, you don't need it anymore."

Obiora slowly shook his head.

His father sighed. "I understand, my son. So, what do you want to do instead?"

Obiora's shyness and nerves had abruptly returned. "I want ... I want to be a personal trainer."

"Huh." His father didn't seem surprised at all, which, for some reason, made Obiora burst out laughing, his relief palpable.

His father's support was strong and unwavering, and Obiora couldn't be happier. He'd been right when he'd told Ejiro that honesty and vulnerability went a long way into bonding relationships, because that conversation left him feeling so much closer to his father afterward. And when he'd broken the news to his mother and brothers, they'd been equally supportive, so supportive in fact he'd felt a little silly for being so afraid of telling them.

He couldn't wait to tell Esther. He couldn't wait to get his licence and actually be a registered trainer—have his clients under *his* name, instead of Esther's.

Obiora's thoughts went to Ejiro. He wondered if Ejiro had spoken to his mother yet, and felt a pinch of worry.

Earlier, after he'd finished eating dinner, he'd texted Ejiro *"I'm about to do it, pray for me"* along with the skull emoji. Ejiro had simply replied with a thumbs up. Obiora had felt a spark of worry; Ejiro hardly ever replied with emojis alone, they were almost always accompanied by a message. But Obiora had told himself Ejiro was probably nervous and possibly didn't feel too chatty as a result. His mother tended to call in the evenings or late in the night after Ejiro had had dinner. Maybe he was so nervous waiting for her call that he couldn't talk right now. That was all right.

The moment he got home, Obiora brought out his phone, and nearly dropped it when the device pinged with a new message.

It was from Ejiro.

Hey. Can I call you?

Of course, love, Obiora replied.

"Hey baby," he answered on the first ring.

"Hi," Ejiro said, his voice thick with tears.

Obiora froze in alarm. "Are you okay? What's wrong?"

Ejiro inhaled shakily, and when he spoke again, Obiora could tell he was trying not to cry. "Things with my mother didn't go so well."

"Baby," Obiora said, his heart fucking breaking. "Fucking hell. I'm so sorry."

"It's fine." Ejiro was clearly crying now, but trying to be quiet. Oh God, his love. His *heart*. He hated that he couldn't do shit—that he couldn't immediately heal his lover's pain right fucking now. "I don't want to talk about it. I just wanted to hear your voice. Be with you."

Obiora didn't even hesitate when he said, "Do you want me to come and get you?"

Ejiro sucked in a sharp breath. "What?"

Obiora turned around and headed back out of his flat, locking the door behind him. "I'm heading to the station right now. You can meet me in the station in Manchester, yeah? I'll pick you up, then you can come stay over at mine for the weekend."

"Obiora." Ejiro was crying again. "You don't ... you don't have to do that."

"Yeah, too late. I'm in a cab," he lied. "You were already going to come over tomorrow, so we're just a little early," he teased gently. "Pack everything you might need for the weekend, okay, baby? I'll stay on the phone."

"Okay. God. Okay. Obiora. Fuck, Obiora."

Obiora's chest fucking hurt. He could hear the confession in the way Ejiro said his name, even if Ejiro didn't say the words outright, and that was enough.

TWENTY-NINE

WHEN EJIRO WOKE UP, HE inhaled a slightly trembling breath and felt like he'd been submerged in soft, golden warmth.

Obiora's arms were wrapped loosely around him, their legs tangled together, and they were sharing the same pillow. Ejiro stared at his boyfriend's sleeping face, his gently closed eyes and soft, pouting mouth, and felt so full of love he could burst with it.

That he'd wanted Obiora so badly last night, and Obiora hadn't even *hesitated*, fuck, Ejiro loved him. After the disastrous phone call with his mother, despite how badly he'd wanted to be with Obiora, Ejiro hadn't wanted to get on the hour-long train ride to Sheffield by himself—the thought alone had felt like torture, though he'd have done it in a heartbeat if Obiora had said he didn't mind. But that *Obiora* had decided to come all the way down to Manchester instead so Ejiro didn't have to be alone, was what made Ejiro feel like his heart was too big to be contained in his chest.

His mother's manipulation—and yes, he was ready to admit that that was what it was—tried to come back to haunt him, but he refused to think about it, he refused to let it ruin this moment.

As he stared, Obiora's breathing changed. His lips slowly tilted into a full-blown smile, his dimple flashing, though he didn't open his eyes. Ejiro's heart skipped a traitorous beat.

"Something on my face?" Obiora asked, his voice rough with sleep.

Ejiro trembled at the sound.

Obiora opened his eyes when Ejiro didn't respond, raising a questioning eyebrow.

"I love you," Ejiro whispered, unable to contain it anymore.

Obiora's eyes widened, and his expression lit up like fireworks. "Baby—" he began, looking so freaking happy it made Ejiro feel slightly ashamed for not telling him sooner.

"I'm sorry," he interrupted quickly, looking away from those dark eyes, his gaze falling on Obiora's throat. "I'm so—I kept holding the words back because the timing never felt right; I wanted to say them at *the* perfect moment, you know? I realise now that that's just unrealistic ... and slightly ridiculous." He laughed awkwardly.

"Aw baby, please don't apologise," Obiora said, one hand lifting to cup Ejiro's chin and tilt his face back up, their eyes locking. His boyfriend looked amused, and so, so fond. "You didn't have to say the words for me to know they were there and they were true; actions do speak louder than words, after all. Also, that's probably the cutest and most romantic thing I have ever heard."

"Shut up," Ejiro groaned. Obiora laughed.

"No, I'm serious. And this *was* the perfect moment, if you think about it." Obiora's eyes darkened, his voice deepening. "I literally just woke up from the best sleep I've had in a while because I had my lover in my arms, and the first thing he tells me is that he loves me. How could it get any better than that?"

Ejiro swallowed the lump in his throat. "Obiora," he whispered.

"I love you," Obiora said, his voice just as low.

"I love you," Ejiro echoed. "I love you. I love you." He wanted to scream it from the rooftops, each declaration leaving him trembling and overwhelmed.

Obiora looked just as dazed, his breaths coming in slightly fast.

"Ejiro," he whispered passionately, then they were kissing.

Ejiro dragged him close, his hands going into Obiora's hair, fingers tangling in the curls. Their mouths were sleep-warm and a bit musty, but they still kissed like it was the last thing they'd do, moulding their lips together and then tangling their tongues in a sensuous dance that left them both panting and trembling.

Desire pooled like lava in Ejiro's stomach, and he whined, shifting restlessly until Obiora pushed against him so he was flat on his back and Obiora was on top of him, pressing his thick, muscled thigh between Ejiro's legs.

Ejiro had to pull back from the kiss to gasp, rocking his hips helplessly against the pressure on his aching length.

"Fuck," Obiora whispered, grinding against him, his own dick a hot brand against Ejiro's hip. He trailed kisses down his jaw, nipping and gently sucking on his suddenly sensitive flesh. "Ejiro," he whispered, pressing his thigh down harder, stealing Ejiro's breath. "What do you want, baby?"

Ejiro swallowed. Obiora was licking his throat, nipping at the sensitive point that joined his neck and shoulder, before sucking hard on the flesh, the feel of it making Ejiro groan and jerk.

"Do you want to stop?" Obiora asked, beginning to pull away.

"No," he admitted desperately, the words ringing with truth. "Don't stop. Obiora, I want you. I want you so much. Please."

Obiora took his lips in another fervent kiss, like the words were too much to bear. They kissed again and again, rolling their hips together—making out until they were literally gasping for breath into each other's mouths, the sound of their lips smacking loud and arousing in the quiet of the morning.

"Obiora," Ejiro groaned when Obiora lifted off him to take off their shirts, before coming back down to join their lips, their bodies meeting skin to skin for the first time. "*Obiora*," Ejiro moaned again, arching against him, wanting the warmth—the intimate press of

Obiora's naked skin against his somehow imprinted on him.

Obiora tugged at his lower lip with his teeth, making Ejiro shudder, the action going straight to his throbbing dick. "Ejiro," Obiora echoed, his voice just as raw.

"I want—" Ejiro broke off, heat flooding his cheeks, even as the arousal in his stomach blazed hotter, his prick throbbing harder.

Obiora lifted up slightly so he was balanced on one elbow, looking down at him with eyes dark with lust. "Yes, baby?"

Ejiro swallowed thickly. "I want ..." His eyes dropped to Obiora's mouth, pink and full, wet and swollen. Fuck, fuck, fuck. He squeezed his legs almost involuntarily around the thigh still lodged in-between them.

Explicit, enthusiastic consent, he reminded himself.

"Your mouth," Ejiro confessed in a shy rush, nails digging into Obiora's biceps. *Oh God.*

"What about my mouth?" Obiora teased huskily, leaning down to nip playfully at Ejiro's jaw.

Ejiro bit his lip, something hot and achy building up between his ribs. "Obiora, don't tease."

Obiora laughed softly. The sound made Ejiro feel like he was falling in love with him all over again.

Obiora balanced his weight on his left arm so he could slide his right hand down Ejiro's chest—brushing a stiff nipple, making Ejiro shiver almost violently at the light touch—slowly, slowly, until he was cupping Ejiro's length through his shorts.

Ejiro felt like he couldn't breathe.

"Here, baby?" Obiora said, still teasing, but his voice was dark, rough. He gave Ejiro's dick a gentle squeeze. "Is this where you want my mouth?"

Ejiro arched against him, almost helplessly. "Please," he whispered, his eyes falling shut, need and shame heating his cheeks. A wet spot formed on his shorts where his dick was beginning to leak.

"Fucking hell, baby," Obiora groaned. "You're so—" Obiora

kissed him, trailing kisses down his throat, his chest, his abs …

"Oh, oh, oh God." Ejiro couldn't stop gasping, rocking his hips; he'd never been this hard in his life.

Obiora pulled down his underwear, and Ejiro helped kick them off his legs.

He felt vulnerable, exposed, so fucking bare—like Obiora was looking into his soul.

Obiora kissed his hip, dragged his teeth against the jut of his hip bone, and Ejiro felt like he'd explode.

"Obiora, Obiora, please, *please*—"

"Jesus." Obiora grunted. His hips kicked into the mattress.

He took Ejiro's dick in his hand, giving it a few strokes that had Ejiro's hips lifting off the mattress, before he took the tip, shiny with pre-come, into his mouth and sucked.

Ejiro cried out, his head falling back against the pillows, his hands flying into Obiora's hair. Obiora hummed encouragingly, taking more of him into his mouth, his tongue flicking against the sensitive underside.

"Oh fuck, oh God." Ejiro sobbed, gripping Obiora's curls, trying desperately not to thrust into that sinful wet heat.

Obiora took him all the way down his throat and *swallowed*. Ejiro bit back a shout, his legs tensing, already on the verge of coming.

Obiora slowly, torturously began to bob his head, one hand pumping, while his mouth pulled and licked and sucked messily. Ejiro's grip on Obiora's hair was so tight he was afraid he'd soon yank the strands from their roots.

Obiora pulled off with a slick sound, his voice sexily rough as he asked, "Is that good, love?" his hand pumping steadily.

The question made Ejiro *burn*. He nodded, a bit frantically. The sight of his slick, straining dick in Obiora's undulating grip was nothing short of *obscene*.

Obiora licked the new wetness pearling at his head, then pressed his lips against the sensitive underside, murmuring hoarsely against his heated flesh, his eyes never leaving Ejiro's, "You can fuck my mouth if you want, baby. I like it."

Oh, fuck. Obiora was already taking him back into his mouth before he could regain his bearings.

It took several moments, but eventually, Ejiro finally let go of his inhibitions.

Fuck, fuck, *God*. He squirmed, twisting his hips, mewling, and then began to move, jerkily pumping his hips into Obiora's mouth, fucking his dick through those plush lips—against that wet, pink tongue.

He looked down, and his heart jolted when he saw that Obiora was watching him with heated, possessive eyes, his cheeks hollowed, mouth stretched obscenely wide, slick with spit.

"I'm gonna—" Ejiro warned, gasping, his back arching. He clawed at Obiora's shoulder, his thighs beginning to shake. "Oh God, oh fuck. Obiora, you're gonna make me—"

Obiora moaned encouragingly, his cheeks hollowing even further, the suction so wet, so tight, and so fucking perfect that Ejiro stiffened abruptly, his nails digging hard into Obiora's scalp.

"*Yes*," he hissed, arching, tilting his head back, heels digging into the mattress as he buried his dick as deep as it could go. Obiora didn't even fucking *gag*. Ejiro's eyes watered. "Yes, yes, yes, *yes—*" he cried, holding Obiora's head down, eyes rolling back in his head as his dick jerked, pulsing furiously as he came so fucking hard he saw stars.

Thanks to the numerous times they'd had sex over the phone, Obiora had probably noticed how Ejiro liked to keep going for a bit even after he'd come; he didn't stop sucking at Ejiro's softening dick until he was whining and curling in on himself at the oversensitivity, pushing weakly at Obiora's head to get him off.

Obiora pulled off with a lewd slurp, and Ejiro immediately reached down to pull him up.

"Come here, baby, come here," he pleaded, his voice rough. Obiora followed the pull of his hands until he was on top of him once more. Ejiro felt wanton as he kissed Obiora deeply, tasting his release in Obiora's mouth. "I love you. I love you."

"I love you," Obiora replied, his voice scraped raw. He was thrusting desperately against Ejiro's hip, his dick hot and hard.

"Obiora," Ejiro whispered. He'd just come, yet he was still fired up; it was in the restless way he was squirming, the way he was spreading his thighs, arching his hips. His dick hadn't even gone fully soft, still mostly hard.

"Fuck, you're so sexy," Obiora whispered, making Ejiro blush. He didn't think he'd like it so much, Obiora complimenting him like this. "What do you want, baby?" Obiora asked gruffly, ignoring his own arousal.

"What do *you* want?" Ejiro retorted shyly, trailing his hand down Obiora's chest, letting his fingers come to a stop on Obiora's hip.

Obiora leaned down to nip the corner of his lip, licking away the sting. "Your hand," he rasped, "on my dick."

Ejiro felt like his cheeks would never recover from his constant blushes. "Fuck. Yes, please."

They both helped Obiora get rid of his underwear. Then Obiora lifted onto his elbows, shifting until he was on his side, giving Ejiro access.

Ejiro pressed close and immediately curled his hand around him, testing his heat and hardness, his thumb finding a vein and tracing it, from the sensitive underside of the head to the base.

"Like that?" he whispered.

Obiora groaned. "Give me your hand." Ejiro obligingly lifted his hand, letting Obiora gently cradle his wrist so he could bring Ejiro's hand up to his mouth.

Then he *licked*, from his inner wrist to the tips of his fingers, and then spat. Ejiro jolted; his entire brain short-circuited, and his dick went from sixty to two hundred in the span of a heartbeat.

"Oh my fucking God."

Obiora replaced his grip on his dick, the glide now obscenely wet and smooth.

"A little tighter, baby," Obiora whispered. "Fuck. *Yes*. Just like that."

Ejiro pumped his grip, slow and tight and exploring, his arousal heightening at the sight and feel of Obiora's pleasure.

"Fuck, fuck, fuck," Obiora rasped, head tilted down, eyes focused on where Ejiro was stroking him, his hips rolling helplessly into Ejiro's grip.

Ejiro swallowed thickly, his mouth falling open the longer he stroked him. It was a headrush, seeing the effect just his *hand* alone had on Obiora. He couldn't stop staring at the frankly lewd sight of the head of Obiora's dick thrusting through his tight fist, the head slightly shiny, slick with pre-come. He stroked his thumb across the wetness, spreading it around the head, and his stomach swooped when Obiora made an agonised sound of pleasure, his hips jerking.

Obiora began to groan helplessly, the movements of his hips quickening. He suddenly wrapped his hand around Ejiro's, stopping his strokes.

"Fuck, Ejiro, baby—wait, wait." He was almost gasping. "I'm—I'm close. *Fuck*."

Ejiro's stomach swooped again. God, he'd always known seeing his partner's pleasure—being the *cause* of it—was a turn on for him, but it seemed to be amped up to one thousand with Obiora.

"Isn't that the point?" Ejiro teased, voice husky.

Like he couldn't help it, Obiora began to move their hands, slowly, torturously over his stiff length. Ejiro shouldn't have found it arousing, Obiora controlling his grip like that. Obiora was so hard, so close Ejiro thought he could actually *feel* his dick throbbing.

"Yeah," Obiora said, lips quirking. He met Ejiro's eyes, his own eyes so fucking dark. "But I want …" Suddenly, it was Obiora's turn to look shy.

Ejiro's heart swelled. "Anything," he whispered. "Anything you want."

"I'd really, really like to fuck you," Obiora admitted, making Ejiro's stomach swoop again. Oh God. "But only if you'd like that."

Ejiro nodded. Managed to swallow the aroused lump in his throat. "Yes, yes, Obiora, please—"

They moved until Obiora was on top of Ejiro once more, between his spread thighs, their lips moulding frantically.

Ejiro moaned, tilting his hips up, planting his feet on the mattress and rocking up until the tip of Obiora's dick was pressed against his entrance.

Obiora gripped his hip in a vice-like hold to stop him, gasping raggedly, arching his own hips.

"Fuck. Tell me again," Obiora seemed to plead.

"Fuck me. Please," Ejiro begged. He opened his eyes, locking them with Obiora's. "I want you. I want to feel you inside me."

"Fucking hell, baby, you're going to be the death of me." Obiora groaned, pressing his dick harder against the tight furl of Ejiro's asshole, almost helplessly. "Anything, baby. Anything you want."

He let go, letting Ejiro fall back onto the mattress, then reached for his bedside table for the lube. Since Ejiro had fingered himself on the phone last time, Ejiro knew Obiora hadn't been able to stop thinking about it; how Ejiro had been so fucking *into* it, gasping and sobbing and fucking himself into a powerful climax.

Obiora leaned down to kiss him when he had the lube and a condom on the bed with them, licking sensually into Ejiro's mouth, taking him apart skilfully with his tongue.

By the time they broke the kiss, gasping for air, Ejiro was practically straining between them, his dick trailing glistening streaks of pre-come across his belly.

Obiora managed by some miracle to keep their eyes locked as he got the lube onto his fingers with shaking hands, rubbing them a little to warm them up.

Ejiro spread his thighs wider, wrapping his arms around Obiora's neck as Obiora pressed his fingers against his hole.

"Obiora," he whispered. He'd never felt so vulnerable.

"Still okay?" Obiora asked softly, not penetrating yet, just gently stroking.

For some reason, the check-in made Ejiro's eyes sting with tears. "Yes," he whispered.

"I love you," Obiora murmured, sinking one finger into his tight heat.

"Oh," Ejiro gasped, his eyelids fluttering. He rolled his hips, positively hungry for it.

"Yeah?" Obiora rasped, his eyes darting from Ejiro's pleasure-filled face to where he was stretched out around his finger.

Ejiro clenched his eyes shut. His throat felt thick; it felt like something in his chest was cracking open. He didn't know why he was on the verge of crying. "Yes. Please. Don't stop."

Obiora gently thrust his finger. "You like that, love?" he asked huskily, leaning down to place a kiss on the corner of his mouth.

Ejiro nodded quickly, eyes still shut.

"I think I'll eat you out next time." Ejiro's eyes flew open, his hips jolting, his hole clenching around the finger inside him. The look in Obiora's eyes was predatory. "Yeah," Obiora said, voice gravelly. "I think you'd like that."

"Fuck," Ejiro whimpered. He began to squirm, rolling his hips into Obiora's movements. He closed his eyes again. All he could sense and feel was Obiora; the scent of his warm, soft skin—like sex and cocoa butter—pressed all against him; his finger gently thrusting inside him; his warm breath puffing against his cheek and the side of his throat, lips sweetly brushing against his skin like the kiss of a butterfly. It felt—it was too— "... much. Too much." But in the best possible way.

Obiora stopped immediately.

Ejiro's eyes flew open. "Wh—?"

"Do you want to stop?" Obiora asked seriously, beginning to pull his finger out.

"No." Ejiro grasped his wrist, stopping him. The tears finally broke free, spilling down his temples. That Obiora had stopped, even though Ejiro hadn't really meant it—that he'd said it was too much and Obiora had—suddenly Ejiro wanted him with a fierceness that was almost excruciating. "Please, God, please—"

"Are you sure?" Obiora eyed his tears worriedly.

It was his heart—his heart was cracking open, spilling red everywhere. "Yes, yes, yes."

Obiora leaned down to kiss him. Ejiro sank into the kiss like a drowning man grasping at straws.

"Another," Ejiro begged, gasping, pressing their foreheads together. "Another finger."

Obiora obeyed, pulling his finger out to get more lube, before sliding two fingers home.

"Yes," Ejiro groaned, his nails digging into Obiora's back, his hips rocking into Obiora's strokes.

All his shyness was gone, blown away by his trust in the fact that no matter what, Obiora would *listen*. He wouldn't just do what he wanted as long as he assumed Ejiro was into it—he'd ask again, he'd check in again, make sure they were always on the same page. The tears were coming faster now.

Obiora was panting. He buried his face in Ejiro's throat, and Ejiro felt him lift his hips off the mattress, possibly to get the pressure off his aching dick.

"God, I can't wait to be inside you," Obiora whispered into his neck. "Can't wait to feel you all around me."

The words drove Ejiro wild, making him gasp and snap his hips harder, his dick so fucking hard.

Obiora curled his fingers with skilled precision, finally rubbing them against the swollen, hypersensitive gland that was his prostate, and Ejiro cried out, his dick jolting and leaking.

"Oh God, now," Ejiro begged, his voice all gravel. "Now, please, now—"

"Are you sure?" Obiora asked, frantic. "You're still so fucking tight." He scissored his fingers, as if to prove his point.

Ejiro gasped, arching into the sensation. "Yes, yes." His eyes met Obiora's, dark with lust. "I want to feel it. I want it—" He blushed furiously "—to hurt a bit."

"JESUS FUCKING CHRIST." OBIORA RAPIDLY pulled his fingers out. He bit his lip hard, shuddering, his lower belly quivering as he rolled the condom on and lubed himself up.

Ejiro pulled him down, pressing their foreheads together as Obiora began to press into him.

"Okay?" Christ, his voice was all growl. He prayed to all the gods and goddesses that existed that he didn't come the second he was inside his lover.

"Don't stop," Ejiro whispered, staring into his eyes, his own eyes glittering.

Obiora honest-to-God whined, his face scrunching up, hips flexing. The head of his dick popped in, and they both let out shuddering breaths.

"Okay?" he asked again, desperately.

"Yes, please, God, I want you, I want you—"

Obiora groaned. "You feel so good."

"*Obiora*," Ejiro moaned. His hands went to Obiora's ass, cupping the globes and pulling him in deeper until he was buried to the hilt.

Obiora's mouth went slack. He tried to wait, tried to let Ejiro adjust, but he'd been on edge for so fucking long he could barely control the frantic way his hips were jolting, his dick so sensitive that the tight, slick clutch of Ejiro's arse around him was almost too much.

"Obiora," Ejiro sobbed. He planted his feet onto the mattress, lifting his hips, moving into Obiora's stuttered thrusts. "Obiora. Obiora. Oh God. Fuck me. Fuck me."

Obiora's dick *pounded*, his balls threatening to pull up.

"Shit!" *Don't come, don't come, don't you dare fucking come.*

He forced himself to slow down and it was heavenly torture, dragging his dick out and then grinding in deep, the action sending Ejiro's breath punching out of him with each deep thrust.

Their eyes were locked again. Ejiro was crying, tears spilling down his temples. "I love you," he said, his heart completely bare. "I love you."

"I love you," Obiora echoed, the intensity scraping him raw.

He twisted his hips, shaking, trying to change the angle, trying to find—

"*Yes*," Ejiro cried out, his ass clamping down hard around his dick, his own length jerking between them, pre-come beginning to stream from his slit like it was a faulty tap.

There we fucking go.

"There, *there*, Obiora, oh my God, oh my *God*—"

"*Fuck*." Obiora hammered his hips, nailing his prick into that spot over and over until Ejiro had to just lie there and *take* it. "You like that, baby? You want it harder?"

"Oh God." Ejiro sounded too fucked-out to be mortified. "Fuck, yes, you can—harder—fuck me harder—fucking give it to me—"

Oh my fucking God. Obiora had to balance on his knees, still gripping Ejiro's hips, slamming into him until the lewd sound of flesh slapping flesh filled the room. Obiora didn't know how he hadn't come yet; he was literally holding back his orgasm by the skin of his teeth.

"Look at you," he growled. "Knew you'd be like this. Knew you'd take my dick so fucking beautifully."

"*Obiora*," Ejiro cried, shoving his hand between them to frantically pull at his dick. He managed barely a few strokes, his dick so fucking *wet* before his arse clamped down tight around Obiora as he came, his body going taut, back arching sinuously.

And Obiora was gone. He fell forward and buried his face in Ejiro's throat, teeth sinking into his shoulder, his hips snapping wildly as he came with a muffled shout.

"Ejiro. *Ejiro.* Jesus *fucking* Christ, baby."

It felt like his orgasm was being wrenched from his body, from his fucking *soul*, his balls cramped up so tightly they hurt.

"Shit," he breathed when it was over, the word drawn out.

They were both shaking. He tried to pull out, but Ejiro's arse clenched around him, and he grabbed Obiora's hips, stopping him.

"Not ... not yet." He blushed.

"Fucking hell." Obiora had to push their hips closer together so his softening dick wouldn't accidentally slip out. He managed to balance himself on one elbow, leaning down to kiss away his lover's tears. "Okay, love? Fucking hell."

"So good," Ejiro said, a little dreamily, panting. "God, that was *so* good."

He sounded genuinely amazed, like he never knew sex could be like this, and Obiora fucking loved him.

"You were right," Ejiro said a little playfully, a little shyly, meeting his eyes. "Consent *is* fucking sexy."

"I love you. You're so fucking cute," Obiora said with a breathless laugh, planting a soft kiss on his jaw. "Do you want to take a shower with me?"

"Yes, please," Ejiro responded. He was grinning, looking so utterly happy—so obviously pleased and satisfied that Obiora couldn't help but preen. "Just as soon as my legs start working again."

Obiora laughed.

THEY SHOWERED, CHANGED THE SHEETS, and went down to make oats, hard boiled eggs, and fried plantain—a Nigerian-style breakfast. Then they were back in bed, clothes off, cuddling and kissing. His hole ached—it'd probably hurt like a bastard later—but right now, he couldn't stop clenching, loving the ache somehow, like Obiora had somehow marked him. He couldn't wait for Obiora to mark him again.

"So, I kind of took all the attention last night," he murmured between kisses. "How did your talk with your dad go?"

"Mhm," Obiora hummed, still kissing him.

Ejiro laughed, giddy. "I love you," he said, because he could.

Obiora smiled against his mouth. "I love you, too, baby. So much."

Obiora continued kissing him.

"*Obiora*," Ejiro said, laughing, but it was a weak complaint, considering that he wasn't stopping him.

Obiora laughed, planting one final smack on his mouth. "Fine, fine. What was the question?"

"You're ridiculous. Your talk with your dad?" Ejiro prompted.

"Oh, right. Yes. It went really great. Turns out he already sort of knew I wanted to leave? And he also had a hunch that I wanted to be a personal trainer. I guess I'm not as good an actor as I thought I was, at least not to my family."

Ejiro's heart melted for him. "I'm so happy for you, baby. That's amazing."

Obiora smiled. "Thank you." His smile dimmed a little. "Do you want to talk about what happened with your mum?"

Ejiro swallowed. "Oh, it was nothing she hasn't said before," he said flippantly, his eyes focused intently on the dimple in Obiora's cheek. "More trite stuff about how much she's done for me and how I owe her because of that. Oh, and I also kind of came out to her? Well, she accused Ajiri of turning me gay, and I didn't deny it, and she had a full-on breakdown. Like, she was literally screaming and crying and telling me that I'd killed her. So. There's that."

"Fucking hell, baby," Obiora said, his voice thick. "That sounds awful."

Ejiro felt his heart crack open. "Yeah. Well."

It was discombobulating, how the same woman who'd coddled him and Ajiri when they were sick, making them pepper soup and spoiling them, letting them stay in bed all day; the same woman who'd come to his primary school to scream bloody murder at the principal when Ejiro had been six years old and had vomited in class and the cleaner had made him get on his hands and knees in the middle of his lesson to wipe the vomit up himself, ignoring his humiliated sobs; the same woman who'd made sure all three of them went on at least one holiday every year—before he and Ajiri had left to the UK for Uni—had turned into ... this.

Everything seemed to have changed after Ajiri had come out.

But ... had it really changed? Or had the veneer simply been pulled back, revealing the ugliness underneath? She'd planned their lives out from the beginning; told them what to study, how to dress; and now that he was thinking about it, she'd even been the one to push them to get their citizenship, citing that it would only open more doors of opportunity for them. She'd written down their entire futures and dismissed their own wants and dreams and desires like she was swatting away at flies, only rewarding them when they did as she bid.

Then Ajiri had had enough, and suddenly, her stance changed. She no longer cared about them getting their citizenship, and wanted Ejiro to come home. She clung to him with a gnarled, clawing grip, and the longer Ejiro had remained in the UK, the darker and uglier she'd become.

How must Ajiri have felt, after their mother's vile rants against her own daughter, to have her twin—by all accounts, her *best friend*—continue to vouch for the woman who'd so easily cut her off without missing a beat?

"Hey, love," Obiora said softly. Ejiro realised he was crying. "Oh, love. Baby. Come here."

Obiora held him, simply held him like he'd done last night, cradling Ejiro tightly like he could somehow put the pieces his mother had shattered back together.

And he did. It hurt, and the pieces remained cracked and jagged, but in Obiora's embrace, Ejiro felt a little more whole.

"All right, love?" Obiora whispered when his sobs had died down, soft lips pressing against his forehead.

Ejiro nodded. Fresh tears pricked at his eyes, but they weren't tears of sadness. He shifted, leaning up so he could kiss Obiora, before pressing their foreheads together, whispering thickly, "I love you."

"I love you, baby," Obiora echoed, staring into his eyes, into his being. "I want ..." Obiora paused, looking strangely nervous. "I want you to meet my family."

Ejiro's eyes widened. "W-What?" he asked weakly.

"Not now, obviously," Obiora said quickly. "I just—I love you, Ejiro. I've never been more serious about anyone in my life. I *need* them to meet you. I want to introduce you to them."

"Obiora," Ejiro said thickly. "I want you to meet mine, too. Blessing's already given you her seal of approval, and Ajiri's happy when *I'm* happy. And I'm *very* happy, Obiora."

Obiora beamed. "I'm glad."

Ejiro trembled. He was overwhelmed in the best way, yet freaking terrified, but he made himself face the intensity burning in Obiora's eyes, the same intensity he could feel beating along with his heart.

"I love you," he said, clutching Obiora close, like he was afraid Obiora would disappear. "I love you. I love you. God, I don't know what to do with this. I've never felt so ... *much*." His throat bobbed as he swallowed. "It's ... honestly kind of terrifying."

"I feel the same way," Obiora whispered. "But there's some comfort to be had, knowing we're in the same boat, isn't there?"

"Yeah." Ejiro nodded. "Yeah." He darted forward to kiss Obiora again, shifting closer, desperate. "Love me. Make love to me."

"Of course, love." Obiora kissed him, and kissed him, and kissed him. "Anything you want."

HOME | ARCHIVE | ABOUT US | CONTACT | SEARCH

CUPID CALLING: IS OBIORA ANOZIE IN A RELATIONSHIP WITH THE CONTESTANT HE CONFESSED TO FALLING IN LOVE WITH?

Episode 7 of the tremendously popular dating TV show CUPID CALLING broke the Internet three weeks ago when one of the contestants confessed to falling in love with a co-competitor. A now deleted Instagram post from the star leaves avid fans wondering, could Obiora's feelings be returned?

Written by Aisha Suleiman

[CUPID CALLING Episode 7 recap provided courtesy of cupidcalling.com.]

WARNING: This post contains spoilers from Episode 7 of CUPID CALLING.

For those who might have been living under a rock—and you have to be, to not have heard about CUPID CALLING, A.K.A Ameri Shae's debut into reality television (it completely takes over the trends on social media for HOURS every time a new episode drops, without fail)— Episode 7 of CUPID CALLING literally broke the internet when it dropped about three weeks ago, after contestant Obiora Anozie— who was supposed to be competing for the heart of Sophia Bailey, the bachelorette—confessed instead to being in love with a co-

competitor.

Avid fans did a re-watch of the entire series in an attempt to figure out the identity of the man who'd stolen the attentions of the handsome contestant, and while a few theories left much to be desired, the general consensus was that Obiora's love interest was none other than sweet, introverted bachelor, Ejiro Odavwaro. Ejiro being eliminated in the very same episode—even though it was for different reasons—only seemed to cement the proof of his being the recipient of Obiora's affections.

[Obiora's 'Highlight Reel' provided courtesy of cupidcalling.com]

However, while this might have proven Ejiro to be Obiora's love interest, the question that left fans buzzing and unsatisfied was whether the former returned the latter's affections.

If you are one of these fans, look no further! The question seems to have FINALLY been answered in the form of a now deleted Instagram post uploaded by Obiora earlier today.

In the photo, who we assume to be Obiora is sitting on a sofa, with another man's jean-clad legs and stockinged-feet stretched out over his sweatpants-clad thighs. Obiora had one hand curled almost possessively on the person's knee, while his other hand presumably took the photo. The caption read:

Days like this; when he's with me <3 Can't believe a freaking TV show is what brought me the love of my life (I can see you smirking from here, Esther, please go away)

Though there were no identifying features in the photograph, fans have taken it upon themselves (tweets below) to interpret Obiora's caption as confirmation that not only is Ejiro the bachelor in question, but he does in fact return Obiora's feelings. His deleting the post not long afterward, according to the fans, only serves to make him look even guiltier.

> **Eva is Heated** @wuji_mp3
> Y'ALL I KNOW WHAT I'M SAYING. THOSE ARE EJIRO'S LEGS. YOU CAN SEE HIS SKIN PEEKING FROM BETWEEN HIS SOCKS AND HIS JEANS, AND NO OTHER BACHELOR WHO WAS AS DARK AS HIM HAD LEGS THAT LONG AND SLIM 🗣🗣🗣
>
> 💬 132   🔁 2.4k   ♡ 17.7k

> **flop era** 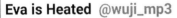 @JA1LTAN
> Obiora confesses he is in love with another contestant > presumably MONTHS after the filming, he posts about a TV show bringing him the love of his life. HELLO?
>
> 💬 825   🔁 4.5k   ♡ 20.7k

> **Ngozi is ia bc school** @shellfishly
> The fact that he deleted the post the second people started putting two and two together literally just cements it for me 💀💀💀
>
> 💬 210   🔁 1.7k   ♡ 3k

CUPID CALLING

> **Dee Dee** 📌 ✓ @makeupbydeedee
> Can't wait for the bachelors tell all episode next week xD Either Obiora and Ejiro are going to come clean, or we're all going to look like idiots xD
>
> 💬 3.2k   🔁 11k   ♡ 32.8k

As <u>makeup youtuber Dee Dee</u> said, this weekend, Netflicks will air the highly anticipated *The Men Tell All* episode, airing LIVE from London, where all the eliminated men from the competition will be coming together to spill some behind the scenes tea, or clarify the parts they played.

Will Obiora and Ejiro come clean? We can only hope!

Don't forget to share your thoughts in the comments! We're already down to the <u>two final bachelors</u>. Who do you think will win Sophia's heart; <u>Chris Wu</u> or <u>Seokjin Shin</u>?

The long-awaited finale of CUPID CALLING will air next week exclusively on <u>Netflicks</u>.

101 COMMENTS **(CLICK TO SHOW)**

THIRTY

"**WELCOME BACK, EVERYONE, TO CUPID** *Calling*!" Ameri Shae said into the mic to the sound of roaring applause. She beamed, looking dazzling in a pale pink pantsuit, her locs pulled up into a neat bun on her head, held in place by a glittering golden hairpin that resembled a tiara. "We're coming to you *live* from London—say hello to the folks at home, people!" She paused so the audience could hoot and holler, before continuing with a grin, "With twenty-seven out of twenty-eight of our eliminated bachelors in attendance!"

The audience applauded again on cue, while the cameras panned to show them, before swinging to show the men in attendance. When the camera landed briefly on him, Ejiro hoped his smile was genuine and not a grimace, though it felt very much like the latter. It had only been four months since they'd filmed the show in Oxford—two since it had started airing on Netflicks—yet it felt like a completely different time, like it could've been years ago instead. Being in front of cameras again shouldn't have felt so alien, but it was all Ejiro could do to act natural and not be as stiff as a board.

Once again, he wished desperately that the seats weren't so far apart; he wished he could have had Obiora pressed against his side to calm his nerves.

He had Obiora seated directly beside him on his left, but each of the men had been given individual seating spaced about a foot apart. Thirteen of them were seated in a semi-circle facing Ameri, while the remaining fourteen of them were seated a step higher behind the other bachelors, so the cameras could capture them all in one swoop.

Since the lead up to the live episode, Obiora had repeatedly told him he didn't have to say or do anything if Ameri asked about their relationship—which she undoubtedly would, given that they'd been trending on and off since episode seven had aired three weeks ago, the speculation made worse when Ejiro had given Obiora permission to post what he'd later realise was an ill-advised photo of the two of them on his Instagram.

He hadn't even been recognisable in the picture—it had just been their legs showing—but the fans had gone absolutely rabid, sharing and reposting and zooming and circling that Obiora deleting the pic did nothing but fan the flames.

Ejiro bit his lower lip as he remembered. Neither he nor Obiora had even been thinking about the show; they'd been dating for six weeks when Obiora had asked Ejiro to move in with him. Ejiro had been gripped by fear; wasn't it too soon? Were they moving too fast? Ajiri had had to sit him down and explain that he shouldn't be living by society's expectations.

"Because what even is *too fast*?" she'd asked with a roll of her eyes. "A month? Two? Six? A year? Fuck all that shit. Honestly."

The next time Ejiro had gone to see Obiora, he'd done so with most of his things in tow. The expression on Obiora's face that day; Ejiro would never forget it. He'd never in his life felt more loved, and seeing how he felt reflected in Obiora's eyes only cemented in that not only had he made the right decision, but he wanted to spend the rest of his life putting that awed, overjoyed look on Obiora's face again and again.

Obiora had posted the picture on a whim; he'd been so, so happy about Ejiro moving in, and he'd wanted to share that happiness with his wider group of friends along with the few members of his class at the gym who followed him on Instagram.

They'd only realised their mistake when the likes and comments and follows started flooding in. They hadn't even been able to discuss the situation before Ameri had gotten wind of it—because of course she had—and had called Obiora immediately to not-so-subtly remind them they were still under contract and their relationship (or lack thereof) could not be publicly spoken about or addressed until either the live episode, or the show itself had finished airing.

The whole thing had made his poor lover panic and delete the pic, and remembering how genuinely stressed out Obiora had been brought a soft, fond smile to Ejiro's lips. God, Obiora could be so freaking endearing without even meaning to be.

"It's okay," Ejiro remembered saying, while Obiora had silently freaked out.

"It's not okay," Obiora argued. "I may have just unintentionally outed you to the *entire* world, Ejiro. This is serious."

"Baby, I gave you permission to post the picture, remember? I knew the risks."

"Yeah, but we thought we were sharing the photo to a *certain* group of people. Fuck, I should've made my Instagram private."

"Yes, because that would have helped," Ejiro had mocked playfully.

Obiora had grinned at him, some of his panic receding in light of Ejiro's teasing. "Don't you snark at me."

They'd kissed, and all was—mostly—forgotten.

Then they'd gotten the call for the details of the live show, and the panic had returned full-force. The fans might have used that picture to jump to conclusions, but Ejiro knew they wouldn't really be satisfied until they had concrete proof, which meant at some point, Ameri was going to ask them about it.

It was at that moment that Ejiro had begun to understand why

Obiora had been panicking so badly. It was one thing to come out to his family and close friends, but on *live* TV? With what would undoubtedly feel like the *whole* world watching? It shouldn't have felt so terrifying, but it did. God, it did.

"You don't have to say anything," Obiora had repeated to him in an intimate whisper when they'd been sequestered in a secluded corner backstage, preparing to come on with the other men. They'd had their foreheads pressed together, hands clasped tightly between them. Obiora was clearly nervous yet trying not to show it in order to be strong for Ejiro, which just made Ejiro love him more. "You can just say no comment, that you'd rather not answer or you could say we're just good friends now, or whatever. You don't owe these people anything."

"Don't I?" Ejiro had asked, not really expecting an answer.

"You don't," Obiora repeated, voice a little hard.

Ejiro swallowed thickly. Before he could respond, they were being called to the main stage.

Obiora kissed him hard. "I love you."

"I love you, too."

Separating from him had felt to Ejiro like tearing out a limb.

Ameri's voice brought him back to the present. "Today, the men tell all! We'll be reviewing highlights of the show so far, and I'll be asking the men certain questions that have popped up every now and then to clarify some behind-the-scenes action. The audience will also be given the opportunity to ask some questions"—said audience clapped and whistled at this—"so, hopefully, we get a better picture of everything that went down. Hope you don't mind, Chad, but I'll start with you."

The audience laughed. Chad grimaced.

"Oh boy, here we go," he said, making the audience laugh again.

"I just have one thing to say: what on earth were you *thinking*?"

The audience burst out laughing, even harder than before, then swelled with applause.

When they eventually quieted down, Chad said, still with that grimace on his face, "Honestly, Ameri, I have no idea."

More laughter and applause burst out, and it set the tone for the rest of the evening. Ameri began from the bottom—from the very first few to be eliminated—and slowly made her way to the top. All the men had made it for the live show except Homophobic Hunter, who hadn't been invited back.

They stopped for a break twice, and throughout the time, Ejiro had to pretend like Obiora was just another bachelor; he had to resist the urge to look at him—*really* look at him—to reach over and touch his hand, or kiss him, or beg for reassurance. It made him hyperaware of how tactile they usually were; it felt unnatural, forcing himself to be apart from him, to keep from touching him. It *hurt*. Like a toothache.

By the time Ameri made it to them, Ejiro was ready to vibrate out of his skin.

"Saving one of the best for last of course." She'd barely finished the sentence when the audience started trying to scream the roof down. "Obiora," she began, to which the screams and wolf whistles actually increased, making Ameri laugh and glance at the audience incredulously.

The sounds eventually died down. Ejiro was painfully, perfectly still. He was sure on the screens, he probably looked unaffected, a small smile on his face, but inside, he was trembling like a newborn giraffe.

Ameri still looked greatly amused. "Obiora, some fans are saying you didn't come onto the show with pure intentions, that is, you held a lot of yourself back when you were with the bachelorette. Now, I'm not saying Sophia's entirely blameless—she did admit to holding back as well when it came to the two of you—but the fans would like to hear things from your point of view."

Ejiro didn't really hear Obiora's answer. He was too busy trying not to look like he was staring and simultaneously like he *wasn't* staring. He had to look at Obiora when he spoke, right? He'd done that for most of the other bachelors, after all. But would looking be weird? Would it give him away? How long could he look that wouldn't be considered revealing?

Ameri asked a few more questions about Obiora's relationship with the other men, his cooking skills, and more, before finally zeroing in on the hot topic of the night.

"So. Obiora. It's time for The Question." The audience "oohed" on cue. "You said, on the night you were eliminated, that you'd fallen in love with one of the other bachelors." They "oohed" again. "Could you tell us a bit more about that? Keep in mind, you've just told us how you held a bit of yourself back because of the hurt you've experienced in previous relationships, so the people want to know: how did this bachelor end up breaking down your walls where Sophia had unsucceeded?"

Ejiro was—if it were possible—even stiller than before. He carefully didn't look in Obiora's direction, but all his senses were on high alert, completely focused on Obiora's answer.

"Well, I wouldn't say he broke down my walls so much as I let them down for him."

Oh. Ejiro tried not to physically melt into his seat, his blush thankfully hidden underneath his dark skin.

The audience awwed. Even without looking at him, Ejiro knew Obiora was probably blushing at the reaction.

Obiora continued, voice soft and serious, "It happened—as most of these situations do—completely out of my control. It started with a simple attraction, which was easy enough to ignore. Then we started to talk more—got to know each other a lot better and before I knew it, I was gone. Head over heels. He's just—such a genuinely sweet soul it would have been harder *not* to fall in love with him."

The audience awwed again, and broke into a light applause. Ejiro wanted to reach out and hold his hand so fucking badly. He wanted Obiora to look at *him*, the way he was probably looking at the camera, his feelings bare for all to see.

Ameri had one hand pressed to her chest, an adoring expression on her face. "That's so, so lovely, Obiora. Thank you so much for sharing. Now, I know the audience is going to crucify me if I don't ask this question"—the crowd laughed—"so here we go: is the bachelor in question in this room?"

There was a pause. "Yes."

The audience was vibrating, Ejiro included.

"I don't want to overstep, or cross any boundaries or abuse your privacy and what not, but again, I *have* to ask: are the two of you in a relationship? Please know that you don't have to answer this question." The audience booed. "They don't," Ameri said, slightly-sharply, though still in a friendly tone. "Their private lives are honestly none of our business. That said, if you don't want to answer the question, just say pass, and we'll move on."

It was so quiet one could hear a pin drop.

And then, like it was scripted, like they'd completely rehearsed it, Ejiro turned to look at Obiora at the same time that Obiora turned to look at him, a slight question in his eyes.

And suddenly, with those eyes on him—despite the cameras, despite the audience and the presence of the other men, and the fact that his twin, Blessing, his friends, Obiora's friends and entire family—despite the fact that everyone he freaking *knew* was probably watching this—with those eyes on him, Ejiro knew he could do anything.

At that moment, he wanted only one thing: he wanted the *entire* world to know that this beautiful, wonderful man was *his*.

"Yes," Ejiro answered to the surprise of the watchers, a little shyly, unable to bear looking at the cameras. He reached out on instinct, something within him settling when Obiora immediately joined their hands, tangling their fingers. "We're in a relationship."

There was a jubilant uproar from the audience. Ejiro was blushing so hard his cheeks were hurting. Obiora's grin was brighter than the sun.

"Oh my God," Ejiro whispered, resisting the urge to hide behind his hands. He couldn't look anywhere but at their joined hands. Within his breast, the mixture of sickening dread and anticipation he'd been feeling was replaced by an almost painful release.

In the moment, and before it, admitting it had seemed so huge. But in the aftermath, all Ejiro felt was relief.

And joy. He glanced at Obiora to find his boyfriend already watching him. They smiled sappily at each other, and *this*, Ejiro thought—this was why it was worth coming out on national TV: the abundant love and passion burning in Obiora's eyes, and the brilliant, overjoyed grin that stretched his full lips.

When the noise got too much, the staff had to come in to force the audience to quiet down.

"Just to clarify"—Ameri's expression was just as bright and excited—"Ejiro, are you saying you're the bachelor in question?"

Obiora squeezed his hand. Ejiro nodded. "I am."

Ameri continued, cutting off the crowd's rising excitement. "And you reciprocated his feelings during the filming?"

Another squeeze. "Yes."

The people had to be quieted down again. He and Obiora probably looked like lovesick fools with how widely they were grinning, though Ejiro's grin was a little shy. They could barely keep their eyes off each other.

"Now, Ejiro, I guess I'll focus on you now." Slight laughter. "If you don't mind answering, how did this come about? Far as anyone knew, at the start of the competition, you were straight."

"Oh." Obiora squeezed his hand again in silent support. Fuck, Ejiro loved him. "I mean, I guess, or, at least, I thought it was. But I'm actually biromantic and demisexual." Fuck, it felt good to say it out loud.

Obiora squeezed his hand again. Ejiro squeezed back, glancing at him and preening at the pride he saw on Obiora's face.

"Could you elaborate on that?"

Ejiro tore his eyes away to focus on Ameri and the cameras, Obiora's grip on his like an anchor. "I don't want to speak for all demisexual people, but personally, for me, it means I only experience sexual attraction when a good deal of mutual trust along with an emotional bond has been formed first."

"And you didn't feel these emotions with Sophia?"

Ejiro tried not to grimace. "I wasn't ready to come out at that time, which is why I didn't mention this, but no, I didn't. My feelings for Obiora sort of overlapped with my falling out with Sophia. When Sophia ..." He had to pause for a moment, because thinking about that kiss still felt awful, though not as bad as it used to be. Obiora's hand tightly gripping his also helped. "When Sophia kissed me, Obiora was actually the one who talked me down. I was panicking and blaming myself, you know?" The audience made a disapproving noise. Ejiro smiled gratefully in their direction. "I blamed myself for not reading her signals, for not responding better to her desires, but Obiora made it clear that the reason I was feeling so upset was that, intentionally or not, Sophia had violated my boundaries. I might've liked her and found her lovely—which I did, and I do—but that didn't necessarily mean I was ready or even *wanted* to take that step."

"And that was the moment everything that *could* have worked with Sophia didn't?" Ameri prompted.

Ejiro nodded. "Yes. Exactly."

"That makes perfect sense," Ameri said, nodding. "Thank you so much for sharing that with us, Ejiro. I'm sad it didn't work out with Sophia, but hey, it seems like you still got a good deal out of the whole thing, am I right?"

Ejiro blushed furiously, even as he said, "You are absolutely right."

The audience cheered.

THE REST OF THE SEGMENT went by in a blur. Sophia came on stage at some point to surprise the men and the audience, and they interacted with her briefly, exchanging regrets, apologies and well wishes, and then it was all finally over.

Some of the men exchanged numbers, wanting to keep in touch. Obiora was still holding Ejiro's hand. After Ejiro had admitted to them being in a relationship—on live fucking TV, no less—all the anxious tension they'd no doubt been feeling all night had rapidly transformed into something else.

It felt like a live wire was sparking between them. Obiora couldn't even *look* at Ejiro for fear that he would literally jump his bones right fucking there.

He couldn't stop picturing it, the resolve and conviction in Ejiro's eyes as he'd said the words, his eyes locked on Obiora. The shy way he'd ducked his head at the audience's wild reaction. The way he'd squeezed Obiora's hand like it was a lifeline. Everything that had come afterward, how easily the words had spilled from his lips.

Something dark and possessive had taken root in Obiora's chest at the realisation that Ejiro had literally just claimed him—claimed *them* —on live TV—proclaimed to most of the entire fucking *world* that Obiora was fucking *his*.

By the time they made it back to the hotel, they were both taut with tension. Each time their eyes met, a frisson of electricity shot through Obiora's body, pooling like liquid warmth in his lower belly.

Obiora wanted to take Ejiro up to their room immediately, but they had to go to the hotel's bar to meet their families; Obiora's brothers and parents, along with Ejiro's twin and her girlfriend, had all made sure to make it to London to support them during the filming. Ameri had offered to have them in the audience, but they'd declined, opting instead to get drunk in the hotel bar while watching the live show on the TV mounted in the room.

"How do you feel?" his mum asked Ejiro, cupping his face in her hands. "That was so, so brave of you. I'm sure it was difficult, coming out like that on TV. I hope you didn't feel pressured?"

"No, I didn't, ma," Ejiro said shyly, respectfully, still bashful with Obiora's family even though they'd pretty much adopted him.

For some reason, the respect and reverence with which Ejiro treated his parents made Obiora want to fuck him even more. He tried desperately not to stare at Ejiro like the man was a walking sex-magnet.

"How many times will I tell you to call me "mummy", eh? Enough of this "ma" nonsense."

"Ifeoma, haba. Stop hounding the poor boy," Obiora's father said, holding an almost empty tumbler of scotch in one hand. "I'm proud of you, Ejiro. I know coming out on TV must've been hard."

"Thank you, sir." His eyes shone with emotion.

"Obiora cried, you know? The first time he told us he was bisexual."

"Okay, daddy," Obiora interjected, blushing. "I think he's heard that story enough times."

"Ah, shuo? And he will hear it again."

They laughed.

Ejiro looked so soft, as he usually did when he interacted with Obiora's parents. It was like he couldn't believe he could have this kind of support from Nigerian parents, which made Obiora feel furious on his behalf at how his mother had messed him up.

Ejiro still hadn't spoken to his mother since that dreadful phone call; she hadn't called him, and he'd refused to call her, admitting to Obiora that if he did, all he'd do was apologise and let her walk all over him again, and he was done with that. That she refused to contact him after everything said she knew this, too.

The relationship was dead and gone in Obiora's opinion, but

Obiora knew Ejiro would need time. At least now that she wasn't hounding him anymore, Ejiro was finally beginning to see and understand the sheer depths of emotional abuse she'd put him and his sister through.

And while he knew that sort of relationship could never be replaced, it felt devastatingly good that his parents could help fill that specific hole in Ejiro's life—or even carve a new space for themselves in his heart.

Ajiri, Blessing, and Obioma were similar in a lot of ways, ribbing him and Ejiro good-naturedly after they were done greeting the parents. Obinna rolled his eyes at their antics, too Grown™ for it all.

They said their goodnights not too long after that.

The door to their hotel room had barely shut when they were crashing into each other's arms.

Ejiro ended up slammed against the closed door, their mouths moulding and meshing, tongues tangling, teeth nipping. Obiora bit at his jaw, his throat, sucked a hickey into his neck that had Ejiro moaning and trembling, gripping Obiora's curls in tight fists. The slight pull of it went straight to Obiora's dick, which was pounding furiously between his legs.

Quickly, he spun Ejiro around to face the door.

"Yes," Ejiro gasped, pressing back against him, his voice raspy. "Oh God, fuck me, fuck me—"

"Shit." Obiora for the sachet of lube and the condom he'd stashed into his wallet "just in-case".

Since Ejiro liked the stretch, liked it to hurt a little, Obiora didn't spend too much time fingering him open before he had the condom on and was sliding home.

"Yes, yes, *yes*, oh my God, oh my God—"

Obiora snapped his hips wildly, one hand on Ejiro's hip, the other braced against the door. He pounded into Ejiro until Ejiro was sobbing incoherently, his pleasure so intense he began to lose the strength in his legs.

Obiora bit his shoulder, shaking, and didn't even try to make it last, dropping his hand from the door so he could reach around and wrap Ejiro's stiff, leaking dick in his grasp.

One tight stroke was all his boyfriend needed, and he was screaming Obiora's name and coming all over his fist.

"Jesus fucking Christ," Obiora groaned as he followed, the feel of Ejiro's ass milking his prick too much to bear.

They collapsed against the door, panting.

"Well," Ejiro said breathlessly.

Obiora laughed. He planted a soft kiss on Ejiro's shoulder, part apology for the teeth marks he could see forming on Ejiro's flesh, and part just because. "I love you."

Ejiro placed a hand on top of Obiora's, where Obiora had one arm wrapped around Ejiro's chest, clutching him close.

"I love you, too."

THEY MANAGED TO SLEEP FOR a few scant hours, and even though it was extremely late, woke up hungry enough to say fuck it and order some food anyway. They remained naked, cuddling and kissing in bed until the food arrived. Ejiro giggled—literally fucking giggled—when Obiora couldn't be arsed to dress up, instead wrapping a sheet around his hips to answer the door.

Ejiro thought eating in bed was disgusting, so he dutifully wrapped a sheet around his own hips and he and Obiora moved to the small seating area in their hotel room. The seating area was right next to the balcony, where they'd been too exhausted to close the curtains after their frenzy against the door.

The bright lights of London bathed Ejiro's features, making him look slightly ethereal. Obiora felt a pang; it had been tough at first, coming back here, but being with Ejiro had made it easier.

"I love you," he said softly.

Ejiro turned to look at him, his eyes swimming with emotion. "I love you, too, Obiora."

God. "Are you okay? I meant to ask earlier."

"What, you mean about the episode thing?"

"I mean the coming out on Live TV thing," Obiora teased, and Ejiro threw a chip at him, making him laugh.

"Honestly? I wanted to. I was terrified. But"—he began to blush—"when you looked at me then? I just … I felt like I could take over the world."

"That's so fucking cheesy," Obiora said, though he was grinning so hard it hurt.

"Shut up," Ejiro laughed, throwing another chip at him.

"Stop wasting your food."

Ejiro threw another chip. Obiora growled and launched himself at Ejiro, straddling his lap and kissing the laugh off his lips.

When he pulled back, Ejiro was looking at him like he'd hung the moon.

"You're right," Obiora murmured.

"Hm?"

Obiora stared into his eyes, his voice an intimate whisper as he said, "Right now, with you looking at me like that, I feel like I can take over the world."

Ejiro wrinkled his nose. "And you were right. That's so freaking cheesy."

Obiora laughed and kissed him.

Cheesy sounded pretty fucking good.

HOME | ARCHIVE | ABOUT US | CONTACT | SEARCH

"THE MEN TELL ALL": THE TOP FIVE FAN QUESTIONS FINALLY ANSWERED!

The highly awaited and highly publicised "The Men Tell All" episode of CUPID CALLING has finally aired, where the contestants have answered the fans' most pressing questions.

Written by Aisha Suleiman

[CUPID CALLING 'The Men Tell All' recap provided courtesy of cupidcalling.com.]

WARNING: This post contains spoilers for CUPID CALLING.

On the cusp of the grand finale, the CUPID CALLING contestants—minus the top two bachelors, Chris Wu and Seokjin Shin—were all brought back together for a live event in London, England, where, as the title states, "The Men Tell All."

For those who have been keeping up with the show since the very beginning, there have been some specific questions and speculations surrounding the show since it aired, and I'm here to tell you that Ameri Shae absolutely did NOT disappoint in getting us some answers during the live show.

So, without further ado, and ICYMI, here are the top five fan questions made by <u>CUPIDS</u>, A.K.A. the avid fans of CUPID CALLING, finally answered!

5) Did Alistair deliberately sabotage his chances with Sophia during the therapy episode?

Short answer: No.

Long answer: In <u>Episode 6</u>, <u>celebrity therapist Sasha Pierce</u> visited the cast of CUPID CALLING to perform a surprise therapy session. The men were obviously blindsided by this, and <u>Alistair took the situation worse than the rest of the men</u>, cracking jokes and refusing to cooperate with either Sophia or Sasha during the session. This frustrated the bachelorette and led to her eliminating him on the spot.

During the live show, Alistair admitted to not being ready at the time to "air his demons", so to speak. Did he handle the situation badly? Sure. But he stated that while he *did* regret that he couldn't have taken his relationship with Sophia further, he ultimately does not regret the way he reacted.

4) Did Sophia and Chris Wu know each other before the show aired?

Short answer: Yes.

Long answer: Right from <u>Episode 1</u>, fans have been wondering if Sophia and the sexy, charismatic Chinese-British contestant <u>Chris Wu</u> knew each other before the filming of CUPID CALLING. So, <u>when Sophia appeared at some point during the live show</u> as a surprise to the bachelors and the audience, a member from the audience didn't hesitate to ask for some clarification.

It turns out that yes, Sophia and Chris Wu did in fact know each other from before; they'd apparently attended the same college for their A levels. They were casual friends—or acquaintances, at best—as when they eventually graduated and went their separate ways, they did not keep in touch until they met again at CUPID CALLING.

What are the chances, eh?

3) Is the tattoo Noah gave Sophia actually real?

Short answer: Yes.

Long answer: In Episode 4, when two times Red Heart winner, tattoo artist, and gorgeous heartthrob Noah took Sophia on a swoony romantic date on his bike, Sophia admired his tattoos and admitted to always wanting one herself. So, what was a tattoo artist to do but offer to design one for her on the spot? I know, right?

A few fans felt this slick move was a stunt orchestrated by the production team, but Sophia put all those doubts to rest during the live show. Once posed with the question, our savvy bachelorette did not hesitate to bare her thigh where, yup, Noah's handiwork lay plain for all to see. Not a stunt at all.

2) Is Jin really royalty?

Short answer: Yes (and no).

Long answer: From his precise mannerisms, to his impeccable wardrobe and his delectable accent, the contestants, the fans, and even the bachelorette herself constantly questioned throughout the show if Seokjin Shin could actually be royalty.

<u>Sophia finally put our theories to rest during the live show</u>, admitting that yes, Jin had privately informed her that he is apparently the adopted son of <u>Lord Ratliffe, A.K.A. the grandson of the Duke of Castlefield</u>. You heard that right, Jin is the adopted great-grandson OF A DUKE.

As an adopted child, and with him <u>not being the heir apparent to Lord Ratliffe</u>, Jin does not and will not bear an official title, but that doesn't mean he isn't seen and treated with the respect his adopted lineage brings. How absolutely dreamy is that? Sophia is one lucky woman!

1) Is Ejiro the bachelor Obiora is in love with?

Short answer: Yes.

Long answer: Finally, the question we've all been waiting for! Out of all the questions on this list, this one <u>generated the most buzz online, trending numerous times</u>, and even <u>bringing in an entire new legion of (mostly LGBTQ+) fans</u> desperate for representation to watch the show.

During the live show—<u>and in a moment that seems completely off script</u>—when <u>Obiora Anozie</u> was posed with the question about the identity of the man who stole his heart, Obiora immediately looked to— you guessed it—<u>Ejiro Odavwaro</u>, seemingly for confirmation. Ejiro then took his hand, and declared to the entire world on live TV and to the delight of both Ameri and the audience, that yes, he is the bachelor in question, and yes, <u>he and Obiora are now in a committed relationship</u>.

Ejiro discovered his sexuality while filming (<u>he is biromantic and demisexual</u>), and Obiora's support and friendship during the filming soon turned the former's feelings from platonic to romantic.

And that's all for now, folks! What questions or theories did you have that you feel the cast didn't answer or address? Share your thoughts in the comments below!

Next week, the long awaited finale of CUPID CALLING will air exclusively on Netflicks.

Who do *you* think will win Sophia's heart: Chris Wu or Seokjin Shin?

63 COMMENTS (CLICK TO SHOW)

EPILOGUE

IT WAS ONE OF THOSE mornings, where Obiora woke up and couldn't believe this was his life. Contentment stretched warm and sweet in his chest like a newborn kitten. As he stared at the unfamiliar wooden canopy of the bed above him, it took him a moment to remember that he and Ejiro weren't in their flat in Sheffield, but in a quaint little hotel in Strafford, in preparation to go for their hot air balloon date. The thought of it immediately made Obiora's breath speed up and his heartbeat start racing.

Ejiro was curled up in his arms, cheek on his chest. His hand was gently stroking a path up and down Obiora's side, the movement being the thing that had slowly brought Obiora awake.

When Ejiro noticed Obiora was awake, he looked up, a small smile on his face.

"Good morning, baby," he murmured, his voice still deep with sleep. He'd probably just woken up himself.

"Morning, love." Obiora smiled, leaning down to peck him lightly on the lips. "What time is it?" It felt like there were a million miniscule acrobats doing somersaults in his stomach.

"Five minutes to seven," Ejiro replied after checking his phone.

"Mm," Obiora murmured, stretching.

He must've failed to look casual, because when he looked down, Ejiro's eyes were dancing with laughter.

"Excited?" Ejiro teased, waggling his eyebrows.

Obiora playfully rolled his eyes. "You already know."

Ejiro laughed, leaning up to kiss him properly.

It was probably supposed to be a longer good-morning kiss, but as it usually was with him and Ejiro, when they were all warm and cosy and cuddled up like this, the kiss soon turned deeper, more passionate.

Ejiro sank his teeth into Obiora's lower lip, making him groan, pleasure flooding his body and making his morning wood throb.

Ejiro pushed his hips forward, pressing his own stiff length against Obiora's thigh. Both of them had taken to sleeping naked, loving the intimacy irregardless of whether or not they had sex, which meant it was easy for Ejiro to begin trailing kisses down his throat.

"Ejiro," Obiora whispered huskily, overwhelmed with love and lust, his hands gently cupping his boyfriend's head.

His breath hissed through his teeth when Ejiro nipped at his hard nipples, soothing the sting with broad strokes of his tongue, before trailing slow, open-mouthed kisses and soft nips down to Obiora's stomach.

By the time he made it to Obiora's dick, Obiora was so hard, several pearls of pre-come had formed, leaking down his slit.

Ejiro looked up at him, and Obiora felt bowled over by the intensity in his gaze. He was taken back to that first time, almost eight months ago now during the filming of *Cupid Calling*, after the first episode where he and Ejiro had sort of been enemies; when Ejiro had ripped him a new one when they'd involuntarily jogged together— the way his gaze had sparked with fire and left Obiora wondering if Ejiro looked that intense when he fucked.

Over the course of the past few months, especially since Ejiro had moved in with him, Obiora was inclined to say yes; Ejiro was *just* as intense, if not even more so, when they were having sex. Having all that fervent passion pinned on him never failed to leave Obiora trembling and breathless, overwhelmed in the best possible way.

"Ejiro," he groaned, arching, his fingers gently sinking into the short, soft coils of Ejiro's hair as Ejiro sensually licked the trail of pre-come sliding down his shaft, then gently took him into the warm cavern of his mouth.

Ejiro moaned around his length, his eyelashes fluttering. That was another thing they'd discovered together: how much Ejiro loved giving head.

Ejiro gently bobbed his head, cheeks hollowing, throat vibrating with encouraging moans, until Obiora was shaking, his hands flexing where they held gently at Ejiro's head. While Obiora didn't mind a bit of rough handling while giving a blowjob, Ejiro preferred gentler, encouraging treatment.

"Fuck, look at you," Obiora whispered hoarsely, gently stroking his hair.

Ejiro's eyes flicked up to meet his, dark with desire.

"Jesus." Obiora rolled his hips gently, very gently, unable to help it, wanting to fuck into that sweet mouth. The sight of his dick slowly slipping in and out of those slick, plump lips was nearly enough to push him over the edge.

He was almost on the brink when Ejiro pulled off with a lewd slurp and climbed astride his hips. He found the small bottle of lube on the nightstand, and poured a generous amount into his palm, before reaching behind him for Obiora's length, which was still slick with his saliva.

"Baby," Obiora groaned, as Ejiro stroked the lube onto his length, held him in position, then sank down, slow and easy, his ass still a bit stretched out from the night before.

"Fuck," Ejiro whimpered, his profanity filter shot to hell.

Despite last night's lovemaking when they'd arrived in the hotel room, Ejiro was still tight, almost painfully so, the feel of it making

Obiora's toes curl.

Ejiro braced one hand on the headboard, the other on Obiora's shoulder, and began to roll his hips, slow and languid.

"Fuck, you're so sexy," Obiora whispered, cupping his hips, digging his heels into the mattress so he could move with him. "Jesus. I love you."

"I love you," Ejiro echoed, his throat scraped raw, his eyelashes wet. "Obiora. Obiora."

"Christ," Obiora grunted, throwing his head back, clenching his eyes shut because *fucking* hell, it felt so good.

They rocked together until they found the perfect angle, which sent Ejiro's breath hitching, his muscles clamping down tight around Obiora's dick.

"Fucking hell." Obiora snapped his hips helplessly, panting. He opened his eyes.

"I love you," Ejiro whispered when their eyes met. He was crying. He did that, too, sometimes, when they made love like this; slow, and sweet, and intense.

"I love you, baby. You're so beautiful. So perfect. I can't believe you're all mine."

Ejiro's breath hitched. "Obiora," he whispered.

"Come here. Kiss me."

Ejiro obeyed, dropping down onto the sheets and joining their lips. He couldn't move properly in this position, so Obiora used the opportunity to take control, bending his knees so his feet were flat on the bed, and fucking up into him.

"Obiora," Ejiro cried at the change in angle, his tears splashing down onto Obiora's own cheeks. "Don't stop, don't stop—"

They weren't kissing anymore, their lips simply pressed together, Obiora's hands gripping Ejiro's hips as he sped up his thrusts, hammering up into him.

Ejiro cried out with each thrust, his voice low, hoarse and sexy. Obiora bit his lip, his fingers digging into Ejiro's hips as he fought to keep from coming too soon.

Ejiro's eyebrows began to furrow, his lips pursing the way they did when he was getting close.

"Yes," Obiora growled, snapping his hips harder, fucking him so hard Ejiro had to brace his hand against the headboard to keep from smacking his forehead against it. "Come on, come on, come on."

"I'm gonna come," he sobbed, his arse already fluttering around Obiora's length, making Obiora grunt and twist his hips, his thrusts stuttering. "Obiora, I'm gonna come."

"Do it, baby," Obiora commanded roughly. "Come on. Come for me."

Ejiro gripped his shoulder, his face scrunching up, his body going taut as he came, completely untouched.

"Fuck!" Obiora threw his head back into the pillows, grinding his prick in deep as Ejiro's orgasm triggered his own, his nails digging into Ejiro's hips.

He managed to shove a hand between their bodies to pump Ejiro's still hard dick, using his come to slick the way.

Ejiro let out a sharp whine, curling in on himself, tightening around Obiora and sending them both shaking with the aftershocks. He didn't stop stroking until Ejiro pushed his hand away, whimpering at the oversensitivity.

Obiora collapsed on the bed, breathing hard and drifting off into the clouds. He came to to Ejiro planting languid kisses on his lips. He smiled into Ejiro's mouth, his eyes stinging as his own emotions went off-kilter, but in a good way.

"Love you," he whispered. "I love you so much."

"I love you, too," Ejiro murmured.

They stayed kissing and holding each other, and didn't leave the bed until they absolutely had to.

Once they did, climbing into the shower together, Obiora's nerves and excitement came back full force, the acrobats that had been dancing in his stomach making a swift return.

Some of his emotions must've shown in his expression, because Ejiro ducked his head, blushing furiously.

"What? Why are you looking at me like that?"

Obiora smiled gently. "I don't know. I just love you."

"Obiora." Ejiro blushed harder. "I love you, too."

They kissed, gently swaying so the spray of the shower could cover them both.

As he got lost in Ejiro's mouth, Obiora prayed for the weather to remain clear, and their journey smooth.

Today had to be absolutely perfect.

TODAY WAS ABSOLUTELY PERFECT. AFTER their shower that morning, they'd gone to the seating area located outside behind the hotel—though Ejiro wouldn't have called it a hotel, it felt more like a luxurious manor in the woods by the riverside—to enjoy the morning air by the small river. Though it was freezing cold—it was mid-February, after all—other guests had had the same idea as well, enjoying hot cups of cocoa and conversing quietly.

The tranquil setting—and their brief, but intense lovemaking of that morning—seemed to set the tone for the rest of the day.

By the time they made it to *Wickers World* for their hot air balloon date, Ejiro was nearly vibrating out of his skin with sheer love and excitement.

It had been a few weeks ago, when Ejiro had surprised Obiora with reservations to go bungee jumping. *Cupid Calling* had since finished airing, but Ejiro hadn't been able to stop thinking about his idea of the perfect date, and how he'd shared it with the wrong person (no offence to Sophia). So he'd decided, *screw* it, and bought the reservations to go with the true love of his life.

Obiora's face when Ejiro had told him his reasoning—Ejiro would never forget it. It was like seeing the sun peeking out from behind a raincloud.

And when Obiora had decided they should go on his own idea of a perfect date as well, Ejiro had very nearly combusted with love for him.

He was aware that the hot air balloon date had been one of the items on Obiora's late girlfriend's bucket list, so Obiora taking him here meant *twice* as much; that Obiora still got to do this with someone he loved meant absolutely everything to Ejiro.

They held hands almost constantly now, regardless of where they were. Ejiro gave Obiora's hand a light squeeze through their gloves, trying not to bounce on his feet as they got checked in.

"Ah, I can't wait," he said. From here he could see the grounds where they were going to lift off, and the scenery looked freaking gorgeous. "I'm not a big fan of flying, but since this is going to be in open air and not a giant metal bird, I think I might enjoy it."

Obiora snorted a laugh. "A giant metal bird?"

"That's what it is, isn't it?" Ejiro deadpanned.

Obiora laughed, Ejiro grinning, tilting his head when Obiora leaned in to kiss him.

Ejiro had researched the place after Obiora had told him about it in order to properly picture it, and he'd seen that the tours were held in groups of ten to twelve—the couple tour was really freaking expensive—but he hadn't really minded, as long as he and Obiora were together.

So imagine his surprise when they were led away from the group toward the edge of the field where a smaller balloon waited.

"Baby," Ejiro said, his voice thick with emotion, squeezing Obiora's hand so hard it must have hurt. Throughout their relationship, he kept thinking he couldn't possibly get any happier than he was at a given moment, then Obiora went ahead and did things like this. "*Baby.*"

Obiora was grinning, looking very fucking satisfied.

"Yeah?" he encouraged, giving Ejiro's hand a squeeze. "I thought you might've liked the more private tour."

"I do," Ejiro said earnestly. "I love it. I love *you*."

"I love you, too, baby."

Ejiro pulled him close for a kiss, wincing a little and laughing at how cold their noses were. Obiora laughed into his mouth, before kissing the smile off his face, and *God* Ejiro loved when he did that—just kissed the laughter off his lips like he wanted to somehow consume the physical evidence of Ejiro's happiness.

Their pilot was a smiling young, white man, with pale round cheeks and curly brown hair framing his face from underneath a beanie pulled down over his ears to protect them from the cold.

Something about the man's smile was contagious. Ejiro had a grin on his face as he set them up inside the balloon, and began talking about how to switch it on.

"There isn't much steering going on," the pilot, who'd introduced himself as Jon, explained. "The balloon follows the wind; we'll enjoy the scenery for about an hour or two, and then land. Easy peasy."

"Easy peasy," Ejiro echoed, making them laugh.

Ejiro exclaimed, unable to help it at the slight jolt as they lifted up, his eyes drinking in everything.

When he glanced at Obiora, his boyfriend was watching him with this sweet, soft look in his face that never failed to make Ejiro blush.

They spent the first few minutes basking in the scenery and in themselves, ignoring Jon's presence behind him. Ejiro had expected Jon to talk through the tour—he'd read on the website about the pilots giving a brief history on the surrounding sites—but Jon was quiet, so quiet he could almost forget the man's presence behind them.

The website had boasted a calm, serene ride, and they'd been right. Ejiro felt almost as if he were floating. They could hear the sound of life below, and see the animals and plants in the surrounding hills. He and Obiora didn't say much, mostly quiet as the balloon slowly advanced, but it was a honeyed silence built from the trust and comfort of being next to someone you loved. The balloon was carried by the air current, which was easy and perfect this morning, thank God.

"I'm going to take some pictures," Ejiro said after a while, smiling brightly.

"Go right ahead, baby."

Ejiro grinned, reaching down to pick his camera bag from the bottom of the basket. It was a little cosy, but it had just enough space that they didn't feel too crowded with Jon behind them.

After securing the strap of his camera around his neck, Ejiro began to take as many photos as possible, wanting to imprint this date on his memory forever. When they'd gone bungee jumping, they'd had the photos they'd taken then enlarged and framed, and Ejiro wanted the same treatment for this date.

He turned to take some playful shots of Obiora, and nearly dropped his camera when he found Obiora down on one knee.

"Obiora," he gasped, his brain short-circuiting as he let the camera go so it flopped uselessly against his chest. He covered his mouth with his hands. "What are you doing?" His voice was unintentionally shrill.

Ejiro glanced at Jon as if for help, and let out a choked-sounding laugh when he saw Jon was currently filming with another camera, a wide grin on his face. There was a small recorder clipped to his hip, and he pressed the play button, soft music streaming into the air between them.

Ejiro looked back at Obiora, his throat thick.

Obiora had taken his gloves off. His hands were trembling, from a mixture of his nerves and the cold, and he was holding up a dark blue velvet ring box.

Ejiro started to cry. "Fuck, fuck, fuck."

The sight of him crying seemed to trigger Obiora's own tear ducts, because he began to cry, too.

"Ejiro ..." he began.

"Oh God," Ejiro said, wiping his eyes with his gloves, trying to stop crying.

"Ejiro," Obiora repeated. "Fucking hell. I had an entire fucking *speech* planned but now that I'm here, in front of you, it's all gone out the damn window."

Ejiro managed a laugh.

"Ejiro. I love you. I didn't believe I could love anyone the way I love you, yet here I am, so full of love I'm practically made of it."

"Oh my God," Ejiro half-groaned and half-sobbed, the declaration cheesy and awful and fucking perfect.

"I love you, and I want to spend the rest of my life loving you. Will you marry me?"

"Yes," Ejiro said immediately. "Yes, please, yes, yes, yes—"

Obiora was on his feet, slamming their mouths together. They kissed furiously, the kiss wet and salty because of their tears, and laughed when they took Ejiro's gloves off, but both their hands were trembling too hard to get the ring on.

But then it was on; a plain rose gold band with four small white diamonds inset into the surface. Ejiro loved it so fucking much.

"I love you. I love you so much," he said, and they were kissing again, the world disappearing around them.

They eventually had to pull apart to breathe, their chests heaving, foreheads pressed together.

Ejiro wiped at his eyes. He laughed a little. "You know, I think I'm still getting used to this biromantic demisexual thing because never in my life did I once imagine I'd get proposed to. I always thought I'd be the one doing the proposing."

"Well, I mean, you can still propose to me if you want; I won't complain."

Ejiro laughed, unable to help but kiss him again. "I just might take you up on that, love."

"It's not too soon?" Obiora murmured, trying and failing to sound casual.

Ejiro's heart ached. "No, baby. If Jon were a priest, I would literally marry you right freaking now."

"I was ordained in 1999," Jon deadpanned.

Ejiro's eyes widened. Obiora's mouth dropped open.

Jon laughed. "I'm kidding, I'm kidding."

"You are awful." Ejiro laughed, shaking his head, his heart pounding.

"I'm going to leave a bad review on TripAdvisor."

"Doesn't that sound a bit harsh, mate?"

They laughed again. They went quiet, holding each other, eyes trailing over the scenery but not really focusing.

Ejiro couldn't stop thinking about his ring—his *engagement* ring—he was *engaged*! He bit back a giddy squeal, holding Obiora tighter, burying his face in Obiora's shoulder. Ajiri and Blessing were going to flip their shit.

Ejiro couldn't help but pull back so he could kiss Obiora again—and again and again and again.

"Picture of the newly engaged couple?" Jon asked when it seemed like he was done filming, and Ejiro and Obiora had taken a brief break from kissing.

"No, I look awful," Ejiro said. His eyes and cheeks were freezing where his tears had trailed and dried up.

"Nonsense," Obiora said, kissing his nose, then his eyelids. "You look perfect."

"You're biased."

"You're damn right I am." Obiora laughed and pulled him closer, chest to chest, holding him so tightly Ejiro forgot all about his tears and the cold.

They stared into each other's eyes as the shutter went off, freezing this moment perfectly in time.

HOME | ARCHIVE | ABOUT US | CONTACT | SEARCH

CUPID CALLING: THE STARS, WHERE ARE THEY NOW?

Cupid Calling took over the hearts of many almost the second the announcement for the series dropped. Here's how the stars are doing, over a year later.

Written by Aisha Suleiman

[CUPID CALLING 'After the Final Heart' episode recap provided courtesy of cupidcalling.com.]

WARNING: This post contains spoilers for CUPID CALLING.

It's been over a year since the events of *Cupid Calling*, the bachelorette-esque TV show that swooped in and stole the hearts of many. For those who haven't heard of the show, Cupid Calling is a reality TV dating competition series where a group of thirty young, handsome bachelors competed for the heart of a sweet and savvy bachelorette, with contestants getting eliminated every week until the bachelorette found her soulmate.

The show fulfilled all the viewers' needs and more; there was drama, there was jealousy, there was heartbreak, and there was even, to the delight of many viewers, two contestants falling in love with each other instead! Through it all, the bachelorette still managed to find her match.

The question everyone is wondering now is, how are the bachelorette, Sophia Bailey, and her chosen bachelor, Seokjin Shin, doing, a year later?

[Photo of Sophia Bailey provided courtesy of Seokjin Shin on Instagram]

There's no heartbreak to be found here, y'all, because Sophia and Jin are doing perfectly fine, as the stars' Instagram pages would let you know.

Both seemed to have fulfilled Sophia's dream to travel the world, and are currently, according to Sophia's Instagram, in Bali, Indonesia, and still happily engaged, if the couple's many sly photos with Sophia's engagement ring dazzling in the shot are anything to go by.

[Photo of Seokjin Shin provided courtesy of Sophia Bailey on Instagram]

And if you were wondering about the OTHER couple the show mistakenly spawned, ahem, Obiora Anozie and Ejiro Odavwaro are not only engaged, but apparently proposed to EACH other! How romantic is that?

[Photo of Obiora and Ejiro provided courtesy of Ejiro Odavwaro on Instagram]

From <u>their social media</u>, Obiora and Ejiro posted separately when <u>the former proposed to the latter in a hot air balloon</u> (!!!) about eight months after *Cupid Calling* had finished airing. For those unaware of the significance of this moment, <u>Obiora had admitted during Episode 7</u> that his idea for a perfect date was to ride in a hot air balloon with the love of his life. *swoons*

Ejiro then <u>proposed on their anniversary six months later,</u> according to him, in the same exact spot when everything between him and Obiora had started feeling "like it could be something real", which was—you guessed it—back in <u>Venice</u>! For those who have no idea what I'm talking about, check out the <u>wildly popular Episode 5 and 6</u> of Cupid Calling on Netflicks, and get back to me. *wink wink*

Let us know in the comments if you thought both couples would have lasted this long! Do you hear wedding bells in their future? Cause we sure do!

101 COMMENTS **(CLICK TO SHOW)**

BONUS EPILOGUE

Can't get enough of Obiora and Ejiro? Get a bonus 7,000+ word epilogue—approximately 29 pages—exclusively on Viano's Patreon!

Obiora and Ejiro visit Venice on their anniversary a few months later, fulfil a few fantasies, and Ejiro plans and enacts the perfect proposal.

ACKNOWLEDGEMENTS

I initially got the idea for CUPID CALLING in early 2017, but didn't actually start writing it until August 2020, where I posted it serially on Patreon until April 2021. As you can see, this was during the height of the pandemic. Because of this, when I started fleshing out the story, my goal really was to write a book that would serve as the perfect escape. While there are some difficult moments for the characters, I feel those moments are far and few between, and are overwhelmingly balanced out by the sweetness of the romance.

The amount of love this book received on Patreon—and eventually, Wattpad and Tapas—was honestly so astounding that, as time passed, I just could not let it go. Finally, this year, with the boost I needed from my close friends and family, I decided to self-publish it so I could share this sweet, swoonworthy story with as many people as I could.

CUPID CALLING is honestly a love letter to the young me who read her first *Mills & Boon* novel and felt her eyes pop as she was introduced to the world of unashamed, unfiltered, unconditional love. This book would not exist without my deep love for the genre, and also not without the support of some of my favourite people.

First of all, I would like to thank my patrons and my readers on wattpad and Tapas: thank you all so, so much for your support, for taking a chance on this book, for your insightful (and oftentimes hilarious) comments, and for giving me the confidence to press publish.

Thank you so, so much to my family; Mummy, Mano, Zino, and Bruno, for your suggestions when I needed ideas for the "episodes"—unfortunately, not all the ideas could make it through (I'm sorry, Zino, but I have no idea how I would have worked in the bachelors playing a game of paintball/laser tag, as amazing as that idea sounded). Thank you for constantly celebrating me, no matter how small the milestone; thank you for always making sure I'm hydrated and keeping to my schedule so I don't burn out. Thank you, thank you, thank you.

And to you, reader, thank you so much for taking the chance to buy CUPID CALLING, and helping fulfil my dream of becoming a self-sufficient, self-published author. As my mother usually says, "One step at a time."

I hope you enjoyed the ride.

ALSO BY VIANO ONIOMOH

For more books filled with swoony romance and BIPOC LGBTQ+ characters, check out Viano's other books:

In FRAGMENTS OF A FALLEN STAR, Moira Karl-Fisher journeys across the sea to find the missing pages of a spell to turn back time.

In THE AURORA CIRCUS, a spirit's plea for help leads Ember Quinn to the magical world of *The Aurora Circus*.

EXCLUSIVE CONTENT ON PATREON

Interested in more content? For as little as $3/month, you get access to over 400,000+ words worth of full-length novels, novellas, and short stories, along with Behind The Scenes content, early cover reveals, early ebook releases, signed physical copies, exclusive merch, and more!

SUBSCRIBE TO VIANO'S NEWSLETTER

Subscribe to Viano's Newsletter for exclusive perks, early cover reveals, giveaways and more, and be the first to get the latest updates about Viano and her work.

ABOUT THE AUTHOR

Viano Oniomoh is a passionate reader and writer, who was born and raised in Nigeria. She spends fifty percent of her time writing, forty percent reading, and the other ten listening to BTS. She may or may not use magic to get everything else in her life done. She also has no idea how to write about herself in the third person.

Stay in touch with Viano via her social media pages and her website linked in the QR code below.

Printed in Great Britain
by Amazon